BOYFRIEND MATERIAL

ALEXIS HALL

Published by Sourcebooks Casablanca, an imprint of Sourcebooks
P.O. Box 4410, Naperville, Illinois 60567-4410
(630) 961-3900
sourcebooks.com

Library of Congress Cataloging-in-Publication
data is on file with the publisher.

Printed and bound in Canada.
MBP 23

To CMC

CHAPTER 1

I'VE NEVER SEEN THE POINT of fancy dress parties. You have two choices: either you make a massive effort and wind up looking like a dick, or you make no effort and wind up looking like a dick. And my problem, as always, was not knowing what kind of dick I wanted to be.

I'd pretty much committed to the no-effort strategy. Then I'd panicked at the last minute, made an ill-fated attempt to track down somewhere that sold costumes, and found myself in one of those weirdly high-streety sex shops that flog red lingerie and pink dildos to people with no real interest in either.

Which is why, when I rocked up to a party already well into the too hot, too loud, too crowded stage of its life cycle, I was wearing a pair of problematically sexualised black lace bunny ears. I swear, I used to be good at this sort of thing. But I was out of practice, and looking like a cut-rate rent boy serving a very specific fetish was not the ideal way to make a triumphant return to the scene. Worse, I'd arrived so late that all the other lonely, shit people had given up and gone home already.

Somewhere in that pit of flashy lights, bleepy music, and sweat were my actual friends. I knew that because our WhatsApp group—currently called Queer Comes The Sun—had devolved into a hundred variations on the theme of "where the fuck is Luc." But all I could see were people I vaguely thought vaguely knew people who vaguely knew me. Wriggling my way to the bar, I squinted at the chalkboard listing the night's bespoke cocktails and eventually ordered a Sloe Comfortable Conversation about Pronouns Up Against the Wall, since it seemed like it would be both nice to drink and accurately descriptive of my chances of scoring that evening. Or, indeed, ever.

I should probably explain why I was sipping on a nonbinary beverage while wearing the world's most middle-class excuse for fetish gear in a basement in Shoreditch. But, honestly, I was beginning to wonder that myself. Basically, there's this guy called Malcom who I know because everybody knows Malcom. I'm pretty sure he's a stockbroker or a banker or whatever, but in the evenings—by which I mean some evenings, by which I mean about one evening a week—he DJs at this transgender/gender-fluid club night called Surf 'n' Turf @ The Cellar. And tonight was his T Party. His Mad Hatter's T Party. Because that's Malcom.

Right now, he was at the back of the room in a purple topper, a striped tailcoat, leather trousers, and not much else, laying down what I think they call "sick beats." Or maybe they don't. Maybe that's something nobody has ever said ever. When I was going through my club-kid phase, I didn't even bother to ask the names of my hookups, let alone make notes on the terminology.

I sighed and turned my attention back to my Comfortable Lack of a Screw. There should really be a word for the feeling you get when you do a thing you don't particularly want to do to support somebody else but then realise they didn't actually need you and nobody would have noticed if you'd stayed home in your pyjamas eating Nutella straight from the jar. Anyway. That. I was feeling that. And probably I should just have left, except then I'd have been the arsehole who showed up for Malcom's T Party, made no effort with his costume, drank an eighth of a drink, and then fucked off without talking to anybody.

Pulling out my phone, I sent a forlorn **"I'm here, where are you?"** message to the group only to see the clock of doom pop up beside it. Who'd have thought an event that took place literally underground and surrounded by concrete would have bad mobile phone reception?

"You do realise"—warm breath brushed my cheek—"that those ears aren't even white?"

I turned to find a stranger standing next to me. Quite a cute stranger, with that pointy, foxy look I've always found weirdly charming. "Yeah, but I *was* late. And you're not wearing a costume at all."

He grinned, looking even pointier and even foxier and even more charming. Then flicked his lapel aside to reveal a sticky label that read 'Nobody.'

"I'm guessing that's an irritatingly obscure reference."

"*'I only wish I had such eyes,' the king remarked in a fretful tone, 'to be able to see Nobody!'*"

"You smug git."

That made him laugh. "Fancy dress parties bring out the worst in me."

It wasn't quite the longest I'd spoken to a guy without fucking the whole thing up, but it was definitely climbing the leaderboard. What was important here was not to panic and try to protect myself by transforming into an unbearable wanker or a gargantuan manslut. "I hate to imagine who they bring out the best in."

"Yeah, that"—another grin, another flash of his teeth—"would be Malcom."

"Everything brings out the best in Malcom. He could make people celebrate having to pay 10p for a carrier bag."

"Please don't give him ideas. By the way…"—he leaned a little closer—"I'm Cam. But since you almost certainly misheard me, I'll answer to any one-syllable name with a vowel in the middle."

"Nice to meet you, Bob."

"You smug git."

Even through the strobes, I caught the glitter of his eyes. And found myself wondering what colour they were away from the shadows and artificial rainbows of the dance floor. That was a bad sign. That was perilously close to liking someone. And look where that had got me.

"You're Luc Fleming, aren't you?" he asked.

Why, hello other shoe. I'd been wondering when you were going to drop. Eff my effing L. "Actually," I said, like I always said, "it's Luc O'Donnell."

"But you are Jon Fleming's kid?"

"What's it to you?"

He blinked. "Well, nothing. But when I asked Angie"— Malcom's girlfriend, currently dressed as Alice because of course she was—"who the hot, grumpy guy was, she said, 'Oh that's Luc. He's Jon Fleming's kid.'"

I didn't like that being the thing people told each other about me. But then again, what was the alternative? That's Luc, his career's in the toilet? That's Luc, he's not had a stable relationship in five years? That's Luc, where did it all go wrong? "Yeah. That's me."

Cam folded his elbows on the bar. "This is exciting. I've never met anyone famous before. Should I be pretending I really like your dad or really hate your dad?"

"I've never even met him." A cursory Google would have told him that, so it wasn't like he was getting a major scoop here. "So I don't particularly care."

"Probably for the best because I can only remember, like, one of his songs. I think it was about having a green ribbon around his hat."

"No, that's Steeleye Span."

"Oh wait. Jon Fleming's Rights of Man."

"Yeah, but I can see how you got them confused."

He gave me a sharp look. "They sound nothing alike, do they?"

"Well, there's a couple of subtle differences. Steeleye's more folk rock, whereas RoM's more prog rock. Steeleye used a lot of violins, whereas Dad's a flautist. Also, the lead singer of Steeleye Span is a woman."

"Okay"—he flicked another smile at me, less abashed than I would have been in his position—"so I don't know what I'm talking about. My dad's a big fan though. He's got all the records. Keeps them in the attic with the bell bottoms he hasn't been able to get into since 1979."

It was beginning to sink in that, about eight million years ago, Cam had described me as hot and grumpy. Except, right now, it was clearly 80/20 in favour of grumpy. "Everyone's dad's a fan of my dad."

"That must mess with your head."

"A bit."

"And it must be even weirder with the TV thing."

"Kind of." I poked listlessly at my drink. "I get recognised more, but 'Hey, your dad's that guy off that stupid talent show' is marginally better than 'Hey, your dad's that guy who was in the news last week for headbutting a policeman, then vomiting on a judge while off his face on heroin and Toilet Duck.'"

"At least it's interesting. The most scandalous thing my dad's ever done was shake a bottle of ketchup without realising the lid was off."

I laughed in spite of myself.

"I can't believe you're giggling at my childhood trauma. The kitchen looked like something out of *Hannibal*. Mum still brings it up every time she's annoyed, even if it's not actually Dad she's annoyed at."

"Yeah, my mum brings up my dad when I piss her off as well. Except it's less 'This is just like the time your father got a tomatoey condiment all over the kitchen' and more 'This is just like the time your father said he'd come home for my birthday, but instead, he stayed in LA snorting cocaine off a prostitute's breasts.'"

Cam blinked. "Eeesh."

Shit. Half a cocktail and a pretty smile, and I was singing like a lovable urchin on a barricade in France. This was the sort of stuff that ended up in the papers. *Jon Fleming's Other Secret Coke Shame.* Or maybe *Like Father, Like Son: Jon Fleming Junior's Childhood Behaviour Compared to Father's Drug-Fuelled Rampages.* Or worst of all, *Still Crazy after All These Years: Odile O'Donnell Rages at Son about '80s Fleming Hooker Binge.* This was why I should never leave the house. Or talk to humans. Especially not humans I wanted to like me.

"Listen," I said, with zero poker face, despite knowing how badly this could go wrong, "my mum's a really good person, and she brought me up on her own, and has gone through a lot so... like...can you please forget I said that?"

He gave me the type of look you give someone when you're mentally shifting them from the box that says "attractive" to the box that says "weird." "I'm not going to *tell her.* I don't even know her. And, yes, I might have come over to hit on you, but we're quite a long way from meeting the parents."

"Sorry. Sorry. I...I'm just protective of her."

"And you think she needs to be protected from random guys you meet in bars?"

Well, I'd ruined this. Because the answer was basically "Yes, in case you go to the tabloids, because that's a thing that actually happens to me," but I couldn't tell him without putting the idea in his head. I mean, assuming it wasn't there already, and he wasn't playing me like a flute or a fiddle, depending which '70s band he thought I was in. So that left option B: Allow this funny, sexy man I'd like to at least try for a one-night stand with to believe I was a paranoid creep who spent way too much time thinking about his mother.

"Um." I swallowed, feeling about as desirable as a roadkill sandwich. "Can we go back to the bit where you'd come over to hit on me?"

There was a longer silence than I would have liked. Then Cam smiled—if slightly warily. "Sure."

Another silence.

"So," I tried. "This hitting-on-me thing you're doing. I've got to say it's pretty minimalist."

"Well, my original plan was to, y'know, try to talk to you a bit and see how it went, and then maybe try to kiss you or something. But you kind of torpedoed that strategy. So now I don't know what to do."

I drooped. "I'm sorry. You didn't do anything wrong. I'm just really bad at..." I tried to find a word that properly encapsulated my recent dating history "...everything."

Perhaps I was imagining it, but I could almost see Cam deciding whether or not he could be arsed with me. To my mild surprise, he seemed to come down on the side of arsed. "Everything?" he repeated, and tweaked the tip of my bunny ear in a fashion I chose to interpret as encouraging.

This was a good sign, right? This had to be a good sign. Or was it a terrible sign? What was wrong with him that he wasn't running away screaming? Okay. No. I was in my head, and that was the worst place for anyone to be, especially me, and I needed to say something light and flirty and right the fuck now. "I might be okay at the kissing."

"Mmm." Cam leaned in a little farther. *Holy shit, he was actually going for this?* "I'm not sure I trust your judgment. Perhaps I'd better check for myself."

"Um. All right?"

So he checked for himself. And I was okay at the kissing. I mean, I thought I was okay at the kissing. God, I hope I was okay at the kissing.

"Well?" I asked a moment later, sounding relaxed, playful, and not at all desperate and insecure.

His face was close enough that I could see all the tantalising details, like the thickness of his eyelashes, the beginnings of stubble along his jaw, and the crinkles at the corners of his lips. "I'm not sure I can draw an accurate conclusion from a single data point."

"Oooh. Sciencey."

We expanded the data set. And by the time we were done, he had me pressed up against the corner of the bar, and my hands were tucked into the back pockets of his jeans in a really half-arsed attempt to pretend I wasn't blatantly feeling him up. Which was when I remembered that he knew my name, and my dad's name, and probably my mum's name, and quite possibly everything that had ever been written about me, and all I had in return was that he was called "Cam" and tasted nice.

"Are you?" I said, breathlessly. And in response to his confused look, "You know, sciencey. You don't look sciencey."

"Oh. No." He grinned, all foxy and delicious. "That was just an excuse to keep kissing you."

"What do you do, then?"

"I freelance, mainly for sites that wish they were BuzzFeed."

I knew it. I fucking knew it. He had been far too eager to overlook my many, many flaws. "You're a journalist."

"That's a pretty generous term for it. I write those lists of x things about y where you won't believe z that everybody hates but seem to read anyway."

Twelve Things You Didn't Know About Luc O'Donnell. Number Eight Will Shock You.

"And, sometimes, I make those quizzes where it's like pick

eight pictures of kittens, and we'll tell you which John Hughes character you are."

The rational version of Luc, the one from the parallel universe where my dad wasn't a famous shithead and my ex-boyfriend hadn't sold all my secrets to Piers Morgan, tried to tell me I was overreacting. Unfortunately, I wasn't listening.

Cam tilted his head quizzically. "What's wrong? Look, I know it's not exactly a sexy job, and I don't even have the comfort of saying 'Someone has to do it' because we totally don't. But you've gone weird again."

"Sorry. It's...complicated."

"Complicated can be interesting." He went up on tiptoes to smooth a lock of hair behind my ear for me. "And we've got the kissing down. We've just got to work on the talking."

I gave what I hoped wasn't a sickly grin. "I'd rather stick with what I'm good at."

"Tell you what. I'll ask you a question, and if I like the answer, you get to kiss me again."

"Um, I'm not sure—"

"Let's start small. You know what I do. How about you?"

My heart was racing. And not in a fun way. But, as questions went, that was harmless, right? It was information at least two hundred spambots already had. "I work for a charity."

"Wow. Noble. I'd say I'd always wanted to do something like that, but I'm far too shallow." He turned his face up to mine, and I kissed him nervously. "Favourite ice cream flavour?"

"Mint choc chip."

Another kiss. "Book that literally everyone else has read but you haven't."

"All of them."

He drew back. "You're not getting kissed for that. It's a total cop-out."

"No seriously. All of them, *To Kill A Mockingbird*, *The Catcher in the Rye*, anything Dickens ever wrote, *All Quiet on the Western Front*, that one about the time-traveller's wife, Harry Potter..."

"You really do own your illiteracy, don't you?"

"Yeah, I'm thinking about moving to America and running for public office."

He laughed and kissed me, staying close this time, body pressed to mine, breath against my skin. "Okay. Weirdest place you've ever had sex."

"Is that for number eight?" I asked, with a bleaty laugh that was meant to show I was incredibly cool and unconcerned.

"Number eight what?"

"You know, twelve celebrities' kids who like to fuck in weird places. Number eight will shock you."

"Wait." He froze. "Do you honestly think I'm kissing you for a *listicle*?"

"No. I mean...no. No."

He gazed at me for a long, horrible moment. "You do, don't you?"

"I told you it was complicated."

"That's not complicated, that's insulting."

"I... It's..." I'd pulled this back before. I could pull it back again. "It wasn't meant to be. It's not about you."

This time, there was no ear tweaking. "How is it *not about me* if you genuinely have this concern about *my* possible behaviour?"

"I just have to be careful." For the record, I sounded extremely dignified when I said this. And not at all pathetic.

"What the hell would I even write? I Met a Has-Been's Kid at a Party? Celebrity's Gay Son Is Gay Shock?"

"Well, it sounds like it'd be a step up from what you usually write."

His mouth fell open, and I realised I might have gone the

tiniest bit too far. "Wow. I was about to say I wasn't sure which of us was the arsehole here, but thanks for clearing that up."

"No, no," I said quickly, "it was always me. Trust me, I know."

"Really not sure that helps. I mean, I can't figure out what's worse. That you think I'd fuck a mildly famous person to get ahead. Or that you think if I was going to make such a profoundly degrading career choice, the person I'd pick to make it with was you."

I swallowed. "All good points. Very well made."

"Shit on a hot tin roof, I should have listened to Angie. You are a world of not worth it."

He stalked off into the crowd, presumably to find someone less fucked up, leaving me alone with my lopsided bunny ears and a profound sense of personal failure. Although I guess I'd accomplished two things tonight: I'd successfully demonstrated my support for a man who in no way needed it, and I'd finally proved beyond all reasonable objection that nobody in their right mind would date me. I was a cagey, grumpy, paranoid mess who would find a way to ruin even the most basic human interaction.

I leaned against the bar and stared at the basement full of strangers having a far better time than me, at least two of whom were probably having a conversation right now about what a terrible human being I was. The way I saw it, I had two options. I could suck it up, act like an adult, find my actual friends, and try to make the best of the evening. Or I could run home, drink alone, and add this to the list of things I was unsuccessfully pretending had never happened.

Two seconds later, I was on the stairs.

Eight seconds later, I was out in the street.

And nineteen seconds later, I was tripping over my own feet and landing flat on my face in the gutter.

Well, wasn't that just the ill-fitting crown on my inbred Hapsburg prince of an evening? And no way was it coming back to haunt me.

CHAPTER 2

IT CAME BACK TO HAUNT me.

And the way it haunted me was a Google alert that threatened to vibrate my phone off the bedside table. And, yes, I'm very aware that tracking what people are saying about you on the internet is generally the act of a tosser or a narcissist, or a narcissistic tosser, but I'd learned the hard way that it's better to know what's out there. I flailed, sending a different piece of vibrating technology— *for gentlemen wishing to explore a more sophisticated kind of pleasure*—spinning to the floor, and finally managed to close my fingers round my phone with all the grace of a teenager trying to hit second base.

I didn't want to look. But if I didn't, I was going to throw up the sticky mess of dread, hope, and uncertainty that had turned my insides to baby food. Probably it was less bad than I feared. Usually it was less bad than I feared. Except occasionally it... wasn't. Peeping through my eyelashes like a small child braving an episode of *Doctor Who* from behind the sofa cushions, I checked my notifications.

And I could breathe again. It was okay. Though obviously in an ideal world, pictures of me lying in the gutter outside The Cellar in my bunny ears *wouldn't* have been splashed across every third-rate gossip site from Celebitchy to Yeeeah. And in a truly ideal world my definition of *okay* wouldn't have sunk quite that low. But, with my life being a never-ending pit of suck, my dismay-dar has gone through some serious recalibrations over the years. I mean, at least the pictures showed me fully clothed and without anybody's cock in my mouth. So, y'know, win.

Today's nail in the coffin of my digital reputation had a strong "like father, like son" theme, because there's a magic porridge pot's worth of footage of Jon Fleming making a tit of himself out there. And I guess "Bad Boy Jonny's Wild Child Son Collapses in Drugs Sex Booze Shame" is a better headline than "Man Trips Over in Street." Sighing, I let my phone thunk to the floor. Turns out, the one thing worse than having a famous father who blew up his career like a champagne supernova is having a famous father who's making a fucking comeback.

I'd just about learned to live with being compared to my reckless, self-destructive absentee father. But now he'd cleaned up his act and was playing the wise, old mentor every Sunday on ITV, I was being compared *unfavourably* to my reckless, self-destructive absentee father. And that was a level of bullshit I was not emotionally prepared for. I should have known better than to read the comments, but my eyes slipped and fell on *wellactually69*, who'd been massively upvoted for suggesting a reality TV show in which Jon Fleming tries to put his junkie son back on the straight and narrow—a show which *theotherjillfrompeckham* declared that she would "watch the shit out of."

I knew, in the grand scheme of things, none of this mattered. The internet was forever, and there was no getting away from that, but by tomorrow, or the day after, I would be below the fold, or whatever the e-equivalent of the fold was. As good as forgotten until the next time someone wanted a twist on the Jon Fleming story. Except I still felt fucking terrible, and the longer I lay there, the fucking terribler I felt.

I tried to take some comfort in the fact that at least Cam hadn't put me on a list of Twelve Pricks Who Will Freak Out on You in a Nightclub. But as comfort went, that landed somewhere between "cold" and "scant." Truth be told, I'd never been the best at self-care. Self-recrimination, I had down. Self-loathing, I could do in my sleep, and often did. So here I was, a twenty-eight-year-old man suddenly feeling an overwhelming need to call his mother because he was sad.

Because the one upside of my dad being who he is, is that my mum is who she is. You can Wiki this stuff, but the tl;dr version is that back in the '80s she was essentially a French-Irish Adele with bigger hair. And at about the time Bros were wondering when they'd be famous and Cliff Richard was spilling mistletoe and wine on a million unsuspecting Christmases, she and Dad were caught up in this love-you-hate-you-can't-live-without-you thing that produced two collaborative albums, one solo album, and me.

Well, technically I came before the solo album, which happened when Dad realised he wanted to be famous and wasted more than he wanted to be in our lives. "Welcome Ghosts" was the last thing Mum ever wrote but, honestly, it was the last thing she had to. Nearly every year the BBC, or ITV, or some movie studio uses a track from it over a sad scene or an angry scene or a scene it doesn't fit, but we'll cash the cheque anyway.

Stumbling out of bed, I adopted out of long-ingrained habit the Quasimodo pose required for anyone over 5'6" to move around my flat without getting clocked in the face by an eave. Which, given I'm 6'4", is the accommodational equivalent of having chosen to drive a Mini Cooper. I'd leased the place with Miles—my ex—back when it had been romantic to live in the twenty-first century equivalent of a garret in Shepherd's Bush. Now it was rapidly becoming pathetic: being alone, stuck in a job that was going nowhere, and still unable to afford a home that wasn't mostly the underside of a roof. Of course, it might also have helped if I'd tidied it, like, ever.

Shoving a pile of socks off the sofa, I curled up and got to FaceTiming. "Allô, Luc, mon caneton," said Mum. "Did you see your father's whole package last night?"

I gave a gasp of actual horror before remembering *The Whole Package* was the name of his stupid TV show. "No. I was out with friends."

"You should watch it. I'm sure it will be on the catch-up."

"I don't want to watch it."

She gave the most Gallic of shrugs. I'm convinced she plays up the French thing, but I can't really blame her for it because all she got from her father was his name. Well, that and a pallor Siouxsie Sioux would envy. In any case, even if having a dad who runs out on you isn't genetic, in our family it's definitely hereditary. "Your father," she declared. "He has not aged well."

"Good to know."

"His head is bald as an egg now and a funny shape. He looks like that chemistry teacher with the cancer."

This was news to me. But then I haven't exactly gone out of my way to keep in contact with my old school. To be honest, I haven't exactly gone out of my way to keep in contact with people who live on the wrong side of London. "Mr. Beezle has cancer?"

"Not him. The other one."

Another thing about my mum: relationship to reality, questionable at best. "Do you mean Walter White?"

"Oui oui. And you know, I think he is too old to be hopping around with a flute these days."

"We're talking about Dad, right? Because otherwise *Breaking Bad* got hella weird in its later seasons."

"Of course your father. He will probably break a hip."

"Well." I grinned. "We can hope."

"He bid on a young lady with a harmonica—it was a good choice, I think, because she was one of the most talented—but she went with one of the boys from Blue instead. I enjoyed that very much."

If left unchecked, Mum could talk about reality TV basically forever. Unfortunately—with *wellactually69* and friends buzzing around my head like internet hornets—my attempt to check her came out as "I got papped yesterday."

"Oh, baby. Again? I'm sorry."

My own shrug was very non-Gallic.

"You know how these things are." Her tone softened reassuringly. "Always a squall in a…a…shot glass."

That made me smile. She always does. "I know. It's just every time it happens, even when it's trivial, it, well, it reminds me."

"You know it was not your fault, what happened. What Miles did, it was not even truly about you."

I snorted. "It was specifically *all* about me."

"Someone else's actions may affect you. But what other people choose to do is about them."

We were both quiet for a moment.. "Will it…will it ever stop hurting?"

"Non." Mum shook her head. "But it will stop mattering."

I wanted to believe her, I really did. She was, after all, living proof of her words.

"Do you want to come round, mon caneton?"

It was only an hour or so away if I cadged a lift from Epsom (1.6 stars on Google) Station. But while I could more-or-less justify ringing my mum every time something bad happened to me, literally running back to her literal house slipped under even my low bar for self-respect.

"Judy and I have found this new show that we are watching," offered Mum in a way that I think was intended to be encouraging.

"Oh?"

"Yes, it is very intriguing. It is called *RuPaul's Drag Race*—have you heard of it? We were not sure we would like it at first because we thought it was about monster trucks. But you can imagine how happy we were when we discovered it was about men who like to dress as women—why are you laughing?"

"Because I love you. Very much."

"You should not be laughing, Luc. You would be very impressed. We are often gagging on their eleganza. That means—"

"I'm familiar with *Drag Race*. Probably more familiar than you." This was what happened when you won an Emmy. Your audience became your audience's mums.

"Then you should come, mon cher."

Mum lives in Pucklethroop-in-the-Wold—this tiny, chocolate box of a village where I grew up—and spends her days getting into scrapes with her best friend, Judith Cholmondely-Pfaffle. "I…" If I stayed home, I could try and achieve grown-up things like plates and clean clothes. Although in practice, I would probably pick at my Google alerts until they bled.

"I am making my special curry."

Okay, that settled it. "Fuck no."

"Luc, I think you are very rude about my special curry."

"Yes, because I prefer my arsehole not on fire."

Mum was pouting. "For a gay, you are far too sensitive about your arsehole."

"How about we don't talk about my arsehole anymore?"

"You brought it up. Anyway, Judy loves my curries."

Sometimes I think Judy must love Mum. God knows why else you would brave her cooking. "Probably because you've spent the last twenty-five years systematically murdering her taste buds."

"Well, you know where we are if you change your mind."

"Thanks, Mum. Talk to you soon."

"Allez, darling. Bises."

Without Mum talking nineteen-to-the-dozen about reality TV, my home was suddenly very quiet, my day very...long seeming. Between work, friends, acquaintances, and sporadic attempts to get laid, I usually managed to use my flat as an overpriced, badly maintained hotel. Turning up only to crash out and leave again the next morning.

Except Sundays. Sundays were tricky. Or had got tricky as the years had got away from me. At university they'd been for brunch and regretting what you'd done on Saturday and sleepy afternoons. Then, one by one, I'd lost my friends to dinners with in-laws or decorating the nursery or the pleasures of a day at home.

It wasn't that I blamed them for their changing lives. And I didn't want what they had. I wasn't cut out for it. Since, as far as I could remember, Sundays with Miles had spun pretty quickly from marathon sexfests to smouldering resentathons. It was just moments like these. When it felt like my world was notifications on my phone.

Notifications I was trying very hard to ignore. Because I knew Mum was right: if I could get through today, they wouldn't matter tomorrow.

Though, as it turned out, we were both wrong.

Super, super wrong.

CHAPTER 3

MONDAY STARTED OUT AS IT usually did—with me late for work and nobody caring because it was that kind of office. I mean, I say *office*. It's actually a house in Southwark that's been half-arsedly converted to the headquarters of the charity I work for. Which happens to be the only charity or, indeed, organisation of any kind that would hire me.

It's the redheaded step-brainchild of an elderly earl with a thing for agriculture and a Cambridge-educated etymologist who I think might be a rogue AI sent from the future. Their mission? Saving dung beetles. And, as a fundraiser, it's my job to convince people that they're better off giving their money to bugs that eat poo instead of pandas, orphans, or—God help us—Comic Relief. I wish I could tell you I'm good at it but, really, there are no metrics to measure something like that. I mean, we haven't gone bust yet. And what I tend to say at interviews for other jobs I don't get is that there isn't another faeces-based environmental charity that raises more money than we do.

Also, we're called the Coleoptera Research and Protection Project. The acronym for which is definitely pronounced CEEARAYPEEPEE. And definitely not CRAPP.

Working at CRAPP has a number of drawbacks: the central heating that blazes all summer and cuts off all winter, the office manager who never lets anybody spend any money on anything for any reason, the computers so old they still run a version of Windows named after a year, to say nothing of the daily realisation that this is my life. But there are some perks. The coffee is pretty decent because the two things Dr. Fairclough cares about are caffeine and invertebrates. And every morning, while I'm waiting for my Renaissance-era PC to boot up, I get to tell jokes to Alex Twaddle. Or rather, I get to tell jokes at Alex Twaddle. While Alex Twaddle blinks at me.

I don't know much about him and I certainly don't know how he got his job, which is, theoretically, executive assistant to Dr. Fairclough. Somebody once told me he had a first-class degree, but didn't say in what or from where.

"So," I said, "there are these two strips of tarmac in a bar…"

Alex blinked. "Strips of tarmac?"

"Yes."

"Are you sure? That doesn't seem to make much sense."

"Just go with it. So there are these two strips of tarmac, and one says to the other, 'Aw man, I'm so hard. All these lorries roll over me, and I don't even feel it.' Then, just as he's finished talking, this piece of red tarmac walks in. And the first piece of tarmac gets up, and runs away, and hides in a corner. And his mate goes over to him and says, 'What are you doing? I thought you were supposed to be hard.' And the first piece of tarmac says, 'Yeah, I'm hard, but that guy's a cycle path.'"

There was long silence.

Alex blinked again. "Why is he frightened of cycle paths? Did he get into an accident?"

"No, it's that he's hard, but the other guy's…a *cycle path*."

"Yes, but why is he frightened of cycle paths?"

Sometimes I lost sight of whether this was my hobby or a punishment I was inflicting on myself. "No, it's a pun, Alex.

Because 'cycle path,' if you say it fast and in a sort of Cockney accent, sounds a bit like 'psychopath.'"

"Oh." He thought about it for a moment or two. "I'm not sure it does, actually."

"You're right, Alex. I'll do better next time."

"By the way," he said, "you've got a meeting with Dr. Fairclough at half ten."

This was not a good sign. "I don't suppose," I began, already sure it was hopeless, "you have any idea why she wants to see me?"

He beamed. "None whatsoever."

"Keep up the good work."

I trudged back downstairs to my office, the prospect of having to interact with Dr. Fairclough hanging over me like a cartoon rain cloud. Don't get me wrong. I have a lot of respect for her—if I'm afflicted by some kind of beetle-related crisis, she'll be my first call—it's just I've got no idea how to talk to her. To be fair, she clearly has no idea how to talk to me either. Or possibly anyone else. The difference is, she doesn't care.

As I crossed the hallway, the floorboards creaking merrily with every step, a voice called out, "That you, Luc?"

Sadly, this was undeniable. "Yes, it's me."

"Do you mind popping in a moment? We're having a bit of a sticky situation with the Twitter."

Team player that I am, I popped. Rhys Jones Bowen— CEEARAYPEEPEE's volunteer coordinator and head of social media outreach—was hunched over his computer, pecking at it with one finger.

"The thing is," he said, "you know how you wanted me to tell everybody about the Beetle Drive?"

The Beetle Drive is our office nickname for the annual dinner, dance, and fundraiser. I've organised it every year for the past three years. The fact it's the big-ticket item on my current job description tells you all you need to know about it. And, for that matter, my job.

I tried very hard to keep my tone neutral. "Yes, I remember mentioning it sometime last month."

"Ah, well, you see. It's like this. I'd misremembered the password, and I was going to get them to send me another one to the email I'd used to set up the account. But as it turned out, I'd misremembered the password for that as well."

"I can see how that would cause problems."

"Now I knew I'd put it on a Post-it note. And I knew I'd put the Post-it note in a book to keep it safe. And I knew the book had a blue cover. But I couldn't remember the title, or who wrote it, or what it was about."

"Couldn't you," I asked carefully, "have reset the password on the email?"

"I could have, but by that stage I was a bit scared to see how far the rabbit hole went."

To be honest, this happens a lot. I mean, not *this* precisely but something along these lines. And I'd probably have been more concerned if our Twitter account had more than 137 followers. "Don't worry about it."

He put out a hand to reassure me. "No, it's okay. See, I was on the loo and I always take a book in with me, and I sometimes leave a couple in there in case I forget, and I see this one on the windowsill with a blue cover and I take it down and I open it and there's the Post-it. And it's a good job I was already sitting down because I fair near shat myself, I was that excited."

"Lucky on both counts." Somewhat keen to move past the toilet, I continued. "So, if you've got the password back, what's the problem?"

"Well, you see, I seem to be running out of letters."

"I emailed you with what to say. It should definitely fit."

"But then I heard about these things called hashtags. Apparently it's very important to use hashtags so people can find your twitters on the Twitter."

To be fair, he wasn't wrong about that. On the other hand, my faith in Rhys Jones Bowen's social media optimisation instincts was not exactly running at a historic high. "Okay?"

"I've been brainstorming a lot of different ideas, and I think this is the tag that describes what we're trying to achieve with the Beetle Drive."

With a quite unwarranted air of triumph, he slid over a piece of paper on which he had painstakingly handwritten:

#ColeopteraResearchAndProtectionProjectAnnual
FundraisingDinnerAndDanceWithSilentAuctionOf
EtymologicalSpecimensAlsoKnownAsTheBeetleDriveAt
TheRoyalAmbassadorsHotelMaryleboneNotTheOneIn
EdinburghTicketsAvailableFromOurWebsiteNow

"And now," he went on, "it's only letting me put another forty-two letters in."

You know, once upon a time, I used to have a really promising career. I've got an MBA, for fuck's sake. I've worked for some of the biggest PR firms in the city. And now I spend my days explaining hashtags to a Celtic twit.

Or not.

"I'll make a graphic," I told him.

He perked up. "Oh, you can Twitter a picture, can you? I read people respond very well to pictures because of visual learning."

"You'll have it by lunchtime."

And, with that, I headed back to my office where my computer was finally up and running, and wheezing like an asthmatic *T. rex*. Checking my email, I was disconcerted to discover a handful of supporters—quite significant supporters—had pulled out of the Beetle Drive. Of course, people were flaky, even more so when you wanted them to give you money, and especially when it was money for dung beetles. But something about this made the hairs on the back of my neck prickle. It was probably random chance. It just didn't *feel* random.

I quickly checked our public footprint, in case our website had been hijacked by amateur pornographers again. And when I found nothing remotely worrying (or interesting), I ended up e-stalking the dropouts like the guy from *A Beautiful Mind*, trying to figure out if there were any connections between them. As far as I could tell, no. Well, they were all rich, white, politically and socially conservative. Like most of our donors.

I'm not saying dung beetles aren't important—Dr. Fairclough has told me at length, several times, why they're important, which has something to do with soil aeration and organic-matter content—but you need a certain level of privilege to care more about high-end bug management than, say, land mines or homeless shelters. Of course, while most of us would say that homeless people are human beings and therefore deserve to be looked after, Dr. Fairclough would argue that homeless people are human beings and, thus, plentiful and ecologically somewhere between insignificant and a net detriment. Unlike dung beetles, which are irreplaceable. Which is why she looks at the data and I talk to the press.

CHAPTER 4

AT 10:30, I DUTIFULLY PRESENTED myself outside Dr. Fairclough's office where Alex made a show of letting me in, even though the door was already open. The room, as ever, was an eerily ordered carnage of books, papers, and etymological samples, as if it was the nest of some particularly academic wasps.

"Sit, O'Donnell."

Yep. That's my boss. Dr. Amelia Fairclough looks like Kate Moss, dresses like Simon Schama, and talks like she's being charged by the word. In many ways, she's an ideal person to work for because her management style involves paying no attention to you unless you actually set something on fire. Which, to be fair, Alex has done twice.

I sat.

"Twaddle"—her gaze flicked sharply to Alex—"minutes."

He jumped. "Oh. Um. Yes. Absolutely. Does anybody have a pen?"

"Over there. Underneath the *Chrysochroa fulminans*."

"Splendid." Alex had the eyes of Bambi's mother. Possibly after she'd been shot. "The what?"

A muscle in Dr. Fairclough's jaw twitched. "The green one."

Ten minutes later, Alex had finally acquired a pen, some paper, a second piece of paper because he'd put his pen through the first one, and a copy of the *Ecology and Evolution of Dung Beetles* (Simmons and Ridsdill-Smith, Wiley-Blackwell, 2011) to rest on.

"Okay," he said. "Ready."

Dr. Fairclough folded her hands on the desk in front of her. "This gives me no pleasure, O'Donnell…"

I couldn't tell if she meant having to talk to me or what she was about to say. Either way, it didn't bode well. "Shit, am I fired?"

"Not yet, but I've had to answer three emails about you today, and that's three more emails than I normally like to answer."

"Emails about me?" I knew where this was going. I'd probably always known. "Is this because of the pictures?"

She gave a curt nod. "Yes. When we took you on, you told us that was behind you."

"It was. I mean, it is. I just made the mistake of going to a party the same night my dad was on ITV."

"The consensus among the press appears to be that you were lying in a drug-fuelled haze in a gutter. In fetish wear."

"I fell over," I said flatly, "in a pair of comedy bunny ears."

"To a certain class of person, that detail adds an especial element of deviance."

In some ways, it felt almost like a relief to get angry. It was better than being terrified I was about to lose my job. "Do I need a lawyer? Because I'm beginning to think this has more to do with my sexuality than my sobriety."

"Of course it does." Dr. Fairclough made an impatient gesture. "It makes you look like entirely the wrong sort of homosexual."

Alex had been watching the conversation as if it was Wimbledon. And I could now hear him murmuring "wrong sort of homosexual" under his breath as he scribbled.

I did my best to offer my reply in the most reasonable tone I could muster. "You know I could really hard-core sue you for this."

"You could," agreed Dr. Fairclough. "But you wouldn't get

another job, and we're not strictly firing you. Besides which, as our fundraiser, you must be acutely aware that we don't have any money, making litigation rather pointless from your end."

"What, so you just brought me here to brighten my day with a little casual homophobia?"

"Come now, O'Donnell." She sighed. "You must know I have no interest in what variety of homosexual you are—incidentally, did you know that aphids are parthenogenetic?—but unfortunately several of our backers do. They, of course, are not all homophobic, and I think rather enjoyed having a delightful young gay wining and dining them. That, however, was rather predicated on you being essentially nonthreatening."

My anger, like every man I'd ever been with, didn't seem inclined to stick around. And had left me feeling tired and pointless. "Actually, that's still homophobic."

"And you may certainly call them up and explain that to them, but I somehow doubt it will make them more inclined to give us their money. And if you are unable to get people to give us their money, then that rather limits your usefulness to our organisation."

Well, now I was scared again. "I thought you said I wasn't going to get fired."

"As long as the Beetle Drive is successful, you may go to whatever bars you please and wear whatever mammalian appendages you like."

"Yay."

"But right now"—she cast me a cold glance—"your public image as some kind of barebacking, coke-snorting, buttockless-trouser-wearing pervert has scared away three of our biggest donors, and I need not remind you, our donor list is straying perilously close to single digits."

Maybe not the best time to tell her about the emails I'd received this morning. "So what am I supposed to do?"

"Rehabilitate yourself fast. You need to go back to being the sort of harmless sodomite that Waitrose shoppers can feel good about introducing to their left-wing friends and smug about introducing to their right-wing friends."

"For the record, I'm really, *really* offended by this."

She shrugged. "Darwin was offended by the *Ichneumonidae*. To his chagrin, they persisted in existing."

If I had a single gnat's testicle of pride, I would have walked out there and then. But I haven't, so I didn't. "I can't control what the tabloids say about me."

"Of course you can," piped up Alex. "It's easy."

We both stared at him.

"Friend of mine from Eton, Mulholland Tarquin Jjones, got into a terrible pickle a couple of years back over a misunderstanding with a stolen car, three prostitutes, and a kilo of heroin. The papers were beastly to him about it, but then he got engaged to a lovely little heiress from Devonshire, and it was all garden parties and spreads in *Hello* from then on."

"Alex," I said slowly. "You know how I'm gay, and this whole conversation has been about me being gay?"

"Well, obviously I mean a boy heiress, not a girl heiress."

"I don't know any heiresses of either gender."

"Don't you?" He looked genuinely confused. "Who do you go to Ascot with?"

I put my head in my hands. I thought I might be about to cry.

Which was when Dr. Fairclough took control of the conversation again. "Twaddle does have a point. With an appropriate boyfriend, I daresay you'd become endearing again very quickly."

I'd been trying very hard not to think about my abysmal failure with Cam at The Cellar. Now the memory of his rejection flooded me with fresh humiliation. "I can't even get an inappropriate boyfriend."

"That is not my problem, O'Donnell. Please leave. Between the emails and this conversation, you've already taken up too much of my morning."

Her attention snapped back to whatever she was doing on her computer with such intensity that I half thought I'd actually stopped existing. Right about then, I wouldn't have cared if I had.

My head was swimming as I left the office. I put a hand to my face and discovered my eyes were wet.

"Gosh," said Alex. "Are you crying?"

"No."

"Do you want a hug?"

"No."

But somehow I ended up in his arms anyway, having my hair awkwardly patted. Alex was supposed to have been a serious cricketer at school or university or something—whatever serious meant for a sport that was basically five days of eating strawberries and walking slowly—and I couldn't help notice he still had the body for it, lean and rangy and solid. On top of which he smelled implausibly wholesome, like freshly cut grass in summer. I pushed my face into his designer cashmere cardigan and made a sound that definitely wasn't a sob.

To his credit, Alex seemed entirely unperturbed by this. "There, there. I know Dr. Fairclough can be a bit of a rotter, but worse things happen at sea."

"Alex." I sniffed and surreptitiously attempted to wipe my nose. "People haven't said 'worse things happen at sea' since 1872."

"Yes, they have. I said it just now. Weren't you listening?"

"You're right. Silly of me."

"Don't worry. I can see you're upset."

Having dragged myself about two inches above rock bottom, I became painfully aware I was crying on the shoulder of the office doofus. "I'm fine. I'm still trying to process the fact that having been basically single for half a fucking decade, I have to get a boyfriend overnight or lose the only job that would have me—working for a charity whose standards for employment are so low that they'd hire you and Rhys."

Alex thought about this for a moment. "You're right. That is terrible. I mean, we're complete duffers."

"Oh, come on," I growled. "At least be offended. Now you're making me feel like a total dick."

"I'm so sorry. I didn't mean to."

There are times when I almost wonder if Alex is secretly a genius and we are but pawns in his grand design. "You're doing this deliberately, aren't you?"

He gave a smile that was either enigmatic or just vacant. "In any case, I'm sure you could get a boyfriend easily. You're nice-looking. You've got a good job. You've even been in the newspapers recently."

"If I could get a boyfriend, I would *have* a boyfriend."

Alex propped his hips against the side of his desk. "Chin up, old thing. We can crack this. Now, do your parents know anybody suitable?"

"You remember that my dad is a recovering druggie on reality TV and my mum is an '80s recluse with exactly one friend?"

"Yes, but I assume they still have a club?"

"They don't."

"Don't worry. Plenty more options." A pause. "Just give me a moment while I think of them."

Oh hello, rock bottom. Nice to see you again. Do you want to be my boyfriend?

After several long moments, Alex perked up like a beagle scenting a rabbit. "What about the chaps you went to school with? Ring them up and ask if any of them has a nice sister. I mean, brother. I mean, gay brother."

"I went to school in a tiny village. There were three people in my year. I'm not in touch with any of them."

"How peculiar." He tilted his head quizzically. "I assumed you must have been a Harrow man."

"You know there are people who went to neither Eton or Harrow?"

"Well yes, obviously. Girls."

I was in no state to explain the socioeconomics of modern Britain to a man so posh he didn't even think it was weird that you pronounced the *t* in Moët but not merlot. "I can't believe I'm going to say this, but can we please get back to you trying to fix my love life?"

"I have to admit I'm a bit stumped." He fell silent, frowning and fiddling with his cuffs. Then, out of nowhere, he beamed at me. "I've thought of something."

Under normal circumstances, I would have taken this with the giant grain of salt it deserved. But I was desperate. "What?"

"Why don't you say you're going out with me?"

"You're not gay. And everyone knows that you're not gay."

He shrugged. "I'll tell them I've changed my mind."

"I'm really not sure that's how it works."

"I thought these things were meant to be fluid nowadays. Twentieth century and all that."

This was not the time to remind Alex what century it was. "Don't you have a girlfriend?" I asked.

"Oh, yes, Miffy. I'd quite forgotten. But she's a terrific girl. She won't mind at all."

"In her place, I would mind. I would mind *a lot*."

"Well, maybe that's why you don't have a boyfriend." He gave me a faintly wounded look. "You sound very demanding."

"Look. I appreciate the offer. But don't you think if you can't remember you've got an actual girlfriend, you might have trouble remembering a fake boyfriend?"

"No, you see that's the clever thing about it. I can pretend that you're my boyfriend, and nobody will think it's strange that I've never mentioned you before because I'm such an utter nincompoop that it could very easily have slipped my mind."

Terrifyingly, he was beginning to make sense. "You know what," I said. "I will genuinely think about it."

"Think about what?"

"Thanks, Alex. You've been a big help."

I made my way slowly back to my office, where I was relieved to discover I hadn't driven off any other donors in the interim. Then I sat at my desk with my head in my hands and wished—

God. I was too fucked up to even know what I was wishing for. Obviously, it would have been nice if my father wasn't on TV and I wasn't in the papers and my job wasn't in jeopardy. But none of those things, either together or individually, were really the problem here. They were just a few more dead seabirds bobbing on the outskirts of the oil spill that was my life.

After all, I couldn't fix the fact my father was Jon Fleming. I couldn't fix that he hadn't wanted me. I couldn't fix falling in love with Miles. And I couldn't fix that he hadn't wanted me either.

It was while I was wallowing that I came to the realisation that Alex hadn't been entirely unhelpful. I mean, he hadn't gone so far as to actually *be* helpful—small steps, small steps—but he was, broadly speaking, right in that people you knew were an effective way to meet people you didn't know.

I grabbed my phone and fired up the WhatsApp group, which somebody had recently rechristened Don't Wanna Be All Bi Myself. After a moment's consideration, I sent a series of siren emojis followed by **Help. Emergency. Queervengers Assemble. Rose & Crown. 6 tonight** and was secretly kind of touched by how quickly the screen lit up with promises to be there.

CHAPTER 5

IT WAS SLIGHTLY SELFISH OF me to choose the Rose & Crown for the meet-up because it was way closer to me than it was to anyone else. But since I was the one having the crisis, I felt entitled. Besides, it was one of my favourite pubs—a gawky seventeenth-century building that looked as though it had been airlifted in from a country village and plonked down in the middle of Blackfriars. With its disconcertingly expansive beer-garden and hanging baskets, it was practically its own little island, the surrounding office blocks almost leaning away from it in embarrassment.

I ordered a beer and a burger and staked a claim to a picnic table outside. As it was what passed for spring in England, the air was a bit nippy, but if Londoners let little things like cold, rain, a slightly worrying level of pollution, and getting crapped on by pigeons bother us, we'd never go outside at all. I was only waiting a couple of minutes before Tom showed up.

Which was ever so slightly awkward as fuck.

Tom isn't, strictly speaking, a friend. He's a friend-in-law, being the long-term partner of the group's Token Straight Girl, Bridget. He's both the hottest and the coolest person I know, on account of looking like Idris Elba's cleaner-cut younger brother and being an actual spy. Well, not exactly. He works for the

Intelligence Division of Customs and Excise, which is one of those agencies that exist but never get in the papers.

It gets even more complicated than that because, technically, I saw him first. We went on a couple of dates and I thought it was going really well, so I introduced him to Bridget, and she fucking stole him from me. Well, she didn't steal him. He just liked her more. And I don't resent it at all. I mean, I do. But I don't. Except when I do.

And probably I shouldn't have hit on him again when he and Bridget went through that bad patch a couple of years ago. They were on a break, so it was less shitty of me than it could have been. And, anyway, all it wound up doing was making him realise how much he loved her and wanted to fix things with her. So that felt great.

Basically Tom does to my self-esteem what he does to people traffickers and gunrunners. Although my self-esteem is way less entrenched.

"Hi," I said, trying not to dig a hole in the grass and wriggle into it like an endangered dung beetle.

Tom gave me a very continental and slightly soul-destroying kiss on the cheek, plonking his beer down next to mine. "Good to see you. It's been a while."

"Yeah. Hasn't it."

I must have accidentally looked traumatised because Tom went on, "Bridge is running late. I mean, obviously."

I laughed nervously. Late is her default. "So. Um. What have you been up to?"

"This and that. Big commercial fraud case. Should be wrapping up fairly soon. What about you?"

From three years of hanging out with Tom, I knew that *commercial fraud* was industry code for something significantly more serious, although I'd never quite worked out what. Which meant having to tell him I was organising a party to raise money for poo bugs was the tiniest bit mortifying.

But, of course, he looked terribly interested and asked a bunch of really insightful questions, half of which I should probably have been asking myself. In any case, it kept the conversation going until the James Royce-Royces arrived.

I met James Royce and James Royce (now James Royce-Royce and James Royce-Royce) at a university LGBTQ+ event. In some ways, it's strange the two of them work so well together because their name is pretty much the only thing they've ever had in common. James Royce-Royce is a bespectacled chef with a way of expressing himself that... Look, I'm trying to find a tactful way to put it, but basically he's just phenomenally camp. James Royce-Royce, on the other hand, looks like a Russian hit man, has a job I don't understand involving unspeakably complex mathematics, and is incredibly shy.

Currently they're trying to adopt, so the conversation very quickly became about the "truly hellacious" (James Royce-Royce's term) amount of paperwork involved in what I'd naively assumed was the straightforward process of getting babies from people who don't want them to people who do want them. I honestly couldn't tell if it was more or less alienating than talking about actual children.

Next we got Priya, a tiny lesbian with multicoloured extensions who somehow managed to pay her bills by welding bits of metal to other bits of metal and selling them in galleries. I'm sure she's genuinely very talented, but I am totally unqualified to judge. She used to be the only other singleton in my immediate friendship group, and many were the evenings we spent drinking cheap prosecco, lamenting our mutual unlovability, and promising to cash out and marry each other if we were both still alone at fifty. But then she betrayed me by falling in love with a married

Medievalist twentysomething years her senior. And then, even more unforgivably, making it work.

"Where the shit were you on Saturday?" She hopped onto the table and glared at me. "We were supposed to be sitting in a corner judging people."

I gave one of those I'm-pretending-not-to-be-mortified shrugs. "Showed up, bought a cocktail, got the knock-back from a pretty hipster, left in disgrace."

"Huh." Priya's mouth quirked into a crooked grin. "So fairly normal evening for you."

"I want you to know that while I do have a comeback, that's actually completely fair."

"Which is why I said it. Anyway, what's this great calamity?"

"Bridget," said James Royce-Royce, "has not yet graced us with her presence."

Priya rolled her eyes. "That's not a calamity. That's business as usual."

Since waiting for Bridge could last anything between twenty minutes and never, I spilled my guts. About the pictures, the donors, and how I was totally fucked job-wise if I didn't get a respectable boyfriend stat.

James Royce-Royce was the first to react. "That," he declared, "is the most outrageous transgression against all forms of decency. You're a fundraiser for an environmental charity, not a contestant on *Love Island*."

"I agree." Gorgeous Not-Dating-Me Tom took a sip of his drink, throat working as he swallowed. "This isn't okay on any level. It's not my area, but you've got a case for an employment tribunal here."

I gave a sad little shrug. "Maybe, but if I tank our fundraising by being too gay, then I won't have an employer to tribune."

"Seems like"—Priya paused to retie the rainbow lace on her Docs—"you've got two options. Get fired or get grafting."

This earned her an over-the-glasses look from James Royce-Royce. "Priya, my darling, we're trying to be emotionally supportive."

"You're trying to be emotionally supportive," she said. "I'm trying to be useful."

"Emotional support is useful, you Technicolour reprobate."

Tom, who didn't have the same fond memories of their bickering, sighed. "I'm sure we can be both. But I'm not sure we should be encouraging Luc to go along with this."

"Look," I told him, "that's super right-on and very kind of you, but I don't think I have a choice. So I need you all to get on board and find me a man."

There was a worryingly long silence.

Finally Tom broke it. "Okay. If that's what you want. But you're going to have to narrow the field a little. What are you looking for?"

"Didn't you hear me? A man. Any man. As long as he can wear a suit, make small talk, and not embarrass me at a fundraiser."

"Luc, I..." He pushed a hand through his hair. "I really am trying to help. But that's a terrible attitude. I mean, what are you expecting me to do? Call up my ex and be like, *Hey, Nish, great news. I've got a friend with incredibly low standards who wants to go out with you?*"

"Well, the last time I had high standards, the guy dumped me for my best friend."

James Royce-Royce sucked in an audible breath. And, suddenly, everyone was studiously looking in different directions.

"Sorry," I muttered. "I... Sorry. I'm a bit upset right now, and I use being a prick as a defence mechanism."

"Not a problem." Tom went back to his beer.

It took me a second or two to realise I wasn't sure if he meant "not a problem because I'm not offended and don't consider you prickish" or "not a problem you're a prick because we're not actually friends." Fucking spies. And it's not like he was wrong. I was asking a lot here.

"The thing is"—I started picking the label off the nearest bottle—"I've not been able to do the relationship thing for...for a while. And probably you're all going to spend the next thirty years arguing with your partners over who gets stuck with me for Christmas. But I can't—"

"Oh, Luc," cried James Royce-Royce, "you'll always be welcome at Casa de Royce-Royce."

"Not entirely the point, but good to know."

"Wait a minute." Priya looked up from her boots and snapped her fingers. "I've got it. Hire someone. I can think of at least thirty people who'd jump on the gig."

"I can't tell if I'm more disturbed that you're recommending I solicit a prostitute or that you apparently already know thirty prostitutes."

She gave me a confused look. "I was mostly thinking of out-of-work actors or performing artists, but whatever works. Though now you mention it, I think Kevin did a bit of escorting in the late 2000s, and Sven still does pro-domming on the side."

"Wow." I put up the world's most sarcastic double-thumbs. "He sounds perfect. Which part of 'trying to keep out of the tabloids' do you not understand?"

"Oh, come on. He's lovely. He's a poet. They won't find out."

"They *always* find out."

"Okay so"—Priya seemed a tad frustrated with me—"when you said a man, any man, you actually meant any man who fits into a very narrow, middle-class, and slightly heteronormative definition of acceptability."

"Yes. I work for an obscure ecological charity. Narrow, middle-class, and slightly heteronormative is our target demographic."

There was another lengthy silence.

"Please," I legit begged, "you must have some friends who are neither sex workers nor too good for me."

Then James Royce-Royce leaned in and whispered something to James Royce-Royce.

James Royce-Royce's face lit up. "That's a splendid idea, sugarplum. He'd be perfect. Except I think he married a chartered accountant from Neasden last July."

James Royce-Royce looked crestfallen.

I yanked the label fully off the beer bottle and crumpled it up. "Right. My options thus far: someone who's probably already married, thirty prostitutes, and a bloke called Nish who used to date Tom and will, therefore, see me as a bit of a comedown."

"I didn't mean," said Tom slowly, "to make you think that I thought that Nish would think he was too good for you. I'd be happy to introduce you. It's just, from his Instagram, I'm pretty sure he's seeing someone."

"Well, I'm fired." I thonked my head onto the table, somewhat harder than I intended.

"Sorry I'm laaaaate." Bridget's voice rang clarion-like across the beer garden, and I turned my face sideways in time to see her wobbling urgently over the grass in her ever-impractical heels. "You won't believe what's happened. Can't really talk about it. But one of our authors was scheduled to have this massively prestigious midnight release tonight and the lorry carrying the books to Foyles went over a bridge into a river and now not only are half of them ruined but the other half have been scavenged by extremely well-organised fans and there are spoilers all over the internet. I think I'm going to get fired." And, with that, she collapsed breathlessly into Tom's lap.

He wrapped his arms around her and pulled her in close. "That's not your fault, Bridge. They're not going to fire you over it."

Bridget Welles: my Token Straight Friend. Always late, always in the middle of a crisis, always on a diet. For whatever reason, she and Tom are genuinely good together. And although I'm messed up about Tom because of my own shit, it's kind of nice that she's found someone who sees what an amazing, loving person she is and who isn't also as gay as a box of ribbons.

"Luc, on the other hand," said Priya, "is definitely going to get fired unless he gets a boyfriend."

Bridge honed in on me like a laser-guided date launcher. "Oh, Luc, I'm so pleased. I've been on at you to get a boyfriend for ages."

I peeled my head off the table. "A+ priorities, Bridge."

"This is the best thing ever." She squeezed her hands together excitedly. "I know the perfect guy."

My heart sank. I knew where this was going. I love Bridget, but she only knows one other gay person outside our immediate social circle. "Don't say Oliver."

"Oliver!"

"I'm not dating Oliver."

Her eyes went big and hurt. "What's wrong with Oliver?"

I'd met Oliver Blackwood exactly twice. The first time, we'd been the only two gay men at one of Bridget's work parties. Someone had come up to us and asked if we were a couple, and Oliver had looked utterly disgusted, and replied, "No, this is just another homosexual I'm standing next to." The second time, I'd been very drunk and very desperate, and invited him to come home with me. My memories of what happened next were hazy, but I'd woken alone the next morning, fully clothed next to a large glass of water. On both occasions, in uniquely humiliating ways, he'd made it very clear that we each had a league, and his was very much out of mine.

"He's... not my type," I tried.

Priya was obviously still narked I'd turned down her prostitutes. "He's exactly the kind of man you said you were looking for. Which is to say, incredibly boring."

"He's not boring," protested Bridge. "He's a barrister...and...
and he's very nice. Lots of people have dated him."

I shuddered. "And that's not a red flag *at all*."

"Alternatively," suggested Tom, "you could look at it like
this: between the two of you, you've had a completely normal,
healthy dating life."

"I don't know why it never works out for him." Bridget
seemed genuinely bewildered that her awful friend was single.
"He's so lovely. And he dresses so well. And his house is so clean
and tastefully decorated."

James Royce-Royce pulled a wry face. "I hate to say it, darling,
but he seems to be exactly what you're looking for. Refusing to
even meet with the man would be deeply ungracious."

"But if he's so fucking perfect," I pointed out, "with his nice
job and his nice house and his nice clothes, what the hell is he
going to want with me?"

"You're nice too." One of Bridget's hands landed consolingly
on mine. "You just try very hard to pretend you aren't. And,
anyway, leave everything to me. I'm super good at this sort of
thing."

I was pretty sure my dating life was about to go off a bridge
and into a river. And quite possibly wind up with spoilers all over
the internet. But, God help me, it looked like Oliver Blackwood
was my best hope.

CHAPTER 6

THREE DAYS LATER, AGAINST MY better judgment and despite my protests, I was getting ready for a date with Oliver Blackwood. The WhatsApp group—One Gay More—was alive with advice, mainly about what I shouldn't wear. Which seemed to amount to everything in my wardrobe. In the end I went with my skinniest jeans, my pointiest shoes, the only shirt I could find that didn't need ironing, and a tailored jacket. I wasn't going to win any fashion awards, but I thought I'd struck a nice balance between "has made no effort" and "is disgustingly desperate." Unfortunately, too much texting, faffing, and selfie-taking for the approval of the peanut gallery had made me late. On the other hand, Oliver was a friend of Bridget's so he'd probably developed a certain tolerance for tardiness over the years.

As I cantered through the door of Quo Vadis—his pick; I wouldn't have dared go for anything so classy—it quickly became apparent he had not, in fact, developed any tolerance for tardiness whatsoever. He was sitting at a corner table, the light from the stained-glass windows dappling over his frown in shades of sapphire and gold. The fingers of one hand tapped impatiently against the tablecloth. The other cradled a pocket watch on a fob, which he was in the process of checking with the air of a man who had done so several times already.

Seriously, though. A fob. Who even?

"I'm so sorry," I panted. "I...I..." Nope, I had nothing. So I had to fall back on the obvious. "I'm late."

"These things happen."

At my arrival he'd risen like we were at a tea dance in the '50s, leaving me totally at a loss for what I was supposed to do in response. Shake his hand? Kiss his cheek? Check with my chaperone? "Should I sit down?"

"Unless"—one of his brows tilted quizzically—"you have another engagement."

Was that a joke? "No. No. I'm, er, all yours."

He made a be-my-guest gesture, and I wriggled gracelessly onto the banquette. Silence stretched between us, as socially discomforting as mozzarella strings. Oliver was much as I remembered him: a cool, clean, modern-art piece of a man entitled *Disapproval in Pinstripes*. And handsome enough to annoy me. My own face looked as if Picasso had created it on a bad day—bits of my mum and my dad thrown together without rhyme or reason. But Oliver had the sort of perfect symmetry that eighteenth-century philosophers would have taken as evidence for the existence of God.

"Are you wearing eyeliner?" he asked.

"What? No."

"Really?"

"Well, it's the kind of thing I think I'd remember. I'm pretty sure this is just what my eyes look like."

He looked slightly affronted. "That's ridiculous."

Thankfully, at this juncture a waiter materialised with the menus, giving us an excuse to ignore each other for a few happy minutes.

"You should start," remarked Oliver, "with the smoked eel sandwich. It's a speciality."

Since the menu came in the form of a broadsheet, with hand-drawn illustrations and a weather report at the top, it took me a moment to find what he was talking about. "It damn well ought to be for a tenner."

"Since I will be paying, that need not concern you."

I squirmed, which made my jeans squeak against the leather. "I'd be more comfortable if we went halfsies."

"I wouldn't, given I chose the restaurant, and I believe Bridget said you work with dung beetles."

"I work *for* dung beetles." Okay, that didn't sound much better. "I mean, I work for their preservation."

Another of his eyebrow twitches. "I wasn't aware they needed preserving."

"Yeah, neither are most people. That's the problem. Science isn't exactly my strong point but the short version is, they're good for the soil and if they go extinct, we'll all starve to death."

"Then you're doing good work, but I know for a fact that even the big-name charities pay far less than the private sector." His eyes—which were a hard, gunmetal grey—held mine so long and so steadily that I actually started sweating. "This is on me. I insist."

It felt weirdly patriarchal but I wasn't sure I was allowed to complain about that, on account of us both being men. "Umm..."

"If it will make you feel better, you could allow me to order for you. This is one of my favourite restaurants and"—he shifted position and accidentally kicked me under the table—"my apologies... I enjoy introducing people to it."

"Are you going to expect me to trim your cigar later?"

"Is that a euphemism?"

"Only in *Gigi*." I sighed. "But fine. I guess you can order for me. If you really want to."

For about 0.2 seconds, he looked perilously close to happy. "I can?"

"Yes. And"—God, why was I always so ungracious?—"sorry. Thank you."

"Do you have any dietary restrictions?"

"Nope. I'll eat anything. Um. Foodwise. That is."

"And..." He hesitated. Then tried to pretend he hadn't. "Are we drinking?"

My heart did the half-dead fish flop it always did when conversation strayed even tangentially close to any of the things that had been said about me over the years. "I know you've got no reason to believe this, but I'm not an alcoholic. Or a sexoholic. Or a drug addict."

There was a lengthy silence. I stared at the crisp, white tablecloth, wanting to die.

"Well," Oliver said at last. "I've one reason to believe it."

In an ideal world, I would have behaved with terrible dignity. In the world I actually lived in, I gave him a sullen glance. "Which is?"

"You told me otherwise. So are we drinking?"

My stomach had gone into a wild free-fall. I hardly knew why. "Can we not, if you don't mind? While I don't have medical problems with alcohol, I do tend to make a bit of a tit of myself when plastered."

"I'm aware."

And to think I'd almost liked him. Although technically I didn't have to like him, I just had to make him think I liked him for long enough that he'd date me for long enough that I wouldn't get fired. It was fine. I could do this. I could be charming. I was naturally charming. I was a quarter Irish and a quarter French. You couldn't get more charming than that.

The waiter returned and, while I sat in sulky silence, Oliver placed our order. The whole experience was slightly strange, since I still hadn't figured out how demeaning I should be finding it. I definitely wouldn't have wanted it to happen regularly. But there was also some pathetic, lonely part of me that enjoyed being so publicly possessed. Especially by a man like Oliver Blackwood. It felt perilously close to being worth something.

"I can't help but notice," I began, when the waiter departed, "that if this fish sarnie is all that and a bag of chips, you aren't having one."

"Yes. Well." Surprisingly, Oliver went a teeny bit pink around the ears. "I'm a vegetarian."

"Then how do you know about the magic eel?"

"I've eaten meat before, and I like it. It's just I've reached the point that I can't justify it ethically."

"But you're cheerfully going to sit there and watch me chow down on bits of dead animal like some kind of creepy carni-voyeur?"

He blinked. "I hadn't thought of it that way. I just wanted you to enjoy the food, and I'd never impose my principles on people who don't necessarily share them."

Was it me, or had he basically said "I think you're behaving unethically, but I assume I can't expect any better from you"? The mature making-this-work-and-saving-my-job reaction would be to let that slide. "Thanks. I always like my dinner served with a sprinkling of sanctimony."

"That's rather unfair." Oliver moved again, and kicked me again. "Especially given you'd have been equally, if not more, offended if I'd ordered vegetarian without asking you. Also, I'm sorry I keep catching you with my feet. Yours are never where I'm expecting them to be."

I gave him one my meanest looks. "These things happen."

The conversation hadn't so much died on us as been taken out back and shot in the head. And I knew I should be playing paramedic but I couldn't quite bring myself to or work out how.

Instead, I crunched on some of the baked salsify and parmesan that had just arrived (which was delicious in spite of the fact I had no idea what salisfy was, and didn't want to give Oliver the satisfaction of asking him) and wondered what it would be like being here with somebody I could actually stand. It was a lovely, cosy place, with the brightly painted windows and caramel leather seating, and the food was clearly going to be amazing. The sort of restaurant you'd come back to for anniversaries and special occasions, and reminisce about the perfect first date you shared there.

The fish sarnie, when it showed up, turned out to be pretty much the most perfect thing I'd ever eaten: buttery sourdough wrapped around smoky slabs of eel, slathered in truly fiery horseradish and Dijon mustard, and served with pickled red onions just sharp enough to cut through the meaty intensity of the fish. I think maybe I genuinely moaned.

"Okay," I said, once I'd inhaled it. "I was too hasty. That was so good I could pretty much marry you now."

Maybe I was seeing the world through eel-tinted glasses, but right then, Oliver's eyes had a touch of silver in them. And were softer than I'd thought. "I'm happy you liked it."

"I could eat one every day for the rest of my life. How could you know these exist and give them up?"

"I...thought it was the right thing to do."

"I can't tell if that's really commendable or really tragic."

He lifted one shoulder in a self-conscious shrug. And the silence between us, while still not comfortable, seemed slightly less jagged. Maybe this was going to be okay. Maybe we'd been saved by a dead fish.

"So...uh..." Still riding my sandwich bliss, I felt slightly more able to make the effort. "I seem to remember you being a lawyer or something?"

"I'm a barrister, yes."

"And what do you...barrist?"

"I—" The toe of his shoe whomped me in the knee. "God. I'm sorry. I've done it again."

"I've got to say, you play one hell of a hard-core game of footsie."

"I assure you, it's been accidental every time."

He looked so mortified I took pity on him. "It's me. I'm all legs." We both peered beneath the tablecloth.

"How about if I..." I suggested, swinging my feet to the right. He shuffled his Italian leather oxfords left. "And I go..."

His ankle brushed against mine as we rearranged ourselves. And it had clearly been way too long since I got laid, because I damn near fainted. Dragging my attention away from our under-table negotiations, I found him watching me with this crooked half-smile—as if we'd single-handedly (-footedly?) brought peace to the Middle East.

And all of a sudden he was a lot more bearable. Enough more bearable that I could almost see myself putting up with a man who smiled like that, and bought me amazing eel sandwiches, even if I didn't have to.

Which was way, way worse than not liking him.

CHAPTER 7

"YOUR...YOUR JOB?" I ASKED WITH all the smoothness of a bowl of granola.

"Ah. Yes. Well, I"—this time, his foot only stroked the side of mine as it jiggled under the table—"specialise in criminal defence. And you might as well get it over with."

"Get what over with?"

"The question that everyone asks when you tell them you work in criminal defence."

This felt uncomfortably like failing an exam. In a blind panic, I blurted out the first thing that came into my head. "Do you have sex in the wig?"

He stared at me. "No, because they're very expensive, very uncomfortable, and I have to wear mine to work."

"Oh." I tried to come up with another question. Except now all I could think of was "Do you have sex in the robe?" and that obviously wasn't going to help.

"The question people usually ask," he went on, like he was the only one in the play who'd remembered his lines, "is how do you live with yourself when you spend your whole life putting rapists and murderers back on the street?"

"Actually, that is a good question."

"Should I answer it?"

"Well, you seem to really want to."

"It's not about whether I want to." His jaw tightened. "It's about whether you're going to think I'm an amoral profiteer if I don't."

I couldn't imagine that he—or anyone—would care that much for my opinion, good, bad, or indifferent. I spread my hands in a go-for-it gesture. "I guess you'd better tell me then."

"The short version is: an adversarial justice system isn't perfect, but it's the best that we've got. Statistically, yes, most people I defend in court are guilty because the police can broadly do their jobs. But even people who probably did it are entitled to a zealous legal defence. And that's a principle to which...to which I am ideologically committed."

Thankfully, while he'd been delivering this monologue—which only needed some stirring background music to reach its full dramatic potential—I was served a truly glorious pie. Beef, as it turned out, almost meltingly soft, swimming in gravy and barely contained by its crisp pastry cap.

"Wow"—I glanced up from the pie and slammed straight into Oliver's hardest, coldest glare—"you seem really defensive about this."

"I just find it helps to be honest from the beginning. This is who I am, and what I do, and I believe in what I do."

I suddenly noticed he'd barely touched his...beetroot, I think it was? Beetroot and other virtuous vegetables. His hands were folded against the table so tightly that his knuckles were white.

"Oliver," I said softly, realising I'd never said his name before, and confused by how intimate it was. "I don't think you're a bad person. Which you must know means next to nothing coming from me, because you only have to pick up a paper or Google my name to know what sort of person *I* am."

"I"—now he looked uncomfortable for a different reason—"I

am aware of your reputation. But if I'm to know you, Lucien, I'd rather it came from you."

Shit. This had got real out of nowhere. How hard could it be to get a guy to like you enough to date you for a few months but not so much that you had to deal with those weird emotion things that fucked with your head, ruined your sleep, and left you crying on the bathroom floor at three in the morning? "Well, for starters, it's Luc."

"Luke?" Somehow I could always tell when people pronounced it with a *k* and an *e*. "It seems a shame when Lucien is such a beautiful name."

"Actually that's the English pronunciation."

"Surely it's not"—he flinched—"*Looshan* as the Americans would have it?"

"No. God no. My mother's French."

"Ah. Lucien, then." He said it perfectly, too, with the half-swallowed softness of the final syllable, smiling at me—the first full smile I'd seen from him, and shocking in its sweetness. "Vraiment? Vous parlez français?"

There's really no excuse for what happened next. I think maybe I just wanted him to keep smiling at me. Because for some reason I said, "Oui oui. Un peu."

And then, to my horror, he rattled off God knew what.

Leaving me to scrape the bottom of the barrel of my GCSE French, for which I'd received a D. "Um...um... Je voudrais aller au cinema avec mes amis? Ou est la salle de bain?"

Utterly perplexed, he pointed. So I was obliged to go the bathroom. And when I slunk back, he immediately confronted me with "You don't speak French at all, do you?"

"No." I hung my head. "I mean, my mother used both when I was growing up, but I still turned out stubbornly monolingual."

"Then why didn't you just say that?"

"I...don't know. I guess I assumed you didn't speak French either?"

"Why on earth would I imply I could speak French, when I couldn't?"

I stuffed a teetering forkful of pie into my mouth. "You're right. That would be a deranged thing to do."

Another of our silences. On a scale of uncomfortable to horrible, I would probably rate this as unpleasant, and I didn't know what to do. I'd definitely succeeded in swinging the needle away from "dangerously intimate." Unfortunately it was now pointing squarely at "not a chance in hell."

I half thought about kicking him. Just to see how he'd react. But that was probably about as weird as randomly pretending I spoke French. God. This was why I was never going to get a proper boyfriend or even a semi-acceptable temporary substitute. I'd lost whatever capacity I ever had to relate to people in a romantic way.

"How come you're so fluent?" I asked in a subcompetent attempt to salvage the evening.

"My, ah"—he poked sheepishly at the remains of his vegetables—"family have a holiday home in Provence."

Of course they did. "Of course you do."

"What do you mean by that?"

I shrugged. "Just, I can imagine it. No wonder you grew up all nice and put-together and perfect." And way too good for me.

"I've certainly never claimed to be perfect, Lucien."

"Oh stop it with the *Lucien*, will you?"

"I'm sorry. I didn't realise you didn't like it."

Except I did like it. That was the problem. I wasn't here to like things. Liking things was trouble. "I told you before," I snarled, "it's Luc. Just Luc."

"Noted."

A few minutes later, with me looking out the window and Oliver looking at his hands, the waiter came to clear our plates. And a few minutes after that, a lemon posset, topped with rhubarb arrived. It was exquisitely simple—this little white ramekin full of sunshine-yellow cream, topped by a pile of pinkish spirals. I felt awful.

"Nothing for you?" I indicated the empty space in front of Oliver.

"I'm not a fan of desserts. But I hope you'll like this one. It's very good."

"If you're not a fan, how do you know it's"—I wriggled my fingers into air quotes—"'very good'?"

"I... That is... I..."

"Do you want to share it with me?" It was the closest I could get, right then, to an apology. Because it wasn't like I could say, *Sorry I'm so desperate for this to work, and so terrified of this working that I'm lashing out at you over things like you being quite nice, and not wholly unattractive, and having had an ordinary childhood.*

He was eyeing the lemon posset the way I've always wanted someone to look at me. "Maybe I could have a little? Let me ask for more cutlery."

"No need."

Okay. It was, at the eleventh and a half hour, time to get my sexy on. I broke the pristine surface of the cream, mounding it perfectly onto the spoon, along with a few pieces of rhubarb. And, holding it out to Oliver, I offered him my very best, most hopeful smile. Whereupon, he took the spoon from my fingers, crushing me so utterly I couldn't even enjoy the way a taste of lemon posset made his whole face go dreamy with bliss.

"Thank you," he said, returning the damn spoon.

I plunged it violently into the pudding, shovelling what remained into my mouth as if it was my mortal enemy.

Oliver watched me, confused once again. "Should I order another one?"

"No, I'm good. Let's get out of here."

"I...I'll get the bill."

God. I was undateable. Genuinely fucking undateable. No wonder Oliver had practically vomited when that randomer at Bridge's party had thought we were going out. No wonder he'd dumped me in bed and run away screaming that time I'd tried to hit on him. No wonder he didn't even trust me to put a spoon of pudding in his mouth.

CHAPTER 8

I WAS STILL IN A daze of self-loathing as we trooped onto Dean Street, where we hovered in mutual uncertainty. All the lovely things I'd eaten had turned to rocks in my stomach. I'd fucked this up. I'd fucked this up so badly. All I'd had to do was smile, be nice to him, convince him for a handful of hours I was a semiworthwhile human being. But no. I'd curled up like a hedgehog on a motorway in front of the only man in London willing to go out with me. And now I was going to get fired.

Oliver cleared his throat. "Well. Thank you for...for that."

He was wearing the full-length overcoat that every posh person in London owned. Except it suited him. Gave him this air of effortless quality. While I was standing there in slutty jeans.

"Anyway," he went on, "I should—"

No. Help. No. If he walked away now, that was it. I'd never see him again. And I'd never have another job again. And my life would be over.

I needed a plan. I didn't have a plan.

So I lost my fucking mind and threw myself at him, fastening my mouth on his with all the grace and charm of a barnacle on a whale's flipper. It lasted seconds before he pushed me away, a knee-buckling blur of heat and softness, that, for the sweetest of moments, tasted of lemon posset.

"What the hell was—*Christ*." In his zeal to get away, Oliver collided with one of the potted plants outside the restaurant, just about managing to grab it before it came crashing down. Which basically meant he'd spent more time voluntarily touching a ficus than he had me.

"It was a kiss," I said, with a nonchalance I was far from feeling. "Why? Haven't you had one before? People sometimes exchange them on dates."

He turned on me with such ferocity that I actually took a step back. "Is this a game to you? What has Bridget told you?"

"What? N-no."

"Tell me what's going on."

"Nothing's going on."

We were sort of dancing down the street at this point, me skipping backwards over the pavement as he stalked after me, shoes clicking and coat flying. There was clearly something very, *very* wrong with me because it was kind of hot.

His eyes gleamed. "*Now*."

I tripped over the kerb as it flattened unexpectedly at a side street. But Oliver caught my wrist before I could fall, yanking me against his body and holding me there. Making me, I guess, equivalent to a plant in his estimation. God, his coat was cosy.

"Please stop playing with me, Luc." Now he just sounded tired. Maybe even a little sad. "What's this really about?"

Fuck. The jig was beyond up. "I...I've been in the papers again recently. So I need a respectable boyfriend or I'll lose my job. Bridge suggested you."

And, of course, Tom had been right all along. It sounded terrible. I ducked my head, barely able to look Oliver in the face.

"I'm sorry," I went on, inadequately. "I'll pay you back for dinner."

He ignored that. "Bridget thought *I'd* be good for *you*?"

"Well"—I flapped a hand at him—"look at you. You're... you're perfect."

"I beg your pardon?"

"Never mind." I had no right to touch anything so nice, but I hid my face against his coat. And he let me. "You've always acted like you thought you were better than me."

I was close enough that I heard him swallow. "Is...is that what you believe?"

"Well, it's true. You are. Happy now?"

"Not remotely."

The pause that followed whistled in my ears like I was falling.

"Explain to me again," said Oliver finally, "why you need a boyfriend?"

It was the least I owed him. "Mainly for this big fundraiser we've got coming up at the end of April. Our donors all think I'm a bad gay."

He frowned. "What's a good gay?"

"Someone like you."

"I see."

"Don't worry about it." I finally managed to peel myself off his coat. "It's not your prob—"

"I'll do it."

My jaw dropped open so hard it clicked. "You what?"

"As it happens, I also have an event coming up that may go more smoothly with someone on my arm. I'll be your public boyfriend, if you'll be mine."

He was insane. He had to be insane. "It's not the same."

"You mean"—one of his cool, grey glances—"I'm to help you with your significant occasion, but you won't help me with mine?"

"No. God no. It's just you're a fancy lawyer—"

"I'm a criminal barrister. Most people think we're the scum of the earth."

"—and I'm the disgraced son of a disgraced rock star. I...I can't hold my drink. I'm unnecessarily mean. I make terrible decisions. You can't possibly want me to accompany you to anything."

His chin came up. "Nevertheless, those are my terms."

"You know you'll end up in the tabloids if you spend too long with me."

"I don't care what people say about me."

I laughed, shocking even myself with how bitter it sounded. "You think that. And then they start saying things."

"I'll take the risk."

"Really?" God. Dizzily, I found myself reaching for his coat again.

"Yes. But if we're to do this, we have to do it properly."

I blinked at him. Properly sounded ominous. I was not good at properly. "You should know I perform very badly in standardised tests."

"I just need you to make an effort to be convincing. I don't care about your past, or internet gossip, but"—and here that stern mouth pressed into a hard line—"I would rather not have to explain to my family that my boyfriend is only pretending."

"Wait. Your family?"

"Yes, it's my parents' ruby wedding anniversary in June. I don't want to go alone."

"Is it," I couldn't help asking, "in Provence?"

"Milton Keynes."

"And you seriously want to take me? To meet your folks?"

"Why not?"

I barked out another laugh. "How long have you got?"

"If you don't want to do it, Luc, you can tell me."

He was never going to call me *Lucien* again, was he? He was going to respect my wishes like some kind of arsehole. "No, no."

I hastily flung up my hands. "I'll do it. I just think you're making a terrible mistake."

"That's for me to decide." He paused, a flush crawling over the sculpted arch of his cheekbones. "Obviously, maintaining the fiction will require a certain degree of physical contact between us. But please don't kiss me again. Not on the mouth, anyway."

"Why? Are you Julia Roberts in *Pretty Woman*?"

His blush deepened. "No. I simply prefer to reserve that intimacy for people I actually like."

"Oh." Sometimes, you can half believe you've been hurt so much you've basically been vaccinated. Rendered immune. And then someone says something like that to you. I forced my mouth into a grin. "Well, as you've seen, that's not a problem for me."

My only consolation was that Oliver didn't look very happy either. "Apparently not."

"But don't worry. Despite recent evidence, I can keep my lips off you."

"Good. Thank you."

Silence sloshed heavily between us.

"So," I asked, "what now?"

"Brunch at mine? This Sunday?"

Twice in a week? He'd be sick of me before we even made it to the Beetle Drive. And I'd either be sick of him or I wouldn't. And "wouldn't" was too scary to handle right now.

"If this is going to work"—he gazed at me solemnly—"we need to get to know each other, Luc."

"You can call me Lucien," I blurted out.

"I thought you said you didn't—"

"It can be your special name for me. I mean"—suddenly, I could barely catch my breath—"your fake special name for me. That's a thing, right? That couples do."

"But I don't want to have a *fake* special name for you that you *genuinely* don't like." There was that light again. Those secret flecks of silver in the cold steel of his eyes. "That would make me a terrible fake boyfriend."

"It's fine. I overreacted. I don't care."

"That's hardly an endorsement."

"I mean I don't mind." Was he going to make me *beg*? Who was I kidding? I was probably going to.

This was why relationships sucked: they made you need shit you'd been perfectly happy not needing. And then they took them away.

He gave me one of those too-searching, too-sincere looks. "Well, if that's what you want."

I nodded, quietly hating myself. "It's what I want."

"Then, I'll see you on Sunday…" He smiled. Oliver Blackwood was smiling. At me. For me. Because of me. "…*Lucien.*"

CHAPTER 9

"SO," I SAID TO ALEX Twaddle, "a man walks into a bar. And he sits down and there's the bowl of peanuts. And a voice comes from the bowl of peanuts, saying *Hey, your hair looks great*. And then this other voice comes from the cigarette machine on the other side of the bar, saying, *No it doesn't, you look like a prick, and so does your mum*."

Alex's eyes widened. "Oh I say. That's a bit much."

"Yeah, keep that in mind because it's sort of integral to the joke. Anyway, the man asks the barman what's going on. And the barman says, *don't worry, the nuts are complimentary but the cigarette machine's out of order*."

"Well, I suppose they wouldn't have bothered to fix it because you're not allowed to smoke in pubs anymore."

I should have seen this coming. "You're right, Alex. It's the accuracy that makes it funnier."

"I'll keep that in mind too." He smiled at me encouragingly. "What's the rest of the joke?"

"That was the joke. The nuts are complimentary, but the cigarette machine is out of order."

"Are you sure that's a joke? It just seems like facts about a bar."

"Once again," I told him, resigned to my fate, "you've hit the nail on the head. I'll try and do better tomorrow."

I toodled back to my office, actually in a pretty good mood for once. My date with Oliver had been, as predicated, a disaster. But, somehow, not in a bad way? And there was something strangely liberating about having a pretend boyfriend because it meant I didn't have to worry about all the usual relationship things. You know, like being shit at them. Even my morning tabloid alert had been borderline positive. Someone had snapped us at the restaurant but, crucially, they'd got the moment before Oliver recoiled from me in disgust. So it had come out looking kind of romantic, with Oliver's coat billowing around us and his face turned up to mine as my lips came down. The headlines were mostly variants of "Package Judge Club Kid Son In New Gent Squeeze Shock," which I liked because it suggested I had good taste in new squeezes. New fake squeezes.

As I sat down and checked the donor lists to see if anyone else had dumped me, the phone rang.

"Oh my God," cried Bridge. "You won't believe what's happened."

"You're right. I probably—"

"I can't really talk about it, but we've just got the English language rights for a really prestigious Swedish author. And everybody has been clamouring to read her debut novel, which is being billed as *A Hundred Years of Solitude* meets *Gone Girl*. But there was a lot of debate amongst the team over whether to give it an English title or stick with the Swedish original, and it all wound up being sorted out very last minute and so now the book's gone to press as *I'm Out of the Office at the Moment. Please Forward Any Translation Work to My Personal Email Address.*"

"I don't know. I think it's got a certain meta-textual cachet."

"I'm going to get fired."

"You've not been fired yet, Bridge. They're not going to fire you over this."

"Oh." She perked up. "That reminds me. How did your date go?"

"It was awful. We have nothing in common. I think I might have sexually assaulted him. But we're going to pretend to give it a go anyway because we're both desperate."

"I knew you'd work it out."

I rolled my eyes, but only because she couldn't see me. "That's not working something out. That's making something up."

"Yes, but you'll slowly discover that you're not as different as you initially assumed, and then he'll surprise you with how thoughtful he is, and then you'll come to his rescue in an unexpected moment of need, and you'll fall madly in love with each other and live happily ever after."

"That's never going to happen. He doesn't even like me."

"What?" I could hear the look on her face. "Why would he agree to go on with a date with you if he didn't like you?"

"Remember that bit where we're both desperate?"

"Luc, I'm sure he likes you. How could anybody not like you? You're lovely."

"He told me he didn't when I tried to kiss him."

She gave a little squeak. "You kissed?"

"No, I attacked him with my lips, and he was so repulsed he jumped into a potted plant."

"Maybe he was surprised."

"I was surprised when you guys threw me a surprise birthday party. Okay, I wasn't surprised because James Royce-Royce accidentally told me. But I didn't pull away in horror, saying *I only go to parties with people I like*."

"Wait. He actually said that?"

"Pretty much, if you replace *go to parties* with *kiss*."

"Oh." There was a moment's silence. "I thought you were just being obsessively negative. You know, like usual."

"No. No. Those were his exact words."

She sighed. "Oliver, Oliver. What are you doing? He can be so hopeless sometimes."

"He's not hopeless. He's an uptight git. Um, like, in general. Not because he was bothered by me nonconsensually kissing him. Okay, let me rephrase: he's an uptight git who, independent of his uptightness and gititude, isn't into me."

"Luc," she cried, "that's not true." Then she gave a weird hiccough. "I mean, he's not an uptight person. He's very... He always wants to do the right thing. And, honestly, I think he's quite lonely."

"I increasingly think some people are meant to be lonely. I'm lonely because I'm a wreck and nobody wants me. He's lonely because he's awful and nobody wants him."

"See. You *do* have something in common."

"Not funny, Bridge."

"Are you seriously telling me there was nothing about the date that went well? Nothing you liked or connected with?"

Well, there was no denying the man had excellent taste in fish sandwiches. And lemon posset. And there was that hidden softness in his eyes sometimes. And his rare smile. And the way he said *Lucien*, like it was just for me. "No," I said firmly. "Absolutely not."

"I don't believe you. You only make such a big deal about hating people when you're secretly into them."

"Look. Can you come to terms with the idea that you know two gay people who wouldn't be good together?"

"I would, except"—her voice lifted plaintively—"you'd be *sooo* good together."

"Okay, I know you can't see it, but I'm holding up the fetishisation card."

"What does that card even look like?"

"It looks like two adorable men in sweaters holding hands under a rainbow."

"I thought you *wanted* to hold hands with an adorable man under a rainbow."

"I do, but the fact you want it almost as much as I do is what makes it creepy."

She let out a melancholy sigh. "I just want you to be happy. Especially after I stole Tom."

"You didn't steal him. He just liked you better." If I said it enough, hopefully one of us would start to believe it.

"Anyway," she went on briskly, "I've got to go. One of our authors emailed to say he had his entire manuscript on a USB stick that was swallowed by a duck."

"Who the fuck is still using USB sticks?"

"Really have to deal with this. Love you. Bye."

I'd got as far as "buh" before the line went dead. To be honest, it was probably about time I started doing my job anyway. Now that Operation Fake Respectable Boyfriend was a go, I was potentially in a position to try to salvage the Beetle Drive. Which, in practice, would mean begging forgiveness from people I didn't think had anything to forgive me for and who wouldn't admit that they thought I needed to be forgiven. The first step would be reaching out and saying "Hi, I know you all think I'm a dirty, junkie pervert, but I've cleaned up my act and renewed my commitment to living my life by a set of standards that you made up for me in your heads. Now please, for the love of God, give us some money so we can save the bugs that eat shit." Except, y'know, without using *any* of those words. Or ideas. Or sentiments.

After a long afternoon, six cups of Fairclough standard coffee, twenty-three drafts, and three breaks—in each of which I had to give the same explanation to Rhys Jones Bowen about how to do double-sided photocopies—I'd composed an appropriately diplomatic email and sent it off. To be honest, I probably wasn't going to get any replies. Then again, it's amazing what rich people will do for free food. So, if I was lucky, I could probably convince at least a couple of them to be less busy on the night of the Beetle Drive than their diaries had hitherto suggested.

Giddy from a rare sense of accomplishment, and swept along by a rush of something that was either optimism or masochism, I unlocked my phone and pinged a message to Oliver: **do fake boyfriends fake text**

I'm not sure what I was expecting in return, but what I got was Not when one of them is due in court. Including the punctuation. Which was mildly better than no reply at all, but mildly worse than a flat no since he'd basically said "No, thanks, also don't forget I've got a better job than you."

It was close to nine that evening, and I was eating kung po chicken in my socks, when he followed it up with Sorry to keep you waiting. I've thought about it and we probably should text each other for the sake of verisimilitude.

I left him hanging for a while to show that I, also, had important life stuff to be getting on with. Never mind that I actually watched four episodes of *Bojack Horseman* and had a vindictive wank before replying **Sorry to keep you waiting and no wonder you're single if the second text you send a guy includes the word verisimilitude**

There was no reply. Even though I sat around 'til half one definitely not caring. I was unexpectedly de-sleeped by a buzzing from my phone at 5:00 a.m.: My apologies. Next time, I'll send a photograph of my penis. And then several further buzzings.

That was a joke.

I should probably make it clear that I'm not intending to send you any pictures.

I've never sent that sort of thing to anybody.

As a lawyer, it's hard not to be aware of the potential consequences.

I was awake now, which normally I'd have found profoundly objectionable. But you'd have to be a way better person than me not to enjoy the hell out of Oliver losing his shit over a purely hypothetical dick pic.

I also realise you're probably asleep at the moment. So perhaps if you could just delete the previous five messages when you wake up.

Of course, I should emphasise that I am not meaning to imply any judgment about people who do choose to send intimate photographs to one another.

It's just not something I'm comfortable with.

Of course if it is something you're comfortable with, I understand.

Not that I'm suggesting you have to send me a picture of your penis.

Oh God, can you please delete every text I've ever sent you.

The influx of messages paused just long enough that I could pop off a reply. **Sorry I'm confused am I getting a dick pic or what**

No!

There was another pause. Then, I'm very embarrassed, Lucien. Please don't make it worse.

I honestly don't know what possessed me. Maybe I felt sorry for him. But he had kind of, admittedly accidentally, made my morning? **I'm looking forward to seeing you tomorrow**

Thank you.

Okay, now I wish I hadn't bothered. Except a second or two later, I got, I'm looking forward to seeing you too.

And while that felt better, it was, if anything, even more confusing.

CHAPTER 10

IT WAS PRETTY TYPICAL FOR my life that when I finally had a brunch date with an attractive, only slightly annoying man, my mum rang.

"A bit busy right now." Busy, in this case, was code for standing in my underpants, trying to find an outfit that said "I'm sexy, yet respectable, and I promise I won't randomly try to kiss you again, but if you change your mind, I'd be up for it." Maybe something in the jumper family? Cuddly, but with a touch of sensuality.

"Luc"—there was an edge of concern in her voice that I really wanted to ignore—"I need you to come right away."

"How right away is right away?" Did I, for example, have time for a couple of rounds of French toast and an eggs Benedict with a hot barrister?

"Please, mon caneton. It is important."

Okay, she had my attention. The thing is, Mum has a crisis every half hour, but she's usually pretty good at signalling the difference between "Judy's lost her watch in a cow" and "There's water coming through the ceiling." I flumped down onto the edge of the bed. "What's wrong?"

"I don't want to say over the phone."

"Mum," I asked, "have you been kidnapped?"

"No. Then I would be saying, *Help, I have been kidnapped.*"

"But you couldn't say that, because the kidnappers wouldn't let you."

She made an exasperated noise. "Don't be silly. The kidnappers would have to let me tell you I'd been kidnapped; otherwise what would be the point of kidnapping me in the first place?" A brief pause. "What you should have asked is, *Have you been replaced by a robot policeman from the future who wants to murder me?*"

I blinked. "Have you?"

"No, but that is what I would say if I had been replaced by a robot policeman from the future who wants to murder you."

"You do know I have an actual date. With an actual man."

"And I'm very happy for you, but this cannot wait."

"Mum," I said firmly, "this is getting weird. What's going on?"

There was a pause, which a paranoid part of me did think felt like the kind of pause you'd leave if you had to nonverbally ask a kidnapper for instructions. "Listen to me, Luc. This is not the same as when I said you had to come immediately because my life was in danger, and it turned out that I just needed you to replace the battery in my smoke alarm. Although I do maintain that I could have died. I am old and I am French. I fall asleep with a cigarette all the time. Also it was making a very annoying noise. It was like Guantanamo Bay."

"How was it like Guant... Actually, never mind."

"Please come over. I'm sorry to do this, but I am playing the 'You have to trust me' card. Because you have to trust me."

Well. That was that. When it came down to it, there was me and Mum, and then there was everybody else. "I'll be there as soon as I can."

I knew the decent thing to do was ring Oliver and try to explain. But I didn't know how—what was I going to say: "Hi, I have this really intense relationship with my mother that probably looks creepy and codependent from the outside so I'm calling off the date I basically begged you to go on with me"? Also, I was a coward. So I texted instead: **Can't make it. Can't explain why. Sorry. Enjoy brunch!**

Then I hastily revised my sartorial choices from "I am going on a date and trying to salvage my reputation" to "I might have to deal with anything from a death in the family to an exploding toilet" and pegged it to the station. While I was on the train, Oliver called and I winced, before nobly diverting him to voicemail. He left one too. Who the fuck does that?

Judy was waiting for me at Epsom in her rickety, green Lotus Seven. I coerced two spaniels into the footwell and slid in underneath the third.

She snapped her goggles into place. "All aboard?"

I'd long since given up expecting her to care either way. And today was no exception. She slammed her foot down with an enthusiasm that, had I not been fully aboard, would have left me smeared all over the road.

"How's Mum?" I yelled, over the rush of the wind and the rattle of the engine and the excitement of the spaniels.

"Bloody distraught."

I nearly threw up my own heart. "Fuck. What's happened?"

"Yara Sofia had a complete breakdown in the lip-synch. And she'd hitherto been so sickeningly fierce."

"And in the real world?"

"Oh, Odile's fine. Fighting fit. Bright-eyed, bushy-tailed, wet nose, glossy coat, all that."

"Then why did she sound upset on the phone?"

"Well, bit of a shock. But you'll find out."

I extricated one of the spaniels from my crotch. "Look, I'm kind of freaking out here. And it would be really helpful if you'd tell me what was going on."

"Nil freakerandum, old thing. But I'm afraid I absolutely have to be like Dad on this one."

"Whose dad?"

"Anybody's dad. You know, *Be like dad, keep mum.*"

"What?" To give Judy her due, she had managed to distract me from the imminent mysterious disaster.

"Sorry. Probably not PC anymore. Probably now you have to say: *Be like dad, keep in touch with your feelings*, or something." She thought for a moment. "Or I suppose for you homosexuals it's *Be like dad, keep dad*. Which is just bally confusing for everybody."

"Yeah, that's what they put on our T-shirts. *Some people are just bally confusing for everybody. Get over it*."

"Anyway. I know it's all a bit wobble-inducing, but stiff upper lip, I'll have you there in no time."

"Honestly, it's fine. Take your—"

The sudden jolt of acceleration ripped away the remains of my protestation. And I spent the next ten minutes trying not to die, juggling spaniels, and clinging to the sides of the vehicle as we careened up hill and down dale, through twisty country lanes and villages that, prior to our passing through them, I'd have characterised as sleepy.

We screeched to a halt outside Mum's, which had once been the village post office, and was now a pretty little detached house called "The Old Post Office" that sat at the end of a road called "Old Post Office Road." That seemed to be how names worked around here. Old Post Office Road was off Main Road, which turned variously into Mill Road, Rectory Road, and Three Fields Road.

"I'll just shove off," announced Judy. "Got to see a chap about his bullocks. Rather fancy them, to be honest."

And, with that, she roared away into the distance, spaniels barking.

Unlatching the gate, I made my way through the slightly overgrown front garden and let myself into the house. I'm not entirely sure what I'd been expecting.

But it definitely wasn't Jon Fleming.

At first, I thought I was having some kind of hallucination. He'd been around when I was very young, but I had no memory of him. So this was effectively the first time I'd seen my, you know, father in person. And I had no way of processing it—just a vague sense of a man wearing a scarf indoors and getting away with it. He and Mum were sitting at the opposite ends of the living room, looking like two people who ran out of things to say a very long time ago.

"What the fuck," I said.

"Luc…" Mum stood, actually wringing her hands. "I know you won't remember him very well, but this is your father."

"I know who he is. What I don't know is why he's here."

"Well, that's why I called. He has something to tell you."

I folded my arms. "If it's 'sorry,' or 'I've always loved you,' or some bullshit like that, he's about twenty-five years too late."

At this, Jon Fleming also got to his feet. As the saying goes, nothing says family like everyone standing around, staring awkwardly at each other. "Lucien," he said. "Or, you prefer Luc, is that right?"

I would have been happy to live my entire life without having to look my dad in the face. Unfortunately—as with so much else—he wasn't giving me the choice. And I will tell you now, it was the weirdest fucking thing. Because the way someone seems in a photograph and the way they really are is this horrible uncanny valley of recognition and strangeness. And it's even worse when you can see bits of yourself in them. My eyes looking back at me. That strange not-quite-blue, not-quite-green.

There was an opportunity here to take the high road. I chose not to. "I'd prefer you didn't talk to me at all."

He sighed, sad and noble in a way he had no right being. That was the problem with being old and having good bone structure. You got this giant whack of unearned dignity. "Luc," he tried again. "I've got cancer."

Of course he did. "So?"

"So it's made me realise some things. Made me think about what's important."

"What, you mean the people you abandoned?"

Mum put a hand on my arm. "Mon cher, I would be the first to agree that your father is a shady caca boudin, but he could die."

"Sorry to repeat myself but *so?*" On some level, I was aware that there was a difference between "not taking the high road" and "taking a road so low that it involved tunnelling straight to hell," but right then, nothing felt even 2 percent real.

"I'm your father," said Jon Fleming. Which his gravelly rock-legend voice somehow transformed from a meaningless platitude into a profound statement of mutual connectedness. "This is my last chance to know you."

There was a buzzing in my head like I'd snorted bees. A lifetime of manipulative movie bullshit had taught me exactly how I was supposed to behave here. I was allowed a brief flash of unconvincing anger, then I'd cry, then he'd cry, then we'd hug, then the camera would pan out and all would be forgiven. I looked him straight in those wise, sorrowful, too-familiar eyes. "Oh, fuck off and die. I mean, fuck off and literally die. You could have done this at any time in the last two decades. You don't get to do it now."

"I know I've let you down." He was nodding sincerely, as though he was trying to tell me he understood what I was saying better than I understood it myself. "But it's taken me a long time to get to where I always should have been."

"Then write a fucking song about it, you arrogant, narcissistic, manipulative, bald wanker."

Then I got the hell out of there. As the door swung closed behind me, I caught Mum's voice saying, "Well, I think that could have gone a lot worse." Which was her all over really.

Pucklethroop-in-the-Wold did, technically, have a taxi service—or at least it had a bloke called Gavin who you could call, and he'd come and pick you up in his car, and charge you about a fiver to take you to one of the three places he was willing to go. But it was actually only a forty-minute walk across the fields to the station. And I was having the sort of hot-ragey-cryey feelings that made avoiding other humans a pretty high priority for me.

I was very slightly calmer by the time I was on a train, whooshing back to London. And, for some reason, I decided that would be a good moment to pick up Oliver's voicemail.

"*Lucien,*" he said, "*I don't know what I was expecting, but this clearly isn't going to work. There isn't going to be an 'in future' but if, in some imaginary future, you were thinking of standing me up again, at least do me the courtesy of inventing a decent excuse. And I'm sure you're finding all this very funny, but it isn't something I need in my life right now.*"

Well. That was...what it was.

I listened to it again. And then immediately wondered why the fuck I'd done that to myself. I guess maybe I was hoping it would be better the second time around.

It wasn't.

The carriage was mostly empty—it was a funny time of day to be heading into the city—so I tucked my face into the crook of my arm and shed some surreptitious tears. I didn't even know what I was crying over. I'd had an argument with a father I didn't remember and been dumped by a guy I wasn't dating. Neither of those things should have hurt.

Didn't hurt.

I wasn't going to let them hurt.

I mean, yes, I was probably going to lose my job, and probably be alone forever, and my father would probably die of cancer, but you know what, fuck everything. I was going to go home, put on my dressing gown, and drink until nothing mattered anymore.

There was fuck all I could do about the other stuff. But I could do that.

CHAPTER 11

TWO HOURS LATER I WAS in Clerkenwell, standing outside one of those dinky Georgian terraces with the wrought-iron railings and the window boxes, holding down Oliver's doorbell as if I was worried it would fall off the wall.

"What," he said, when he finally answered, "is wrong with you?"

"So many, many things. But I'm really sorry and I don't want to fake break up."

His eyes narrowed. "Have you been crying?"

"No."

Ignoring my obvious and pointless lie, he stepped out of the doorway. "Oh, for God's sake, come in."

Inside, Casa de Blackwood was everything I'd expected in some ways and nothing like I'd expected in others. It was tiny and immaculate, all white-painted walls and stripped wooden floors, with flashes of jewel-bright colour from rugs and throw pillows. Effortlessly homey and grown up and shit, leaving me jealous and intimidated and weirdly yearny.

Oliver closed his laptop and hurriedly tidied away a selection of already neatly stacked papers before settling onto the far end of the two-seater sofa. He was in what I guessed to be his casual mode: well-fitting jeans and a light-blue cashmere jumper, and bare feet, which I found strangely intimate. I mean, not in a fetishy way. Just in a "This is what I look like when people aren't around" way.

"I don't understand you, Lucien." He rubbed at his temples despairingly. "You ditch me with no explanation—by text, because a phone call would apparently be too much. And then you turn up on my doorstep, still with no explanation because a phone call would apparently not be enough."

I tried to pick a not-avoiding-or-crowding-you spot on the sofa and sat in it, knocking my knee against his anyway. "I should have phoned. Like, both times. Except, I guess, if I'd phoned the first time, I wouldn't have had to phone this time."

"What happened? I honestly thought you couldn't be bothered."

"I'm not that much of a flake. I get that the evidence is kind of against me here. But I do need this...this"—I gave an inarticulate wave—"thing we're doing. And I'll try to do better if you give me another chance."

Oliver's eyes were at their silverest—soft and stern at the same time. "How can you expect me to trust you'll do better next time, when you still won't talk to me about this time?"

"I had some family shit. I thought it was important but it wasn't. It won't happen again. And you signed up for a fake boyfriend, not a real basket case."

"I knew what I was getting into."

I wasn't quite strong enough for Oliver's opinion of me right now. "Look, I get I'm not what you're looking for, but can you please stop throwing it in my face?"

"I... That..." He seemed genuinely flustered. "That wasn't what I meant. I was just trying to say that I didn't expect you to be something you weren't."

"What, like remotely reliable or sane?"

"Like easy or ordinary."

I stared at him. I think my mouth might actually have been hanging open.

"Lucien," he went on, "I realise we're not friends, and that, perhaps, we're not naturally suited to one another. That, given the opportunity, you'd have chosen to be with anybody else rather than me. But"—he shifted uncomfortably—"we've agreed to be part of each other's lives, and I can't do this if you can't be open with me."

"My dad's got cancer," I blurted out.

Oliver looked at me the way I'd like to imagine *I'd* look at somebody who'd just told me their dad had cancer, but blatantly wouldn't. "I'm so sorry. Of course you had to be with him. Why on earth didn't you say that at the beginning?"

"Well, because I didn't know. My mum just told me something important was happening, and I believed her because...I'll always believe her. And I didn't tell you because I thought you'd think it was weird."

"Why would I think it's weird that you love your mother?"

"I don't know. I always worry it makes me sound like Norman Bates."

His hand settled warmly on my knee, and while I probably should have, I didn't see any reason to shake him off. "It's very admirable of you. And I appreciate your honesty."

"Thanks. I... Thanks." Wow, Oliver being nice to me was way harder to deal with than Oliver being angry with me.

"Is it all right if I ask about your father? Is there anything I can do?"

"Yeah, you can *not* ask about my father."

He patted my knee in this gently sympathetic way that I could never have managed without it feeling like a come-on. "I understand. It's a family matter and I shouldn't intrude."

I'm sure he wasn't trying to make me feel bad. But he was

doing a really good job of it regardless. "It's not that. I just hate the fucker."

"I see. I mean"—he blinked—"I don't. He's your father and he's got cancer."

"He still walked out on Mum and me. Come on, you must know this."

"Know what?"

"Odile O'Donnell and Jon Fleming. Big passion, big breakup, small kid. Do you not read the papers? Hasn't Bridge told you?"

"I was aware you were peripherally famous. I didn't consider it relevant."

We were quiet a moment. God knows what was going through his head. And I was just confused. I'd always resented people thinking they knew who I was from something they'd read or seen or heard on a podcast, but I'd also apparently got used to it. So used to it that having to actually tell a person about my life was a little bit scary.

"I can't decide," I said, finally, "if this is really sweet or really apathetic of you."

"I'm pretending to date *you*. Not your parents."

I shrugged. "Most people think my parents are the most interesting thing about me."

"Perhaps that's because you don't let them know you."

"The last person who knew me… Never mind." No way was I going there. Not today. Not ever again. I let out a shaky breath. "Point is, my dad's a dick who treated my mum like shit, and now he's doing this big comeback where everyone's acting like it's okay, and it's not okay, and it fucks me off."

Oliver's brow wrinkled. "I can see how that would be difficult. But if he truly might die, you should probably be sure you aren't making any choices you can't unmake."

"What's that supposed to mean?"

"Just that, if the worst happens, and afterwards you regret not giving him a chance, there'll be nothing you can do about it."

"What if that's a risk I'm willing to take?"

"It's your call."

"Would you think less of me?" I coughed. "Well, even less of me."

"I don't think badly of you, Lucien."

"Apart from being the sort of self-involved arsehole who'd stand up his date for fun."

At this, he went a little pink. "I'm sorry. I was upset and said some unfair things. Though in my defence, I'm not sure how you expected me to factor in the possibility that your behaviour was a result of your having received a cryptic message from your reclusive rock icon mother and having then learned that your estranged father, whose recent return to the limelight you profoundly resent, has a life-threatening illness."

"Pro tip: Apologise or make excuses. Don't do both."

"You're right." Oliver leaned toward me a little, his breath whispering across my cheek. "I'm sorry I hurt you."

It would have taken only the slightest of movements to kiss him. And I very nearly did because this whole conversation was taking me down a rabbit hole of feelings and memories and *urgh*— stuff I had trouble sharing with my actual friends. But he'd made it pretty clear he wasn't up for that, so instead, I had to say, "I'm sorry I hurt you too."

There was a long silence, with us both hovering awkwardly on the edge of each other's personal space.

"Are we really bad at this?" I asked. "We've been fake dating for three days and we've already fake broken up once."

"Yes, but we fake resolved our difficulties and fake got back together, and I'm hoping it's made us fake stronger."

I laughed. Which was crazy because this was Oliver Blackwood, the stuffiest man in the universe. "You know, I was genuinely looking forward to brunch."

"Well…" He gave me an uncertain smile. "You're here now. And everything's still in the fridge."

"It's nearly six. That's not brunch, it's…brinner?"

"Does it matter?"

"Wow. You rebel, you."

"Oh yes, that's me. Sticking two fingers up at society and its normative concept of mealtimes."

"So." I tried to sound casual, but I was about to touch on something very serious indeed. "This…brunch…brinner…punk-rock rejection of the egg-based status quo… Will there be French toast?"

Oliver flicked up a brow. "There could be. If you're very good."

"I can be good. What sort of good did you have in mind?"

"I wasn't… I mean, um… I mean, that is… Maybe you can set the table?"

I hid a smile behind my hand, because I didn't want him to think I was mocking him, even if I kind of was. But I guess this was exactly what I'd signed up for: a man who probably owned napkin rings. After all, the *Mail* was unlikely to run with "Rock Star Love Child In Wrong Fork Shame."

What I hadn't expected, though, was how nice, how safe, how right it would feel.

CHAPTER 12

I DID, IN FACT, SET the table—though, thankfully, there were no napkin rings. We ate in Oliver's kitchen, at a tiny circular table about three feet away from the hob, with our knees touching underneath it, because apparently we were doomed to an eternity with our legs tangled up together. I'd secretly enjoyed watching him cook for me—heating oil, chopping garnish, and breaking eggs with the same care and precision he brought to everything else. Also there was no denying he was easy on the eyes when he wasn't judging me. Which I was starting to suspect he did way less often than I'd imagined.

"So, how many of me were you expecting?" I asked, surveying the bounty of eggs and waffles and blueberries and multiple varieties of toast, French included.

He blushed. "I got a little carried away. It's been a while since I've had anyone to cook for."

"I suppose, since we're meant to be dating, we should know this sort of stuff about each other. How long's a while?"

"Six months, give or take."

"That's not a while. That's practically a now."

"It's longer than I prefer to go without a partner."

I stared at him over my eggs Benedict. "What, are you some kind of relationship junkie?"

"Well, when were you last with somebody?"

"Define *with*."

"The fact you're even asking says quite a lot."

"Fine." I scowled. "Nearly five years."

He gave a thin smile. "Perhaps it would be best if we refrained from passing comment on each other's choices."

"This is an amazing brinner," I said, by way of a preemptive peace offering. Then launched straight into "So why did you break up?"

"I'm...not entirely sure. He said he just wasn't happy anymore."

"Ouch."

He shrugged. "There comes a point when enough people have said, *It's not you, it's me* that you begin to suspect it may, in fact, be you."

"Why? What's wrong with you? Do you hog the duvet? Are you secretly racist? Do you think Roger Moore was a better Bond than Connery?"

"No. Good God no. Although I do think Moore is somewhat underrated." Handling the serving spoon with irritating deftness, Oliver poured a perfect spiral of cream onto his poppy-seed waffle. "I honestly believed it was working. But then I always do."

I snapped my fingers. "Ah. You must be terrible in bed."

"Clearly." He gave me a wry look. "Another mystery solved."

"Dammit. I was hoping you'd get defensive and I'd at least find out something dirty about you."

"Why Lucien, for someone who's made it abundantly clear that he's not interested, you seem quite fascinated with my sex life."

Heat rushed to my face. "I'm...not."

"If you say so."

"No, really. It's..." *Urgh*, this was a mess. Partly because I was maybe a bit more curious than I wanted to admit. Oliver was so self-possessed that it was hard not to wonder what he was like when he let go. *If* he let go. What it would be like to inspire that kind of recklessness in him. "I'm just sort of aware that anything you wanted to know about me you could Google."

"Would it be the truth, though?"

I cringed. "Some of it. And not only the good stuff."

"If there's one thing I've learned in my line of work, it's that 'some of the truth' is the most misleading thing you can hear. Anything I want to know about you, I'll ask."

"What about," I said in a small voice, "when you're mad at me? When you're looking for reasons to think the worst of me."

"And you believe I'll need the papers to help me with that?"

I shot him an outraged glare, but for some reason I ended up smiling instead. Something about the way he was looking at me took the sting from his words. "Is that what passes for reassurance in your world?"

"I don't know. Is it working?"

"Weirdly, maybe a little bit?" I distracted myself with the French toast—which was rich and sweet and dripping with maple syrup. "You'll end up looking, though. Everyone always does."

"Do you really think I have nothing better to do with my time than web-stalk the e-list children of c-list celebrities?"

"Again, with the…mean comforting. What the hell is that about?"

"I, well, I wasn't sure you'd accept any other kind." He looked slightly abashed, chasing a blueberry round and round his plate.

Honestly, he might have been right. But I wasn't going to give him the satisfaction of admitting it. "Try me."

"I'm not going to make you any promises because that just gives all this nonsense more power over you. But—"

"It's easy for you to call it nonsense. You don't live with it."

He gave an exasperated little huff. "See. I said you wouldn't want my reassurance."

"You haven't given me any reassurance. You've told me you aren't going to make any promises and dicked on my pain."

"It wasn't my intent to dick."

We eyed each other warily over the battlefield of our breakfast foods. In many ways, our second date was going as badly as our first. Hell, in many ways it was going worse, since I'd arrived six hours late and been dumped before I got there. But it felt different. Somehow even being annoyed with him brought with it this strange warmth.

"Anyway," Oliver went on, "you didn't let me finish."

"And I'm usually so considerate in that regard."

Up went that brow of his. "Good to know."

And, for some reason, *I* blushed.

He gave a little cough. "As I was saying, I recognise that the penumbra of public commentary is significant to you and has affected your life. But it is nonsense to me, and always will be, compared to you."

"Okay..." I made an odd hoarse noise. "You were right. Go back to being snarky."

"I really don't think I'll look, Lucien. I have no wish to hurt you."

"I get I have bad taste in men, but I've managed to mostly avoid dating guys who actively want to screw me over. It's not about wanting or not wanting to hurt me. But"—I tried to sound jaded and resigned, rather than horribly, horribly exposed—"you know how it is. People get curious. Or they get frustrated. Or they do that thing where they think they're going to read it, then impress me with how totally okay with it they are, but they just get freaked out and I just feel fucked up."

"Then if you can't trust in my good intentions, at least trust that I'm as much of a pompous arse as you think I am and would, therefore, never touch a tabloid."

"I don't think you're a pompous arse."

"According to Bridget, it was the first thing you said about me."

Actually, it was the second. The first was, "If I'd known your only other gay friend was that hot, I'd have agreed to meet him months ago." Of course, that had been before the "homosexual who's standing next to me" incident. I shuffled uncomfortably in my seat. "Oh yeah. Looking back, I was probably a bit harsh on you."

"Really?" he asked in a tone of hope tinged with suspicion.

"Well, I wouldn't say you were a full-on pompous arse. Maybe more of a supercilious butt cheek."

To my surprise, he laughed—a deep, full-throated laugh that made the hairs on my arms stand up in unexpected pleasure. "I can live with that. Now"—he propped his elbows on the table, moving in a little closer—"what else should fake boyfriends know about each other?"

"You're the one with all the relationship experience. You tell me."

"That's the thing about relationships. If you've not had many, you've got limited basis for comparison. If you've had a lot, you're clearly doing something wrong."

"You're the one who insisted we had to get to know each other." I smirked at him. "You know, for *verisimilitude*."

"Are you ever going to let me live that down?"

I gave it a moment's thought. "No."

"Fine." He sighed. "Birthdays?"

"Don't bother. I'll forget it. I can't be fucked with birthdays, including my own."

"Well, I would remember."

"God," I groaned. "I bet you'd get me an incredibly thoughtful gift as well. And make me feel awful."

His lips twitched. "I would make a point of it."

"Anyway, it's July. So we'll have fake decided we're not compatible and fake broken up long before it becomes an issue."

"Oh." For a split second, he looked almost disappointed. "Your turn."

"I don't remember agreeing to take turns."

"I generally find most situations are improved by reciprocation."

"Versatile, are you?" I widened my eyes innocently.

"Behave yourself, Lucien."

Well, that wasn't sexy. Nope. Definitely not. Not at all. A sweet little shiver whooshed the length of my spine.

"Um." My mind had gone blank. "Hobbies and stuff? What do you do when you're not working?"

"Usually I *am* working. The law is a demanding profession."

"For the record, saying things like 'The law is a demanding profession' is what made me think you were pompous."

"Well, I'm sorry," he said in the tone of someone who wasn't sorry at all. "But I didn't know how else to convey that I have a fulfilling but challenging job that takes up a lot of my time."

"You could have gone with that."

"Dear me. We've been dating for less than three days, and you're already trying to change me."

"Why would I want you to change when it's so much fun taking the piss out of you?"

"I..." His brow wrinkled. "Thank you. I think. I can't tell if that was a compliment."

It was probably just because I'm a bad person that I was finding him slightly endearing right now. "Yeah. That's kind of the game. But, come on, you must do something that doesn't involve wigs and hammers."

"I cook, I read, I spend time with friends, I try to stay healthy."

Oh yay. So I hadn't been imagining the body under those conservative suits. I mean, not that I was imagining it. At least, not very much.

His gaze caught mine. "What about you?"

"Me? You know, the usual. Stay out too late, drink too much, cause the people who care about me needless anxiety."

"And what do you *actually* do?"

I really wanted to look away. But for some reason I couldn't. His eyes kept promising me things I was sure I didn't want. "I've been in a bit of a slump. For a while. I still do stuff—I was out last Saturday—but I never seem to have anything to show for it."

There was the rabbit hole again, and the last thing I wanted was for Oliver to ask a thoughtful follow-up question that would take me further down it.

"Your turn," I yipped, grinning wildly, as if my life being basically wrecked was a hilarious anecdote.

His fingers tapped lightly against the table for a moment or two as he seemed to give the matter far too much consideration. "With the caveat that I would be interested irrespective of your parents' celebrity, could you tell me a little of your background?"

"That sounds like a job interview, not a boyfriend interview."

"I can't help being curious. I've known *of* you for years. But we've never really talked before."

"Yeah, because you made it pretty damn clear you wanted nothing to do with me."

"I would dispute that characterisation but, either way, I do now."

I made a sullen, embarrassingly adolescent noise. "Whatever. Uneventful childhood, promising career, went off the rails, here I am."

"I'm sorry," he said, which was not the reaction I was expecting. "This was too artificial a structure for personal conversation."

Shrug. Apparently I was still in teenager mode. "There's no conversation to have."

"If that's your preference."

"What about you?"

"What would you like to know?"

I'd been hoping talking about him would feel less revealing than talking about me. Turned out, it didn't. I made a sound that could roughly be expressed as "*Urdunuh*."

"Well," he offered gamely. "Like yours, my childhood was very uneventful. My father's an accountant, my mother used to be a professor at LSE, and they're both kind and supportive people. I have a brother, Christopher, who's a doctor, as is his wife, Mia."

"Well, aren't you a bunch of high achievers."

"We've been very lucky. And we were raised to believe that we should pursue something we believed in."

"Which is what led you to law?"

He nodded. "Indeed. I'm not sure it's entirely what my parents had in mind, but I think it's right for me."

"If I murdered someone," I told him, discovering, to my surprise, that I meant it, "I would totally want you to be my lawyer."

"Then the first piece of advice I should give you is don't tell me if you've murdered someone."

"Surely people don't do that?"

"You'd be surprised. Defendants have no legal training of their own. They don't always know what will implicate them and what won't. I'm not speaking from experience, incidentally." He gave me a small smile. "My second piece of advice is that if you are ever accused of murder, you should hire somebody significantly more experienced than I am."

"You mean you've never done one?"

"Contrary to what you might think, homicide is actually quite rare. And one tends to come to it later in one's career."

"Then what sort of cases do you work on?"

"Whatever comes. I don't get to choose. It's often rather banal."

I shot him a quizzical look. "I thought this was your big passion."

"It is."

"You just described it as *rather banal.*"

"I meant, it can seem banal to other people. If your only experience of the law is television courtroom dramas, the reality that I spend my days defending teenagers who were caught shoplifting nail varnish and small-time criminals who've overreached themselves can be somewhat disappointing." He stood and started gathering up the empty plates and bowls. "Socially, it's a bit of a lose-lose. Either people think I spend all day putting killers and rapists back on the street for the money, or they think I'm terribly dull."

Without thinking about it, I rose to help, our hands tangling among the brinnerware. "Maybe we can split the difference and say you're spending your days putting teenage shoplifters back on the street for the money."

"Maybe we can split the difference and say I spend my days making sure a single error of judgment doesn't ruin a young person's life."

I flicked a stray blueberry at him, and it bounced off his nose.

"Your point being?" he asked.

Clearing up. I was very busy clearing up. "You...you really do care about this stuff, don't you?"

"And that observation led you to assault me with soft fruit?"

"Objection. Badgering the witness."

"You know that's not a thing in this country?"

I gasped. "Then what do you do when counsel is testifying?"

"You either trust the judge to know what they're doing— which they usually do, even the mad ones—or you very politely say something along the lines of 'M'lud, I believe the honourable counsel for the prosecution is testifying.'"

"And to think"—here I heaved a deep sigh—"I was imagining you leaping up and laying the legal smackdown on the smug suits from the AG's office."

"Do you mean sterling public servants from the Crown Prosecution Service?"

"Dammit, Oliver." His name tasted bright and sharp on my tongue. Sugar and cinnamon. "You're kind of sucking the fun out of the criminal justice system."

Very deliberately, he picked up another blueberry and launched it at me. It pinged off my eyebrow.

"What was that for?" I asked with what I hoped came across as feigned petulance.

His mouth was curling into a smile as slow and warm as maple syrup. "You deserved it."

CHAPTER 13

OLIVER WASHED UP, AND I mostly got in the way, which was how I handled domestic tasks.

"Um," I said, hooking my thumbs in my pockets in a futile attempt to look casual. "Thanks for the food. And for not dumping me and stuff. I suppose I should…"

Oliver also hooked his thumbs in his pockets. Then immediately took them out again, as if he had no idea why he'd done it. "You don't have to. I mean if you aren't… There are some things we should probably discuss. About logistics."

This was more the Oliver I'd been expecting. I guess I'd got a temporary upgrade on account of my dad having cancer. "Logistics, huh? You'll turn a boy's head with talk like that."

"I'm not trying to turn your head, Lucien. I'm trying to make sure this doesn't blow up in both of our faces."

I made an insouciant gesture that involved knocking over the tiny vase of flowers that Oliver had just replaced on the table. "Shit. Sorry. But, how complicated is this? We carry on with our lives and tell anyone who asks that we're dating."

"That's rather my point, though. Do we tell anyone who asks? What about Bridget?"

"Yeah"—I tried to fix the flowers and failed utterly—"she kind of already knows the truth."

"And were you going to mention this at any point? Or were you just going to let me make a fool of myself in front of her as I naively committed to the pretence we were both supposed to be maintaining."

"Bridge is the exception. We can't keep secrets from Bridge. She's my straight best friend. There's a code."

Oliver leaned past me and made two small adjustments to the flowers, transforming them from shabby and accusing to radiant and lovely. "But to everyone else we're really dating?"

"Absolutely. I mean, there's a guy at work who's sort of in on it."

"A guy at the work for whose benefit this whole deception is being practiced?"

"Well, it was his idea, so it was unavoidable. Besides"—I nearly got insouciant again, but then thought better of it—"he's got the brains of a raspberry pavlova. He's probably already forgotten."

He sighed. "Fine. So to everyone except Bridget and this gentleman you work with, we're really dating?"

"I can't lie to my mum obviously."

Another sigh. "So to everyone except Bridget, a gentleman you work with, and your mother, we're really dating?"

"Well, my other friends might not buy it. You know, because I've told them all I hate you. And after years of my love life being a car crash in a dumpster fire it's pretty fucking convenient I've ended up in a stable, long-term relationship just when I needed to do exactly that to not be fired."

"And"—Oliver's eyebrows got all mean and pointy—"they're more likely to conclude that we concocted an elaborate fictional relationship than that you changed your mind about me?"

"It doesn't have to be elaborate. You're the one who's making it elaborate."

"While you're putting no thought into it whatsoever."

"Yep, that's how I roll."

He folded his arms ominously. "In case you've forgotten, there are two of us in this fake relationship. And it won't be a very successful fake relationship without real work."

"Jesus, Oliver." In my frustration, the flowers got it again. "I might as well actually be dating you."

At this point, he edged me out of the kitchen and started reconstructing his centrepiece in a way I found, frankly, passive-aggressive. "As we've agreed, that is an outcome neither of us want."

"You're right. That would be awful." Except for the French toast. And his cuddly Sunday afternoon jumper. And the rare moments when he'd forget he thought I was a dick.

"Still, now we're committed, we should do this properly." He jammed a tulip into place slightly too hard, splitting the stem. "And that means not telling everybody that the whole affair is a pathetic hoax invented by two lonely men. And also getting used to spending time together like we would if we genuinely got on."

I was starting to fear for the rest of the flowers so I sidled back up to the table and pried them from his fingers. "I'm sorry I let the cat very slightly out the bag. I won't do it again."

He was silent for a long moment so I started sticking things back into the vase. They didn't look good, but at least nothing snapped.

"And," I added grudgingly, "we can do all the logistics and stuff that you think we need. Just let me know when you want to...logist with me and I'll be there."

"I'm sure we can negotiate matters as they arise. And you're still welcome to stay. If you'd like. If you have no other engagements."

Engagements? Oh, Oliver. "There was this tea dance I was meant to go to in 1953, but I can probably skip it."

"I should warn you"—he gave me a cool look, apparently unimpressed by my dazzling wit—"I shall be quite busy with work."

"Can I help?" Honestly, I'm not a big fan of helping in general.

But it seemed only polite to offer. And anything was better than going back to my empty, barely habitable flat and thinking about how the father I hated-slash-was-indifferent-to might be dead soon.

"Not remotely. It's confidential, you have no legal training, and I saw the mess you made of the washing up."

"Right. So I'll sort of…sit then? In the name of learning to put up with each other."

"I wouldn't put it quite like that." He seemed to give up on the flowers. "And please make yourself at home. You can read, or watch television, or… Actually, I'm sorry, this was an awful invitation."

I shrugged. "It's probably what I'd be doing anyway. Just in a nicer house with more of my clothes on."

"Keeping your clothes on is probably for the best."

"Don't worry. I know the drill: no kissing, no dick pics, no nudity."

"Yes. Well." His hands moved absently. "I think any of those would unnecessarily complicate the fake boyfriend situation."

"And I'm never unnecessary or complicated."

There was an uncomfortable pause.

"So," he asked finally, "are you staying?"

And, God knows why, I nodded.

We settled down in the living room, me sprawled out on the sofa, and Oliver sitting cross-legged on the floor, surrounded by papers, with his laptop balanced on his knee. It wasn't exactly awkward, but it wasn't exactly not awkward either. We were still figuring out how to talk to each other without having a fight, so working out how to enjoy a comfortable silence was a bit next level for us. Or maybe it was just me. Oliver had vanished into the law—his head lowered and his fingers flurrying occasionally across the keys—and for all I knew, he'd already forgotten I existed.

Snagging the remote, I turned on the TV, sheepishly installed

ITV Catchup and bopped through the recentlys until I found *The Whole Package*. There were two episodes now. Joy.

I pressed Play.

And was immediately treated to a thirty-second montage of how great my dad was: clips of him performing interspersed with sound bites from people I assumed were famous music types, but either far too old or far too young for me to have any idea who they were, and all saying stuff like "Jon Fleming is a legend in this business" and "Jon Fleming is the elder statesman of rock music— prog, folk, classic, he can do it all" and "Jon Fleming's been my hero for thirty years." I almost turned it off, but then another montage kicked in and I realised they were saying basically the same things about Simon from Blue.

Once they'd finished shamelessly promoting the judges, we cut to the studio where the four of them performed a frankly bizarre take on Erasure's "Always" before a live audience who reacted like it was a cross between Live Aid and the Sermon on the Mount. My unqualified hot take was that it was the kind of track that could just about take a spurious flute solo, but definitely did not need a rap break from Professor Green.

After that, they got into the show proper which, it being the first ever episode, included a really pace-killing explanation of the format that I only half understood, and the presenter—who I was pretty sure wasn't Holly Willoughby but could have been—didn't understand at all. There was something involving points, and bidding, and the judges getting a wild card they could use to steal people, and sometimes the contestants got to pick which judge they went with, but mostly they didn't. And, finally, someone came on and wailed out an aggressively emotional version of "Hallelujah" before being snapped up by one of the Pussycat Dolls.

They filled an hour, plus ad breaks, cycling through variants on the six people who are always on these shows: the cocky guy who nobody wants and is nowhere near as good as he thinks he is, the forgettable one who gets picked up but is destined to be cut in the first of the head-to-heads, the one with the tragic backstory, the quirky one who will go out in the quarter final but will wind up doing better than the actual winner, the one you're supposed to underestimate but blatantly won't because Susan Boyle happened, and the good-looking, talented one who the public will uniformly hate for being too good-looking and talented. Between the performances and the saccharine vid packages about people's mums and hometowns, the judges had the sort of banter you'd expect from people who'd never met and had nothing in common except having reached a point in their careers where judging a reality TV show was their best option.

It was annoyingly watchable, is what I'm saying. And even Oliver would glance up occasionally to offer a comment. Apparently he hadn't got the memo that the only socially acceptable way to watch reality TV was ironically because he kept saying things like, "I was very concerned for the shy girl with the NHS glasses and the braces, but I was very moved by the way she sang 'Fields of Gold.'" And then I'd wish I had a blueberry to throw at him.

We got to a bit where Jon Fleming bid heavily on a girl with a harmonica (quirky one: will go out in quarter finals) only for Simon from Blue to play his wild card early and steal her out from under him. And it was the best moment so far by a mile. My dad tried to act all chill about it, but you could tell he was pissed off. Which meant, for about thirty seconds, I became a massive fan of Simon from Blue, while also not being able to name a single one of his songs.

I'm not entirely sure why—it could have been masochism, or Stockholm syndrome, or secretly feeling kind of cosy—but I queued up the second episode. It was pretty much identical in format to the first: the judges still didn't know how to talk to each other, the presenter still didn't seem to understand the rules, and the contestants were still telling heartwarming stories about their dead grandmas and day jobs at Tesco's. We kicked off with a mum of three throwing everything she had at a two-minute version of "At Last," which nobody went for, but then insisted afterwards they should have gone for before promptly forgetting about her. Then we got a seventeen-year-old boy, peeking shyly from behind the world's floppiest fringe, black-painted nails on fingers curled tightly round the mic, who gave a weirdly fragile and affecting performance of "Running Up That Hill."

"Oh," remarked Oliver, glancing up from his laptop, "that was rather good."

Apparently the judges thought so, too, and Ashley Roberts and Professor Green got into a slightly crazy bidding war for him that ended with Ashley Roberts pulling out and then Jon Fleming—with a sense of the dramatic honed over a career that, as the intro kept telling us, had spanned five decades—jumping out of his chair to play his wild card. This left the kid, Leo from Billericay, free to choose between the professor and my dad.

Obviously, the show cut straight to a commercial break, and we came back after an ad for car insurance with the tense music still playing, and Jon Fleming about to launch into his "pick me" speech.

He'd gone back to his seat and was sitting with an elbow on the armrest, and his cheek against his fingers, his blue-green eyes fixed intently on Leo from Billericay. "What was in your head," he asked, in that nonspecifically regional burr that always made him sound so worldly and sincere, "while you were singing that?"

Leo squirmed behind his fringe and muttered something the mic completely failed to catch.

"Take your time, son," Jon Fleming told him.

The camera jumped briefly to the other judges, who were all wearing their best this-is-a-moment faces.

"My dad..." Leo managed "...he died. Last year. And we never really agreed about a lot of stuff. But music was, like, the thing that really brought us together."

There was a perfect televisual pause. Jon Fleming leaned forward. "That was a beautiful performance. I could tell how much the song meant to you, and how much of your heart you put into it. I'm sure your dad would have been proud of you."

What.

The.

Fuck.

Okay, I felt very sorry for Leo from Billericay, because he was clearly bereaved, and having a shit relationship with an absent father sucked. But it didn't change the fact that *my* absent father was having a redemptive bonding experience with some prick from Essex on national TV while I watched from the sofa of my fake boyfriend's house.

Oliver glanced over. "Are you all right?"

"Yeahimfinewhywouldntibe?"

"No reason. But if hypothetically you stopped being fine and wanted to, I don't know, talk about anything, I'm right here."

On the screen, Leo from Billericay was biting his lip in that trying-not-to-cry way that made him look brave and noble and fan-favouritey, and Jon Fleming was explaining how much he wanted him on his team.

"Not a lot of people know this about me," he said, "but I never knew my own father. He died on the Western Front before I was born, and I always regretted not having that connection in my life."

No. Not a lot of people did know that. *I* didn't know that. Essentially making Leo from Billericay—and for that matter, Simon from Blue, and how many the fuck million people watched this show live—closer to my dad than I was. It was getting increasingly hard not to be actively glad that the fucker had cancer.

Anyway, of course Leo from Billericay picked Jon Fleming to be his mentor. I came this close to cutting my losses and turning the show off, but that would have felt weirdly like letting my dad win. I'm not sure *what* it felt like letting him win, but I knew I wanted to stop him winning it. So, instead, I stared blankly at the screen while the carousel of hopefuls continued.

I was pretty sure I was getting a headache. What with Oliver and Jon Fleming, and Leo from Billericay, and my job hanging by a thread, there was too much in my brain. And the more I tried to deal with any of it, the more it just swirled around like clay in the hands of an inexperienced potter. So I shut my eyes for a moment, telling myself things would make more sense when I opened them.

CHAPTER 14

"LUCIEN?"

I opened my eyes to find Oliver right in my face. "Wuthuh?"

"I think you fell asleep."

"I did not." I jerked into a sitting position, nearly headbutting Oliver in the process. There was no way I was letting him think I was the sort of person who spent his evenings passed out in front of the TV. "What time is it?"

"A little after ten."

"Really? Shit. You should have woken me sooner. I mean, not woken me. Reminded me."

"I'm sorry." Tentatively he unstuck a strand of hair from where it had plastered itself over my brow. "But you've had a long day. I didn't want to disturb you."

A glance around the living room revealed that Oliver had finished his work, probably some time ago, and packed everything neatly away around me. Fuck. "I can't believe I turned up on your doorstep out of nowhere, insisted you continue pretending to date me, whined about my dad's cancer, got in a massive argument about logistics, made you watch reality TV, and then fell asleep."

"You also threw a blueberry at me."

"You should dump me."

"I tried that already. It didn't take."

"Seriously. If you want out, I'll be reasonable this time."

Oliver held my gaze for a long moment. "I don't want out."

Relief bubbled through me like indigestion. "What the fuck is wrong with you?"

"I thought we'd established that fairly clearly. I'm stuffy, pompous, boring, and desperate. Nobody else will have me."

"But you make amazing French toast."

"Yes"—his expression grew charmingly rueful—"I'm starting to think that's the only reason my relationships lasted as long as they did."

For some reason, I was suddenly very aware I wasn't allowed to kiss him.

"There's still time to catch the last Tube," he went on, "or I can call you a cab, if you like."

"It's fine. I can grab an Uber if I need to."

"I'd rather you didn't. Their business model is deeply unethical."

I rolled my eyes. "I think we've just worked out why nobody's going out with you."

"Because I don't use Uber? That seems fairly specific."

"Because you've got an opinion about *everything*."

"Don't most people have opinions?"

At least I wasn't thinking about kissing him anymore. "I don't mean opinions like 'I enjoy cheese.' Or 'John Lennon is overrated.' I mean opinions like 'You shouldn't use Uber because of the workers' and 'You shouldn't eat meat because of the environment.' You know, opinions that make people feel bad about themselves."

He blinked. "I don't want anyone to feel bad about themselves or that they have to make the same choices I do—"

"Oliver, you just told me not to get an Uber."

"Actually, I said I'd rather you didn't get an Uber. You can still get an Uber if you want to."

"Yeah"—somehow we'd got all close again, making me aware of the heat of him, the shapes his mouth made when he was arguing with me—"except you'll look down on me if I do."

"No, I won't. I'll accept you don't have the same priorities I do."

"But your priorities are clearly right."

His brow furrowed. "I think now I'm confused. If you agree with me, what's the problem?"

"Okay." I drew in a calming breath. "Let me try to explain. Most of the people who aren't you understand that capitalism is exploitative and climate change is a problem and that choices we make can support things that are bad or unjust. But we survive by a precarious strategy of not thinking about it. And reminding us of that makes us sad, and we don't like being sad, so we get angry."

"Oh." He looked crestfallen. "I can see that being terribly unappealing."

"It's also kind of admirable," I admitted reluctantly. "In a really infuriating way."

"I don't mean to cherry-pick, but did you just call me admirable?"

"You must have imagined it. And now, ironically, I'll *have* to get an Uber because I can't make the train and I've got no cash for a cab."

He cleared his throat. "You could stay the night if you wanted."

"Wow, you are seriously committed to me not supporting Uber's business model."

"No, I just thought it might be… That is." A self-conscious little shrug. "For the sake of verisimilitude."

"Who do you think is going to notice where I sleep? Do you think we're being monitored by the FBI?"

"I believe surveillance outside the United States is more likely to be carried out by the CIA, but actually I was mostly considering the paparazzi."

That was a fair point. They'd caught me leaving various people's houses on various mornings down the years.

"And it would be no inconvenience," he added awkwardly. "I have a spare toothbrush, and can sleep on the sofa."

"I can't make you sleep on the sofa in your own house."

"I can't make you sleep on the sofa when you're a guest."

There was a long silence.

"Well," I pointed out, "if neither of us can sleep on the sofa, then either I go home or..."

Oliver faffed with a sleeve of his jumper. "I think we're mature enough to share a bed without incident."

"Look, I know what happened outside the restaurant was a bit much, but I usually wait for an invitation before I jump on someone. I'm an incident-free zone, I promise."

"Then, it's getting late. I suggest we head upstairs."

And, just like that, I'd apparently agreed to spend the night with Oliver. Well. Not *with* Oliver. More sort of in Oliver's general vicinity.

Except, right then, no matter how hard I tried to convince myself otherwise, there didn't feel like much of a difference.

———

It should have come as no surprise to me that Oliver owned actual pyjamas. In dark-blue tartan. Also that he made his bed like an actual grown-up, instead of throwing a duvet vaguely in the direction of a duvet cover, somewhere near a mattress.

"What are you staring at?" he asked.

"I'd assumed people stopped buying nightwear in 1957. You look like Rupert Bear."

"I don't remember Rupert Bear wearing anything remotely resembling this."

"No, but he would have, if it had been available."

"That seems specious."

I struck what I assumed to be a lawyerly pose. "M'lud. The honourable counsel for the prosecution is being specious."

"I think"—Oliver seemed to be giving this far more consideration than it deserved—"unless you had established expertise in the field, your speculation as to what Rupert Bear would have worn, had he been given the opportunity, would not be admissible in court."

"M'lud. The honourable gentleman is being mean to me."

He pursed his lips peevishly. "You're the one who said I looked like Rupert Bear."

"That's not mean. Rupert Bear is cute."

"Given he's also a cartoon bear, I'm still not certain I can take it as a compliment. And I happen to have a spare pair of pyjamas if you'd like to borrow them."

"What. No. I'm not a child in a Disney movie."

"So will you be sleeping fully clothed or completely naked?"

"I...did not think this through." I flailed mentally for a moment. "Look, do you have a spare top or something?"

He rummaged around in a drawer and threw me a plain, grey T-shirt that had clearly been ironed. Refraining—with some difficulty—from further comment, I retreated to the bathroom to change. Normally, I put a bit more thought into what underwear I have on the first time a guy's going to see it, not least because it might end up in the papers. One of the few upsides of my self-destructive manslut phase is a largeish collection of sexy underpants—I mean, sexy in the sense of making my dick look big and my arse look perky, not in the sense of crotchless or edible. Of course, today, safe in the knowledge that they would go entirely unobserved, I was wearing my comfiest pair of schlumping shorts.

They were a slightly faded blue, with tiny hedgehogs picked out on them in white. Oliver's T-shirt, which smelled of fabric softener and virtue, was long enough that it mostly covered the design, but it was a good thing I definitely didn't want to get it on with him because Mrs. Tiggy-Winkle—the hedgehog design, that's not what I call my penis—would have nuked my chances.

By the time I emerged, Oliver was already in bed, propped up against the headboard, his nose buried in a copy of *A Thousand Splendid Suns*. I darted from the doorway and dived under the covers, wriggling myself into a sitting position and trying to get close enough it wasn't weird but not so close it was weird.

"I feel like Morecambe and Wise," I said.

Oliver turned a page.

"You know you're wearing pyjamas wrong, right?"

He didn't look up. "Oh?"

"Yeah, you're supposed to just wear the bottoms, and have them hanging low on your hips, displaying your perfectly chiselled V-cut."

"Maybe next time."

I thought about this for a moment. "Are you saying you *have* a perfectly chiselled V-cut?"

"I'm not sure that's any of your business."

"What if someone asks? I should know for verisimilitude."

The corners of his mouth twitched slightly. "You can say I'm a gentleman and we haven't got that far."

"You"—I gave a thwarted sigh—"are a terrible fake boyfriend."

"I'm building fake anticipation."

"You'd better be fake worth it."

"I am."

I hadn't quite been expecting that and didn't quite know how to reply. So I just sat there, trying not to think too hard about what Oliver's idea of "worth it" might be.

"Good book?" I asked, to distract myself.

"Relatively." Oliver glanced my way briefly. "You're being very talkative."

"You're being very...not talkative."

"It's bedtime. I'm going to read and then go to sleep."

"Again, starting to see why people don't stick around."

"For God's sake, Lucien," he snapped. "We've made an agreement to be useful to each other, I have work in the morning, and you're in my bed, wearing rather skimpy hedgehog boxers. I'm trying to maintain some sense of normalcy."

"If it's upsetting you that much, I can take my skimpy boxers and leave."

He put the book on the bedside table and did that massaging-his-temples thing I was seeing way too often. "I'm sorry. I don't want you to leave. Shall we try to sleep?"

"Um. Okay."

He flicked the light off abruptly, and I tried to settle myself down without impinging on his personal space or sense of propriety. His bed was firmer than mine, but also way nicer, and probably way cleaner. I could just about catch the scent of him from the sheets—fresh and warm, like if bread was a person—and I could just about feel the shape of him beside me. Comforting and distracting at the same time. Damn him.

Minutes or hours crept by. Determined to be a good sleeping partner, I was assailed by a thousand itches, niggles, and a terrible fear of farting. Oliver's breath was steady enough that I became hyperaware of my own, which was on the edge of going full Darth Vader. And then my brain started thinking stuff, and wouldn't stop.

"Oliver," I said. "My dad's got cancer."

I was fully prepared for him to tell me to shut up and go to sleep, or to kick me out entirely but instead, he rolled over. "I imagine that's going to take some getting used to."

"I don't want to get used to it. I don't want to know him at all. And if I do have to know him, it's deeply unfair I have to know him as a bloke with a cancer." I snuffled in the darkness. "He opted out of being my father. Why does he expect me to opt in just for the shit bit?"

"He's probably scared."

"He was never there when *I* was scared."

"No, he was clearly a bad father. And you can punish him for it if you want to, but do you honestly think that will help?"

"Help who?"

"Anyone, but I'm thinking mainly of you." Under the plausible deniability of the bedclothes, his fingertips brushed mine. "It must have been hard to go through life after he abandoned you. But I'm not sure it'll be easier to go through life after you've abandoned him."

I was silent for a long time. "Do you really think I should see him?"

"It's your decision, and I'll support you either way, but yes. I think you should."

I made a plaintive noise.

"After all," he went on, "if it goes badly, you can walk away at any time."

"It's just…it's going to be all hard and messy."

"Lots of things are. Many of them are still worth doing."

It was a sign of quite how fucked up I was feeling that I didn't try to make a joke out of *hard, messy* or, indeed, *worth doing*.

"Will you," I asked, "will you come with me? If I go."

"Of course."

"You know for…"

"Verisimilitude," he finished.

He still hadn't moved his hand. I didn't ask him to.

CHAPTER 15

"OKAY, ALEX," I SAID. "HOW do you get four elephants in a Mini?"

He thought about this for longer than it should have required. "Well, I mean, elephants are very big so normally you wouldn't expect that even one of them would fit in a Mini. But if they were very small—if they were, for example, baby elephants—then I suppose you'd put two in the front and two in the back?"

"Um…y-yes. That's right."

"Oh good. Have we got to the joke yet?"

"Nearly. So how do you get four giraffes in a Mini?"

"Once again, giraffes are very large but we seem to be ignoring that for the purposes of this exercise. So I'd expect two in the… Oh no, wait. Of course, you'd have to take the elephants out first, assuming it was the same Mini."

My universe was imploding. "Also right. Okay, final question."

"This is splendid. It's making a lot more sense than the jokes you usually tell me."

"Glad to hear it. Anyway. Final question. How do you get two whales in a Mini?"

Another pause. "Gosh. It's not really my area of expertise, but I think it's up the M4 and over the Severn Bridge. Maybe you should check with Rhys, though, because he's from there."

I was about to say something along the lines of "Well, this

has been fun," meaning, of course, "I don't know what's just happened" when Alex cupped a hand theatrically round his mouth and shouted, "Rhys, can we borrow you for a second?"

Rhys Jones Bowen poked his head around the door of the glorified cupboard that we called the "outreach office." "What can I do you for, boys?"

"Luc wants to know how to get to Wales in a Mini," explained Alex.

"Well, I don't see why it matters if you're in a Mini or not." Rhys Jones Bowen had even more of a look of perplexed helpfulness than usual. "But usually you'd go up the M4 and over the Severn Bridge. I mean if you were going somewhere in south Wales, like Cardiff or Swansea. But if you were going somewhere in north Wales like Rhyl or Colwyn Bay, you'd be better off going up the M40 via Birmingham."

"Thank you?" I offered.

"Are you going to Wales then, Luc? Best country in the world."

"Er, no. I was trying to tell Alex a joke."

Rhys Jones Bowen's face fell. "I don't see what's funny about wanting to go to Wales. I've known you for a long time, young Luc, and all these years I've never had you pegged for a racist."

"No, it's a pun. It's a series of jokes about trying to get incongruously large animals into a small car, and it ends with how do you get two whales in a Mini."

"But we've just told you that," complained Alex. "It's straight up the M4 and over the Severn Bridge."

"Unless you're headed north," added Rhys Jones Bowen, "in which case you take the M40 via Birmingham."

I threw my hands up in a gesture of surrender. "Okay, I've got the information now. Thank you both very much. Rhys, it was not my intent to speak ill of your homeland."

"It's all right, Luc. I quite understand." He nodded in a

reassuring way. "And if you did want a trip up to God's own kingdom, I've got a friend who's got a lovely little place outside of Pwllheli that he'll let you have at mates' rates for three hundred quid a week."

Alex gave a little gasp. "Why don't you take your new boyfriend?"

"Yeah, the whole idea of a getting a new boyfriend, which you ought to remember because it was your fucking idea, is to be seen dating someone appropriate. I'm not sure even the most farsighted paparazzi are going to be lurking around rural Wales just on the off chance I'm over there for a weekender."

"Ah. Well. We could do that thing they do in Westminster."

"Fiddle my expense claims?" I suggested. "Send pictures of my penis to journalists pretending to be teenage girls?"

"Oh Luc, I'm sure both of those situations were taken very much out of context by an unfair press establishment."

"So what are you talking about?"

"We should leak it. The next time you're having dinner with the CFO of an international news organisation, casually let it slip that you're planning to go to Wales."

I stifled a sigh. "Do we really need to have the 'what sorts of people the average human being has dinner with' conversation again?"

"Well, gentlemen," announced Rhys Jones Bowen, correctly concluding that he didn't have much more to contribute to the conversation. "I think I've done enough good here for one day. If you need me, I'll be updating our Myspace page."

And with that, he ambled off, providing me with a narrow window in which to steer things in a less ludicrous direction. "The trouble is, Alex, I'm not sure the plan's working. And now I say it out loud, I don't know why I ever thought it would."

He gave one of his slow, bewildered blinks. "Not working how?"

"Well, I've managed to avoid getting flayed in the press for the last week or so, but I've tried reaching out to some of the donors we lost and nobody's biting. So they either haven't noticed I'm respectable now or they don't care."

"I'm sure they care, old thing. They care so much they dropped you like a light-fingered footman. You just need to get their attention."

"The only attention I know how to get is the wrong kind of attention."

Alex opened his mouth.

"And if you say, oh it's easy, ring up the Duchess of Kensington, I will stick this biro up your nose."

"Don't be silly. I'd never say that. There is no Duchess of Kensington."

"You know what I mean." He probably didn't. "You have a whole bunch of nice society people you can reach out to, and they'll get you in *Hello!* or *Tatler* or *Horse & Hound* or something. I can get in the *Daily Mail* by sucking somebody off in a fire escape."

"Actually, I was going to suggest that you come with me to the club. Miffy's always got men following her with cameras. I mean"—he wrinkled his nose—"I think they're mostly journalists, although there was that awkward business with the kidnapping last February."

"Sorry. Did your girlfriend get kidnapped?"

"Silly business. They thought her father was the Duke of Argyll when he's actually the Earl of Coombecamden. How we laughed."

I decided to let that go. "So you're telling me that if I hang out with you, I'll either get my picture in better-quality magazines or I'll be abducted by international criminals."

"Which will also get you in the papers. So I think that's what the kids today are calling a win-win."

For the sake of my sanity, I decided now was not the time to explain to Alex what slang was and, more to the point, what it wasn't. "I'll see if he's free," I said and then retreated to my office via the coffee machine.

Since Sunday, Oliver and I had been sporadically fake-texting, which was becoming increasingly indistinguishable from real texting. My phone was never far from my hand, and my sense of time had distorted around my understanding of Oliver's schedule. He always sent me something first thing in the morning, usually an apology for the continued absence of dick pics, then it would be silence 'til lunchtime because important law stuff was happening, and sometimes he would work through lunch so I wouldn't hear from him at all. Come the evening, he'd check in before and after hitting the gym, and diligently ignore my request for updates on his V-cut. And once he was in bed, I'd bombard him with as many annoying questions as I could think of about whatever he was reading, usually based on the Wikipedia plot summary I'd just Googled. All of which was a long-winded way of saying I was surprised when he rang me at eleven thirty.

"Is this a butt-dialling," I asked, "or is someone dead?"

"Neither. I've had a bad morning, and I thought it would look suspicious if I didn't call the person I'm supposed to be dating."

"So you thought they'd notice you not calling me, but they wouldn't notice you saying 'supposed to be dating' aloud on the phone?"

"You're right." He was quiet a moment. "I think, perhaps, I just wanted someone to talk to."

"And you picked *me*?"

"I thought giving you an opportunity to laugh at my expense might make me feel better."

"You're a strange man, Oliver Blackwood. But if you want to be laughed at, I won't let you down. What happened?"

"Sometimes people don't help themselves."

"Okay, there'd better be more to this, or I *am* going to let you down."

He appeared to be taking calming breaths. "You may be aware that occasionally defendants change their stories, and this tends to get brought up in court. My client today was asked why, when originally questioned regarding a recent robbery, he'd claimed that he was with an associate of his. Who, for the sake of this anecdote, I shall call Barry."

There was something about the way Oliver was relating this to me in his best "I care deeply about the right to a fair trial even for petty criminals" voice that made me giggle before I was probably supposed to.

"What are you laughing at?"

"Your expense. I thought we'd established."

"But," he protested, "I haven't said anything funny yet."

"That's what you think. Do go on."

"You're making me self-conscious."

"I'm sorry. I'm just happy to hear from you."

"Oh." A long silence. Then Oliver cleared his throat. "Anyway, my client was asked why he had previously said he was with Barry when he was now claiming to have been alone. And my client said he got confused. And so the council for the prosecution asked why he got confused. To which my client explained that he got confused because, and I quote, 'Me and Barry get arrested together all the time.'"

"Did you shout objection?"

"We've been over this. And even if that were a feature of the British judicial system, what would I have said? Objection, my client is an idiot?"

"Okay then. Did you do that thing where you rub your temples and look really sad and disappointed?"

"I don't recall doing so. But I couldn't swear that I did not."

"So what did you do?"

"I lost. Although I flatter myself that I made the best of a bad situation by attempting to characterise my client as, and once more I quote, 'a man so honest that he voluntarily introduces prior arrests not in evidence.'"

At this point, I just gave up and burst out laughing. "You're such a trier."

"I'm glad I could amuse you at least. It means I've done somebody some good today."

"Oh, come on. It wasn't your fault. You defended the guy as well as you could."

"Yes, but if one must lose, one prefers to lose honourably rather than ignominiously."

"Y'know, I was going to be sympathetic, right until you started referring to yourself as *one*."

He gave a little chuckle. "One is sorry."

"One fucking well better be. One isn't the fucking queen."

"Will you come for a drink with me after work?" he said. It wasn't exactly a blurt, but it had definite blurty qualities. "That is, I think we should be seen together more often. For the sake of the project."

"The project? This isn't an episode of *Doctor Who*. But if you're that keen to preserve the integrity of Operation Cantaloupe, we've had an invitation to an expensive private members' club from the biggest nitwit in the Home Counties."

"Does this sort of thing happen often in your line of work?"

"Not so much," I admitted. "My get-a-respectable-boyfriend plan isn't doing what it's supposed to because none of our donors have noticed. And my very lovely, very posh, but very, very silly coworker has suggested we go out with him and his partner in order to generate a little bit of society buzz. But we absolutely don't have to do it. To be honest, it's probably a bad idea anyway."

"We should go." I was beginning to recognise Oliver's decisive voice. "The entire purpose of this exercise is to improve your public image. If we started turning down opportunities to do that, I'd be remiss in my fake boyfriend duties."

"Are you sure? There'll be other opportunities to score fake boyfriend points."

"I'm sure. Besides, meeting your coworkers is what a real boyfriend would do."

"You're going to regret that. But it's too late. I'll text you the… Will you fake dump me if I say 'deets'?"

"Without hesitation."

I hung up a few minutes later and delivered the news to Alex, who, once he remembered that he'd invited us, seemed genuinely delighted.

Next on my list of personal things to do on company time was—and I could not believe I was even thinking about this—get in touch with my father. I'd been putting it off since Sunday, but Oliver was the kind of thoughtful bastard who'd probably ask how it was going and I didn't want to have to tell him I'd wussed it.

Of course, now I came to it, I realised that I didn't have any way to contact Jon Fleming, and the thing about famous people is they're actually pretty hard to reach. Probably the quickest and most effective strategy I could have tried was asking Mum, but quick and effective wasn't really what I was aiming for. Basically, what I needed was a way of trying to get in touch with my dad that left me with as little chance as possible of having to be in touch with my dad.

So I got his manager's name off his website and his manager's number off his manager's website. The manager in question turned out to be a guy named Reggie Mangold, who by the looks of things had been a hotshot in the '80s, though now Jon Fleming was by far his biggest client. Very, very slowly I poked the number into my office phone and hoped for an answering machine.

"Mangold Talent," said a gruff Cockney voice that definitely wasn't an answering machine. "Mangold speaking."

"Um. Hi. I need to talk to Jon Fleming."

"Oh, well. In that case, I'll put you through directly. Please hold."

The absence of hold music and the sarcasm dripping from his tone suggested that I was not, in fact, about to be put through directly. "No, really. He asked to speak to me."

"Unless you've got way nicer tits than you sound like you've got, I very much doubt that."

"I'm his son."

"Pull the other one, mate, it's got bells on."

"My name is Luc O'Donnell. My mother is Odile O'Donnell. Jon Fleming actually is my father and does actually want to speak to me."

Reggie Mangold wheezed a smoker's laugh. "If I had a quid for every little shit who's tried that on me, I'd have eight pound forty-seven."

"Okay, so you don't believe me. That's fine. But if you could just tell him I called, that would be peachy."

"I will certainly do that. I'm writing your message down right now in my imaginary notebook. Are we spelling O'Donnell with two *l*'s or three?"

"Two *n*'s. Two *l*'s. And it's about the cancer thing."

And then I hung up, which gave me a sense of satisfaction that briefly counteracted the nausea. Key word being *briefly*. Honestly, I wasn't sure what was worse: having to reach out to my waste of a father in the first place, or trying to reach out to him and discovering he'd made no effort to actually let me. And, yes, I'd gone about it in a slightly half-arsed way, but you'd think telling your manager that he might get a call from your son at some point fell somewhere between "bare" and "minimum" on the trying-to-connect-with-your-long-lost-family scale.

It was gradually sinking in that if Dad did kick the bucket, my last, and pretty much only, words to him would have been "fuck off and literally die." And I resented how shitty that made me feel about myself because, while a lot of people had an absolute right to make me feel shitty on account of the many years I've spent systematically letting them down, Jon Fleming was just some prick I'd never met.

This was the problem with, well, I was going to say "the world" or "relationships" or "humanity in general," but I guess I really meant me. Because when I let someone into my life, it went one of two ways: either they carried on putting up with me, even though I'm clearly not worth putting up with. Or else they pissed all over me and walked out, occasionally popping back to piss on me some more.

Around this point, remembering I had—for the moment—still got a job, and that job involved more than sitting in my office, making personal calls, and wallowing in self-pity, I checked my email.

Dear Mr. O'Donnell,

I have been a supporter of CRAPP for many years and have always believed that my not-insignificant contributions were being well directed towards a worthwhile cause. Having seen your recent personal conduct and made my own independent researches into your, frankly, sordid history I am forced to conclude that this belief was misguided. I do not give money to charities in order that they can pay people to gallivant off on homosexual drug binges. I am withholding all donations to your organisation for as long as it remains associated with you or your lifestyle.

Sincerely,

J. Clayborne,

MBE

Needless to say, he had cc'ed it to Dr. Fairclough, the rest of the office, and possibly his entire address book.

I was just making a detailed plan to slink home, drink heavily, and pass out under a pile of at least three duvets when Alex popped his head around the door.

"Ready to go, old chap? Bit tricky to get a reservation at this notice but, you know, a fellow's always willing to call in a marker for a fellow who needs it."

Oh yes. That. Fuck.

CHAPTER 16

ALEX'S CLUB WAS CALLED CADWALLADER'S and it was exactly like you'd expect a club called Cadwallader's to be. Lurking discreetly behind a door just off St James's Street, it was made entirely of oak, leather, and men who'd been occupying the same armchair since 1922. Seeing no way to get out of the social engagement that had been arranged purely for my benefit at very short notice, I'd gone ahead with Alex.

He'd left a note with someone I thought was an honest-to-goodness butler that we were expecting guests later, and was now leading me up a staircase of Hogwartsian proportions, all gleaming mahogany and blue velvet carpeting. From there, we passed between a set of actual marble pillars and into what a little plaque informed me was the Bonar Law Room. It was sparsely occupied, allowing Alex to lay claim to a sizeable sofa directly underneath an even more sizeable portrait of the queen.

I perched on a nearby chair, uncomfortable partly because the chair itself was surprisingly hard, given that it probably cost more than my laptop, partly because my day was turning into a string of back-to-back rejections, and partly because of the surroundings. The room appeared to have been decorated on the assumption that its inhabitants would have an aneurysm if they realised we didn't have an empire anymore. I'd never seen so many chandeliers in one place, even counting that time I'd accidentally gone to the opera.

"Well, isn't this cosy." Alex beamed at me. "Would you like anything while we wait for the ladies? I mean, my lady and your boylady."

"I'm not sure 'boylady' is the correct term."

"Terribly sorry. Still a bit of a novel sitch. Not that it isn't fearfully nice that you're a homosexual. Just never brought one to the club before. After all, they only let ladies in three years ago. They can't join, of course. That way madness lies, let us shun that. And, actually, thinking about it, it must be terribly jolly for one's lady to be a gentleman. You can go to all the same clubs, have the same tailor, play on the same polo team. No metaphor intended."

"You know," I said, "I think I will have a drink."

He leaned over the back of the sofa and made an obscure posh gesture at a soberly dressing butling person who, I'd swear, hadn't been standing there ten seconds ago. "The usual, James."

"Um, what's the usual?" I had enough experience with high-society bullshit that I knew "the usual" could have been anything from a sweet white wine to live herring that you had to eat with a soup spoon.

Alex looked momentarily confused, even by his standards. "Haven't the foggiest. Can never quite remember, but don't have the heart to tell the staff."

A few minutes later, we were served two thistle-shaped glasses full of a honey-coloured liquid that I was pretty sure was something in the sherry family.

Taking a sip, Alex made a face and then set the drink down on a coffee table. "Ah yes. It's this stuff. Dreadful."

I really wanted to ask Alex how he had wound up with his "usual" being a drink he didn't actually like, but I was terrified that he might answer me. And I was saved in any case by Oliver's arrival. He was looking all sleek and professional in another of his three-piece suits—charcoal grey, this time—and it wouldn't have been totally unfair to say I was overjoyed to see him. And maybe it was because I'd had spent the last half hour alone with Alex, or maybe it was because Oliver was the only other person in the place who wasn't a peer, a Tory, or a Tory peer, or maybe... Oh, who I was kidding? I was just glad he was here. So I could tell him how I'd tried to do the right thing by my dad, and his manager hadn't even believed I was me. How some prick with an MBE had sent me another one of those not-homophobic-but-clearly-homophobic emails I was so sick of being polite and gracious about. How absurd it was that we were drinking wine none of us could identify under a royalist portrait the size of Cornwall. How I'd missed him.

That was when I realised that although Oliver and I were meant to be a couple, we'd failed to establish any rules for interacting in public. Well, unless you counted "Don't kiss me" and "Stop telling everyone the whole thing's a sham." And I guess in my head somehow it'd be straight back to French toast, and silly texts, and Oliver's hand in mine in the dark. But that didn't happen.

I stood up awkwardly and he stood awkwardly in front of me.

"Hello, um..." He paused for way too long. "Darling?"

"His name's Luc," offered Alex, helpfully. "Don't worry, I forget all the time too."

Nice going, us. Undetectable fake boyfriending. "Oliver, this is my colleague Alex Twaddle."

Alex stood up to shake Oliver's hand—looking way more comfortable with him than I did. "Of the Devonshire Twaddles."

"Alex, this is my...um...boyfriend, Oliver Blackwood."

"Are you sure?" Alex glanced between us. "I thought you didn't have a boyfriend. Didn't we have this entire plan where you were going to find someone to pretend to be your boyfriend because you didn't have a boyfriend?"

I sank down into my chair. "Yes. We did. And this is him."

"Ah. With you." He transparently was not with us. "How about a drink, Oliver?"

"That would be lovely." Oliver settled onto the sofa next to Alex, crossing one leg elegantly over the other, and looking very much at ease.

While I was teetering on the edge of my crap chair like I was waiting outside the headmaster's office. At least the headmaster's office of the kind of school Alex and Oliver had probably gone to. They probably had portraits of the queen everywhere. They probably used them as blackboards. Fuck. I might as well go home and leave my fake boyfriend to bond with the office ninny.

"Did you say the Devonshire Twaddles?" enquired Oliver smoothly. "Any relation to Richard Twaddle?"

"My father actually, God rest his soul."

I stared at him. "Alex, you never told me your dad died."

"Oh, he didn't. Why would you think that?"

"Because…never mind."

"So"—Alex turned back to Oliver—"how do you know the old bugger?"

"I don't know him, but he's a big advocate for restricting the right to trial by jury so I have a sort of professional interest."

"That sounds like him. Talks about it round the dinner table all the time. Says they cost the government a huge amount of money, that people are only in favour of them because of silly sentimentality, and they spread tuberculosis."

"I'm not sure," said Oliver, "but I think you might be getting jury trials mixed up with badgers."

Alex snapped his fingers. "That's them. He can't stand the things. Little black-and-white furry bastards causing unnecessary delays in our already overstrained criminal justice system."

Oliver opened his mouth, then closed it again. At which point we were mercifully interrupted by James returning with another glass of whatever Alex's usual was.

"Thank you." Oliver sampled the drink decorously. "Ah. What a fine amontillado. I feel quite spoiled."

Trust Oliver Blackwood to be able to identify sherry by taste. It was fast becoming apparent that what I'd hoped would be me and him against the posh dingbat was actually him and the posh dingbat against me.

Alex slid his own glass over. "Have mine if you like. Can't abide it."

"That's very generous of you, but I think I'll stick to one drink at a time for now."

"You don't need to stand on ceremony here, old chap." At this juncture, Alex decided to pat my fake boyfriend's knee. "Lord Ainsworth usually has a glass in each hand the moment he walks through the door. That's why they call him Double Fisting Ainsworth. At least, I think it is. Could be something to do with the prostitutes."

"Yes," agreed Oliver. "It's always hard to tell, isn't it?"

"So." My voice was much louder than I expected it to be. "What's the problem with jury trials?"

They both glanced at me, with eerily similar expressions of mild concern. Probably, with my inappropriate volume and my awkward segue, I'd deeply embarrassed both of them. But at least Oliver had remembered I exist.

He fixed his cool, silver-grey gaze on me. "Well, as far as I'm concerned, nothing. I think they form a vital part of our democracy. I believe Lord Twaddle would advance the argument that they're slow, inefficient, and leave complex decisions in the hands of people who don't know what they're doing."

"Also"—Alex wagged a finger—"they leave terrible holes all over... Sorry. Badgers again. Do disregard."

This was honestly not an issue I'd given any thought to ever. But, goddamn it, Oliver was *my* fake boyfriend, not Alex Fucking Twaddle's. We were going to have a pleasant conversation over sherry if it killed us both. "I suppose," I arse-pulled, "that if I'd been accused of something I didn't do, I'd be far more willing to trust a legal professional than twelve randomers. I mean, have you met people?"

Oliver gave a faint smile. "That's an understandable position but, interestingly, one that is seldom shared by lawyers."

"Seriously?" I asked. "Do you really want to leave your fate in the hands of a dozen people you don't know, none of who want to be there, on the off chance one of them pulls a Henry Fonda?"

"In real life, juries aren't made up of eleven bigots and an angel. And I would far rather leave my fate in the hands of a cross-section of the public than a single person who sees the law entirely in abstract terms."

I adopted what I hoped was a thoughtful pose, but was largely motivated by a desire to stop my left buttock going to sleep. "But don't you *want* someone to see the law in abstract terms?" What was that line from *Legally Blonde*? "Didn't Socrates say, 'The law is reason free from passion'?"

"Actually, it was Aristotle. And he was wrong. Or rather, he was right in a way, but the law is only one part of justice."

Oliver was looking distractingly intense. I guess I could admit that, under most circumstances, he was a better-than-okay looking man. But when he was being passionate about shit, and his eyes got all sharp and his mouth got all interesting, he probably got upgraded to hot. And this was just about the worst possible time to start noticing that because, while I was noticing how attractive he could be, he was noticing what a complete piece of human garbage I was.

"Oh?" I said intelligently, while not staring.

"The point of a jury trial is that reasonable people—and before you say anything, most people *are* reasonable—get to decide whether the defendant truly deserves to be punished for their actions. The letter of the law is, at best, half of that question. The other half is compassion."

"That's the cheesiest thing I've ever heard."

I think what I'd meant was, *That's the most adorable thing I've ever heard.* But I couldn't admit that and now wished I'd said nothing because Oliver had snapped closed like a fan in the hands of an angry drag queen. "Fortunately I don't need you to validate my beliefs."

Great. Now I had Dad, a random donor, and Oliver all coming at my self-esteem from different directions. And, yes, I deserved it in Oliver's case, but that wasn't making me feel any better.

"This is jolly interesting," piped up Alex. At this point the odds were fifty-fifty that he still thought we were talking about badgers. "But I can't help feel a chap is still better off with a judge. I mean, just seems more likely to be a chap's sort of chap, you know?"

Oliver turned back to him with an effortless smile. "In your specific case, Alex, I very much agree."

"Gosh. Really? Well, look at me. See, I'm always a bit less wrong than people think. Like a stopped clock. Oh I say, it's Miffy."

Alex leapt to his feet, followed more gracefully by Oliver with the instinctive courtesy of the properly brought up. I stumbled after them, listing a little because of the buttock issue.

"Hello, boys." An immaculate gift box of a woman—mostly eyes, cheekbones, and cashmere—was gliding towards us. "So sorry I'm late. Had a beastly time getting through the photographers."

There followed a brief flurry as she and Alex exchanged a surprisingly complex sequence of air kisses. "Don't worry, old girl. I kept them entertained. This is Oliver Blackwood—he's a lawyer. Frightfully clever fellow."

More air kisses, which Oliver fielded expertly. Because apparently everybody got to touch my boyfriend—I mean, my fake boyfriend—except me.

"And this is Luc O'Donnell, who I've told you all about."

She came in to kiss me and I moved my head wrong and we banged noses. "Gosh," she said. "You look very young to be Speaker of the House."

"Um. No. That's not me."

"Are you sure? That's definitely who Ally was telling me about."

"Is it possible," I asked, "he's told you about more than one person?"

She blinked. "Possibly, but that would get terribly confusing."

"Anyway"—that was Alex again, and for possibly the first time in my entire life I was relieved he was speaking—"Luc and Oliver are boyfriends. Only not really. They just have to pretend until the Beetle Drive. It's the most tremendous wheeze." He blushed modestly. "My idea actually."

"Oh, Ally. You *are* a smarty-pants."

"Only don't tell anybody because it's a gigantic secret."

She tapped the side of her head. "*Video et taceo.*"

"And this," Alex went on, "is my... I say, Miffy, are we engaged?"

"I don't recall. I feel like we probably should be. Let's say we are for now and work out the details later."

"In which case, this is my fiancée Clara Fortescue-Lettice."

I knew I was going to regret this. But I said it anyway. "I thought she was called Miffy?"

"Yes." Alex gave me a what-is-wrong-with-you look. "Miffy, short for Clara."

"But it's the same number of sylla... Never mind."

Alex drew Miffy-Short-for-Clara's arm through his with easy confidence. "Shall we tootle into the dining room?"

"Yes, let's," she agreed. "I could eat an entire dressage team."

Oliver and I eyed each other nervously, uncertain if we had a linking-arms type of relationship, before falling into step beside each other like estranged relatives at a funeral. Yep. I'd been demoted from "Don't kiss me" to "I cannot bear the thought of physical contact with you."

"So," remarked Miffy as we made our way down another absurdly opulent corridor, "what have you boys been nattering about?"

Alex glanced briefly towards us. "Actually it's been fascinating. Oliver was just telling us about the merits and drawbacks of jury trials."

"That *does* sound fascinating. My father's against them, of course. Terrible for dairy farmers."

Oliver moved his hand swiftly to his mouth as if to stifle a cough. But I was 99 percent certain he was smiling. Unfortunately he wouldn't look at me, so I couldn't even share that.

CHAPTER 17

IT TURNED OUT THERE WERE two dining halls—the Eden Room and the Gascoyne-Cecil Room—but Alex found the Eden Room, in his words, "chummier." Although what precisely was chummy about mustard-yellow walls, wainscoting, and massive portraits of severe-looking men dressed entirely in black, I couldn't say. The menu offered roast chicken, roast beef, roast pork, beef Wellington, roast pheasant, game pie, and roast venison.

"Ah," exclaimed Alex, "lovely. Just like school dinners."

I gave him a look. Maybe if I focused on how annoying I found Alex, I'd find myself more bearable. "Often had pheasant at school, did you, Alex?"

"Not often. You know, once or twice a week maybe."

I glanced at Oliver, who was scrutinising the menu as if he hoped he'd somehow missed the non-dead-animal option. Was this a fake boyfriend job? It was probably a fake boyfriend job. And if I did it right, he might start paying attention to me. Fuck, I was pathetic.

"I should have mentioned," I said gallantly, "Oliver's a vegetarian."

"I'm so sorry." Miffy gazed at him with genuine concern. "What happened? Is there anything anyone can do?"

Oliver gave a wry smile. "I'm afraid not. But please don't worry, I'll manage."

"No no," Alex protested. "I'm sure it's fine. Let's ask James." He made a gesture and a completely different butling person who still, apparently, answered to the name James appeared at his elbow. "I say, James. Queer business. Seems I've accidentally brought a vegetarian."

James did one of those mini-bows straight off *Downton Abbey*. "I'm sure the chef can accommodate the lady, sir."

"I'm not a vegetarian." Miffy's eyes widened in outrage. "My father's an earl."

"I do apologise, madam."

Oliver made a charmingly bashful gesture. "I'm afraid I'm the difficulty, James. If you could arrange something along the lines of a garden salad, that would be more than sufficient."

He took the rest of our orders, and twenty minutes later we were surrounded by various meats, most of them roasted, some of them in pastry, and Oliver had an actually quite pleasant-looking pile of leaves. I mean, I wouldn't personally have wanted it for dinner, but I guess it served him right for having ethics.

Alex regarded Oliver with a pained expression. "Are you absolutely sure you're all right with that? Miffy and I have plenty of Wellington if you want some."

"It's fine. I'm enjoying my salad."

"If it's the meatiness that's an issue, we could mix it up with the cabbage."

"I think it would still contain meat?"

So, my cunning plan to win Oliver over by being sensitive to his needs and respectful of his choices? That had failed hard. I pointedly shovelled a large scoop of game pie into my mouth. After all, if food was going in, words couldn't be coming out. Which, given my contribution to the conversation so far, was probably best for everyone.

Miffy reappeared from behind the beef Wellington. "Well, I'm sorry. I just think that's silly. I mean, what would we do with meat if we didn't eat it? Just let it go off?"

"Well, that's actually quite a complicated question." Oliver deftly speared a radish. "And the answer is mostly that we'd slaughter fewer animals."

"Then wouldn't there be too many animals? What would we do with all the cows?"

"I think we'd breed fewer cows as well."

"Bit of a rum deal for the cows then, isn't it?" she exclaimed. "To say nothing of the farmers. We have some jolly lovely farmers on our land. They make a beautiful showing at the harvest festival and give us such nice hams at Christmas. And here you are trying to put them all out of work. It's rather rotten of you, Oliver."

"You see"—Alex wagged his fork playfully—"you've set her off on one now. And she's right, you know. I don't think you've thought this through."

Still determinedly masticating, I stole a peek at Oliver to see how was taking this, and he seemed surprisingly comfortable. Well, he *was* a barrister. He'd had a lot of practice being polite to posh people. "I do admit that the economic implications of large-scale shifts in the national diet are more complicated than people often give them credit for being. But the vast majority of meat we eat nowadays is unlikely to have been produced by the type of farmer you're talking about, and industrialised agriculture is actually quite a significant threat to the countryside."

There was a pause.

"Oh," said Alex. "Maybe you have thought it through. Didn't I say he was frightfully clever?"

Miffy nodded. "Yes, he's splendid. I think you chose an excellent fake boyfriend, Ally."

"Hang on." I nearly choked on shortcrust. "He's not Ally's...I mean, Alex's fake boyfriend. He's my fake boyfriend. Also we should probably stop loudly saying the word 'fake' because it's kind of giving the game away."

Alex had reverted to his ordinary state of confusion. "Are you completely sure? Because I definitely remember it being my idea."

"Yes, it was an idea for how *I* could fix *my* reputation."

"It seems a shame." Miffy had finished her beef Wellington and was making inroads into Alex's. "Ally and Ollie seem to be getting on terribly well. Of course, their couple name would be Ollivander, which I'm sure I've heard somewhere before."

"I think," offered Oliver, "it's the name of the wand-maker from Harry Potter."

Suddenly, Alex let out a joyful yelp. "So it is. I should have spotted that immediately. I've read the whole series thirty-eight times. Didn't mean to. Just, by the time I got to the end, I forgot how it started. Only thing I've read more is *The Republic*."

"Yeah." I tried to catch Oliver's eye and failed. "I can see how those two fandoms overlap."

Alex was still beaming like he had a coat hanger in his mouth. "It brings back such happy memories. When the films came out, I got all my college pals together, and we sat in the front row of the cinema and shouted 'House' every time the old alma mater popped up on screen."

This was one of those gatekeepery anecdotes that you needed an English/Posh Git dictionary to make any sense of. Why was Alex's house in a Harry Potter movie?

"Oh"—Oliver, of course, had read the English/Posh Git dictionary at the age of four and now had his tell-me-more face on, which I really preferred him to be directing at me—"so you're a Christ Church man?"

That made more sense. Although if there was anyone I'd have believed went to Hogwarts, it was Alex.

"For my sins. Same as Pater. And Mater, for that matter. Bit of a family tradish, actually. Great-great-great-great-great-great-great-great-great-great..." Alex started ticking them off on his fingers "...great-great-great-great-great-great-great-great grand-papa used to go on the lash with Cardinal Woolsey. I mean, until he got exiled. No fun after that."

Oliver was still attending courteously. Polite bastard. "No, I can't imagine he would be."

"So what about you? You didn't go to the other place, did you? Could explain rather a lot."

Miffy elbowed him.

"I mean," Alex added hastily, "the vegetarianism. Not the homosexuality."

"Oriel."

And they were back to their private code. I'd just about worked out that House was an Oxford thing. So where was the other place? Was it hell? If so, *Hi, weather's lovely down here.* And as far as I knew, Oriel was either a songbird or a biscuit. What was even happening right now?

This, right here, was why somebody like Oliver would never date somebody like me in real life.

Alex nodded approvingly. "Good show. Knew lots of splendid chaps from Oriel. Mostly rugger fellows, you know. Did you go in for that?"

"No," said Oliver. "I was very committed to my studies. I'm afraid I was rather boring at college."

"You're rather boring now," I muttered, perhaps a teensy bit louder than I meant to.

Which made Oliver look at me, finally. But not in the way I wanted.

"Luc," cried Miffy. "I thought Oliver was supposed to be your boyfriend. That's a beastly way to talk about him."

Now Alex was glaring at me as well. "Well said, old thing.

Can't go around badmouthing the ladies like that. I mean, gentle-men. I mean, your gentleman."

"If I were you"—Miffy patted Oliver on the hand—"I'd kick him to the kerb, girlfriend. Boyfriend. Oh I say, that doesn't work."

"I'm inclined to agree, Miffles." Alex wagged his fork sternly. "I would never have suggested Luc get a boyfriend if I knew he was going to rag on the fellow. You should probably leave him and go out with me instead. Hashtag Ollivander."

Miffy nodded. "Yes, do go out with Ally. I could have one of you on each arm. It'd be the most ripping lark."

"For fuck's sake"—once again, I was slightly louder than I meant to be—"stop trying to steal my boyfriend. You don't even like men."

Alex gave me a genuinely wounded look. "Of course I like men. All my friends are men. My father's a man. You're the one who's being horrid to everybody. Telling Oliver he's boring when he's an Oxford fellow and has been dashed good company all evening. And now implying I'm the sort of chap who doesn't get along with other chaps. When really"—here, Alex turned downright haughty—"it's becoming very clear to me that *you're* the sort of chap who doesn't get along with other chaps. I really feel I ought to apologise, Oliver."

"Do me a favour." I stood up. "Don't apologise for *my* behaviour to *my* boyfriend. I've had nothing but fucking Oxford talk for this entire fucking meal. I know it's stupid to complain about feeling excluded from your little private club when we are literally sitting in a little private club but, sorry, it's been a long day and, yes, you're trying to do me a favour, but I'm having the worst fucking evening and…and I'm going to the toilet."

I stormed off, discovered I had no idea where the loos were, asked one of the Jameses, and made an embarrassing U-turn. Once I was safely in the gents—which were tasteful but simplistic like they were saying "Only Americans and the middle classes feel the need to put marble in a water closet"—I stood at the sink and did that thing people do in movies where they brace themselves on the counter and stare meaningfully at their reflection.

Turns out, it didn't help. It was just a dick, looking at a dick, asking why he was always such a dick.

What was I even doing? Oliver Blackwood was a dull, annoying man I was pretending to date, and Alex Twaddle was an overprivileged buffoon who regularly stapled his trousers to his desk. What did I care if they got on with each other better than they got on with me?

Ooh, ooh, tally-ho toodle pip, which college were you at where did you sit at the annual duck following ceremony go fuck yourselves you self-satisfied pair of testes.

Okay, so calling them names didn't help either.

And, actually, Oliver wasn't dull. And he was only a little bit annoying. And Alex was terribly annoying, but he'd done nothing but try to help me. Maybe, and I'd suspected this for a while now, I was fundamentally unhelpable. Because somewhere along the line, I'd turned getting ahead of the story into a lifestyle.

When Miles had thrown me to the tabloid sharks, I'd been completely unprepared, and the only way I'd survived was by making sure that there was enough chum in the water that they'd only eat what I wanted them to. It had only half worked, but by the time I figured that out, the habit was so ingrained that I was doing the same with people.

The truth was, things were easier that way. It meant whatever happened wasn't really about me. It was about this shadow person who partied and fucked and didn't give a shit. So what did it matter if someone didn't like him? Didn't want him. Let him down or sold him out.

Except he wasn't dating Oliver—pretending to date Oliver—*I* was. And so, suddenly it all mattered again, and I wasn't sure I could cope with it mattering. The door swung open, and for a biscuit crumb of a second I hoped it might be Oliver coming to rescue me. And that was precisely the sort of crap I wanted out of my head. Anyway, it didn't matter because it wasn't Oliver. It was an old guy in tweed who looked like Father Christmas if Father Christmas only had a naughty list.

"Who are you?" he barked.

I jumped. "Luc? Luc O'Donnell?"

"Weren't you once up before me for public defecation?"

"What? No. I defecate very privately."

Evil Father Christmas narrowed his eyes. "I never forget a face, young man, and I don't like yours. Besides, never trusted the Irish."

"Um." Probably I should have stood up for my mother's father's people but I increasingly wanted to get the hell out of there. Unfortunately Racist Santa was blocking the exit. "Sorry about the...face. I really need to—"

"What are you doing here anyway?"

"Using the...facilities?"

"Loitering. That's what you're doing. Lurking in a communal lavatory like you're waiting for Jeremy Thorpe."

"I really just want to go back to my friends."

I managed to sidle past him with my hands in the air like I was being arrested. His head did almost a full exorcist as his cold, dead eyes followed me out. "I'm watching you O'Toole. Never forget a face. Never forget a name."

Back at the table, my so-called companions were enjoying my absence.

"—quarter blue for tiddlywinks in the end," Alex was saying cheerfully. "Miffy's the real sportsman. I mean, sportslady. Suppose we'd better be politically correct about these things. Full blue for lacrosse, don't you know. Invited to join Team GB but turned it down, didn't you, old girl? Wanted to focus on... Oh I say, what is it you do, Miffy?"

I sat down, trying to figure out if I was relieved or pissed off that everyone was carrying on as if I hadn't made an enormous scene.

Miffy tapped her perfect lips with a perfect nail. "Now you come to mention it, I have no idea. I think I've got an office somewhere, and I might be launching some kind of line, but mostly I just get invited to parties. Not like Ally, who's got an actual, you know, job. Which everybody thinks is terribly funny. But he goes in every day, which is so good of him, isn't it?"

This would have been a great time for me to be mature and say sorry. "I'm not sure," I said instead, "'good of him' is the right phrase. Maybe more 'contractually obligated' of him?"

"Are you quite certain?" Alex tilted his head like a bewildered parrot. "That doesn't seem quite cricket. Chap makes a commitment, chap follows through on it. One doesn't need to get all legal about things—no offence, Oliver."

"None taken." Of course Oliver wasn't taking offence. Oliver was an angel. While I was a slime demon from the planet Jerkface.

"Well, I say it's splendid. And, of course"—here Miffy bestowed a dazzling smile on me, which in the circumstances felt an awful lot like a participation trophy—"you're splendid too, Luc. Since you do the same job."

Great. So now not only did Oliver know that my job wasn't something I was passionate about, the way he was about his, but he was also going to think you could do it with about three functioning brain cells.

"Oh no," exclaimed Alex. "Luc's much more important than I am. No clue what he does, but it seems terribly complicated and involves, oh, what do you call them? Things with the little boxes?"

Miffy wrinkled her nose thoughtfully. "Cricket teams?"

"Not quite, old girl. Spreadsheets, that's the word. I just muck about with the photocopier, check we don't have more than two meetings in the same room at the same time, and keep Daisy alive."

"Who's Daisy?" asked Oliver, still ignoring me but, let's be honest, I probably deserved it.

"She's the aloe vera I'm growing in the filing cabinet. Our social media chappie burns himself on the coffee machine quite a lot, and Nurse always used aloe vera on us when we were small and it's jolly efficacious. In fact, I'm thinking we might need two because the poor dear is looking quite denuded in the leaf department."

"On another topic," I announced, changing the subject with all the grace and subtlety of someone saying *Can we change the subject now*, "a scary old man went for me in the bathroom. I mean, yelled at me. Not, like, tried to hit on me."

"Thank you for clarifying that." It was Oliver's driest tone. So far Operation Come Across as a Total Prick was running ahead of schedule.

Alex frowned. "How very rum. Did you do anything to provoke him?"

My apology window had closed an aloe vera ago. So I was basically stuck with sort of pretending I hadn't been awful, even though I blatantly had, and trying to find the mythical middle ground between making it worse and overcompensating. "Nice to know you're taking his side already. But, for the record, no. I was minding my own business by the sink when this mad old coot barged in and—"

"Alex, m'boy," bellowed the mad old coot, materialising behind me like the serial killer in a horror movie. "How's the old man?"

"Can't complain, Randy. Can't complain."

"Very much enjoyed his speech in the Lords recently about, oh, what was it…"

"Badgers?"

"No, not badgers. Those other, what do you call them… immigrants."

"Ah yes. Sounds like Daddy. Oh"—Alex gave a little start—"by the way, I should introduce you. You remember Clara, of course."

"'Course I do. Never forget a face."

"And these are my friends, Luc and Oliver."

His eyes lasered over us and I wilted in my seat. "Pleasure. Any friend of a Twaddle is a friend of mine. But I should warn you, stay out the bathroom—there's a mad Irish bastard ambushing people in there."

"Actually, Your Honour," said Oliver, in his best *If it please m'lud, counsel is testifying* voice, "we've met. I had a client before you last month."

"Nonsense. Never forget a face. Got no idea who you are." A pause. "Still"—he brightened—"did we get the bugger?"

"I was counsel for the defence, Your Honour, and the defence was, in this instance, successful."

The judge scowled at Oliver, who met his look with studied mildness. "Well. Suppose we can't catch 'em all. I'll leave you to your dinner. See you at the Swan Upping, Alex, if not before."

And, with that, the Right Honourable Racist doddered off.

"I say," exclaimed Alex, turning to me, "it seems Randy met the same strange man that you did. Do you think we've got an intruder? Shall I tell somebody?"

"I suspect," offered Oliver, "that won't be necessary."

"Are you sure? I mean, you know, can't be too careful and all that."

"I have no doubt Justice Mayhew dealt with the miscreant appropriately."

Alex gave a fond smile. "He's a feisty old bugger, isn't he?"

"That's certainly one way to put it."

There was a brief silence, which Oliver delicately steered us over by asking if everyone was ready to move on to dessert. "I couldn't help but notice," he went on, "the jam roly-poly on the menu. I've always been rather partial."

Alex bounced in his seat like a poorly trained beagle. "I'm a dick man, myself. Thick and solid, and piping hot, and slathered in what the French call crème anglaise."

I was still having way too many Oliver-related emotions, but I couldn't not steal a peek at him. And, of course, he didn't look even the slightest bit as if he was about to die of laughter in a room named after a dead Tory.

"I'll admit"—oh God help me, his eyes were legitimately twinkling—"that does sound good."

Miffy looked rather dreamy. "You know, I was just thinking, I really fancy a tart."

Were they doing this deliberately? They *had* to be doing this deliberately.

In any case, it turned out they could talk about pudding basically indefinitely, swapping childhood anecdotes, and squabbling over the merits of cobblers versus crumbles. They had, at least, finally hit on a topic—or rather, Oliver had introduced them to a topic—that I knew more than nothing about. And if I'd been a better person, I would have given them my hot take on which order you put the jam and cream on a scone. (It's jam, then cream). Unfortunately I'm a mediocre person at best. And so sat there, trying not to sulk into my pineapple upside-down cake.

We finished up our desserts, and I was about to be relieved that it was nearly over when one of the Jameses came around with cheese, then coffee, then brandy, then cigars. We eventually exhausted the topic of pudding, but Oliver kept stubbornly guiding the conversation back towards accessible subjects. I was sure he meant well and, after the fuss I'd made, wanted to make sure I was included.

But between my dad, my job, Justice Mayhew, and all the ways I'd made a complete mess of tonight, I didn't quite have the energy to be grateful.

CHAPTER 18

EIGHTY-SEVEN THOUSAND, FIVE HUNDRED AND sixty-four gazillion hours later, we were finally allowed to leave the Cadwallader Club. Given how terribly the evening had gone, I was really looking forward to taking a quiet cab ride home, sticking my head under a duvet, and dying. But, of course, the whole point of the evening had been to get me photographed standing next to socially acceptable people. Which meant the moment we stepped outside, we were swarmed by a mixture of high-end paparazzi and low-end journalists.

My vision sheeted white as far too many cameras went off in my face. I froze. Normally when people took my picture, they had the decency to sneak around so they could catch me fucking against a wheelie bin or vomiting in a pub car park. This was a whole other level of attention. And I'd not particularly liked the old level.

"Who are you wearing?" someone yelled from the crowd.

Okay. They were definitely not talking to me. My clothes were much closer to a "what" than a "who."

Miffy tossed back her hair and reeled off something incomprehensible that I assumed was a list of designers.

This was fine. I was fine. I just had to look vaguely like I belonged in this nice world where nice people could have nice things. How hard could it be?

"Have you set a date yet?"

"The eighteenth."

Relax. But not too relaxed. Smile. But not too much. I tried to remind myself that journalists were like tyrannosauruses. Their vision was based on movement.

"Eighteenth of what?"

"Yes," Miffy said.

Were they getting closer? I was sure they were getting closer. Also not sure I could breathe. I must have been photographed enough by now, right? Good publicity was starting to feel worse than bad publicity. At least bad publicity, or the sort of bad publicity I was used to, didn't pin you into a corner and yell at you.

I scanned the jostling horseshoe of newspersons, looking for a gap between the bodies. But I could hardly see for the after-images, and the idea of being grabbed at and pulled at as I tried to force my way through a pack of strangers made my stomach twist. I was this close to throwing up. On camera. Again. Another crackle of silver, and when the starbursts faded, I realised I was looking this one guy straight in the eye. I tried to turn away, but it was too late. "Is that Jon Fleming's kid?" he yelled. "You into Rights of Man, Miffy?"

Oh shit oh shit oh shit.

"I'd so love to chat"—her voice ebbed and flowed in my ears like the tide—"but I have to see a horse about a man."

"Which horse?"

"Which man?"

Another lightning storm of flashes—this time pointed much more squarely at me. I threw an arm across my face like a vampire trying to dab.

"What's the matter, Luc?"

"Overindulged?"

"Making the old man proud?"

"N-n-no comment," I muttered.

"Have you joined the Cadwallader Club?"

"What have you been drinking?"

"Are you turning over a new leaf?"

No way was any of that not a trap. "No...no comment."

"Cat got your tongue, Luc?"

"Are you coked up right now?"

"Where's your bunny ears?"

"That's enough." There was suddenly an arm around my waist. And then I was being drawn against Oliver's side—right up against that warm, gorgeous, um, coat. It was the most pathetic thing I'd ever done, possibly the most pathetic thing in the world, but I turned in to him and hid my face against his neck. The scent of his hair, so clean and, somehow, so *him*, slowed the panicked racing of my heart.

"What're you hiding from?"

"Come on, mate. Give us a smile."

"Who's your boyfriend?"

"My name is Oliver Blackwood." He didn't shout, but he didn't have to. There was something about the way he spoke that sliced through the clamour. "I'm a barrister at Middle Temple, and I suggest you get out of my way."

"How'd you meet?"

"How long do you think you're going to last?"

"Have you done him in an alley yet?"

I was basically made of day-old spaghetti at this point, but Oliver got me through the crowd. It wasn't as bad as I'd imagined. Mostly people fell back, and when they didn't, a look at Oliver's face seemed to make them reconsider. And, all the time, I sheltered in the circle of his arm, and nothing touched me but him.

Eventually, though, we got far enough and I calmed down enough that I became very aware of what a total arse I must have looked, clinging to Oliver and trembling like a kitten.

"Okay," I said, making a bid to pull away, "we're clear. You can let me go now."

Oliver's hold tightened. "They're still following. Endure me a little longer."

As ever, Oliver wasn't the issue. The problem was me, and how good this could have felt if I'd let it. "We can't do this forever. Just get me to the Tube and I'll sort myself out from there."

"You're obviously shaken. We're getting a taxi."

Wait. What did he think was happening? "Hang on, what's this *we*?"

"I'm taking you home. Now stop arguing with me in front of the press."

"Fine," I grumbled. "We can argue on the way."

Oliver flagged down a passing cab which, of course, actually stopped for him instead of speeding past with an air of contempt. He bundled me into the back, and I reluctantly gave my address. Then off we went.

Knowing Oliver would probably disapprove if I didn't, I resentfully fastened my seat belt. "Look, I appreciate the whole chivalry bit. But you are absolutely not coming into my flat."

"Not even"—his eyebrow flicked up nastily—"if I appear unannounced on the doorstep after standing you up?"

"That was a very different situation."

"Which doesn't alter the fact that I've welcomed you into my home and you're pushing me away from yours."

"Well, I'm sorry. Let's chalk this up to one more example of you being a fundamentally better person than me."

"That wasn't what I meant. Although"—his expression grew grave in the flicker of the city lights—"I found your behaviour tonight somewhat...surprising."

"Because I was supposed to sit there and take it while you completely ignored me in order to chat up Alex Fucking Twaddle?"

Now he did the *Lucien is being terrible* temple-massaging thing. "I wasn't ignoring you. I was trying to make a good impression because I understood that to be the purpose of the exercise."

"Then you succeeded," I retorted with more vehemence that perhaps made sense in context. "They clearly thought you were just ducky."

"I'm confused. You're angry because I did too well at reflecting positively on your taste in boyfriends?"

"Yes. I mean. No. I mean. Fuck you, Oliver."

"I don't see how that's helpful."

"It's not meant to be helpful." My voice bounced off the walls of the taxi. "I'm angry. I don't understand why you're not angry too. Because this was clearly a shit evening for both of us."

"Actually, I thought your friends were rather charming, as long as you didn't expect them to be anything they weren't. What made it a *shit evening* for me was your eagerness to demonstrate how little you think of me."

I...had not expected that. And, for a moment, I didn't know what to say. "Um, what?"

"I'm very conscious that you wouldn't be with me if you had any other choice. But this will not work if you can't hide your contempt for me in public."

Oh God. I was the worst human. "I tease you all the time."

"It felt different tonight."

I wanted to say that was on him. Except it wasn't. I guess I hadn't expected him to notice. Let alone care. *Fuuuck.* "I'm sorry, okay?"

"Thank you for the apology. But, right now, I'm not sure it's helping."

Yeah, that had been a bit lacklustre. "Look"—I addressed myself to the floor—"I really don't believe any of the shit I said."

"You acted as if you believed it."

"Because I...I thought it was going to be different."

"*What* was going to be different?"

"I thought it would be like when it's just the two of us. But you wouldn't look at me. You didn't know how to touch me. And you were supposed to be bonding with me over what a posh twerp Alex is. Not bonding with him over how I didn't go to Oxford."

There was a long silence.

"Lucien," said Oliver, in the soft, low voice that made me want to curl up inside him. Like, not in a serial-killer way. Like, in a blankety way. "I think I owe you an apology too. I never meant to make you feel uncomfortable or excluded, and I will admit I didn't quite know how to act in front of your friends because, well, I've never had to pretend to be someone's boyfriend before." He paused. "Especially in front of a pair of... What did you call them? Posh twerps who think the National Minimum Wage is the Duchess of Marlborough's prize racehorse."

A laugh startled out of me.

"You see." Oliver gave me a rather smug look. "I can be mean too."

"Yeah, but where was it when I needed it?"

"I like to make you smile, Lucien. I don't like to make other people feel small."

"I guess I can live with that." I took off my seat belt and slid over towards him.

"You should be wearing your seat belt. It's a legal requirement."

I let my head rest ever so lightly, almost accidentally, against his shoulder. "Oh shut up, Oliver."

CHAPTER 19

SOMEHOW, AGAINST ALL REASON AND sense of self-preservation, I invited Oliver into my flat. I mean, to give him his due, he didn't immediately drop dead from disgust and E. coli.

"I'm aware," he said, "that you sometimes consider me judgmental. But I honestly can't understand how you live like this."

"It's easy. All I do is I touch something, and whether it sparks joy or not, I just leave it exactly where it is."

"I'm not certain I'd recommend touching anything in this building."

I took off my jacket and, with more situational awareness than I would have credited myself with, threw it immediately over the most embarrassing pile of underpants. "I tried to save you. But you wouldn't be warned. You're basically Bluebeard's wife at this point."

"I thought you were ashamed of me." Oliver was still staring aghast at the impressive collection of takeaway containers that I was definitely going to get around to washing so that I could then definitely get around to recycling them. "But it turns out you were quite rightly ashamed of yourself."

"That's where you're wrong. Shame is for people with self-respect."

He put his fingers to his brow again in his so-sad-and-disappointed gesture that was not becoming endearing in the slightest. "At least Bluebeard kept his dead wives neatly in one cupboard."

"I know you're probably regretting our fake relationship pretty hard right now, but please don't dump me again."

"No, no." Oliver stiffened his shoulders like he was in a wartime propaganda poster. "It took me a moment. But I'm over it."

"You can leave if you want to."

He looked very briefly tempted. But then went back to being all *Your country needs you.* "For the sake of appearances, we should make sure we don't repeat tonight's mistakes. I don't think either of us had thought through how to be together in public."

"Wow"—I threw myself listlessly onto the sofa, which was mostly clear apart from two pairs of socks and a blanket—"I really underestimated how much work this was going to involve."

"Yes, well, as the kids say: Suck it up, buttercup. Now do you think we should hold hands?"

"Did you actually say, 'Suck it up, buttercup'?"

"I thought pointing out that this is a lot of work for me too, and that I'm not complaining, while an accurate observation, would have made me sound like a prig."

I eyed him, half-irritated, half-amused. "Good call."

"So are we holding hands or not?"

If nothing else, you had to kind of admire his ability to stick to a point. "Um…I genuinely have no idea."

"It involves minimum actual intimacy, but makes it clear we're together if we happen to get photographed."

"Well, I do love me some minimum actual intimacy."

Oliver frowned at me. "Stop being frivolous, Lucien, and hold my damn hand."

I stood up, picked my way back through a slalom of mugs, and held his damn hand.

"Hmm." Oliver adjusted his grip several times. "This seems forced."

"Yeah, I feel like I'm being dragged round the supermarket by my mum."

"So, no to hand-holding. Try taking my arm."

"Don't you mean your *damn* arm?"

He blinked aggressively. "Just. Do it."

I took his arm. Still weird. "Now it's more like I'm a maiden aunt at a garden party."

"So I either make you feel like a child or an old lady? How very flattering."

"It's not you." I un-took his arm. "It's the situation."

"Then we'll have to be one of those couples who never touch each other when anybody's looking."

"But," I whined, "I don't want to be one of those couples. I don't even want to *pretend* to be one of those couples."

"In which case, I suggest you work out some way you can bear to touch me."

"Okay." I couldn't think of anything clever so I said the first thing that came into my head. "Why don't we have sex?"

His mouth twisted quizzically. "I don't think that would be appropriate at a fundraiser."

Well. In for a penny, in for pound. "No. I mean, like now."

"I beg your pardon?"

"Jesus, Oliver." I rolled my eyes. "Who responds to a come-on with *I beg your pardon*?"

"That wasn't a come-on. That was… I don't even know what that was."

"I just thought," I said with a shrug I told myself wasn't at all self-conscious, "if we had sex, we might be less awkward about touching each other."

"Ah yes. Because sex is renowned for making things less complicated."

"Okay. Bad idea. You asked me how we could be more

comfortable touching in public, and I came up with a suggestion. Excuse me for thinking outside the box."

He turned away from me, looking like he was about to start pacing, except my floor wasn't pace-friendly at the best of times. So he just fidgeted for a while. "I realise that you did not meet me when I was at the pinnacle of my self-esteem, but it still takes more to get me into bed than 'Why don't we have sex. I mean, like now.'"

"We had dinner first."

"Dinner at which you freely admit you were a dick to me and to your friends."

Yeah, probably not the time to be making jokes. But I was trying hard not to dwell on the fact that I'd been shot down by Oliver Blackwood *again*. "Tell you what. Let's stop talking about how much you don't want to have sex with me."

"I'm sorry." His expression softened slightly, not that it made me feel any better. "I know it's unfashionable, but I don't think sex is something you should do just because it's convenient."

"Why? Is everyone supposed to wait until they've got this deep, meaningful connection and can gaze into each other's eyes while they make tender love by an open fire?"

He visibly unsoftened. "You really do think I'm a god-awful prude, don't you?"

"Yes. No. Maybe." Oh God. How could I make this sound less...messed up and needy. "I'm just not used to a hookup being a big deal, so it feels kind of personal that you keep refusing to shag me."

"What do you mean, *keep*?"

"Bridget's birthday. Couple of years ago. We nearly got together, but instead, you pissed off and left me."

He gazed at me with obvious incredulity. "Sorry, are you insulted that I didn't date-rape you?"

"You what?" I gave him a shocked look back.

"I remember that evening, and you were completely out of it. I don't think you knew who I was, much less what you were doing."

"For fuck's sake," I snapped. "I've had a lot of drunk sex. I'd have been fine."

"Oh, Lucien, how can I explain this?" For some reason, he sounded sad. "I don't want *fine*. Fine isn't enough. It's not about the open fire or whatever other clichés you can conjure up, but yes, I want a connection. I want you to care as much as I care. I want you to need it and want it and mean it. I want it to *matter*."

He had to stop talking. Or I was going to...I don't know...cry or something. He had no idea what he was asking for. I had no idea how to give it to him. "I'm sure that's all...lovely." My mouth was so dry it was making my words click. "But with me, what you get is fine. And that's all there is."

There was a really, really, really long silence.

"Then it's probably for the best that none of this is real."

"Um. Yeah. For the best."

There was a really, really, really, *really* long silence. Then Oliver put his arm round me, tucking me against his side. And, God knows the hell why, I let myself be tucked. "Will this do?"

"D-do for what?"

"Touching. In public." He cleared his throat. "Not all the time, obviously. It would make going through doors difficult."

Right now, I could live without doors. I turned my head, for the smallest of moments, breathing him in. And almost thought, imagined probably, his lips brushed my temple.

"I guess it'll do," I said. Because what else could I say? That the moments when it nearly worked made all the times it didn't feel just a little worse.

All the same, it took every scrap of pride I possessed not to follow him when he stepped away.

"So." I shoved my hands into my pockets in case they went reaching after him. "What now? Obviously you won't want to stay in my shitty apartment."

"I will admit, I have some concerns about the state of your bedroom. But if I'm caught leaving, it may look as if we've broken up."

"Do you ever half-arse anything?"

He thought about it. "I gave up about two-thirds of the way through *Wolf Hall*."

"Why?"

"I don't know, really. It's quite long and involved, and I think I got distracted. Isn't that precisely what half-arsing entails?"

Out of nowhere, I was laughing. "I can't believe I'm pretending to date someone who just used the phrase 'precisely what half-arsing entails.'"

"Would you believe me if I said I did it deliberately for your amusement?"

"Nope." I did not want him to hold me again. I did not want him to hold me again. I did not want him to hold me again. "That's just how you talk."

"It may be, but you do appear to derive a unique enjoyment from it."

"Okay. That one was deliberate."

He offered me a slow smile—not the effortless one he used so freely in public, but something real and warm and almost reluctant, making his eyes shine from the inside like a lamp left in a window on a dark night. "All right. I'm prepared for the worst. Show me your bedroom."

———————

"I was not," Oliver said, a few minutes later, "prepared for the worst."

"Oh, come on. It's not that bad."

"When did you last change your sheets?"

"I change my sheets."

He folded his arms. "That's not an answer. And if you can't remember, it's been too long."

"Fine. I'll change my sheets. Just, y'know, I might need to do some laundry first." I tried not to look at my clothes, which were a little bit everywhere. "Maybe quite a lot of laundry."

"We are taking a taxi back to mine. Right now."

"Wow. This is turning into an episode of *Queer Eye* only with fewer hot men, and without the heartwarming bit where they make you feel good about yourself."

"I'm truly sorry. I wasn't intending to judge, but this situation, frankly, demands judgment. I mean, how can you not be miserable living here?"

I threw my hands up in exasperation. "I'm confused. What on earth has given you the impression I'm not miserable?"

"Lucien—"

"Also," I rushed on, not sure if I was more afraid of him saying something nice or something mean, "your house might be clean, but you're clearly not happy either. At least I admit it."

A touch of pink had crept across the top of Oliver's starkly defined cheekbones. "Yes, I'm lonely. I sometimes feel I haven't achieved what I should have achieved. On the basis of quite a lot of evidence, I worry that I'm not very easy to care for. But I'm not trying to hide that. I'm just trying to cope with it."

God, I hated it when he was all strong and vulnerable and honest and decent, and everything I wasn't. "You're not... *completely* difficult to care for. And I think I might have some clean sheets that I bought the last time I realised I didn't have any clean sheets."

"Thank you. I know I'm sometimes a bit of a control freak."

"Really?" I gave him a big-eyed look. "I've never noticed."

We stripped my bed, which I honestly think was less gross than Oliver was making out, although I super wished my, um, personal pleasure device hadn't bounced out of the sheets and landed right at Oliver's feet like a dog wanting to go walkies. Except, y'know, up my bum. I shoved it hastily in my bedside drawer which, unfortunately, involved revealing yet more of my, now I thought about it, depressingly onanistic collection.

Whether out of embarrassment or gallantry, Oliver said nothing. Just got on with crimping down the edges of my new sheets until they were glass smooth and hotel room perfect. From there, he changed the pillowcases and the duvet cover, even bothering to do up the little poppers at the bottom which I was pretty sure no human being ever, ever did. And, finally, he started taking off his clothes.

I stared blankly. Or not so blankly. "What are you doing?"

"I'm not sleeping in a three-piece suit, and meaning no disrespect, I don't especially want to borrow any of"—he made a circular gesture that encompassed the various piles of crap strewn across my floor—"this."

"That's fair." A thought occurred to me. "Hey, does this mean I finally get to meet the V-cut?"

He gave a weird little cough. "You will be passing acquaintances at best."

"I'll take it."

I bounced onto my newly Oliver-approved bed and knelt there, rumpling the duvet, and gazing somewhat shamelessly as Oliver undid his shirt.

"Lucien," he said. "What you're doing right now looks suspiciously like ogling."

I cupped my hands round my mouth. "Off. Off. Off."

"I'm not a stripper."

"You're literally stripping right now. I'm just encouraging you."

"What you're doing is embarrassing me."

He removed the shirt, folded it neatly, realised there was nowhere to put it, and stood there in confusion.

But.

Oh holy God.

You normally had to pay money to see something like that. I mean, we were talking grooves, ridges, just the right amount of hair—fuzzy, not furry—and even a couple of playful little veins snaking up from beneath the waistband of his trousers.

Fuck. I wanted to *lick* him.

Double fuck. I suddenly realised I could never *ever* take my clothes off in front of this man.

"What's the matter now?" asked Oliver. "And where can I put my shirt?"

"I...I...I'll find you a hanger." And some kind of, I don't know, beekeeping outfit for me. Something nicely covering.

I ran out of the room and changed into the biggest, baggiest T-shirt I could find, along with my loosest, least formfitting pair of lounge pants. I mean, don't get me wrong. I was fine with how I looked. I'd had no complaints body-wise from anyone, and there'd been plenty of complaints about other things so it wasn't a reticence issue. But Oliver was the sort of fantasy I usually didn't even bother to have because I thought it was just too unrealistic. And I had no idea what a man who looked like that could possibly see in me.

Oh wait.

He didn't have to see anything. That was the deal.

By the time I got back to the bedroom, Oliver was waiting for me in a pair of black boxer briefs that somehow managed to be sensible in a sexy way, his suit over one arm and his shirt in his other hand. In a moment of panic, I threw a hanger at him and jumped under the covers.

I definitely wasn't watching Oliver as he arranged his garments to his satisfaction and hung them up in my otherwise completely empty wardrobe. Fuck it, who was I trying to fool. I *was* watching because he was gorgeous and I totally wanted to do him and I'd totally wanted to do him even before I knew the V-cut wasn't a joke.

This was bad. This was very, very bad.

What felt like hours later, I was lying in the dark next to Oliver, not touching him, and trying not to think about touching him. Which meant, instead, I was thinking about everything else. Like how much he was doing for me, when he didn't have to, and how badly I kept treating him in return. And how scary this could all get if I let it.

"Oliver," I said.

"Yes, Lucien?"

"I really am sorry. For tonight."

"It's fine. Go to sleep."

More time passed.

"Oliver," I said.

"Yes, Lucien?" Slightly less patiently.

"I just...don't understand why you care. What I think."

The bed shifted as he rolled over, and I was suddenly very conscious how close we were. "Why wouldn't I?"

"Well, because you're this...incredible lawyer-slash-swimwear-model guy—"

"Excuse me?"

"I mean, metaphorically. I mean, not the lawyer bit. That is your actual job. Fuck. Look, I'm just saying, you're conventionally successful and conventionally attractive. And you're a good person. And I'm...not."

"You're not a bad person, partly because there are no bad people and partly—"

"Wait. What about, like, murderers?"

"The vast majority of murderers murder one person and either regret it for the rest of their lives or have a reason for doing it that you would probably sympathise with. The first thing you learn as a criminal barrister is bad things are not the exclusive province of bad people."

I guess it was some kind of masochistic penance for having called him cheesy earlier, but I heard myself telling him, "You're hot when you're being idealistic."

"I'm hot all the time, Lucien. As you've just observed, I look like a swimwear model."

Fuck. No. Help. Now he was making me laugh.

"Speaking of which," he went on, "you surely can't doubt your own..." He wriggled nervously and I wished I could see the expression on his face, because lost-for-words Oliver was one of my favourite Olivers. "Appeal?"

"You'd be amazed what I can doubt." This right here was why you had sex. So you were too tired to randomly tell people personal shit at three in the morning. "Besides, when all you see of yourself is what the tabloids show you, it's hard to believe in anything else."

I felt the faintest stirring of air close to my face, as if he'd reached out to me but thought better of it. "You're beautiful, Lucien. I've always thought so. Like an early self-portrait of Robert Mapplethorpe. Um"—I practically *heard* him blush—"not the one with the bullwhip in his anus, obviously."

I wasn't sure, but I thought Oliver Blackwood had just called me beautiful. I had to be gracious and calm and mature. "Pro tip: When you're complimenting someone, avoid the word 'anus.'"

He chuckled. "Duly noted. Now, seriously, go to sleep. We both have work in the morning."

"You've met Alex. Consciousness is barely a requirement in my office."

"Is there some reason you're intent on keeping me awake?"

"N-no… I don't know." He was right. I was being weird. Why was I being weird? "Do you really think I'm beautiful?"

"At this very moment, I think you're annoying. But, in general, yes."

"I haven't even said thank you for getting me away from those reporters."

He sighed, his breath warm under the duvet we shared. "I'll take your silence as gratitude."

"Sorry… I…um…sorry."

I turned onto my side. Then onto my other side. Then onto my back. Before flipping to the side I'd tried to begin with.

"Lucien." Oliver's voice rumbled through the dark. "Come here."

"What? Why? Come where?"

"Never mind. I'm here." Then Oliver folded himself around me, all strong arms and smooth skin and the thud of his heart against my back. "You're okay."

I lay still, my body not sure whether it wanted to run screaming for the door or just sort of…melt everywhere. "Um, what's going on?"

"You're going to sleep."

There was no way that was happening. This was too much. It was far too much.

Except, as it turned out, he was right, and it wasn't, and I was.

CHAPTER 20

"SO," I SAID TO ALEX the next morning, "I'm really sorry that I was such a dick last night."

He gazed at me expectantly. "And?"

"Well, um, I should have been nicer to you."

"And?"

"And..." Wow, he was seriously committed to holding this over me. "...I'm a bad friend and a terrible coworker?"

"Oh." He frowned. "I'm afraid to say that I just don't get it at all. I mean, the one about going to Wales wasn't funny, but at least it made sense."

"It wasn't a joke, Alex. I was trying to apologise for last night. I thought maybe my use of the words 'sorry' and 'last night' might have clued you in."

"In that case, think nothing of it, old boy. And, honestly, it's my fault. I should have said something at the time. Because we skipped the fish course, you should have skipped the fish fork."

I gave up. "Okay. Great. Glad we cleared the air. Sorry again about the fish fork."

"Happens to the best of us. Why, once at high table I had a moment of mental abstraction and tried to use a salad fork to eat cooked vegetables. And everyone had a jolly good laugh at my expense."

"Gosh. Yes. The mental image alone is hilarious."

"Isn't it? I mean the tines are completely the wrong length."

"The tines," I offered, with a confidence my history with Alex did not at all support, "they are a-changin'."

He gave me a blank look. "I suppose so. That's why you swap forks between courses."

Back at my desk, I ran through what was becoming a slightly depressing morning ritual: drink coffee, worry about alienating more donors, check scandal sheets. As it turned out, I was barely in them, and not just because I was mostly hidden against Oliver's body. Pretty much every article was about Miffy—what she was wearing, where she was going, when she and Alex might be getting married. Oliver and I were blissfully relegated to the "also withs" although some enterprising intern had managed to unearth the designer of Oliver's coat. And you knew it was the right kind of press coverage when people wrote more about what you were wearing than what you were doing. I even got a glancing mention in *Horse & Hound*, despite being neither.

This just left me to deal with the endless stream of unnecessary crises that always afflicted the Beetle Drive, like the time Rhys Jones Bowen told me the venue was double-booked because he'd got the Royal Ambassadors Hotel Marylebone mixed up with the LaserQuest he was trying to arrange for his friend's stag-do. Or the time the printed invitations went missing and we thought they'd got lost in the post, but it turned out Alex had just been using the box as a footstool for three months. And let's not forget when Dr. Fairclough briefly cancelled the entire event because she decided that the term *beetle* was insufficiently scientifically rigorous, and backed down only when we reminded her that it wasn't actually in the official name of the event.

Today, it was Barbara Clench, our dogmatically frugal office manager, questioning the necessity of releasing funds for the purposes of, y'know, operating our fundraiser. Which meant I was tied up with email for most the day, since our ability to successfully cowork was built upon a mutual understanding that we would never, ever speak to each other in person.

Dear Luc,

   I've been looking at the costings for the hotel and am wondering if we really need it.

Kind regards,

Barbara

Dear Barbara,

   Yes. It's where we're having the event.

Kind regards,

Luc

Dear Luc,

   I've been thinking about that, and was wondering if it wouldn't be more practical for donors to remain at home and contribute by telephone during a preapproved window.

Kind regards,

Barbara

Dear Barbara,

   I appreciate your commitment to helping the Beetle Drive run smoothly. Unfortunately, the invitations have already been printed, and the event has been advertised as a "dinner and dance" and not as a "stay at home and phone us maybe." The cost of the hotel should be more than covered by the ticket price.

Kind regards,

Luc

Dear Luc,

Could we at least choose a cheaper hotel?

Kind regards,

Barbara

Dear Barbara,

No.

Kind regards,

Luc

Dear Luc,

I consider your last email inappropriately curt. I would take this matter up with our Human Resources Department, but we do not have one.

Kind regards,

Barbara

PS—Thank you for raising a requisition request for a new stapler. This requisition request has been denied.

Dear Barbara,

Perhaps you could ask the Office Manager if we could release sufficient resources to hire a Human Resources Department. Maybe I could also borrow a stapler from them.

Kind regards,
Luc

Dear Luc,

There is no room in the workplace for facetiousness.

I refer you to last month's memo on the new paper-fastening policy. For financial and environmental reasons, we are requiring all documents to be bound with recyclable treasury tags. We expect these to be reused wherever possible.

Kind regards,
Barbara

Dear Barbara,

Please pay the hotel. The manager just called me, and we are at risk of losing the room.

Kind regards,
Luc

PS—We have run out of treasury tags.

Dear Luc,
   If you have run out of treasury tags, please submit a requisition form.

                                        Kind regards,
                                        Barbara

I was just composing a devastating reply, because I absolutely had one and it was absolutely a good use of office time, when my phone buzzed. It was a text from Oliver which, the preview helpfully informed me, began with the words *Bad news.*

Oh fuck. Oh fuck oh fuck oh fuck.

Without my telling it to, my brain started filling in a hundred different ways that sentence could end. And it probably said something about what a messed-up place I was in Oliver-wise that it went straight to "We're breaking up" rather than "My grandma's died" or "I have syphilis."

He was though, wasn't he? I'd been a total maniac last night. He'd had to rescue me from reporters and then cuddle me until I went to sleep like I was a highly strung puppy. And in the morning, I'd woken up sprawled all over him, and made a huge fuss about him leaving, which had obviously been because I was still half-asleep and not thinking straight, but given how sleep-halved and not-straight-thinking I'd been, I remembered making some pretty forceful arguments. After all that, *I* wanted to break up with me, and I *was* me.

In the end I did the mature thing: put my phone in my drawer without reading the message and went for coffee. Under normal circumstances, I would never have been relieved to see Rhys Jones

Bowen doing anything, but the fact he was already installed at the coffee machine meant that this whole operation was going to take about three times longer than it would have otherwise, and that was exactly what I needed.

"Thank goodness you're here, Luc," he exclaimed. "I can never remember. Is it water in the front and coffee in the back, or the other way round?"

"Coffee goes in the little basket that's got leftover coffee in it. And the water goes in the bit at the back that's already half-full of water."

"Ah, you see, that's what I was thinking. But you know when you get one of those things and you always get it the wrong way round, and then even when you get it right, you trip yourself and do it the other way anyway."

I was about to say "no" in my most withering tone but actually, that *was* kind of a thing. I got it myself with the number of *m*'s in *accommodation*. And the number of *c*'s for that matter. Besides, Oliver would have disapproved. Oliver who'd just sent me a text saying he had bad news, which I was going to have to look at some point, and deal with, and probably be hurt by and—shit, what was the point of a displacement activity if it didn't displace anything.

"I know what you mean," I said. And slid into a useful waiting position, while Rhys Jones Bowen navigated the intricacies of the, to be fair, somewhat complicated coffee machine.

"Oh bother." He knocked the back of his hand against the steamer nozzle. "I always forget that's there. It's going to blister now, and that's my typing hand as well."

I stifled a sigh. "Why don't you go and see Alex for some aloe vera. I'll finish up here and leave your coffee on the desk."

There was a bewildered pause.

"That's very decent of you, Luc." For someone paying me a

mild compliment, he sounded worryingly surprised. "Is everything all right? Have you been visited by the ghost of office workers past?"

"What? No. I'm…I'm a helpful person."

"No, you aren't. You're a total pillock. But I'll take the coffee anyway, thank you very much."

He ambled off in search of a burn remedy, and I finished reloading the coffee machine. While I waited for it to percolate, I searched the sink, cupboards, and draining board for any clean mugs, and found none. This was the problem with good deeds: they escalated. I was in the middle of scrubbing a particularly stubborn ring from Rhys's prized Welsh dragon mug when Dr. Fairclough stuck her head through the door and said, "Black, no sugar, since you're making."

Gah. Except no, not gah. Perfect.

Still waiting for the coffee to percolate, I went back to my office, really seriously intending to check my phone like an adult with a sense of proportion. But, fuck, what if bad news meant the papers had taken last night's outing and spun it into something awful for both of us? *Drunk Rock Kid Abducts Lawyer Shock.* Or maybe one of Oliver's exes had flown back in from Paris to say "Darling, I've just remembered you're the most wonderful person I've ever met, and I should never have left you. Let's run away together immediately." Well, I'd never know unless I looked.

I didn't look. The drawer sat accusingly shut while I fired up Outlook and through gritted fingers typed a much more conciliatory reply to Barbara.

Dear Barbara,

   Please forgive my earlier rudeness. I'm making a round of teas/coffees for the office. Would you like one?

                                                                Luc

Dear Luc,
  No.

                                        Kind regards,
                                        Barbara

On this *one* occasion, I'll admit I deserved that.

Olive branch returned to sender, I sloped back to the kitchen where I poured two coffees—black for Dr. Fairclough, milk and too much sugar for Rhys Jones Bowen—and went about my deliveries. I was holding out some hope that I could wring a few minutes of idle conversation out of them which, in Dr. Fairclough's case at least, I should have realised was a hope so vain that Carly Simon could have written a famously enigmatic song about it. Normally, I'd have been able to count on Rhys Jones Bowen, but he was distracted getting a botanical burn treatment from Alex. All of which left me with no option but to read Oliver's text. And when I put it like that, I felt really silly for reacting to it so strongly.

Although not so silly that my phone didn't sit on my desk for another five minutes while I started it. If, for whatever reason, Oliver had decided he couldn't do this, it probably wouldn't ruin my life. I'd had some good publicity already. And by the time the tabloids noticed they hadn't seen us together for a while, it'd be too late for them to run the inevitable *Gay Playboy Fleming Kid Drives Away Nice Lawyer Man* headlines before the Beetle Drive. Besides, if Oliver was breaking it off, it said more about the situation than it did about me. And, honestly, we'd be both better off not having to navigate this whole weird pretending-to-be-going-out-with-each-other thing that I should never have agreed to do in the first place.

This was for the best. Definitely for the best.

I took a deep breath and opened the text:

Bad news, it read. Big case. I'm afraid I'll be quite busy for the next week.

Oh, fuck me. What kind of technologically illiterate prick starts a message "bad news" when the news is average at worst? I was so goddamn relieved I was actually angry. Of course, Oliver had probably failed to factor in my deeply ingrained—and repeatedly validated—belief that everything good in my life was just waiting for the perfect moment to fuck off and leave me.

There was also the slimmest of chances that I might have been being a bit of a drama queen.

Once my hands had stopped trembling, I sent back: **Is this just a polite way of saying you need time to recover from my flat?**

I won't lie. It was fairly terrible. But there were some compensations.

Like what? I asked.

You.

I stared at the word for a really long time.

Remember this is fake. Remember this is fake. Remember this is fake.

CHAPTER 21

IT WAS THE LONGEST WEEK ever. Which made no sense because I'd only had a pretend boyfriend for ten minutes. And it wasn't like I'd ever been Mr. Knows What to Do with Himself—it's just that before Oliver came along, I'd been resigned to a lifetime of cruising Grindr, then freaking out in case I got recognised and ended up in the papers again, and deciding instead to spend my evenings half-dressed under a pile of blankets binge-watching Scandi-noir on Netflix and hating myself. And now I…I don't know… I guess I wasn't?

He still texted because, of course he would. Though mainly he said things like, Grabbing a bagel. Case is complicated. Can't discuss it. Apologies for lack of dick pic. Which was lovely for about three seconds, and then just made me miss him. And what was with that? Was my life really so empty that Oliver could just walk into it, sit down, and start taking up space? I mean, it probably was. But somehow, even after so little time, I couldn't imagine anyone doing that but him. After all, who else could be that annoying? And thoughtful. And protective. And secretly kind of funny. And—bugger.

At nine o'clock on Tuesday night, halfway through an episode of *Bordertown*, which I'd been paying no attention to, I came abruptly to the conclusion that all my problems would be solved if I tidied my flat. At nine thirty-six on Tuesday, I came abruptly to the conclusion that this had been the worst idea ever. I'd started trying to put things in places, but the places where I wanted to put the things were already full of things that weren't the things that were supposed to go in those places, so I had to take the things out of the places, but there were no places to put the things that came from the places, so then I tried to put things back in the places but they wouldn't go back in the places, which meant now I had more things and nowhere to put the things, and some of the things were clean and some of the things were very much not clean, and the very much not clean things were getting mixed up with the clean things and everything was terrible and I wanted to die.

I tried to lie on the floor and sob pathetically, but there was no room. So I lay on my bed, which I'm sure still smelled faintly of Oliver, and sobbed pathetically there instead.

Nice going, Luc. Very not a loser.

What was wrong with me? Why was I putting myself through this? This was all Oliver's fault with his you-are-special eyes and his you're-beautiful-Lucien bullshit, half convincing me I was worth something. When I knew exactly what I was worth down to the nearest fucking penny.

Then my phone rang, and I was in such a mess that I accidentally answered it.

"Is that you, Luc?" gravelled my fucking dad.

"Um." I bolted upright, wiping away snot and tears and trying desperately not to sound like I'd been crying my eyes out. "Speaking."

"I'm sorry about Reggie. He has to deal with a lot of shit for me."

That made two of us. "It's fine. I…"

"I'm glad you reached out to me. I know this is difficult for you."

No shit. "Yeah, but I probably shouldn't have told you to fuck off and literally die."

"You're right to be angry. Besides"—he gave a 'I have lived and experienced and discovered where my joy is' laugh—"it's what your mother would have done when she was your age. It's what I would have done too."

"Stop that right now. You don't get to look for any of you in me."

A moment of silence. And I honestly wasn't sure I was hoping he'd push it or not. That he'd fight for me.

"If that's the way you want it to be," he said.

"It's the way I want it to be." I took a deep breath. "So what happens now?"

"Like I said at your mother's, I want to get to know you. How that happens, if that happens, is up to you."

"Sorry. Since I never intended to meet the father who walked out on me when I was three, I didn't have this planned out in advance."

"Well, how about this. We're filming at the farmhouse in a couple of weeks. Why don't you come down on the Sunday? We should be done by then, and we'll have time to talk."

I was vaguely aware my dad had an absurd rock-star farmhouse-slash-studio-slash-creative-retreat somewhere in Lancashire, near where he grew up. "Fine. Send me the details. And," I added, quite aggressively, "I'll be bringing my boyfriend. Is that a problem?"

"Not at all. If he's important to you, I'd like to meet him."

That kind of took the wind out of my sails. I wasn't exactly *hoping* my dad would turn out to be a homophobe, but I'd got really comfortable believing bad things about him. "Oh. Okay."

"It was good to talk to you, Luc. I'll see you soon."

I hung up. It was the only power move I had left, but I was going to use it. Unfortunately, using it left me so exhausted, especially after my utter failure to make a meaningful difference to my existence, that I just pulled the duvet over my head and passed out in my clothes.

The next time I looked at my phone, it was a hell of a lot later, and I'd slept through twelve texts from Oliver and my alarm. The texts said:

> I miss you.
>
> Sorry. Was that too much?
>
> I know it's only been a few days.
>
> Maybe this is why people don't want to go out with me.
>
> Not that you're really going out with me anyway.
>
> I hope I didn't sound presumptuous.
>
> I'm probably sounding really weird now.
>
> I'm assuming you're not texting back because you're still asleep. Not because you think I'm disgustingly clingy.
>
> If you're awake and think I'm disgusting clingy, could you at least tell me?
>
> Right. You're probably asleep.
>
> And now you're going to wake up and read all this and I'm going to die of embarrassment.
>
> Sorry.

And the alarm said "You're going to be late for work, cockface." But I still paused long enough to reply to Oliver.

> **I was missing you too but then you sent me a million texts and it was like you were in the room**
>
> **Also. Still no dick pic?**
>
> **Also we're meeting my dad Sunday after next. Hope that's okay**

Somehow, despite my flat still looking like a bomb had thought about going off but got too depressed and just sat in the corner eating Pringles and crying, I was in an oddly good mood. I think maybe I just liked waking up to Oliver.

As usual, showing up late at the office didn't exactly mean much except I was conscious of the smallest pricklings of guilt, and I missed my telling-a-joke-to-Alex window, which was sort of a disappointment and a relief at the same time. Throwing myself into what I laughably called my work, I was...cautiously pleased to discover an email from a pair of donors who had previously withdrawn their support from the Beetle Drive.

> Dear Luc,
>
> Thanks so much for your email. Adam just heard today that our Johrei retreat has fallen through so we might be able to make the Beetle Drive after all. We'd love to take up your invitation for lunch and catch up.
>
> Namaste
> Tamara

Oh God. I didn't really have favourite or least favourite donors because, and I'm aware I say this as someone who's lived his whole life on the royalties from an album his mum wrote in the '80s, rich people are pricks. Adam and Tamara Clarke's particular flavour of prickishness was that they had got richer than any human being had a right to get while constantly banging on about how fucking ethical they were and glossing over the fact that they got their start-up capital because he was an investment banker in about 2008. They ran this chain of vegan-lifestyle whole-food eateries called Gaia. Because of course they were called Gaia.

And, now I thought about it, it also meant I had to work out somewhere to take them that not only would Barbara Clench release the funds to pay for, but that didn't serve animal products, wasn't owned by the client, and wouldn't look like a pointed attempt to support their competition.

I heaved a despairing sigh. "Well, fuck me sideways with a baked aubergine."

"Something I can help you with, Luc?" Rhys Jones Bowen, who had been passing on the way to either the coffee machine or the burns unit, stuck his head round the door. "I mean, not with that. Not that I'm judging."

"It was a rhetorical aubergine, Rhys."

"I'm not sure that makes it any better. Now what's the issue?"

"Just"—I waved a dismissive hand—"donor stuff."

He came in uninvited and plonked himself in the spare chair. "Well, let me hear it. A problem shared is a problem two people have."

"I'm afraid you're not going to be able to do much good here. Not unless you happen to know a cheap but not insultingly cheap, ideally slightly trendy and indie, but not threateningly trendy and indie, specifically vegan café-slash-restaurant that I can take Adam and Tamara Clarke to."

"Oh, that's easy. Just take them to Bronwyn's."

My mouth sagged for a moment. "Who's Bronwyn?"

"Friend of mine from way back. She's a vegan, and she's doing a pop-up."

"Okay," I said hesitantly, "that sounds promising. Just to check, is this pop-up happening in Aberystwyth?"

"Luc, I find it offensive the way you assume I only know about things in Wales. It's happening in Islington. Although she is *from* Aberystwyth."

"And she's definitely vegan? Not, like, a volcanologist or a veterinarian?"

"I'm finding your lack of confidence a little bit hurtful, Luc." He did, in fact, look fairly hurt. "We do have vegans in Wales. And I don't just mean the sheep."

"Sorry."

"That last bit was a joke. I'm allowed to make it because I'm *from* Wales. And so you can laugh."

The moment, such as it had ever been, had very much passed. But he was doing me a favour—maybe—so I forced out a wheezing noise I hoped sounded moderately amused.

"But, no," Rhys went on defensively, "she's definitely vegan. I remember because she used to be vegetarian but then she explained that she felt that it wasn't ethically defensible to be vegetarian but not vegan owing to the complex interdependence of animal exploitation in industrialised farming. For example, Luc, did you know that there are two types of chickens, one for laying eggs, and one for eating, and because we only need the girl chickens for the eggs, the boy egg chickens just get thrown in a big blender and used for cat food?"

"Um. I didn't know that. Thank you for ruining eggs for me."

"Yeah but they're brilliant with soldiers, though, aren't they?"

As in most conversations with Rhys Jones Bowen, I really wasn't sure how we'd got here. "Anyway, back to you saving my vegan bacon substitute. This Bronwyn who used to be a vegetarian from Aberystwyth and is now a vegan in Islington, is she...how do I put this...actually any good?"

He scratched absently at his beard. "She won the South Wales Echo Food and Drink Award a couple of years back. Though she did marry an Englishwoman so her taste is questionable."

"Wait. Bronwyn's a lesbian?"

"It'd be a bit strange of her to marry a woman if she wasn't."

"No, I just kind of assumed all your friends would be more..."

"That's quite homophobic of you, Luc, if you don't mind my saying." He climbed to his feet and ambled back into the corridor, pausing on the threshold to give me a stern look. "You're not the only gay in the village, you know."

Well, that was me told.

———————

That evening, as I was pushing the mess around my flat like a half-arsed Sisyphus, I got a text and an attachment from Oliver. And was briefly really excited until I found myself staring into the kindly, twinkly eyes of the late Sir Richard Attenborough.

Wtf is this? I sent back.

A dick pic.

You are not funny, I told him, laughing. **And I definitely don't miss you now**

A few minutes later: I'm glad you chose to reach out to your father.

I'm not

I can see you're handling this well.

I'm insecure. Tell me how mature I'm being

I think—and somehow I could hear him like a voice-over—genuinely mature people don't demand praise for being mature.

Baby steps, I typed. **Praise me anyway**

You're being very mature and I'm very impressed.

Was that your sarcastic voice? I read that in your sarcastic voice

I am actually proud of you. I just thought it would sound patronising to say it.

You must have noticed I have zero self-respect

A pause. I don't think that's true. I think you've just forgotten where you put it.

Well you've seen my flat

Normally we'd wrap up here, with him saying something semi-nice to me and me not knowing how to cope with it. But tonight for some reason I wasn't quite ready to let go.

I know you can't talk about it blah blah blah. But you okay? Work okay? Everything okay?

Wow. Look at me playing it cool. Like a fucking cucumber.

There was a longer-than-average Oliver pause.

Oh fuck, I'd pushed it too far. Or he'd fallen asleep.

Yes, he said finally. I'm just not used to

He left that half sentence hanging for a really long time. Then: Sorry. I pressed Send too early.

Okay, he was not getting away with that. **I'd like the second half please**

I didn't mean to send the first half.

Well. You have. And as five-word phrases go I'M JUST NOT USED TO is nearly as bad as WE NEED TO TALK ABOUT

Sorry. Sorry.

OLIVER!!!

I'm just not used to having something in my life that's as important to me as my job.

I typed out **You're really taking this fake boyfriend business seriously aren't you?** But didn't have the heart to send it. Instead, I tried, **What about your gazillion other relationships?**

They were different. And, while my thumb was midswipe, By the way, I think we should have lunch tomorrow.

And again, before I could answer: I mean if it's agreeable.

I'm just very aware the aim of this exercise was to generate positive publicity for you.

Which we can't if we aren't seen in public.

So we have lunch

As I suggested

In my other text.

So he'd panicked then.

As a world-class panicker, I was well-placed to read the signs. There were a bunch of things I could have done. I could have teased him or pressed him or fucked with him. But none of them seemed right just then. So I...I let it go. **That sounds great**, I sent, **but what about your case?**

If you'd be so good as to bring me something. A wrap or something. I thought we could eat it on a bench.

Play your cards right I'll get you a packet of crisps to go with it

That won't be necessary, thank you. A pause. You're teasing me, aren't you?

I guess you'll find out tomorrow

Meet me by the Gladstone statue at 1. We'll go somewhere nice and photographable.

God he was…thoughtful. And in whatever the texting equivalent to silence was that followed his last message, I sat on my sofa with my knees tucked under my chin, my brain churning restlessly. It was that weird space where I didn't actually know what I was thinking, only that thinking was kind of happening. But afterwards there came this calm, like fine rain on a too-hot day.

Hell, I had a lunch date. With a barrister. A fake lunch date, admittedly. But a real barrister.

And suddenly my job didn't look quite as crap.

And my flat didn't look quite as impossible.

And I didn't feel quite as hollow.

Grabbing my phone again, I jumped into the WhatsApp group, which was currently called All About That Ace, and sent out a quick cry for help: **Have been too bad at adulting for too long. Flat is unliveable in. Fake boyfriend horrified. HLEP!**

Priya was the first to respond with Luc, do you only ever message us when you want something?

Followed by Bridget. ILL COME HELP YOU. JUST SAY WHEN WHERE. HOW IS FAKE BOYFRIEND?????

Oh dear. So much for not telling all my friends. Maybe I could ask them to keep extra special double quiet about it. What was that saying? Three can keep a secret if two of them try really, really hard.

My flat, I typed. **This weekend. I'll pay you in pizza. Though frankly that might make things worse**

Do NOT order pizza! Somehow James Royce-Royce sounded camp even in text. The big chains are all run by Nazis. And also the pizza's terrible. I will make a picnic and bring it with me.

TIDY PARTY!!!!!!! Bridge, of course. I think she'd had her caps lock stuck on since 2002. IM SO EXCITED!!!!! HOW IS FAKE BOYFRIEND?????

Then Priya: You just want me for my truck, don't you?

I bet, I couldn't help myself, **you say that to all the girls**

HOW IS FAKE BOYFRIEND?????

What I say to all the girls is that's my sculpture. Wanna fuck?

LUC IM GOING OT KEEP ASKING YOU HOW THINGS ARE WITH OLIVER UNTIL YOU ANSWR OR MY THUMBS FALL OFF

I took pity on her. Or maybe on everyone else. **It's wonderful. We're getting married. Why do you think I need to clean my flat?**

YOUR BEING SARCASTIC THAT MEANS YOU SECRETLY LIKE HIM!!! SEE YOU ON SAT CANT WAIT!!!

From there the conversation moved on to other things, and I stuck it out for long enough to prove that, whatever Priya said, I didn't only talk to my friends when I needed something from them. Then a bit longer to prove that I wasn't just sticking around to prove I didn't only talk to my friends when I needed something from them. Then a little bit longer than that because I realised Priya had been right all along and I was a bad person. And, besides, it was nice. I hadn't realised how far I'd drifted from them, because they'd kept sculling towards me anyway. But I had. And I shouldn't have.

CHAPTER 22

PICTURES OF ME AND OLIVER having lunch on a bench near a statue of Gladstone didn't exactly make headlines—*Two Men Eat Sandwiches* was never going to get the traction of *Minor Celebrity Vomits on Other Minor Celebrity*—but they were out there, showing me off in all my nice-boyfriend-having, nonthreatening glory. We did lunch again on Friday, without much expectation of anyone caring, but we felt we should keep up appearances anyway. And also I, y'know, liked, y'know, seeing, y'know, him. And stuff. True, it wasn't going to last because come a discreet time after his parents' anniversary, we'd be going our separate ways with no need to ever speak to each other ever again, but maybe that was...a good thing? It turned out that there was way less pressure when it was all just pretending. And for now I didn't have to think too hard about what I'd do when the pretending stopped.

Saturday rolled around and, despite Bridge's all-caps assurance that she couldn't wait to come and tidy my flat, I wasn't entirely surprised to get a call from her at nine in the morning.

"Luc," she wailed. "I'm so sorry. I super wanted to come round for the tidy party. But you will not believe what's happened."

"Tell me what's happened."

"I can't really talk about it, but you know The Elf-Swords of

Luminera? Robert Kennington, series of twenty-something fantasy novels that've been going since the late '70s."

"Didn't he die?"

"Yes. Back in 2009, but he gave his notes to Richard Kavanagh, and *he* was going to write the last three books in the series. But then the first one had to be split into three other books for publication, and the other two have been broken into a quadrilogy and tetralogy—"

"Aren't those both sets of four?"

"There's a technical difference, but I don't have time to go into it right now. Anyway, the point is, it was all going really well, and Netflix was interested in optioning books three, seven, and nine, and we were trying to get them to look at one, two, and six and I think they were about to pick them up. But now Kavanagh has also died. And Raymond Carlisle and Roger Clayborn are both saying that he wanted them to take over, and they're refusing to collaborate with each other."

"Yeah," I said, "that sounds...complicated."

"I know. And I'm probably going to be on a conference call all day. If I can't get them to work it out, I'm definitely going to get fired."

I rolled my eyes, only because she couldn't see me. "You're not going to get fired, Bridge. You never get fired. They keep getting you to deal with this sort of nonsense because you're actually fantastic at your job."

There was a long silence. "Are you feeling okay?"

"Fine. Why?"

"I can't remember the last time you said something nice about, well, anything."

I thought about this for slightly longer than I was comfortable having to think about it. "When you got that new haircut. The one with the cute fringe. I told you it looked really good on you."

"That was three years ago."

I gasped. "It was not."

"Luc, I can remember when fringes were in."

"Jesus." I sank down onto the arm of my sofa. "I'm sorry."

"It's all right. I'm saving these stories for when I'm best man at your wedding."

"You might be saving them for a long time."

"Then it's going to be a very long speech. And I have to go. But please tell me how much you like Oliver first."

"Nothing," I insisted, "is happening with Oliver."

She squeaked happily. "Ah, but you're not complaining about how pompous and boring he is. That means it's going exactly according to plan. Must dash. Ciao, darling."

She was gone before I could ciao back.

Twenty minutes later, the James Royce-Royces appeared, James Royce-Royce with an actual picnic basket.

"Oh, Luc." He gazed around in dismay. "I hadn't realised it had got this bad. I'm not sure I'll feel safe eating in here."

"People eat in *fields*," I pointed out. "Like, places where cows shit. No cows have shit in my flat."

"Are you familiar, sweet pea, with the term 'damning with faint praise'?"

"Did you come here to help or take the piss?"

He shrugged. "I thought I'd try a bit of both."

A rumble outside heralded the arrival of Priya, her girlfriend, and her pickup truck. I mean, the rumbling was the truck. Her girlfriend was scary in other ways, what with being a legit grown-up and everything. By the time all five of us were crammed into my front room, surrounded by the detritus of the last five years, I was feeling pretty epically low.

"Welp." I made a helpless gesture. "This is my life. And I wish I hadn't invited you to come and look at it."

"You know," said Priya. "I'd normally say something mean. But you're so pathetic right now, it wouldn't be satisfying."

Her girlfriend, whose name was Theresa, but who I had a hard time thinking of as anything but Professor Lang, elbowed her in the ribs. "That's still mean, dear."

"You like me when I'm mean."

James Royce-Royce shooed at them gently. "I'd tell you to get a room, but as we can see, there isn't one."

"It's not that bad." Professor Lang picked up a sofa cushion and then put it down again very quickly. "I lived in worse in my student days."

"Luc's twenty-eight." Ah, I could always count on Priya to boost me up when I was down.

"Well"—to my surprise, Professor Lang shot me a mischievous smile—"considering that when I was twenty-eight, I was lying to my husband, denying my sexuality, and pretending work would solve all my problems, I don't feel in any position to judge."

I stared at them both. "I have no idea how Priya wound up with someone so much less of an arsehole than her."

"I'm a tortured artist," Priya shot back. "And I'm fucking incredible in bed. Now how do we tackle the pile of unadulterated skank you call your home?"

There was a humiliatingly long silence.

Then James Royce-Royce spoke up unexpectedly. "We prioritise things that need to be thrown away. Recycling over there"—he pointed to a moderately empty corner—"refuse over there"—another point, another corner—"waste, electronic and electrical on that table. Then Priya, Luc, and Theresa will go to the dump, while James and I start on the dishes. By the time you get back, there'll be enough space to be going through the laundry. Clean"—it was pointing time again—"dirty whites, dirty colours. From there we'll regroup and start on the surfaces."

We all took a moment to remind ourselves that there were some jobs James Royce-Royce was scarily good at.

"You see," said James Royce-Royce, kissing his husband's cheek extravagantly, "isn't he fabulous?"

We got to work and, holy shit, was it work. Having a system helped a lot, but it turned out I'd dropped a lot of things over the years, metaphorically and literally, and picking them all up and figuring out how best to dispose of them was surprisingly draining. It didn't help that Priya kept sarcastically double-checking whether I was sure I wanted to get rid of something with such obvious sentimental value as the empty Twiglets tube from last Christmas or a lone Mr. Grumpy sock with a hole in the toe. Then we piled the pickup shamefully full of crap and drove it down to the tip.

I nearly sent Oliver a picture of our neatly sorted recycling piles so I could show off how sensible and mature I was being, but then I realised how much I wanted to surprise him with how sensible and mature I was being. He'd made it painfully clear sex was very much off the table, but maybe if I managed to get at least some of my shit together, he might like me enough to kiss me.

Not that I really had any right to expect that or ask for that or imagine how it might feel. Except now I'd had the thought, I didn't entirely want to let it go. Which was an epic red flag. I'd built my whole life around not wanting things I couldn't have and, yes, that had left me alone and bitter in a messy flat, but I was still worried the alternative was worse.

By the time we'd got back from the dump, the washing machine was thrashing through the first of what would likely be approximately twenty-seven thousand loads, and James Royce-Royce had spread a red-and-white-checked picnic blanket across my newly visible living room floor. It was laden with goodies, and there were even clean plates to eat them off. Been a while since I'd seen those.

We all flopped down and waited semipatiently for James Royce-Royce to introduce the food. I'd never quite figured out if it was a chef thing or a him thing, but he got borderline huffy if you tried to eat something he'd made for you before he'd told you all about it.

"So," he announced, "this is a traditional pork pie with hot-water crust pastry. Sorry, not suitable for Priya, but it's a picnic. You can't have a picnic without a pork pie."

Priya gave him a look. "Yes. That is absolutely true. I have all these magical childhood memories of how every summer I'd go out into the park with my family and my mum would make roti and samosas and a raita and a pie none of us could eat. Then when we got home, we'd lend it to the Jewish family next door so they could take it out on *their* next picnic."

"I'm sorry, darling. That was culturally insensitive of me. But I did make you a lovely quiche."

"Ooh." She perked up. "Is it the broccoli and goat cheese one?"

"Caramelised red onion, cream, and Stilton."

"Okay, I'm sold. You can keep your pie, infidels."

"There's also," went on James Royce-Royce, with typical ceremony, "a kale Waldorf salad with buttermilk dressing, a selection of handmade dips, including the hummus you were so fond of last time, Theresa, some of my home-made bread, naturally, and a range of local cheeses. Then, to finish, we have individual raspberry fools in mason jars. And, don't worry Luc, I brought my own spoons."

Priya dragged a cooler out from behind my sofa. "Well, I brought beer." She struck a Royce-Royceian pose. "It's a sumptuous hops-based beverage served in a bottle."

"I'm seeing what you're doing there, Priya." He mock-glowered at her over the top of his black-rimmed hipster frames. "And since I've already blotted my cultural copybook, I've always wondered why you're okay with alcohol but not with pigs."

"You want the long answer or the short answer?"

"What's the short answer?"

"Fuck you, James." She grinned.

"And," he asked warily, "the long answer?"

"Because in case you haven't noticed, I'm not a very good Muslim. I fuck women, I drink alcohol, and I don't believe in God. But I grew up not eating pork, and so it still feels weird to eat an animal that rolls around in its own shit all day."

"Actually, pigs are very clean animals."

"Yeah"—she shrugged—"still not gonna eat 'em."

There was a brief period of calm while we all attempted to put a dent in James Royce-Royce's characteristically excessive picnic.

Eventually, Theresa—who clearly had better manners than the rest of us—said, "Priya tells me you have a new boyfriend, Luc. Will he be joining us?"

"He's got a work thing." I waved a hunk of James Royce-Royce's delicious home-made bread slightly sheepishly. "He's a barrister."

"What speciality?"

Help. I hadn't prepared for the quiz. "Um...criminal stuff? He defends them and stuff."

"That's very admirable. I had a friend from university who went into criminal law, but he recently moved into consultancy. I understand it can be very draining and not particularly lucrative."

"Well, Oliver's got a lot of passion for it. I can't imagine him wanting to do anything else really."

She looked thoughtful for a moment. "Then he's lucky. Although in my experience there's no one thing you need to make you happy."

"Is this," said Priya, "your way of telling me you want a threesome?"

Theresa gave her a wry smile. "Absolutely. In front of your friends at a picnic in a flat that still looks a little bit like the

Siege of Constantinople is exactly how I'd choose to have that conversation."

"That sounds like it's probably bad"—I went for another piece of infidel pie—"but I don't actually know what the Siege of Constantinople looked like."

Theresa looked thoughtful again. I guess thoughtful was kind of the default in academia. "To be fair, it depends which siege you're talking about, but I was thinking of the one in 1204."

"Oh good. Because if it had been any of the other ones, I'd have been deeply offended."

From which point the conversation degenerated into a mixture of quite a sophisticated description of the sack of Constantinople during the Fourth Crusade (from Theresa) and some rather juvenile speculation about the presence, or otherwise, of my stripy underpants at the event (from everybody else). I would have tried to steer us onto practically any other topic, except knowing my friends, any other topic would have been just as bad. So, while they were trying to work out which bits of my laundry would be most useful against a crusading army, I found myself surreptitiously checking my phone. Turned out while I'd been dragging bags of rubbish between flat and truck and truck and dump, I'd missed a text from Oliver.

He'd sent me a picture of Richard Chamberlain.

Nice Dick, I sent back.

"Oh my God, Luc," cried James Royce-Royce. "What's happened to your mouth?"

I glanced up, startled. "If there's hummus on my face, just tell me."

"It's far worse than that. You were *smiling*."

"W-was I?"

"At *your phone*."

From the uncomfortable hot feeling and the way everyone was

looking at me, I was pretty sure I was blushing. "I saw something funny on the internet."

"Wow." Priya put on her extra specially sardonic face she only used when I was being a total numpty. "A+ lying. Really good detail. Really sells it."

"It was a cat. Being scared of...something."

"It's cucumbers. It's always cumbers. And that was not a cat-meme smile. That was an 'I've got a sweet message from someone I like' smile."

I threw my hands up. "Fine. Oliver sent me a dick pic, okay?"

There was a long silence.

"Well." James Royce-Royce drew in a long breath. "I enjoy a good penis as much as the next man, but I don't normally go misty-eyed over them."

Somewhat shamefacedly, I turned my phone around and showed them the young Richard Chamberlain in a brown velvet coat, holding a glass slipper. "It's...sort of...a joke we have."

Suddenly, with the exception of Theresa—who was looking very slightly confused—everyone had their phones out. And my own lit up with notifications from the WhatsApp group, which had just been renamed Don't Luc Back in Anger.

Bridget we have something very important to tell you

Luc and Oliver are totally in wuv

We are not!

He sent him a dick pic and he got all smiley over it

WHAT THAT MAKMES NO SENSE OLIVER WOULD NEVER DO
    THAT!!!!1

It was a picture of Richard Chamberlain

Which means they have private jokes. They're getting married
    in August.

YAAAAAAY

Nobody is marrying anybody. It's just a bit of friendly banter about men called Richard. It doesn't mean ANYTHING

IM REALLY CONFUSED BY THE MEN CALLED RICHARD THING

I think it's a pun on dick pic. It's about Luc's level.

OMG THAT IS SO SWEEEEET LUC SEND HIM A DICK PIC BACK RIGH TNOW

I'm not sending my boyfriend either a picture of my penis or a picture of a famous guy called Richard just because my friends told me to

OH MY GOD YOU CALL HIM YOUR BOYFRIEND!!!

ALSO G2G

ONE OF MY AUTHORS IS BEIN G SUED BY THE STATE OF WYOMING

Also my girlfriend is in the room and we're ignoring her and she's too fucking polite to mention it

I was used to my friends teasing me about basically everything—it was how we related to each other—but that afternoon they'd hit a survivalist's bunker's worth of ammunition. Apparently the idea of me actually giving a shit about someone was such a novelty that it supported an endless stream of jokes, jibes, and ribbings. And, for some reason, I was totally defenceless, reduced to stuttering and blushing, when I was sure once upon a time it would all have just bounced straight off my armour of apathy.

It took a bit of getting used to because I'd spent a long time pretending I was invulnerable. But they were so obviously happy for me, and their goal was so obviously to get me to admit that I was happy for myself, that even I couldn't quite justify being a prick to them about it. Which meant they got to laugh at me, and I got to take it...and it didn't entirely suck.

CHAPTER 23

I WOKE UP THE NEXT day in a clean flat, which was fucking weird. It was almost like I'd moved house—I didn't recognise anything, or know where anything was, and there was this sense of emptiness I hadn't been conscious of since Miles moved out. Although there was also a sense of possibility that was completely new.

It was so fresh and exciting that I got out of bed without my customary five-more-minutes-whoops-it's-noon. I even considered putting actual clothes on, but I didn't want to overwhelm myself with too much maturity all at once and shrugged into my dressing gown instead. What I did do, though, was make the bed. Not as well as Oliver would have but well enough that he wouldn't rub his temples in dismay at the sight of it.

I was in the kitchen, making coffee very, very carefully so as not to get grounds all over the now-shiny countertops when my phone rang.

"Allô, Luc, mon caneton," said Mum.

"Hi, Mum. What's up?"

"I just wanted to say how proud I am that you made the effort with your father."

"I…" I sighed. "I guess it was the right thing to do."

"Of course it was the right thing to do. He has the cancer. But

I would have supported you if you wanted to do the wrong thing as well."

"Supported me. But not been proud of me."

"Oh no, I would still have been proud. I admit that a tiny of part of me wishes I had the courage to tell him to go fuck himself."

"You wrote an entire album telling him to go fuck himself."

"Yes, but he did not have the cancer then."

"Well"—sandwiching my phone between my ear and shoulder, I tried to hold the cafetière steady while I pressed the plunger, but I must have overfilled it because it still geysered out the top—"we don't know how it's going to go. I may still tell him to go fuck himself."

"That's fair. But I do also have a bone to pick with you, mon cher."

I dabbed desperately at the countertops with what was left of the kitchen roll James Royce-Royce had brought with him. "Why? What have I done?"

"What you have done is not tell me that you have a boyfriend. And, worse, you have told your father. When we both know your father is objectively a complete oyster dick."

"A complete what?"

"It loses something in translation. And that is not the point. The point is I am very upset that you have been keeping secrets from me."

"I'm not—" In my eagerness to mop up my minor coffee spill-age, I knocked over the rest of the cafetière. *Fuck.*

"You had an important piece of information to tell me about having a boyfriend, and you did not tell me about having a boyfriend. How is this not a secret?"

"I told you I had a date."

"Luc, that is chopping up hairs."

Okay, there were two crises. Mum thought I was lying to her, and I'd already trashed my kitchen. I abandoned the coffee for now and headed back to the living room, where I lay down on the sofa so I couldn't damage anything else. "Look, I'm sorry I didn't tell you. It's actually a bit more complicated than that."

"Mon dieu, he's married, he's in the wardrobe, you're secretly straight and seeing a woman—you know, I would love you anyway, even if you were a straight."

"No. No, it's none of those things."

"Wait, I have it. You're not really dating anybody, you've just persuaded some poor man to pretend to be your boyfriend because you are tired of everyone thinking you are lonely and pathetic."

"Um." The problem with Mum was that she knew me far too well. "Actually, yeah. That one. Only nobody thinks I'm lonely and pathetic. As it happens, I have a very important work function that I need to take someone to."

A sigh gusted over the line. "What are you doing, mon caneton? This is not normal behaviour, even when your parents are estranged rock stars from the '80s."

"I know, I know. But somehow it's wound up being the most functional relationship I think I've ever had. Please don't jinx it for me."

"Oh no, this is all my fault. I did not model positive romantic choices for you when you were growing up and now you are dating a fake man."

"He's not a fake man." I sat upright so abruptly I twisted the cushion half off the sofa. "He's a real man."

"Is he even really a gay? Probably you are going to fall for him, and then it is going to turn out he is engaged to this duke, and you are going to try and steal him away from the duke, and the duke will try to have you killed, and he will have consumption and try to make you think he doesn't love you when really he does and—"

"Mum, is that *Moulin Rouge?*"

"It could happen. I'm not saying there will be singing. But I'm worried this fake gay will break your heart."

I put my head in my hands. "Can you please stop using 'gay' as a noun?"

"First I'm not meant to use it as a pejorative. Now I'm not meant to use it as a noun. This is very hard for me."

"Look. Mum." Time for my best calm and rational voice. "I'm so sorry I didn't explain this to you earlier. Oliver's a real person, and he's not Nicole Kidman, and we've got an arrangement where we're going to pretend to be dating for a couple of months, just to make both our lives easier."

There was a long silence. "I'm just worried that someone will hurt you again."

"Yeah well. So was I for a long time, and I think that was hurting me more."

There was another long silence. Followed by "Then I want to meet him."

"What part," I asked, "of fake boyfriend did you miss?"

"I didn't miss anything. I especially did not miss the part when you said this was the most functional relationship you had ever had."

Look at me being hoist by my own petard. "It's still not real."

"I pay my bills with songs written by a girl I can barely remember being. Real is not something that interests me very much."

After twenty-eight years I'd reached the point that I only ever argued with Mum to see how I'd lose. "Fine. I'll ask him. He's working right now."

"Does he live in Canada?"

"No. He lives in Clerkenwell."

She made a Gallic noise. "You should come see me anyway. Judy and I are about to start a new season of the *Drag Race*, and we would like you to spill the hot tea on the queens for us."

"I…" I glanced around my slowly de-pristining flat. If I carried on at this rate, by the time Oliver saw it, the place would be a tip again. "I'll come over tonight."

"Yippee."

"Mum, nobody says 'yippee.'"

"Are you sure? I read it in a phrasebook in 1974. Anyway, Judy and I will see you this evening. I will make my special curry."

"Do not make your special curry."

Too late. She'd gone.

I spent the rest of the day taking twice as long to do everything—since now doing anything in my flat required me to tidy up afterwards or else undo all my friends' hard work. And before I'd even had the chance to milk it for Oliver points. I was just getting ready to hoy for Epsom when my phone rang *again*.

"Sorry to call unexpectedly," said Oliver.

I was glad I was alone so I could grin like an idiot without a running commentary. "Why, do you normally book your calls in advance? Do you call ahead? Are you like, *Hi, this is Oliver, I'm just ringing you up to say I'm going to be ringing you up.*"

There was a tiny pause. "I did not think through how silly that was going to sound. I'm just aware that I told you I was going to be working this weekend, so you might be busy, and I wanted to be respectful of that."

"*I Wanted to Be Respectful of That* is totally the title of your sex tape."

"Well," he murmured, "I can imagine worse titles."

"Can you? Can you really? Because I very much cannot."

"*St. Winifred's School Choir Presents There's No One Quite Like Grandma*?"

My mouth dropped open. "You are a sick man."

"My apologies. I was just trying to prove a point."

"I'd say you'd ruined that song for me, but it was kind of pre-ruined by its own existence."

"Lucien"—he suddenly sounded deadly serious and, despite the lesson I should have learned from the bad news text, I still felt faintly nauseous—"I called because I've done all the work I can on my case and I'd...I'd like to see you this evening. If that's...agreeable."

My heart stopped trying to choke itself to death. "Jesus, Oliver. Don't use that voice unless you're dumping someone or telling them their cat died. Also, did you just say...'if that's agreeable'?"

"I panicked."

"Also: title of your next sex tape."

"*If That's Agreeable* or *I Panicked*?"

"Both."

"I take it you're too busy? And I know we saw each other on Friday, and the papers are likely to be sick of you for at least another week... I'm sorry, I should have planned this better. And *please* don't say that's the title of my third sex tape."

I could have teased him about his imaginary sex tapes literally forever. But there was the whole wanting-to-see-me thing. Which was...perfect? "I...I'm not... It's not that I don't..." Shit. I was coming perilously close to telling Oliver that I'd rather see him than watch old episodes of *Drag Race* with my mother, her best friend, and her best friend's spaniels. Which, now I thought about, wasn't the tremendous compliment I'd built it up to be in my head. Still couldn't say it, though. "I've kind of accidentally told my mum I'll go see her tonight."

"I would like you to formally acknowledge that I have taken the moral high road and shall not suggest that *Accidentally Told My Mum I'll Go See Her Tonight* is the title of *your* sex tape."

"Oh, hell no," I protested. "You don't get credit for pretending you're not making the joke you're clearly making."

"Plausible deniability, Lucien. Plausible deniability." How could I *hear* him smiling? "But you should visit your mother. I know how much she means to you."

"I mean... You could..." Help. Words were happening. And I couldn't seem to stop them "Come? If you wanted to. It'll be awful, because Mum already thinks you're Nicole Kidman—don't ask—and she's making a curry, which she does not know how to do, but won't admit she doesn't know how to do, and her best friend is...this... Actually, I don't even know how to describe her. But she once told me she'd shot an elephant in her nightdress. And when I said, 'What was an elephant doing wearing your night-dress?' she said, 'It broke into my tent, and I think it got draped over its trunk.'"

"I recommend you breathe at some point in the very near future."

He had a point. I breathed. "Anyway, you really can sit this one out. I'm pretty sure it's too early in our fake relationship for you to be meeting my mother."

"Well, aren't I going to be meeting your father next week?"

"That's different. I care about my mum."

"I'd like to meet her, if it wouldn't make you uncomfortable."

I opened my mouth, realised I had no idea what I was going to say, and finally settled on, "Okay then."

Given I was already late, Oliver suggested we rendezvous at Waterloo, which I suggested sounded like a terrible love song from the forties. Then I texted Mum to let her know I'd be bringing my fake boyfriend, threw on my coat, dashed out the door, and tried not to think too hard about what it meant that I wanted Oliver to meet my mother.

CHAPTER 24

HALF AN HOUR LATER I was sitting on a train with Oliver. And it was weird. The problem was that being on public transport with someone for more than a couple of stops on the Tube fell down the uncanny butt crack between necessity and social occasion. I mean, it was basically just the two of you, sitting down facing each other, for about as long as you would if you were in a restaurant, only with much worse surroundings and without food to give the whole thing focus. Worse, I was worried I was going to blurt out something awful like "I missed you" or "I tidied my flat for you."

"So," I said. "How's the case?"

"I'm afraid I can't—"

"Talk about it?"

"Precisely."

A pause, both of us looking anywhere except at each other.

"And—" he crossed one leg over the other and then uncrossed it when he kicked me in the knee—"your work? It's going well, I take it?"

"Actually yes. By the low bar it sets for itself. The Beetle Drive hasn't accidentally been relocated to a warehouse in Tooting Bec. Nothing's caught fire in at least a couple of weeks. And some of the donors I scared off by doing the bad gay might deign to come back to us."

"I'm glad the plan seems to be working. But I confess I'm increasingly uncomfortable with the assumptions that seem to underlie it."

"You'd better not be getting cold feet on a train halfway to my mum's."

"I'm not. I just don't think you should have to be dating someone like me for it to be acceptable to be someone like you."

I finally met his eyes again. How had I ever found them cold? "I know, right? And what especially grinds my gonads is that it's not even my, I will admit, real and extensive personality flaws they object to. It's that they think I might have casual sex sometimes. Which, ironically, I'd be doing more of if I was in a healthier place emotionally."

"I hope you wouldn't." He blinked several times. "That is, not in a sex-negative way. Just that, as far as I know, we never agreed this was going to be an open fake relationship."

"What would that even be? Are you telling me that you don't want me to have fake sex with other people when I'm fake dating you?"

"Well, I hadn't given it much thought. But, if we were really dating, I'd want to be monogamous because that's just, well, my preference. And so if you're going to pretend to date me, I'm afraid you'll have to pretend to be monogamous. Which, I suppose, when the press are following you, is going to be an awful lot like being genuinely monogamous. Is that"—he seemed to be trying to sink through the seat—"going to be a problem?"

"I wish I could say *yes* because I'm beating them off with a stick. But in practice, it just slightly changes the reason I'm not getting laid."

"I thought when you said you hadn't been in a relationship you meant, um, you hadn't been in a relationship. Rather than you weren't..."

I stared at him, daring him to finish that sentence.

"...getting any? As it were."

I had to laugh. *As it were* indeed. "And I bet you couldn't imagine me being any more of a loser."

"You know I don't think you're a loser. But I don't understand why you'd have difficulty...um..." He seemed to be flailing again.

"As it were?"

"In this area."

This would have been a brilliant opportunity to build a deeper and more lasting relationship, based on trust, honesty, and mutual understanding. I could have told him about Miles. About partying like there was no tomorrow. And then waking up one day and finding out there definitely, definitely was. Oliver would have understood. It was kind of his whole jam.

"It's complicated," I said instead.

And he didn't push it, because of course he wouldn't push it, and I almost wanted him to—just so I could get it over with. But that was also the worst thing I could possibly imagine. So we went back to silence for the rest of the trip. Fun times.

I'd never been so glad to see Epsom Station (facilities lacking according to Google). Hopefully the woeful inadequacy of the station at which you couldn't even use your fucking Oyster card would take my mind off my woefully inadequate attempts to emotionally connect with my fake boyfriend. We de-trained ourselves and struck out across the fields towards Pucklethroop-in-the-Wold.

The sun was just setting, making everything soft and golden and shiny, like it was taunting me with romance. And Oliver was all casual again: another crisp pair of jeans, into which his distractingly fabulous arse was wholesomely nestled, and a cream, cable knit jumper that made him look like he belonged on a Tumblr feed called fuckyeahguysinknitwear.

He paused with one foot on an actual stile, the wind ruffling playfully through his hair, making me briefly resentful that the fucking atmosphere was getting more action with my fake boyfriend than I was. "I've been thinking," he said. "We should probably refine our boyfriend act a little before the Beetle Drive."

"Um. What?" I was not staring at…anything. Especially not anything crotch-related. But. The stile. He had one leg on a stile. No jury in the land would convict me.

"I don't want to let you down and… Lucien, my eyes are up here."

"Then stop…being in my face with your…jeans."

He took his foot off the stile. "We work well when it's just the two of us, but we should practice being together in company."

"Is this"—I gave him a sly look—"your way of saying you want to spend more time with me?"

"No. My way of saying I want to spend more time with you was when I rang you up earlier today and asked if I could spend some time with you."

"Oh. Right. Yeah." Something struck me. "Hang on, are you telling me you want to spend more time with me?"

"Would you still believe me if I claimed it was verisimilitude?"

"Maybe. I have very low self-esteem."

Probably aware I was watching super intently, he climbed self-consciously over the stile and waited for me on the other side. I hopped over after, taking his hand without really thinking about it as I came down.

"Of course I want to spend time with you," he said, still holding my hand. "I'd like you to come as my date to Jennifer's thirtieth birthday in a couple of weeks."

We headed for Mum's. I didn't mention the hand thing in case it went away.

"Who's Jennifer?"

"An old friend from university. She and her husband are having a few of us round for dinner."

I gave him a suspicious look. "Are these your straight friends?"

"I don't generally categorise my friends by sexuality."

"Do you only *have* straight friends?"

"I know Tom. And...and you."

"Tom doesn't count. I mean, not because he's bisexual. I mean, because he's dating Bridget. I mean, not that dating a woman makes him less bisexual. I'm just saying, he's not your friend. *She's* your friend. And I'm the rando you're pretending to date, so I'm pretty sure I don't count either."

He smoothed down his adorably wind-tousled hair. "My friends are just the people who happen to be my friends. There are a lot of straight people in the world. I like some of them."

"Oh my God." I gazed at him in horror. "You're like one of those documentaries about, I don't know, a pig that got lost on the edge of the village and wound up being raised by gorillas."

"I...I think that might be insulting."

"Pigs are cute."

"It's more that you seem to object to my not choosing my friends based solely on who they do, or don't, want to sleep with."

"But do they not just...not get you?"

"Lucien, most of the time *you* don't get me." His fingers twisted restlessly against mine. "I tried to do the...the community thing. But I went to one LGBTQ+—well, LGB as it was in those days— mixer at university, realised I had nothing in common with any of these people except my sexual orientation, and never went back."

I half laughed, not because I thought it was funny, but because it was so alien to my experience. "When I turned up at mine, I felt like I'd come home."

"And I'm glad for you. But I made different choices, and I'd rather you didn't see them as mistakes."

Honestly, it didn't make sense to me. But I also didn't want to upset Oliver—and I was still slightly stinging from being told I didn't understand him. Well, I didn't. But I wanted to.

I gave his hand a squeeze. "I'm sorry. I'd love to go to your straight-people party with you."

"Thank you." His lips twitched. "Just a quick word of advice: if you're at a straight-people party, you should try to avoid referring to it as a straight-people party."

I tsked. "God, it's political correctness gone mad."

We tromped through the next couple of fields, which—with the one we'd just been through—made up the three fields that ran onto Three Fields Road.

"Nearly there." I pointed down the winding track. "Main Road's down that way. And Mum's just round the corner."

Oliver made a noise that probably wasn't a hiccough but did a good impression of one.

"Are you okay?" I asked.

"I'm…I'm…a little nervous."

"You should be. Mum's curries are… Oh fuck, I didn't tell her you're vegetarian."

"It's fine. I can make an exception."

"Do *not* make an exception. In fact, if you could, please pretend you don't want me eating meat either. You would be doing my lower intestines a massive favour."

"I'm not sure coming across as the sort of man who polices her son's diet would endear me to your mother."

I thought about it for a moment. "I'm willing to take that risk."

"I'm very much not."

"Are you"—I peeked over at him—"actually worried about meeting my mum?"

His hand was a little clammy. "What if she doesn't like me? She might not think I'm good enough for you."

"Well, if you don't walk out, leaving me alone with a three-year-old kid, you'll be doing way better by me than my dad did by her so, y'know, not a lot to lose here."

"Lucien"—he gave another anxiety hiccough—"I'm serious."

"So am I." I stopped and turned to face him. "Look, you're... I can't believe you're making me say this. But you're great. You're clever and thoughtful and hot and you went to fucking Oxford and you're a fucking lawyer. You're not dying of consumption or promised to a duke—don't ask—and...you're nice to me. And that's really all that matters to her."

He gazed at me for a long moment. I had no idea what he was thinking, but suddenly I was all to pieces. My mouth had gone dry and my pulse had gone wild and, in that moment, the only thing I wanted in the world was for him to—

"Come on," he said. "We'll be late."

CHAPTER 25

I WAS ABOUT TO PUT my key in the lock when the front door flew open, almost as if my mum had been lurking behind it, watching the road through the stained-glass inset. Like a total creeper.

"Luc, mon caneton," she cried. And then turned her attention, viperlike, to Oliver. "And you must be the fake boyfriend."

I sighed. "This is Oliver, Mum. Oliver, this is my mum."

"I'm very pleased to meet you, Ms. O'Donnell." From anyone else, that would have sounded stilted. With Oliver, it was just the way he talked.

"Please call me Odile. You are most welcome."

Okay. This was going well.

"But," went on Mum, "you must clear something up for me."

Or maybe not.

"Luc tells me that you are a fake boyfriend but not a fake gay. If that is the case, why are you not going out with my son for real? What is wrong with him?"

"Mum." I flailed on the doorstep. "What are you doing? You don't even know Oliver, and now you're trying to browbeat him into dating me."

"He looks nice. Clean, tall, he's wearing a good jumper."

"I can't believe you're trying to pimp me out to a complete stranger because you like his jumper. He could be a serial killer."

"I'm...I'm not," said Oliver quickly. "Just for the record."

She glared at me. "It is the principle. Even if he is a serial killer, he should still want to go out with you."

"To reiterate," said Oliver. "I'm not a serial killer."

"That does not answer my question. I want to know what is wrong with my son that you are only willing to pretend to go out with him. I mean, look at him. He's lovely. A bit untidy, I suppose, and his nose is a little large, but you know what they say about men with big noses."

Oliver gave a little cough. "They make good sommeliers?"

"Exactement. Also they have big penises."

"Mum," I exploded. "I'm twenty-eight. You've got to stop embarrassing me in front of boys."

"I'm not being embarrassing. I'm saying nice things. I said you had a big penis. Everybody loves a big penis."

"Stop. Saying. Penis."

"It's just a word, Luc. Don't be so English. I raised you better than that." She turned to Oliver. "Luc's father, you know, he had a huge penis."

To my horror, Oliver got the kind of thoughtful look you never want your boyfriend to get over your dad's dick. "Had? What's happened to it since?"

"I don't know, but I like to think either the drugs shrivelled it up or it got squeezed into nothing by a groupie's vagina."

"Mum," I loud-muttered, like she was hugging me in front of my school friends.

"Awww, mon cher. I'm sorry I embarrassed you." She patted my cheek. Embarrassingly. And then turned to the boy she was embarrassing me in front of. "You'd better come in, Oliver."

I trailed after them into the hall, which was about the right size for Mum, slightly too small for Mum and me, and far too small for Mum, me, Oliver, and the four spaniels who bolted through from the front room and started nosing eagerly at him as the newest object in the building. He did that thing that people who are good with dogs do where they crouch down and the dogs squirm all over them, tails wagging and ears flopping, and it's adorable and domestic and *bleurgh*. And Oliver was blatantly going to want a dog in the future, wasn't he? Probably from a shelter. And it'd have, like, three legs, but he'd train it to catch Frisbees as well as a dog with four legs, and he'd be in the park with it, throwing Frisbees, and this really hot guy would come up to him and be, like, "Hey, nice dog, wanna fuck?" And he'd be like "Sure, because your mother's never said the word 'penis' in front of me" and then they'd get a lovely semidetached in Cheltenham and Oliver would make French toast every morning and they'd walk the dog together, hand-in-hand, and have meaningful conversations about ethics and—

"Come on," yelled Judy. "Stop dawdling in the hallway. I want to meet Luc's new beau."

We bundled into the front room, Oliver doing a better job of navigating spaniels than I did, or, indeed, had ever done. "You must be Baroness Cholmondely-Pfaffle," he said, with his usual effortless courtesy. "I've heard so much about you."

"Pish-posh. Call me Judy. And I haven't heard a damn thing about you because Luc doesn't think it's worth telling us things, do you, Luc?"

I slumped onto the sofa, as I'd been doing my entire life. "I'm sorry I didn't tell you about my fake boyfriend soon enough."

"It's your loss. I know all about having a fake boyfriend."

"Do you?" I asked warily. "Do you really?"

Mum—who had only interacted with about three people since the dawn of the millennium—seemed to have decided "hospitality" meant "poking." She poked Oliver towards me. "Sit down, Oliver. Sit down. Make yourself at home."

"Oh yes," Judy went on, "just after my coming-out in '56, I

spent three months pretending to be engaged to this lovely Russian fellow."

Oliver lowered himself gingerly down beside me, and all the spaniels tried to get into his lap simultaneously. Honestly, couldn't blame 'em.

"Charles, Camilla"—Judy snapped her fingers—"Michael of Kent. Down. Leave the poor fellow alone."

Charles, Camilla, and Michael of Kent slunk abashedly to the floor, leaving Oliver with a single more manageable spaniel. A spaniel that currently had its forepaws on his shoulders and was licking his nose lovingly, while staring deeply into his eyes. If I'd tried to do that, he'd have told me he wanted it to mean something.

"He said…" If Judy let rampaging dogs get in the way of an anecdote, she'd had never have said anything "…it was very important that people believed he had a legitimate reason for staying in England and interacting with the aristocracy. You can keep Eugenie. She's rather a love. Looking back on it, I think he might have been in the KGB."

"The spaniel?" asked Oliver.

"Vladislav. They pulled him out of the Thames in the end, with a small-calibre bullet in his brain. Poor fellow. I say, you're not working for the, well, I suppose it would be the FSB now, wouldn't it?"

"No. But that's what I'd say if I was in the FSB."

"He's not in the FSB," I interrupted before Judy could get ideas in her head. "Or the KGB. Or the NKVD. Or SPECTRE. Or Hydra. He's a barrister. And he's nice. Now leave him alone."

Mum, who had been flitting back and forth from the kitchen, stuck her head through the door. "We are just interested."

"In whether he's a spy?"

"In general. He's a guest. Besides, you haven't brought a boy home in a very long time."

"And," I grumbled, "I'm starting to remember why."

Oliver made a placating gesture from behind Eugenie. "Really, it's fine. Thank you for your hospitality."

"Oh now, doesn't he have lovely manners," announced Judy, as if Oliver wasn't in the room. "I like him much more than that Miles. He had a sly look, like my third husband."

"Miles?" Oliver tilted his head with gentle curiosity.

Fuck. I was about to have a horrible experience that could almost certainly have been avoided if I'd been more honest with the guy to begin with. It's like there was a moral here or something.

Judy banged her fist against the arm of her chair, somewhat startling Michael of Kent. "He was a wrong'un from the start. Charming, of course, but I always knew he was going to—"

"Judy"—that was Mum, coming to my rescue, just like always...okay, like about 90 percent of the time, when she wasn't the problem—"we are here to eat my special curry and watch the drag race. We are not here to talk about that man."

"Then dish up, old girl. It must be ready by now."

"My special curry, she cannot be rushed."

"It's been in the slow cooker since you got up this morning. If it was any less rushed, it'd be catatonic."

My mum threw up her hands. "It is called a slow cooker. It is slow. If it was not slow, it would be called a fast cooker. Or maybe just a cooker."

Oliver dislodged Eugenie and climbed to his feet. "Can I help at all?"

Mum and Judy gazed at him adoringly. God, he gave good parent. Worse, I was pretty sure he meant it.

"By the way," I said. "I should have mentioned this earlier, but Oliver's vegetarian."

He gave me a genuinely betrayed look, as if I'd respected his ethical choices just to make him look bad in front of my mother. "Please don't worry. It's not a problem."

"Of course it's not a problem." Mum somehow managed to turn *bof* into a gesture. "I'll pick the meat out in the kitchen."

Judy shook her head. "Don't be a ninny, Odile. That's very disrespectful. What you should do is fish the vegetables out and serve them separately."

"I assure you," Oliver protested, "neither is necessary."

Mum turned to me. "You see? Why are you making such a big fuss over nothing, Luc? You are embarrassing yourself."

She barrelled off again. And Oliver, mouthing a "sorry" in my direction, trotted after her. I held out a tempting pay-attention-to-me hand to Eugenie, but all I got for my trouble was a disdainful glance before she scampered out in pursuit of Oliver.

Well, fine. My perfect fake boyfriend and the cute dog could go and play with my mother in the kitchen while I was stuck in the front room with a serial divorcee in her mideighties.

"Just us, eh?" Judy had that "I'm about to start a long anecdote, and there's nothing you can do about it" look in her eye. "I never did tell you what happened with those bullocks, did I?"

I surrendered with as much grace as I could muster. Which, admittedly, wasn't very much. "You didn't. How were they?"

"Terrible disappointment. I went to see the chap, expecting him to have a nice, big healthy pair of bullocks for me to get my hands on. But when I got there, I found I'd been quite misled."

"Yeah. It happens."

"I know. We went all the way down to his paddock and he got them out for me, and frankly they were substandard. About half the size I'd expected. I mean, I think there was something wrong with them, to tell you the truth. The one on the left had this strange swelling, and the one on the right was listing most unfortunately."

"It sounds," I offered tentatively, "like you were better off leaving them alone."

"That's what I thought. Obviously I gave them a good

once-over anyway just in case. Nice firm pat-down and all that. But in the end I had to tell the fellow 'No, I'm sorry, but I will not be handling your oddly shaped bullocks.'"

To my tremendous relief, Mum, Oliver, and Eugenie came back in with the curry before Judy could explain how he'd gone on to try to interest her in his prize rooster. Oliver handed a bowl of curry to Judy, and then he, Mum, and I squidged onto the sofa like three not especially wise monkeys.

"Has this got banana in it?" I asked, prodding nervously at what I hesitated to call my dinner.

Mum shrugged. "They put bananas in curries all the time."

"In specific curries. Curries where the rest of the ingredients are chosen to complement banana."

"It's like tofu or beef. It absorbs the flavour."

"It's delicious, Odile," declared Judy, loyally. "Best one you've ever made."

We fell silent as we grappled with Mum's cooking. I wasn't exactly a wizard in the kitchen myself, but I think Mum was an *evil* wizard in the kitchen. It took skill, and years of practice, to be as consistently and specifically terrible at food as she was.

"So." Oliver could have been doing his social lube thing as usual or, maybe, he'd just realised that if he was talking, he didn't have to be eating. His eyes were definitely watering. "Um. Is that your guitar?"

It was. And it usually lived in the attic. I'd like to think I would have noticed if I hadn't been so distracted by, well, everything else.

"Ah oui. Luc's father wants me to collaborate with him on a new album."

I choked on curry. I mean, I'd been choking on curry already, but this time the reaction was emotional, rather than chemical. "You didn't tell me that."

"Well, you didn't tell me you had a fake boyfriend."

"That's different. Oliver didn't walk out on us twenty-five years ago and isn't a complete arsehole."

"I'm not even sure I'm going to do it, mon caneton." Mum forked up a curried banana with what appeared to be genuine relish. "I haven't written in years. I think I've run out of things to say."

Judy glanced up from her almost-empty bowl. No wonder the queen was still going—they clearly made the aristocracy out of concrete. "'Course you haven't. Just need to get back on the horse, that's all."

"I'm not sure the horse is what I remember it being. Horses get old, too, you know. Sometimes, it's kinder to leave them out in the field, eating the apples."

"I can't believe you're even thinking about this." I stopped slightly short of yelling. "Obviously, if you want to write music, that's great. But why do you have to do it with Jon Fucking Fleming?"

"We always had something together. And this may be the last chance I get."

I plonked what was left of my curry on the side table. This was a perfect excuse not to eat it, but I was also kind of too angry for food right now. "You mean, the last chance *he'll* get. He's blatantly using you."

"So? I could use him back."

"It's true," added Judy. "You're never more popular than when you're dead. Look at Diana."

"Yeah but"—I accidentally elbowed Oliver in my effort to gesticulate—"you'll have to spend time with him. He doesn't deserve to spend time with you."

"Luc, I decide who I spend time with. Not you."

I opened my mouth. Then closed it again. "Sorry. I...just...sorry."

"Don't worry, mon cher. You don't have to look after me." She stood up decisively. "Now, shall we tidy away the dinner things and then gag on the fierce queens?"

CHAPTER 26

PARTLY OUT OF A DESIRE not to look like a terrible son and partly because I needed a change of scenery, I persuaded Mum to let me deal with the cleanup. It wasn't until I got into the kitchen that I remembered quite what carnage my mum was capable of creating, especially when she was making the special curry.

"I can see where you get it from," said Oliver, coming in behind me, with Eugenie trailing behind him.

I dumped the bowls next to the sink, which was full of other things that should in no way have been necessary to produce anything like what we'd just eaten. "I'm sorry." I kept on staring at the washing up, too scared to look at Oliver, in case he was horrified or disappointed or confused or contemptuous. "This is awful, isn't it?"

"Of course it's not awful. They're your family, and you clearly all care about each other a lot."

"Yeah but we've talked about my dad's penis, served you a literally inedible nonvegetarian curry, and then I had a fight with my mum I really wish you hadn't seen."

His arms went round me, in that enfoldy sort of way he was so good at, and he pressed against my back. "It's certainly very different from what I'm used to. But I don't...I don't think it's bad. It's *honest*."

"I shouldn't have freaked out about Jon Fleming."

"You had a slightly emotional disagreement that I could tell came from a good place."

I let myself lean into him, his chin settling neatly onto my shoulder as if it belonged there. "You can't want any of this."

"If I didn't want this, I wouldn't have come."

"It must be so weird to you, though." Turning, I discovered too late that it brought us way too close, way too quickly. Probably I should have moved away, but between the sink and the currypocalypse, there was nowhere for me to go. And, anyway, I wasn't totally sure I wanted to. "I mean, you have two fully functional parents, and neither of them have ever been in jail or on TV. I bet you don't row in public or ask if people are in the KGB two seconds after meeting them."

He laughed softly, his breath warm and sweet against my lips—oddly sweet, actually, considering the curry. Must have been the banana. "No, we don't. And I admit, I'm quite glad we don't. But it doesn't mean that it's wrong you do. People express love in different ways."

"And apparently I do it by being a dick."

"Then"—God, his mouth right now wasn't stern in the slightest—"you must care for me very deeply."

"I..." I was actually *dying*. I was going to blush myself to death.

"Boys," bellowed Mum, "we are tired of waiting for you, and we are starting our engines. You do not want to miss the entrances. They are a very important part of the experience."

We startled away from each other, almost guiltily, and hurried back to the living room.

"Come, come." Mum waved us onto the sofa. "This is my first viewing party. I am very proud."

I couldn't quite imagine anything worse than sitting between my mum and my boyfriend—I mean, my fake boyfriend who I might have accidentally spurted feels onto in the kitchen—on the sofa, while we watched *RuPaul's Drag Race* with her best friend and four spaniels named after minor royals. So I sat on the floor instead, slightly closer to Oliver's leg than was probably strictly necessary. Also I didn't quite have the heart to tell Mum that me, Judy, and Oliver didn't really add up to a viewing party. We were more like some people watching television.

Apparently Mum and Judy were up to season six already, which shouldn't have surprised me because, as far as I could tell, Mum and Judy's standard evening was Netflix and chill, only not a euphemism. At least, I assumed it wasn't a euphemism. Probably best not think too much about that. They got all of one queen in before the running commentary started, and for the next two full episodes, Judy and Mum were ranking the death drops, making inaccurate predictions about who would go out, and asking us earnestly which boys we thought looked nicest.

Mum paused before episode three autoplayed. "How are enjoying the *Drag Race*, Oliver? You are not too confused?"

"No," he said, "I think I'm keeping up."

"We should probably explain that the woman who does the judging at the end and the man in the workroom at the start are actually the same person."

I put my head in my hands.

"At the beginning, we thought it was like *Project Runway* and the man at the beginning is like Tim Gunn and the woman at the end is like Heidi Klum. But then Judy realised that they seem to have the same name, and that because it is a show all about men putting on dresses, she probably is actually the same man only in a dress."

I looked up again. "Nothing gets past you, does it, Mum?"

"Yes," agreed Oliver, ever polite, "the name did tip me off."

"Seriously, Oliver," I asked, nervously, "how *are* you finding the show? We can leave at any time. Any time at all."

He made a hmming noise. "We don't have to go. I'm enjoying myself. And the show is…interesting."

"You are so right, Oliver." Mum turned to him enthusiastically. Odds were about 60/40 in favour of her next line being wildly inappropriate. "I had not known there were so many different sorts of gays. In my day we had Elton John and Boy George, and that was it."

"Freddie Mercury?" I offered.

Judy's mouth dropped open. "He was never? But he had a moustache and everything."

"Famously so, I'm afraid."

"Well, stone me if you don't learn something new every day." She turned to Oliver with a terrifyingly *interested* look in her eye. Oh God. "What about you, old man? Have you ever sissied that walk?"

"Do you mean," he asked, "have I ever done drag?"

"Is that an insensitive question? They're doing it on TV now, so I assumed it was fine."

Oliver did his contemplative frown. "I'm not sure I want to set myself up as an authority on what's insensitive. I mean, for what it's worth, most people don't, and I personally never have. It's honestly not something I see the appeal of."

There was a small pause.

"Well, it's all larks, isn't it?" said Judy. "Like those parties we used to have in the '50s where the boys would get up in dresses and the girls would get up suits, and then we'd drink far too much fizz, sneak off into the bushes, and do naughty things to each other."

Oh dear. I was perilously close to using the phrase "it exists on a spectrum" to Mum and Judy. "It's complicated," I tried instead. "What's a lark for one person can be really important for another. And really problematic for someone else."

"I think for me"—Oliver shifted slightly uncomfortably—"and I should stress I'm speaking entirely personally, I've never wholly identified with that particular way of signalling your identity. Which always makes me feel like I'm letting the side down a little bit."

Mum patted him reassuringly. "Oh, Oliver, that is a sad way to think. I am sure you are one of the best gays."

I glanced back to find Oliver looking faintly flustered. "Mum, stop ranking homosexuals. It doesn't work like that."

"I am not ranking anybody. I'm just saying, you should not have to feel bad because you do not like to watch men in dresses telling blue jokes. I mean, I enjoy it, but I am French."

"Yeah," I said, "very important part of French culture that. Along with Edith Piaf, Cézanne, and the Eiffel Tower."

"Eh, have you seen what our kings used to wear? Their faces were beat for the gods and their heels were sickening."

Oliver laughed. "Thank you. I think."

"It is true. You should never let anyone tell you it is wrong to be how you are." Mum was watching him with an expression I recognised from every childhood setback I'd ever had. "It is like the special curry. Luc has been telling me for years that it has too much spice, that I should not put sausage meat in it, and that I should never make it for guests."

"Where are you going with this story?" I asked. "Because all those things are true and your curry is terrible."

"Where I am going with this, mon caneton, is that I don't give a shit. It is my curry, and I will make it the way I fucking well want to. And that is the way Oliver should live his life. Because the people who matter will love you anyway."

"I..." For the first time since I'd known him, Oliver seemed genuinely speechless.

"Come along." Mum reached for the remote. "Let us watch episode three. The queens are going to be in a horror movie."

Apparently deciding that bzns had become srs, Judy got up and dimmed the lights. As we all settled in for what was probably going to become a *Drag Race* marathon, I really wasn't sure how I felt or was meant to be feeling. Life with Mum and Judy had been this bubble I'd kept other people away from, partly because I was worried they wouldn't understand, but also because, I guess, in some odd way, I wanted it to stay mine. This private space where Mum would always be cooking—or saying—something awful, and she and Judy would always be far too into whatever hobby or book or TV show had caught their attention this week, and I would always be welcome and safe and loved.

I'd brought Miles to visit, of course, but I'd never tried to make him part of our world. We'd usually gone down to the village pub and had scampi and chips on our best behaviour. But here I was with Oliver, and while it was a little exposing and a little unnerving, it was also... What's the word? Nice. And he hadn't run away yet, despite Mum and Judy being at pretty much peak Mum and Judy.

I let my head rest against his knee, and, somewhere between the mini-challenge and the runway, Oliver's hand began stroking softly through my hair.

CHAPTER 27

OLIVER WAS STILL BUSY WITH his case (which he couldn't talk about, but refused to let me pretend was a murder) for the next few days. And I, of course, had a weekend with my dad looming and, as a fabulous aperitif for that three-course shit banquet, I also had to meet Adam and Tamara Clarke. Hopefully at an excitingly trendy pop-up vegan dining experience, rather than something Rhys Jones Bowen had just made up in his head.

I got there well ahead of time so that I could scope the place out and, in an absolute emergency, come up with a flimsy excuse to cancel. Thankfully, it seemed to be legit. Yes, from the outside the venue was your typical, generic pop-up space—a white-painted shop front with a sign over the awning reading "By Bronwyn"— but inside it was full of hanging baskets and repurposed furniture that hopefully the Clarkes would find ethical and carbon neutral and stuff.

When I'd given my name to the teenage hippie running front of house, I was ushered into a cosy corner and given a compli- mentary bowl of, um, seeds? Which was kind of the worst, because I didn't particularly want to eat them, but they were there so I was definitely going to, and I'd probably have finished them before my intended schmoozees had arrived. I was trying, and failing, to stop picking at the seeds—they were actually quite well seasoned, insofar as you could season something that was itself basically seasoning—when a large woman in chef's whites, her abundant chestnut hair stuffed into a hairnet, came over to greet me.

"You must be Luc," she said. "I'm Bronwyn. Rhys told me all about you."

"Look. Whatever he said, I'm not actually racist against Welsh people."

"Oh, you probably are. You English are all the same."

"And how," I asked, "is that okay?"

"I think you'll find it's a complex question of intersectionality. But basically my people never invaded your country and tried to eradicate your language."

I slumped lower on the upcycled whisky barrel I was sitting on. "Okay. Good point. Thanks for taking the booking."

"That's okay. Rhys said you were a hopeless berk and you'd be fired if this didn't go perfectly."

"Nice to know you're both on my side. So what's good?"

"It's all good." She grinned. "I'm amazing at my job."

"Let me rephrase. Suppose I was a committed meat-eater trying to impress two potential donors who run a chain of vegan cafés. What can I order that will make it look like I know what the fuck I'm doing?"

"Well, if you want something relatively predictable, then you could go for the sunflower seed and cashew burger, but that might make you look like you're really wishing you could have a steak."

"No offence, but I probably really will be wishing I could have a steak."

"Yes, that is a little bit offensive considering you're in my restaurant. If you want to pretend you actually know what a vegetable is, you could go for the jackfruit Caesar or the tomato lasagne. And if you're feeling adventurous, you could try the sesame-rolled tofu."

"Thanks. I do have some self-loathing issues, but I don't think I'm quite ready for bean curd."

"Little bit of advice if I may, Luc. Stop talking like this when your guests are here. They won't like it."

"Yeah, I know. I'm just trying to get it out my system before I have to be polite to the Clarkes."

Her face contorted. "What, you mean the Gaia people?"

"Not a fan? Are they like the Starbucks of veganism?"

"It's not so much that. But they're very… Well, let's say I do this because I think eating animal products is unnecessarily cruel and an avoidable environmental catastrophe. I don't do it because I want to bathe the world in healing goddess energy and flog yoga mats."

I gave her a faintly alarmed look. "You're not going to say that to them, right?"

"Of the two of us, which was the one dissing tofu in front of a vegan chef?"

"I thought I was more dissing myself, but fair enough."

"Anyway, I'll leave you to the… Oh, you've eaten all the seeds."

Fuck. I had. "I don't suppose I could have some more? What do you put on them, anyway? Crack cocaine?"

"Salt, mostly, and a few spices."

"They're really moreish."

"I know, and they don't even come out of a dead cow."

A few minutes after she'd gone back to the kitchen, and the teenager had replenished the seeds, Adam and Tamara wafted in, looking willowy, bronzed, and smug. They Namasted at me and sat down across the table, making it feel unpleasantly like a job interview. Which, I suppose, in a way it was.

"Oh, this is charming," said Tamara. "Well done, you."

I put on my best smile. "Yes, the chef's been on my radar for a while. And when I heard she was doing a pop-up, I thought of you immediately."

"I feel like it's been a while since we've spoken." Adam popped a seed into his mouth. He was handsome in this weird picture-in-the-attic sort of way. The last time I'd Googled him, he'd been in his early fifties but he looked like he could have been anything between thirty and about six thousand and nine.

"It has." I was pretty sure Adam was hinting that I hadn't stroked their egos enough recently so I fell back on the strategy of making an excuse that sounds like a compliment. "But now the franchise rollout is underway, I'll be a lot less worried about bothering you. I hear it's going well?"

Tamara, who was just enough younger than Adam that it came across as creepy but not so much younger than you didn't feel judgmental for thinking it was creepy, pressed a hand coyly to what I strongly suspected was a chakra. "We've been very blessed."

"If you put good energy in the universe," Adam added, "good energy comes back to you."

God. By the time this was over, I was going to have a near-fatal buildup of unused sarcasm. "I think that's a really positive philosophy, and I know it's one you've always lived by."

"We very much feel we have a duty to set a positive example." That was Tamara.

Adam nodded approvingly. "It's particularly important to me because I used to work in a very negative industry, and even with Tamara's help, it took me a long time to come through that."

At this point, I got a momentary reprieve when the teenager came over to take our orders, and Adam and Tamara gave him the third degree over where the restaurant's ingredients were sourced from and which bits specifically were organic. I half wondered if it would have been a better strategy to take them somewhere less in line with their values so they could have the satisfaction of being unsatisfied with it. In the end, I went with the jackfruit

Caesar—despite not knowing what jackfruit was—because I figured it was a good compromise between making an effort and trying too hard.

"Anyway"—Tamara leaned forward earnestly—"we're really glad to have this opportunity to speak to you, Luc. As you know, we find the work that Coleoptera Research Project does in restoring the natural balance of the earth to be incredibly important."

I tried to match her earnest for earnest. "Thank you. We've always been very grateful for your generosity. But, more than that, we've always felt you had a real understanding of our mission."

"That's really great to hear," said Adam. "The thing is though, Luc, our values are central to our way of life."

"And…" Now it was Tamara's turn "…some of the things we've been hearing recently have actually been quite concerning to us."

"Like we were saying earlier. We think it's really important to put out the right sort of energy."

"And, obviously, nature really matters to us. And being in harmony with nature and with ourselves."

"And, so, being frank and strictly off the record, we've been a little bit worried that some elements of your lifestyle are not necessarily compatible with what we see as healthy and positive living."

I was pretty sure that they could have gone on like this for at least another hour but, mercifully, it seemed like they thought they'd made their point. And now they were gazing expectantly at me.

Somehow, I didn't throw the seeds at them.

"I completely see where you're coming from," I told them. "And, being frank and strictly off the record, I've not been in the best place recently. But I've taken time to reflect and look inward, and although I think it's going to be quite a slow, holistic process, I'm beginning to take steps to really realign myself with where I'm supposed to be in life."

Tamara reached across the table and laid her hand across mine like a benediction. "That's really centred of you, Luc. Not a lot of people have the courage to do that."

"Just to be clear"—Adam suddenly looked a little bit uncomfortable—"it's not about the gay thing."

A nod from Tamara. "We have lots of gay friends."

I widened my eyes in a look of reassuring disbelief that I had been practicing for way too long. "You know, it never even crossed my mind that it might be."

A couple of hours later, they'd gone, having formally un-pulled-out of the Beetle Drive—which, y'know, they could do because their Johrei retreat wasn't happening. I celebrated and/or consoled myself with a terrifyingly good chocolate caramel brownie. Like, seriously. Better than a real—I mean nonvegan—chocolate caramel brownie. My working theory was that getting a dessert from a vegan restaurant was like having sex with someone less attractive than you—they knew it was a tough sell, so they tried harder.

"How was the jackfruit?" asked Bronwyn, popping up beside me.

"Surprisingly good. There was even a thirty-second window when I stopped wishing it was meat."

She folded her arms. "You've been bottling that up, haven't you?"

"Yes. Yes, I have. They are the worst people, Bronwyn."

"I blame the yoga. All that time in facedown dog's not good for you."

"They actually used the phrase 'It's not the gay thing.'"

"Oh, so it was the gay thing then?"

"Yeah." I hoovered up the last crumbs of brownie. "They've got to that place where they've realised being homophobic is bad, but haven't quite reconciled that with the fact they're a bit suspicious of gay people."

Bronwyn oofed. "Are you going to need another brownie?"

"I think I might actually. This is on expenses. And I kind of feel like work owes me."

She did, in fact, bring me another brownie. And I did, in fact, eat it.

"Oh, by the way," she said, swinging herself onto a repurposed wine crate, "I had a text from Rhys. He wants to know if you're getting fired or not. He does worry about you, Luc. On account of how you're such a bellend."

"I think it went okay. Bellend or not, I'm depressingly good at pandering to straight people when I have to."

"Well, it's a living, isn't it? Probably better than digging a hole."

I squirmed. "You don't think it's...messed up?"

"No point asking me. I'm not the gay pope. You do it. What do you think?"

I carried on squirming. "It's not a massive part of my job. It just feels like it right now."

"You mean," she offered, helpfully, "because you were in the newspapers being a massive junkie slutbag?"

"Excuse me. I've recently been in the newspapers having a very nice boyfriend."

"Yes, but that's only for pretendsies, isn't it?"

I face-palmed. "Has Rhys told everyone in Wales about this?"

"Oh, I doubt it. I don't think he knows anyone in Llanfyllin. Anyway—"she stood up again—"you should bring your fake boyfriend here on a fake date. I'll even serve him a fake burger."

"He is actually vegetarian."

"There you go, then. Hopefully I'll get some publicity out of it, and you'll get to enjoy my food without the casual homophobia."

Now she mentioned it, Oliver would really like this place, and since all I'd managed to bring him during our lunch dates were two identically average avocado wraps from Pret, I owed him some nice food at some point. Plus I could let him order for me, and I'd get to watch him being all earnest and gastronomical and—

Publicity, that was the main thing. I mean, I was sure going to vegan restaurants with the lawyer you were monogamously dating was donor-friendly behaviour.

"Thanks," I said. "That'd be...um...great."

She nodded. "I'll get you the bill."

I wriggled my phone out my pocket and discovered I had a picture of Richard Armitage waiting for me. Which was definitely my kind of dick.

Want to come to a pop-up vegan restaurant with me? I sent.

And few minutes later I got back, Of course. Is this for work or broader reputation management?

Both. Because it was. But also, it wasn't. **You'll like it though**

That's very thoughtful of you, Lucien.

It wasn't. It was very thoughtful of a Welsh lesbian. Still, it was the closest I'd come to trying for a very long time. And that was scary as fuck.

Just not quite scary enough to stop me.

CHAPTER 28

I HADN'T THOUGHT MUCH ABOUT how to get to my dad's. My plan, such as it was, had been to put it completely out of my mind until Saturday night, then panic, and maybe discover I couldn't make it after all. Oliver, however, had not only pre-Googled the route but rented a car for the weekend. Which was very considerate. And also infuriating.

With an eye for logistics that could have seemed romantic if you squinted—and our relationship wasn't a total fiction—he suggested that it would be most efficient if I was to stay at his place the night before. I'd have found the idea intensely appealing except I was finding the together-not-togetherness of our arrangement increasingly difficult to navigate. My brain didn't know what to do with a kind, considerate, supportive man except tell me to get out, get out now before he uses what you've given him to hurt you. Which, obviously, I couldn't because we both needed this and we'd made a deal.

It would have been so much easier if we were just fucking. Then, he'd be a guy I was having sex with and I'd know what it meant—and, yes, afterwards he could go to the papers and tell them a bunch of dirty sex anecdotes. But, at this point, that was barely news, and I'd take it any day over stories about how much I loved my mum or how much my dad had screwed me up or the fact I had a tragic French toast fixation. Stuff about *me*.

Anyway, I took him to By Bronwyn on Saturday evening, and shamelessly showed off my knowledge of vegan cuisine for about twelve seconds before he gave me an "I call bullshit" look and asked me what a jackfruit was. So I admitted I didn't have a clue and asked him to order for me, which made him far happier than that should make anyone. He had the rolled tofu, and showing far too much insight into my preferences, he got me the burger I'd have felt too shallow ordering for myself. And it was actually a really nice evening—we talked about Oliver's case, now it was finished, and I did my impression of Adam and Tamara Clarke, and somehow halfway through a bottle of vegan wine (because apparently most wine contains fish bladder for some fucking reason), we got onto the finer points of *Drag Race*. And from there to basically everything, the conversation twisting and meandering and turning back on itself the way it normally only did with my oldest and closest friends.

Of course Oliver insisted he didn't want dessert, and then ate half of my brownie anyway, after a minor scuffle over who got to hold the spoon.

"What the hell is wrong with you?" I asked, when he tried to take it from my fingers. *Again.*

"I can feed myself, Lucien."

"You can order your own fucking dessert as well."

"I told you. I'm not a big fan of dessert."

I glared at him. "You're giving my brownie puppy eyes."

"I...I..." He was blushing. "I feel awkward not eating while you're eating."

"Oliver. Is that a lie?"

The blush deepened. "'Lie' seems a very strong word. It might be a little...misleading."

"You can't have this both ways. You can either get the virtue points for not eating cake, or you can eat cake. And you can see which side of that equation I fall on."

"I suppose I just feel I shouldn't."

Only Oliver could turn a brownie into an ethical quandary. Well, Oliver and Julia Roberts. "You'll still be a good person if you have dessert."

"Yes, well." He gave one of his self-conscious squirms. "There are also practical considerations."

"What, are you literally allergic to enjoying yourself?"

"In a manner of speaking. The, um, V-cut you so admire doesn't maintain itself."

I stared at him, suddenly feeling guilty. I guess even though I knew rationally that you didn't get a body like that without basically killing yourself, I'd still taken it for granted. "If it helps, you'll still get to keep turning me down for sex even if you start looking a bit more like a normal person."

"You say that. But it wasn't until I had my shirt off that you expressed any interest whatsoever."

"Not true. What about Bridget's birthday?"

"That doesn't count. You were so drunk I suspect you would have had sex with a bag of crisps."

"Also not true. And...for the record"—I slugged back some vegan wine—"I've actually been into you for quite a long time. The V-cut was just a convenient excuse. Now if you don't want to eat brownies because of your choices about your body, that's fine. But if you want the fucking brownie, then we can share the fucking brownie."

There was a long silence.

"I...I think," said Oliver, "I want the brownie."

"Fine. But as punishment for not having the guts to order your own, I'm going to feed it to you in a sexy way."

Aaaand the blush was back. "Do you have to?"

"Well. No." I smiled at him across the table. "But I'm going to anyway."

"I think you'll find it's not a sexy food."

"I've seen you eat a lemon posset. I'm going to find this sexy whether you like it or not."

"Fine." He gave me a cold stare. "Give it to me, baby. Give it to me hard."

"You see, you're trying to put me off. But it's not working."

I leaned over the table and slipped a morsel of brownie into his slightly horrified mouth. But within seconds he had that gorgeous, blissed-out Oliver Eating Dessert look. It wasn't until we got home afterwards, and we were lying decorously in bed next to each other, that I realised getting all sensual and chocolatey with a guy who was never going to shag me had been an epic strategic error. Because suddenly all I could think about were his lips and his eyes gone soft with pleasure and the brush of his breath over my fingertips. And I was losing my fucking mind. But I was in *his* house, and he was *right there*, so I couldn't even wank it off.

I don't think I slept well. And, on top of that, Oliver made me get up at seven. Which, it is no exaggeration to say, was the worst thing that had ever happened to any human being. And I acted like it, hiding under the covers, whimpering, and calling him names.

"But"—he actually put his hands on his hips—"I made French toast."

I peered at him from beneath the pillow I'd wedged over my head. "Really? Really *really*?"

"Yes. Although, having just called me an offensively perky breakfast tyrant, I'm not sure you deserve any."

"I'm sorry." I sat up. "I didn't realise you'd actually *made* breakfast."

"Well, I have."

"And there's actually French toast?"

"Yes. There's actually French toast."

"For me?"

"Lucien, I don't understand why you're obsessed with glorified eggy bread."

I think I was blushing. "I don't know. It's just got this domestic bliss vibe to it that I find, um, nice?"

"I see."

"And, honestly," I admitted, "I never imagined anyone would actually make it for me."

He brushed the hair out of my eyes almost absentmindedly. "You know, you're sometimes very sweet."

"I…" *Fuck.* I didn't know what to do with myself. "All right, all right. I'm getting up."

Forty minutes later, with me reluctantly showered but full of French toast, we were on the road, bound for Lancashire. And I was slowly coming to terms with the fact that Oliver and I had signed up to take a four-hour car journey together. Or rather, Oliver had signed up to spend four hours driving me to see my dad in a car he was renting. And, once again, I was having to face up to the fact that he was taking this fake boyfriend gig way more seriously than any actual boyfriend I'd ever had.

"Um." I squirmed. "Thanks for doing this. I think in my head Lancashire wasn't quite this…far."

"Well, I did encourage you to reach out to your father, so I suppose I really brought this on myself."

"I know I've barely met the guy, but this feels so typical of him."

"What do you mean?"

"Oh, you know. Making a big song and dance about wanting to reconnect and then dragging me all the way to Lancashire to do it. I mean, what if I didn't have a fake boyfriend who could drive? This'd be crap."

"Thankfully, you do have a fake boyfriend who can drive."

I cast him a sidelong glance. "I know. And I'd offer to make it up to you, but you keep turning me down."

"Just an observation, Lucien. There are other ways to make things up to people than sex."

"So you say. I remain sceptical."

He gave a little cough. "How are you feeling about seeing your father?"

"Inconvenienced."

And, ever the epitome of tact, Oliver didn't push it. "Would you mind if I put on a podcast?" he asked.

Obviously Oliver was a podcast person. "Okay, but if it's a TED Talk or the *New Yorker* fiction podcast, I'm walking to Lancashire."

"What's wrong with the *New Yorker* fiction podcast?"

"It's the *New Yorker* fiction podcast."

He plugged his phone into the dock, and the car filled up with Twilight-Zoney music and the weirdly sonorous voice of an American man.

"Okay," I told him, "can we add *This American Life* to the no-fucking-way list?"

"Welcome to Night Vale," said the weirdly sonorous American man.

I stared at Oliver's serene profile. "What is happening?"

"It's *Welcome to Night Vale*."

"Yeah, I got that from the guy using the words 'welcome to Night Vale.' Why are you listening to it?"

He gave a little shrug. "I like it?"

"I figured that on account of you choosing to play it in the car for what will be a four-hour journey. I just didn't think it was the kind of thing you'd even have heard of."

"Clearly I have hidden depths. Also I'm rather invested in Cecil and Carlos."

"Genuinely? Do you *ship them*? Do you have a Tumblr as well?"

"I don't know what any of those words mean."

"I'd have believed that, right up until the point I discovered you're into *Welcome to Night Vale*."

"What can I say? I sometimes need a break from listening to documentaries about current affairs and looking down on people."

I was about to retort but something held me back. "Did I do the bad teasing again?"

"Maybe. I just didn't realise you'd find it so shocking that I had an interest outside the law and the news."

"I'm sorry. I...I like seeing other sides of you."

"Is the side you normally see so objectionable?"

"No," I grumbled. "I like that too. Is this why you don't have casual sex?"

He blinked. "Because of *Welcome to Night Vale*?"

"Because you're waiting for someone with perfect hair."

"Yes. That is the reason." He paused. "That, and instructions from the Glow Cloud."

CHAPTER 29

BETWEEN CECIL'S HONEYED TONES AND the fact I'd got up at seven, I might have fallen asleep. Oliver shook me gently awake, and I peeled myself out the car somewhere round the back of Dad's insultingly idyllic rock-star farmhouse. To my complete lack of surprise, the parking area where we'd stashed the rental was very, very full of what looked an awful lot like a working film crew. I mean, there was even a motherfucking food truck, from which a bald man in a leather jacket was getting a baked potato.

"Well," I said, "I'm really looking forward to spending some quality time with my emotionally distant father."

Oliver's arm went round my waist. It was worrying how natural that was beginning to feel. "I'm sure this will all be wrapped up soon."

"It should have been wrapped up yesterday."

"Then I suspect it's overrun, which is hardly his fault."

"I'll blame him if I want to."

We crunched over the gravel and between some outbuildings— all thatched and charming, although at least one of them had obviously soundproofed windows—and managed to nearly reach the front door before we were accosted by security.

"What do you think you're doing?"

I sighed. "I've been asking myself that since we left London."

"Sorry, mate." The man put up a hand. "You can't be here."

"We were invited," said Oliver. "This is Luc O'Donnell."

"If you're not on the show, you can't be here."

I half managed to turn away, but Oliver's arm was making it difficult. "Oh, what a shame. Let's go. If we hurry, we can make that lovely service station in time for dinner."

"Luc"—Oliver wheeled me back around—"you've come a long way. Don't give up now."

"But I like giving up. It's my single biggest talent."

Sadly, Oliver wasn't having any of it. He fixed the security guard with his best lawyer look. "Mr... I'm sorry, I didn't catch your name."

"Briggs," offered the security guard.

"Mr. Briggs, this is Jon Fleming's son. He has been invited and, therefore, has a right to be here. While I appreciate that it is your job to tell us to go away, we aren't going to. If you try to physically prevent us from seeing Mr. Fleming, that will be assault. Now I'm going to walk past you into the house, and I recommend you go and speak to your manager."

Personally, even putting aside how little I wanted to be there, I wouldn't have chosen the course of action that had "get assaulted" as a possible consequence. Oliver, apparently, didn't have a problem with it. We walked round the guy and into the house.

Where we were immediately yelled at by a red-haired woman in her early fifties. "Cut. Cut. Who the fuck opened the door?"

We were standing in what, when it wasn't full of boom mics and angry people, would have been a gorgeously rustic entrance hall, with stripped wooden floorboards, slightly faded rugs, and an enormous fireplace set into a stone wall.

"My apologies for the interruption," Oliver said, unperturbed. "We're here to see Jon Fleming. But there seems to be a schedule clash."

"I don't care if you're here to see the fucking Dalai Lama. You don't walk onto my set."

At this moment, Jon Fleming stepped through from the room beyond—a sitting room decorated in the same style, which somehow managed to look cosy despite also being enormous.

"Sorry. Sorry." He made what James Royce-Royce would call a mea-culpa gesture. "They're with me. Geraldine, you okay with them sitting in?"

"Fine." She glared at us. "Just be quiet and don't touch anything."

"Well"—I sighed sadly—"there goes my plan to scream and lick the furniture."

Jon Fleming gave me a look of sincere contrition, though I was sure that he was neither sincere nor contrite. "I'll be with you soon, Luc. I know this wasn't what you expected."

"Actually. It's pretty much *exactly* what I expected. Take as long as you need."

It took him five fucking hours.

Most of it, he spent mentoring Leo from Billericay through a soulful acoustic rendition of "Young and Beautiful." They were sitting on one of the expansively homey sofas—Leo from Billericay, with his guitar cradled on his knee like it was a dying lamb, and Dad watching him intently with this look that said "I believe in you, son."

I knew shit all about music but Dad was depressingly good at this stuff. He kept making insightful, but non-pushy technical suggestions and offering the sort of praise and support that stayed with you for a lifetime. And, incidentally, also made for great TV moments. At one point he even guided Leo from Billericay's fingers into a better position to transition between chords.

And then we had to clear the entrance hall so Leo from Billericay could sit by the fireplace and tell the camera how amazing my dad was and how important their relationship had become to him. Which took several takes because they kept asking him for more emotion. By the end he was on the verge on tears, although whether that was because it had been such a meaningful experience for him, or because he'd been sat under hot lights for the whole afternoon with nothing to eat or drink while people shouted at him, I couldn't say. Well, I could. But I didn't really care.

While they were doing whatever TV slang for tidying up is—folding the pooches or clearing the banana—I slunk off to steal a baked potato from ITV. It did not make me feel substantially better. But finally Oliver, Jon Fleming, my stolen baked potato, and I were sitting round the kitchen table, sharing an uncomfortable moment.

"So," I said, "what with you filming pretty much constantly since we got here, I couldn't introduce you to my boyfriend."

"I'm Oliver Blackwood." Oliver offered his hand, and my father gave it a firm shake. "It's good to meet you."

Jon Fleming gave him slow nod that said *You have been judged and found worthy.* "And you, Oliver. I'm glad you could come. Both of you."

"Well"—I made a gesture that came as close as I could get to "fuck you" without literally giving him the finger—"that's nice, but we'll be leaving soon."

"You can stay the night if you want. You can take the annexe. You'll have your own space."

Part of me wanted to say yes if only because I was pretty sure he was banking on me saying no. "We've got work."

"Another time, then."

"What other time? We had to rent a car for this, and we spent the whole afternoon watching you shoot a shitty TV show."

He looked grave and regretful—which, when you were a bald man in your seventies with more charisma than conscience, was very easy to do. "This wasn't what I wanted. And I'm sorry my work got in the way."

"What *did* you want?" I stabbed my potato with a wooden spork. "What was the plan here?"

"There isn't a plan, Luc. I just thought it would be good for us to spend some time together, in this place. It was something I wanted to share with you."

I...had no idea what to say to that. Jon Fleming had given me nothing my whole life. And now he suddenly wanted to share, what, Lancashire?

"It's a very beautiful part of the country," offered Oliver. God, he made the effort. Every. Single. Time.

"It is. But it's more than that. It's about roots. It's about where I come from. Where you come from."

Okay. Now I had something to say. "*I* come from a village near Epsom. Where I was raised by the parent who didn't walk out on me."

Jon Fleming didn't flinch. "I know you needed me in your life, and I know it was wrong of me not to be there. But I can't change the past. I can only try to do what's right in this moment."

"Are you..." It genuinely upset me that I was having to say this. "Are you even sorry?"

He stroked his chin. "I think being sorry is too easy. I made my choices and I'm living with them."

"Um. That sounds a lot like a no."

"If I'd said yes, what would it change?"

"I don't know." I made a show of mulling it over. "I might not think you're a colossal prick."

"Lucien..." Oliver's fingers brushed my wrist.

"You can think what you like of me," said Jon Fleming. "You've got that right."

There was this pressure building inside me, hot and bitter, like I was going to cry or vomit. The problem was, he was being so reasonable. But all I could hear was *I don't give a shit*. "I'm supposed to be your son. Don't you care how I feel about you?"

"Of course I do. But I learned a long time ago you can't control other people's feelings."

My potato wasn't protecting me anymore. I pushed it away and put my head in my hands.

"With respect, Mr. Fleming." Oliver somehow managed to sound both as conciliatory and as unyielding as my dad. "I think it's a mistake to apply the same standards to magazine reviewers and your own family."

"That's not what I meant." I got the impression that Jon Fleming was not a big fan of being challenged. "Luc's a grown man. I'm not going to try to change his opinions of anything, least of all myself."

I could feel Oliver's stillness beside me. "It's very much not my place to say," he murmured, "but that position might come across as trying to evade your responsibility for considering the impact your actions have on other people."

There was a small, unhappy silence. Then Jon Fleming said, "I understand why you feel that way."

"For fuck's sake." I looked up. "I can't believe you responded to being called on your bullshit with the same bullshit."

"You're angry." He was still fucking nodding.

"Wow, you've got a real insight into the human condition there, Dad. I can see why ITV thinks you're a music legend."

He folded his hands on the tabletop, long, gnarled fingers interlacing. "I know you're looking for something from me, Luc, but if it's for me to say I regret choosing my career over my family, then I can't. I'll admit I hurt you, I'll admit I hurt your mother. I'll even say I was selfish, because I was, but what I did was right for me."

"Then what," I pleaded, feeling way more like a child than I was comfortable with, "am I doing here?"

"What's right for you. And if that's walking away and never speaking to me, I'll accept that."

"So you've asked me to make an eight-hour round trip to tell me you support my right to decide whether I come and see you? That is fucked up."

"I see that. It's just I'm increasingly aware of how few opportunities I might have left."

I sighed. "Credit to you, Dad. You really know how to play the cancer card."

"I'm only being honest."

We stared at each other, locked in this weird stalemate. I shouldn't have come. The last thing I needed was Jon Fleming finding new and creative ways to tell me he'd never wanted me. And now I couldn't even walk away without feeling like the bad guy. My fingers folded desperately over Oliver's arm.

"You're not being honest," he said. "You're being truthful. I'm a barrister. I know the difference."

Jon Fleming glanced at Oliver, somewhat warily. "I'm afraid you've lost me."

"I mean everything you're saying is perfectly unobjectionable when taken at face value. But you're trying to make us accept an entirely false equivalence between you abandoning your three-year-old child and Lucien holding you accountable for a choice you admit to making freely. They are not, in fact, the same thing."

At this, my dad gave a wry smile, though it didn't reach his eyes. "I know better than to argue with a lawyer."

"You mean I'm right, but you can't admit it, so you're making a joke about my profession and hoping Luc will mistake it for a rebuttal."

"Okay"—Jon Fleming made an everybody-settle-down gesture—"I can see things are getting heated."

"They're not getting heated at all," returned Oliver coldly. "You and I are remaining perfectly calm. The problem is you've been profoundly upsetting your son for the last ten minutes."

"You've said your piece, and I admire you for that. But this is between me and Lucien."

I jumped up so sharply the chair fell over and crashed with incredible force onto what I'm sure were authentic Lancastrian flagstones. "You do not get to call me Lucien. And you don't get to do"—I waved my hands in a way that I hoped encompassed the everythingness of everything—"*this* anymore. *You* reached out to *me*. Yet somehow I've wound up being the one who makes all the effort and the one who has to take responsibility when it crashes and burns."

"I—"

"And if you say 'I understand where you're coming from' or 'I hear you' or anything remotely like it, then even though you're an old man with cancer, I will fucking deck you so help me God."

He opened his arms in a way that looked half like he was channelling Jesus and half like he was saying 'Come at me, bro.' "You want to take a shot, go right ahead."

I was strangely relieved to discover that I had no actual desire to hit him. "I can see," I drawled out, in my best Jon Fleming voice, "why that might be something you want me to do. But I'm afraid I can't give you what you're looking for."

Maybe I was imagining it, but I thought my dad looked almost disappointed.

"Look," I went on. "This is on you. Either you make an actual effort to spend some actual time with me somewhere I can actually get to. Or I walk out of here right now, and you can enjoy dying of cancer alone."

Jon Fleming was silent a moment. "I probably deserved that."

"I don't care if you did. It's just how things are going to be. So, what do you say?"

"I'll be in London again in a couple days. I'll come see you then."

I let out a really long breath. "Fine. Come on, Oliver. Let's go home."

CHAPTER 30

WE GOT UNDERWAY IN SILENCE.

"Do you mind," I said, "if we skip *Night Vale* for now?"

"Not at all."

The soft thrum of the engine filled up the car. And, beneath it, the steady rhythm of Oliver's breath. I rested my head against the window and watched the motorway streaking past in a grey haze.

"Are you—"

"Can I put some music on?" I asked.

"Of course."

I stuffed my phone into the dock and fired up Spotify. For some reason that might well have been a cry for therapy, I had this urge to listen to one of Jon Fleming's old albums. Half-reluctantly, half-anxiously I swiped "Rights of Man" into the search bar. And holy fuck, my dad had been on a lot of shit over the years. Not counting several best-ofs, remixes, and decade-anniversary collections, there were about thirty albums there, including *The Hills Rise Wild*, which was one of the ones he'd done with Mum. And which I was never ever *ever* playing.

I dithered between the *The Long Walk Home*, which was his latest release, and *Leviathan*, which was the one everyone's heard of and that won a Grammy in 1989, and eventually settled on *Leviathan*. There was brief pause as the title track buffered. And then the speakers began belting out a level of angry prog rock that they really hadn't been designed to cope with.

To be honest, I'm not sure *I'd* been designed to cope with it either.

I'd gone through a phase when I was about thirteen of obsessively listening to Jon Fleming's music. Then I'd decided I never wanted to listen to it again, which meant hearing it now was a fucking weird experience. Because I remembered it perfectly—not only the music, but how it had felt, being that age, and having a dad who was at once so accessible and so absent. He was completely *in* his music. And, even now, when I'd just spent an hour yelling at him, not in my life at all.

Oliver's eyes slid briefly to mine. "Is this…"

"Yeah."

"It's, um. Loud."

"Yeah, he was loud in the '80s. In the '70s, it was all trees and tambourines."

Another interlude of cynical growling and heavy guitars.

"Forgive my ignorance," said Oliver, "but what's it even about?"

"According to Mum—and we can double-check on Wikipedia if you like, because it didn't exist when I last listened to this album—it's about Thatcherite Britain. Y'know, because everything in the '80s in this country was about Thatcherite Britain."

"Does it have anything to do with Hobbes's *Leviathan*?"

"Um. Probably? I mean, unless we're talking about the cartoon tiger, in which case, still maybe, I have no idea."

Oliver gave one of his little chuckles. "Well, he called his band 'Rights of Man.' So I assume he had some interest in the philosophy of the seventeenth and eighteenth centuries."

"Oh fuck." I thunked back against the headrest. "Does everybody know more about my dad than I do?"

"I don't know more about your father. I just know more about the Enlightenment."

"Yeah, I'm not sure I'm finding that very comforting. It just means you know more about my dad *and* more about history."

"You know"—another swift look—"I didn't mean it that way."

"I do. But I enjoy poking your middle-class guilt."

"In which case, you should be pleased to hear I'm feeling at the very least ambivalent right now for encouraging you to reach out to him."

"You're right. This was a disaster and it's all your fault."

He flinched. "Lucien, I—"

"I'm joking, Oliver. None of this is on you. It's on Jon Fucking Fleming. And"—uh, why did he keep making me say this stuff—"I'm glad you were there. It would have been way worse without you."

The next track was gentler and flutey-er. "Livingstone Road" I could annoyingly still remember.

"I'm sorry," he said, after a moment, "it didn't go better."

"It was never going to."

"And you aren't...too hurt?"

If anyone else had asked me, or if Oliver had asked two weeks ago, I'd probably have said something like *Jon Fleming stopped being able to hurt me a long time ago.* "Not too hurt but...yeah."

"It's hard for me to understand why anyone wouldn't want you in their life."

I snorted. "Have you met me?"

"Please don't laugh this off. I mean it."

"I know. It's just easier to push people away than watch them leave." The words hung there, and I wished I could suck them back into my mouth. "Anyway," I went on quickly, "you were still right. If I hadn't tried, I'd have spent my whole life as the bastard who abandoned his dying father."

"You wouldn't have been. It might still have felt that way, but you wouldn't have been." A pause. "What will you do next?"

"Fuck knows. See what happens when he calls."

"You've done all the right things, Lucien. It's down to him now. Although, frankly, I don't think he deserves you."

Fuck. I really needed him to stop being nice to me. Well, stop or never stop.

I let *Leviathan* run to the end, and then Spotify decided I wanted to listen to Uriah Heep so we...listened to Uriah Heep. And a four-hour algorithmically guided journey through '80s progressive rock later, most of which I spent not quite asleep but near enough to it that I didn't have to think about anything, we got back to mine.

"Do..." I did my best to sound nonchalant. "Do you want to stay?"

He looked over at me, his expression unreadable in the shadows from the streetlamps. "Do you want me to?"

I was too tired to fight it and too washed out to pretend. "Yes."

"I'll find somewhere to park and meet you upstairs."

Normally, this would have been my opportunity to try and contain the worst evidence of my god-awful lifestyle but, actually, I'd been super careful lately and had managed to keep my flat looking almost as nice as it had when my friends had left. Which meant now I had nothing to do except stand awkwardly in front of my sofa and wait for Oliver. And that was how he found me, still in my coat and plonked like a lemon on the rug Priya had given me to tie the room together.

"Um," I said. "Surprise?"

He glanced from me to the lack of filth to me again. "You cleaned?"

"Yes. I mean, I had help."

"You didn't do this for me, did you?"

"For myself. And a bit for you."

He looked genuinely overwhelmed. "Oh, Lucien."

"It's...it's not a big de—"

He kissed me. And it was the most Oliver kiss, his hands cupping my face gently to draw me to him, and his lips covering mine with a deliberate care that was its own kind of passion. The way you'd eat a really expensive chocolate, savouring it because you knew you might never get another. He smelled of familiarity, of homecoming, and of the night I'd spent wrapped in his arms. And he made me feel so fucking *precious* I wasn't sure I could bear it.

Except I also didn't want it to end. This moment of finding something I'd long since given up looking for. Maybe even stopped believing in. The wild impossible sweetness of somebody kissing you for you—because of you—and everything outside the press of bodies, the ripple of breath, the stroke of tongues drifting away like old leaves in autumn.

It was a kiss to make you invincible: hot and slow and deep and perfect. And for a little while, for as long as Oliver was touching me, I forgot to need anything else. I clutched helplessly at the lapels of his coat. "W-what is even happening right now?"

"I rather hoped it was obvious." The mouth that had moved on mine curled into its softest smile.

"Yes but. Yes but. You said you only kiss people you like."

At this, he went very pink very quickly. "It's true, but I'm sorry I said that to you. Because I do like you. As it happens, I've always liked you. I just thought you'd find me ridiculous if you knew how much."

"Oh come on"—my head was reeling—"when have I needed your help to find you ridiculous?"

"You make a good point."

"So kiss me again."

I wasn't used to Oliver doing what I told him, but I guess it was a special occasion. Or the tidying had gone to his head. In any case, he didn't stay careful long: we ended up on the sofa, Oliver between my legs, his hands pinning mine against the cushions, everything a tangle of harsh breath and arching bodies and way, way too many clothes. And, God, his kisses. Deep, drowning, desperate kisses. Like he'd been told the world was ending and for some bizarre reason he'd decided I was the last thing he wanted to do.

"And here I thought," I gasped, "you were supposed to be a good boy."

He gazed down at me. With his hair mussed, and his mouth red, and his eyes dark with passion, he looked very bad indeed. "And here I thought you were far too socially conscious to entertain that sort of sex-negative stereotype."

"I am. I'm socially conscious *as balls*. I just meant…this wasn't a side of you I ever thought I'd see."

"Well, you weren't meant to." His expression grew solemn again. "We agreed…that is…what we're doing. It's not supposed to be—"

I wasn't sure what he was going to say next, but I knew I didn't want to hear it. Tomorrow we could go back to acting like this was nothing. But tonight…I don't know…I guess I was too tired for my own bullshit. "Oliver, please. Let's stop pretending. You were amazing today. You've been amazing all along."

He was blushing. "I've done what we agreed. That's all."

"Okay, then. But you've made me happier than, well, anybody. In a really long time. And I'm not trying to mess with what we've got or make you do anything you don't want to do. Only I…I guess I wanted you to…to know?"

"Lucien…"

"Um," I asked, after a very long pause, "were you intending to finish that sentence?"

He laughed. "I'm sorry. It's just this isn't a side of you I ever thought *I'd* see."

"Yeah." Him and me both. "I'm not used to...any of this. Being with someone and being able to count on them, and wanting them to be able to count on me."

"If it's any consolation, I'm not quite used to this either."

"But haven't you had loads of boyfriends?"

"Yes, but"—his eyes slid away from mine for a moment—"I never quite felt I was enough for any of them."

"That makes zero sense."

"Well," he said, smiling, "you do keep telling me you have low standards."

"Hey, I was being self-deprecating. Keyword 'self.'"

He leaned in and kissed me again—a fleeting brush of his lips against mine. Normally I didn't do sweet but, well, Oliver.

"So"—I was a bit worried I'd jinx it but I had to ask the question—"is kissing part of the arrangement now?"

"If it...if you...wouldn't mind."

I heaved a heavy sigh. "Since you *insist*."

"I'm serious, Lucien."

"I know you are, and it's adorable. Yes, I think we should add a kissing subclause to the fake boyfriend contract."

His lips twitched. "I shall draft one first thing in the morning."

Honestly, I could have taken a lot more teenage-level sofa action with Oliver, but we'd driven to Lancaster and back, and my dad had been a total cock to both of us, and we technically had grown-up jobs to go in the morning, all of which added up to bedtime. Besides, I didn't have any books, so Oliver would be forced to rely on me for entertainment, and now we'd negotiated kissing, I intended to be pretty darn entertaining.

Gentleman that I was, I let Oliver use the bathroom first and then slipped in to clean my teeth and make sure I didn't need a shower before I attempted to get snuggly with the attractive man I'd brought home with me. I was at the toothbrush-in-mouth stage when I realised my phone was flashing pretty insistently and, without really thinking about it, I checked my alerts. The problem was, Google had been pretty kind to me recently with its Celeb's Kid Doesn't Fuck Up Much stories, which meant my guard was way further down than it should have been. And so *A Life Like Ordinary: The Here Nor There of Luc O'Donnell* by Cameron Spenser kicked me right in the teeth.

Luc O'Donnell isn't famous, it began. Even his parents—the so-called "celebrities" in this celebrity lifestyle piece have names more likely to provoke a "who" or an "I thought he was dead" than the universal snap of recognition that you get with the genuinely celebrated. When I met him at a party a month or so back, a mutual friend had told me his dad was that guy from that reality TV show ("that guy" being Jon Fleming and "that reality TV show" being *The Whole Package* insofar as those details matter). At the time, despite what we're constantly being told about our "media obsessed culture," neither the guy nor the show meant much to me, but it seemed like as good an icebreaker as any, so I went up to him.

Okay, this was okay. This was just facts. It was facts about a specific thing that had happened to me recently involving a guy who had sworn blind he wouldn't do something like this, but it was just facts.

"Hi," I began. "You're Jon Fleming's kid, right?"

I'll never forget the way he looked at me with these intense blue-green eyes—come-to-bed eyes they'd have been called about a decade and a half ago—full of hope and fear and suspicion all at once. Here was a man, I thought, who's never known what it's like to be nobody. And I hadn't realised until that moment what a burden that must be. It's a cliché to say that fame has taken the place of religion in the twenty-first century, the Beyoncés and the Brangelinas of our world filling the void left by the gods and heroes of antiquity, but like most clichés there's an element of truth to it. And the gods of old were merciless. For every Theseus who slays the Minotaur and returns home in triumph there's an Ariadne abandoned on the island of Naxos. There's an Aegeus casting himself into the ocean at the sight of a black sail.

This was still okay. This had to be okay. It was just air. Just words. Just self-serving waffle about nothing. But those were my eyes he was talking about. My fucking eyes.

In another life, I like to think that Luc O'Donnell and I might have worked out. In the short time I knew him, I saw a man with endless potential trapped in a maze he couldn't even name. And from time to time I think how many tens of thousands like him there must be in the world—insignificant on a planet of billions but a staggering number when considered as a whole—all stumbling about blinded by reflected glory, never knowing where to step or what to trust, blessed and cursed by the Midas touch of our digital-era divinity.

I read the other day that he's seeing somebody new, that he's getting his life back on track. But the more I think about it, the less I believe there was ever a track for him to be on. I hope I'm wrong. I hope he's happy. But when I see his name in the papers, I think back to those strange, haunted eyes. And I wonder.

I put my toothbrush carefully down by the sink. Then I sank down on the cold bathroom floor, put my back to the door, and pulled my knees up to my chest.

CHAPTER 31

"LUCIEN? IS EVERYTHING ALL RIGHT?" Oliver was still tapping politely on the bathroom door. I wasn't sure when he'd started.

I wiped my eyes with the sleeve of my T-shirt. "I'm fine."

"Are you sure? You've been in there rather a long time."

"I said I'm fine."

There was a sort of dithery noise from outside. "I want to respect your privacy, but I'm becoming increasingly concerned. Are you ill?"

"No. If I was ill, I would have said *I'm ill*. I said I was fine because I'm fine."

"You don't sound fine." It was Oliver's most patient of patient voices. "And if I'm being honest, this doesn't seem like fine behaviour."

"Well, it's how I'm behaving."

Then came a soft *thunk* like he'd put his head against the door. "And I'm not challenging that, it's just… I know that a lot has happened today, and if you're upset about anything, then I'd hope you could talk to me about it."

With a somewhat louder *thunk*, I put my own head back rather harder than I'd expected. The sudden jolt of pain *felt* like it clarified things, but probably didn't. "I know you do, Oliver, but I've talked to you too much already."

"If you mean this evening, I... I don't know what to say. I liked having that connection with you—I liked knowing I mattered—and I don't think that's something either of us should regret."

"Shouldn't isn't the same as won't."

"You're right. Neither of us can be certain we aren't going to look back in five years' time and think this was the worst idea we ever had. But that's a risk I'm willing to live with."

I scraped pointlessly at the grouting between the floor tiles. "That's because when you regret something, you do it on your own in a house with a cup of tea and a bottle of gin. When I regret something, I do it on page eight of the *Daily Mirror*."

"I'm aware this is a concern for you, Lucien, but—"

"This is more than a fucking concern. It's my life." My nail snagged and tore awkwardly, a half-moon of blood gathering on my fingertip. "You don't understand what it's like. Every stupid thing I've done. Every time I've been dumped. Every time I've been used. Every time I've been even a little bit vulnerable. That's *forever*. For anyone. It's not even a proper story. It's the article you read over someone's shoulder on the Tube. It's the half headline you catch as you walk past a newspaper you're not buying. It's something you scroll through when you're having a shit."

There was a long, long silence. "What's happened?"

"*You've* happened," I snapped. "You've fucked me up and made me think things could be different and they can never be different."

Another, even longer silence. "I'm sorry you feel that way. But whatever is going on right now is clearly about more than just me."

"Maybe, but you're the bit I can deal with right now."

"And you're dealing with me by having an argument through a bathroom door?"

"I'm dealing with you by telling you this isn't working. Apparently even a fake relationship is beyond me."

"If you're going to dump me, Lucien"—Oliver had become very, very cold—"will you at least do it to my face instead of through two inches of plywood?"

Hiding my face against my knees, I definitely wasn't crying. "Sorry. This is what you get. You can't say I didn't warn you."

"You did, but I hoped you'd think I deserved better."

"No, I'm that much of an arsehole. Now get out of my flat."

The faintest of sounds, like maybe Oliver had been about to try the handle and then thought better of it. "Lucien, I... Please don't."

"Oh fuck off, Oliver."

He didn't reply. From my white ceramic cell, I listened to him dressing, heard his footsteps walking away, heard the front door closing behind him.

For a while I was too fucked up to do anything. Then I was too fucked up to do anything except ring Bridget. So I rang Bridget.

She picked up straight away. "What's wrong?"

"Me," I said. "I'm what's wrong."

"What's going on?" Bridge's phone was just sensitive enough to pick up Tom's sleepy voice.

"It's an emergency," she told him.

He groaned. "They're books, Bridge. What problems can they possibly have at half one in the morning?"

"It's not a publishing emergency. It's a friend emergency."

"In which case, I love you. And you're the best and loyalest person I know. But I'm going to sleep in the spare room."

"You don't have to. I'll be quick."

"No you won't. And I don't want you to."

Down the slightly shitty connection I caught the rustle of bedclothes and a kiss goodbye. And then Bridge was back on the line. "Okay, I'm here. Tell me what's up."

I opened my mouth and then realised I had no idea what to say. "Oliver's gone."

A slight pause. "I don't know how to say this without it sounding bad but...what did you do now?"

"Thanks." I let out a laugh that sounded more like a sob. "You're my rock."

"I *am* your rock. Which is why I know you make really bad decisions."

"It wasn't a decision," I wailed. "It just sort of happened."

"What just sort of happened?"

"I told him he'd fucked me up and to fuck off."

"Um." Bridge gave me the audible equivalent of her confused face. "Why?"

The more I thought about it, the more I wasn't sure. "I'm in the *Guardian*, Bridge. The fucking *Guardian*."

"I thought the whole point of dating Oliver was to get better press? After all, it's a broadsheet. They'd probably only run a celebrity sex story if it was about an MP or a Royal."

"It was worse than a sex story. It was a thought-provoking opinion piece about what a broken victim of celebrity culture I am written by that guy I failed to pull at Malcom's T Party."

"Should I look?"

"Why the hell not?" I huddled further into a corner of the bathroom. "Everyone else will."

"I meant, would reading it help me support you better."

I mumbled something along the lines of *urnuhnuh*.

"Okay I'm going in."

A pause, while she switched apps and read the article, during which I shivered and sweated and felt sick.

"Wow," she said. "What an utter wanker."

That was less consoling than I'd hoped it would be. "He's right, though, isn't he? I'm this half-person wreckage of someone else's fame, who'll never have a normal life or a normal relationship or—"

"Luc, stop it. I work in publishing, I can spot articulate guff a mile away."

"It's how I feel, though. And he must have seen it, and now the whole world can too." I pressed my cheek against the wall, hoping the chill would help somehow. "It's not just a picture of me getting off or throwing up. It's...Miles all over again."

"It's not at all like Miles. This is someone who met you for five seconds and decided to use your name to sell a completely generic article about nothing in particular. Besides, you only need that many classical allusions if you have a very tiny penis."

I gave a weird hiccoughy laugh. "Thanks for that. Here, I thought I was having a crisis, but it turned out all I was looking for was an opportunity to insult a stranger's dick."

"Comfort comes in many forms."

Perhaps it did, but it left in many forms too. "Look, I wish I was better at not caring. And, actually, I've worked fucking hard at not caring. Except then I started caring and look where it's got me."

"Where has it got you?" she asked gently. "If you mean on the phone with me at two in the morning, that's been a constant of both our lives for as long as I can remember."

"Bridge, when we're on our deathbeds, I hope the last thing we do is ring each other. But I kind of meant Oliver."

"Yes, what happened? This article has nothing to do with him."

"I know, but"—I tried to assemble my thoughts, which remained stubbornly unassembled—"he was nice to me, and that made me feel safe, and maybe not worthless. And so I got all soft and happy and shit. And then this happened and I couldn't cope. And it's going to keep happening, and I'm going to keep not being able to cope as long as I'm trying to live like a normal person."

Bridget let out a long, sad sigh. "I love you, Luc, and that does sound terrible. But I don't think 'make yourself miserable' is the one-size-fits-all solution you think it is."

"It's worked so far."

"Do you really believe you'd have felt better about that article if you'd read it alone in a flat full of empty Pringles tubes?"

"Well, at least I wouldn't have had to break up with someone through a bathroom door."

"You didn't *have* to break up with him. You *chose* to break up with him."

I ground my forehead against the tiles. "What else was I supposed to do?"

"Well, this might be quite a radical notion." I could always tell when Bridge was making a huge effort not to sound cross with me. I was telling it right now. "But did it at all occur to you that you could have told him something upsetting had happened, and then have a conversation about it?"

"No."

"Do you not think maybe that might have been a good idea? Do you not think maybe that might have helped?"

"It's not so simple." Shit, I was crying again. "Not for me."

"It could be, Luc. You just have to let it."

"Yes, but I don't know how. I saw this thing in the paper, and suddenly I felt as if I'd spent the last month wandering around with all my clothes off, and I hadn't even noticed."

"But you liked being with Oliver."

"I did," I snuffled. "I really did. But it's not worth this."

She made a supportively confused noise. "I don't understand. What this? The article would have come out anyway. And you can't break up with someone so you don't have to break up with him."

"No, it's neither of those. It's both of those. It's this whole big everything. Fuck, I'm such a fuckup."

"You're not a fuckup, Luc. You sometimes do fucked-up things. But, and I mean this in the nicest possible way, I still don't have a clue what you're talking about."

I tugged at the ragged edge of my nail with my teeth. "I told you, it's everything. I can't... I'm not... Relationships. I can't relationships. Not anymore."

"There's not a magic formula," she said. "It's hard for all of us—you've seen how many times I've messed it up—but you just have to keep trying."

Sliding the rest of the way down the wall, I curled up on the bathroom floor, with the phone tucked against my shoulder. "It's not that. It's...bigger than that. It's..."

"It's what?"

"It's me." I had that creeping nausea again that isn't quite about your body. "I hate how being with someone makes me feel."

There was a little pause. Then Bridge asked, "How do you mean?"

"Like I've left the gas on."

"Um. I'm sort of glad you can't see my face now. Because I still have no idea what you're talking about."

I did that thing where you pull your knees and elbows in, and try to get so small you disappear. "Oh, you know. Like I'm going to come home one day and my whole world will have burned down."

"Well"—she made a pained sound—"I don't really know what to say to that."

"That's because there's nothing you can say. It's just the way it is."

"Okay," she announced, with the unwarranted confidence of a World War I general sending his men over the top, "I've got things to say."

"Bridge..."

"No, listen. There is actually a choice here. And the choice is, either you never trust anybody ever again, and pretend that stops people hurting you when clearly it doesn't. Or, um, don't do that.

And maybe your house will burn down. But, at least you'll be warm. And probably the next place will be better. And come with an induction hob."

I couldn't tell whether Bridget's strategy of distracting me from my problems by being odd was deliberate or not. "I think you've drifted from 'giving me a pep talk' into 'advocating arson.'"

"I'm advocating taking a chance on a nice man who you're clearly into and who'll treat you well. And if you think that's arson, then yay, arson."

"But I've already dumped him."

"Then undump him."

"It's not that—"

"If you say 'It's not that simple' one more time, I'm going to get in an Uber, come over there, and poke you sharply in the ribs."

I gave another weird weepy laugh. "Don't call an Uber. Their business practices are unethical."

"The point is, this is all fixable. If you want to be with Oliver, you can be with Oliver."

"But should he be with me, though? I mean, he drove me all the way to Lancashire to see my dad, stood up to my dad for me, drove me all the way home again, and then I broke up with him through a bathroom door."

"I agree," conceded Bridget, "that wasn't ideal. And you probably hurt his feelings quite badly. But, ultimately, whether he wants to be with you is his decision."

"And you don't think maybe he'll decide *not* to go out with the crying man in the toilet?"

"I think people surprise you and, really, what do you have to lose?"

"Pride? Dignity? Self-respect?"

"Luc, you and I both know you have none of those things."

She'd made me laugh again—I was pretty sure it was her

superpower. "That doesn't mean I want to give Oliver Blackwood a chance to kick me hard in the feels."

"I know you don't. But from what you've said, he sort of deserves one. And, anyway, it might go well."

"Yeah," I muttered, "that's what they said about the invasion of Iraq."

"We're talking about asking a cute boy to give you a second chance. Not starting a war."

"You have no idea how many second chances he's already had to give me."

"Which means he clearly likes you. Now go and tell him you're sorry, and that you like him back, because you obviously are and you obviously do."

"But I'll fuck it up or he'll not want to see me or—"

"Or you'll be unbelievably happy together. And if it goes wrong, we'll figure it out like always."

That was about 50 percent comforting, 50 percent embarrassing. "You shouldn't have to keep scraping me off the floor."

"That's what friends do. Scrape each other off the floor and hold your hair back when you're being sick in the toilet."

"You're so sentimental, Bridge."

"Holding someone's hair while they throw up is one of the most loving things you can do for them."

"You know, you could just drink less?"

"I could, but I choose not to."

I mumbled something.

"What was that?"

"Iloveyoubridget."

"I love you too, Luc. Now go get your man."

"At three a.m.? How will that help?"

"It's romantic. You're chasing after him in the rain."

"It's not raining."

"Don't ruin this for me."

"And you don't think he'd prefer a polite text after we've both had a decent night's sleep?"

She squeaked in exasperation. "No. And, besides, he won't be sleeping. He'll be staring out the window, wondering if you're looking at the same moon he is."

"How could we be looking at different moons? Also he can't see the moon, because it's apparently raining."

"Okay, now you're just stalling so I'm hanging up."

She hung up.

After she'd gone, I slowly uncurled. I still wasn't quite ready to stand up or leave the bathroom, but I was taking my victories where I could find them. As enthusiastic as Bridge had been about the plan, I wasn't sure that showing up at Oliver's doorstep at stupid o'clock in the morning would come across as quite as romantic and spontaneous as she was hoping, especially since I'd done it before—although at least then it had been at a slightly more sociable time. In my defence, on that occasion he'd dumped me so, in a way, we were one for one. If we ignored the fact that he'd dumped me specifically because of my behaviour and I'd dumped him, um, specifically because of my behaviour.

And while I got what Bridge was saying about letting him choose whether he wanted to deal with my bullshit or not, I couldn't shake the sense that we'd hit a level of bullshittery that would make the choice kind of a no-brainer. Because this was what he was getting: someone who'd spent five years burying himself in cynicism and apathy, and honestly hadn't been so great before then either. I didn't want to be that person for Oliver, I didn't want to lash out or run away every time I thought something might hurt me, but it was going to take more than a month of fake-dating and a couple of rounds of French toast to dig my way out.

It would be easier for everyone if I never spoke to him again.

But Bridge was right, he deserved better than easy. And if that meant I had to stand there on his doorstep *again*, and say I was sorry *again*, then I guess I'd do it. And maybe this time I could let him see me, all the ways I was messy and hurt and lost, and all the ways he made me better. Maybe he deserved that too.

Twenty minutes later—against my better judgment—I was in a cab on my way to Clerkenwell.

CHAPTER 32

I WAS STANDING ON THE pavement outside Oliver's, trying to figure out exactly how bad an idea this had been, when it started to rain. Which, at the very least, got in the way of my plan to dither helplessly for twenty minutes before wussing out and going home. I mean, I still hadn't completely written off Operation Wuss Out but, somehow, there I was, unsexily damp and terrified, ringing Oliver's doorbell at four in the morning.

Oh shit, what had I done?

I stared at Oliver's pretty glass panels, wondering if it was too late to run away like a kid playing a prank. And then the door opened, and Oliver was standing there in his stripiest pyjamas, his face pale and his eyes red-rimmed.

"What are you doing here?" he said in a "this is the last thing I need right now" sort of voice.

With no idea how to answer that, I called up Cam's article on my phone and jammed it in Oliver's face like an FBI agent in a movie.

"What's this?" He squinted.

"It's an article about what a loser I am by some guy I met for five minutes a month ago."

"When you woke me up," said Oliver, "at a time so unsociable it can't even be called the middle of the night because that was about two hours back, I'd hoped you might at least be coming to apologise. I didn't expect that you'd be asking me to do background reading on a wet smartphone."

Fuck, I was fucking this up. "I am," I tried. "I mean, I do. I apologise. But I wanted you to know why I flipped out. For context."

"Ah yes." He gave me one of his cold looks. "The most important part of any apology."

Rainwater slithered from the tips of my hair and down my face. "Oliver, I'm sorry. I'm really sorry. I'm sorry for pushing you away. I'm sorry for losing my shit. I'm sorry for locking myself in the bathroom like an emo teen at a bad party. I'm sorry I suck at apologies. I'm sorry I've been a crap fake boyfriend. And I'm sorry I keep showing up on your doorstep begging you to give me another chance."

"It's not that I don't appreciate the gesture...well, gestures"—he was doing the temple-rubbing thing that meant he had no idea how to deal with me—"but I don't understand why this keeps happening. Honestly, I don't even understand what happened tonight."

"Which is why," I yelled, brandishing the phone again, "I tried to give you context."

He glanced from me to the phone and back again. "You should probably come in."

I came in and stood in his hallway dripping. Neither of us seemed entirely sure what was meant to happen next.

Then Oliver said, "Why don't you take a moment to dry off. And I'll have a look at this article, if you're still comfortable with that."

I wasn't comfortable with that at all, but having shoved it under his nose, it was a bit late to back out now. Besides, I was committed to being honest and transparent and oh, help.

Trying not to panic, I let Oliver shepherd me upstairs, where he took a towel from the airing cupboard because, of course, he had an airing cupboard. And, of course, the towel was all fluffy and sweet-smelling. I hugged it needily.

He gave me a little nudge towards the bathroom. "There's a dressing gown behind the door. I'll be in the kitchen."

Feeling both drier and floatier, I came down a few minutes later, wrapped up in navy-blue fleece, and found Oliver at the table frowning at my phone.

"Lucien"—he looked up with a less encouraging expression than I might have hoped—"I'm still confused. From your reaction, I assumed you'd read something that, at the very least, put one of our careers in danger. This is a contentless piece of self-serving fluff by an obvious hack."

I slid awkwardly onto a chair opposite. "I know, but it felt really true in the moment."

"I'd say I'm not unsympathetic, but since you locked yourself in a bathroom and dumped me over it, I am finding sympathy difficult."

"I...I get that."

Oliver crossed one leg over the other, looking prim and serious. "I think what I need you to understand is that even though we are not in an official relationship, we have made a commitment to each other that we are both relying on. And when you behave unreliably it has real consequences for me, logistically and"—he gave a tight little cough—"emotionally."

This was everything I thought I didn't like about Oliver Blackwood: severe, stern, headmastery and not in a kinky way, and with that faint edge of superiority that suggested he would never flake out or fuck up. But I knew him better now and I knew I'd hurt him. "I realise I've treated you badly, and I realise my many, many issues aren't an excuse for that. And I wish I could tell you I won't do this again, but I can't because I'm worried I will."

"While I appreciate your honesty," he said, still rather coldly, "I'm not sure where that leaves us."

"I can't tell you where it leaves you, but where it leaves me is I want to give this another go and I'll try to do better."

"Lucien…" He gave a soft sigh. "I really don't want to go alone to my parents' anniversary. But it's a little late for me to find anybody else now."

That wasn't quite the falling back into my arms Bridget had led me to expect. "If that's what you need, and that's all you want, I can still do that for you. I think I know you well enough that I could pass as your boyfriend for one party, even if we don't speak until then."

"What about your work function?"

"It'll be fine." I shrugged. "I've got most of the donors back. And, you know, I'm starting to think that if they come for my personal life again, I might actually be able to face taking them to an employment tribunal."

Oliver was looking at me, his eyes all silver-grey and searching. "Why couldn't you before?"

"Because getting fired just felt like something I deserved."

"And it doesn't now?"

"Sometimes. But not so much."

"What changed?" he asked, with a quizzical look.

I groaned. "Don't make me say it."

"Say what?" His foot flickered impatiently. "You'll have to forgive me if I'm not at my most perspicacious, but I've only had three hours sleep."

"Which I notice is still enough sleep to say 'perspicacious.' Oliver, *you*. It was you. You're what changed. And now I've blown it. And I'm sad."

He softened for about a second. And then unsoftened abruptly. "If I've been such a positive influence, why on earth did you dump me through a bathroom door over a nothing article in a newspaper famed for its misspellings?"

"I think what you're underestimating here is how much better I can get and still be a complete disaster."

"You're not a complete disaster, Lucien. I just don't want to be going through this again in a fortnight—and you haven't been able to give me any reassurance that I won't."

I took a deep breath. "Okay. Look, the truth is, we're both terrible at relationships. That's how we got into this position in the first place. But it feels to me that you're asking for the wrong thing."

"Is that so?" He raised an unconvinced eyebrow. "I flatter myself that I'm asking for something quite reasonable, which is that our relationship, fake or otherwise, isn't going to be constantly punctuated by your appearing on my doorstep apologising for your shitty behaviour."

"And I see why that's not great. Except I'm not sure it's the real problem. I don't know how to promise you that I won't overreact, or lash out, or say something I shouldn't. All I can promise, and I really think it's what I should be promising, is that I'll be honest with you about...about what's going on with me." This was hell. I'm pretty sure this was hell. "That's what I should have done tonight. And that's why we're here."

There was a long silence. It was fifty-fifty whether this was good silence or bad silence.

"All right." Oliver eyed me warily. "So if you had been honest with me, as you've suggested, what would you have said?"

I opened my mouth. Nothing came out.

"I think," Oliver murmured, "we've discovered the flaw in this plan."

"No. No. Give me a minute. I can do this. I can trust someone. With, like, my feelings and shit."

Why was this so hard? I mean, it was Oliver. Basically the most decent person I'd met in the last decade who I wasn't already friends with. Fuck.

"Um," I tried. "This is probably going to sound totally bizarre, but do you mind if I go in your bathroom?"

"Sorry, I assume you're not asking to use the facilities?"

"No I...I think I'd just like to go in there."

"If you dump me through a door again, I'll be very angry."

"I'm not going to. And my end goal is to get to the stage where we can have this kind of conversation in the same room. But, y'know, baby steps?"

He made a defeated gesture. "Fine. If that's what you need."

So I went to Oliver's bathroom, locked the door behind me, and sat on the floor with my back to it. "You can still hear me, right?"

"Loud and clear."

"Okay." Breathe. Breathe. I had to breathe. "This...whatever it is...that we're having, it's...the best thing that's happened to me in five years. And I know it's supposed to be fake, but it's not felt that way to me for... I don't know. A while. And that's, I guess, rearranged my messed-upness in ways that are overall really, really...good. But I also feel vulnerable and frightened, like, all the time."

The door shuddered slightly, which took me a moment to interpret. But then I thought maybe Oliver was sitting on the other side of it, with his back to mine. "I... Lucien. I don't know what to say."

"You don't have to. Just, um, listen or something."

"Of course."

"So when I saw that article, it brought up all this old stuff that I... Yeah. You see, my last boyfriend—Miles...we were together all through university and a little bit after. And I think it was one of those relationships where the stuff that keeps you together at uni doesn't work in the real world. We were sort of going through a rough patch, but I guess I didn't know how rough, because he went and sold his story...my story...our story...to the *Daily*—I can't even remember which. For fifty fucking grand."

I heard Oliver draw in a breath. "I'm sorry. That must have felt awful."

"Pretty much. What I couldn't hack was... I thought when you're in love, it's supposed to be safe, isn't it? You're supposed to be able to do things and try things and make mistakes, and it'll be okay because you know who you are to each other. I genuinely believed we had that, but he took it and flogged it to the press, and they turned five years of my life into a couple of threesomes and that one time we did cocaine at a party in Soho."

"Thank you for telling me," Oliver whispered through the door. "This is clearly very difficult for you, and I appreciate your trust."

I should have been done. But, somehow, now I'd started talking about this shit, I couldn't stop. "He met my mum. I told him about my family, about my dad, how I felt, what I wanted, what I was scared of. And he made it all so ugly and so cheap. And now everyone thinks that's who I am. And half the time I believe it too."

"You shouldn't. And I know that's easy to say and harder to believe, but you're far more than pictures in papers, and a couple of sad little articles written by sad little men."

"Maybe, but it came back on Mum as well. She's gone through enough without the tabloids turning her into a crazy has-been."

"Of course," he said softly, "I don't know her as well as you. But she seems...resilient to say the least."

"That's not the point. She shouldn't have to pay because I trust the wrong people."

"One person. Who betrayed you. Which is on him."

My head fell back gently against the door. "The thing is, I didn't even see it coming. I thought I knew him. Better than anyone. And he still..."

"Again, that's about him, and his choices. Not about you and yours."

"Rationally, I know that. I just don't know when it's going to happen again."

"And so you haven't been with anyone since?"

"Basically." I tried to pick at Oliver's floor like I had my own, but the grouting was too clean. "It was liberating at first. It felt like the worst had already happened, so I thought I might as well do anything I wanted. Except, then, doing what I wanted became steering into people's worst assumptions about me. And before I knew it, I'd lost my job, alienated most of my friends, and my health was trashed and my house was a tip."

I felt another ripple through the door—it was weirdly comforting, like he was touching me. "I had no idea how difficult it's been for you. I'm so sorry, Lucien."

"Don't be. Because then I met you."

Leaving the bathroom still seemed like a terrifying prospect, but I was coming to the conclusion that waiting wouldn't make it less terrifying. And while Oliver's toilet was way nicer than, say, mine, I hadn't quite sunk low enough that I'd be happy to live there for the rest of my life. I got shakily to my feet, opened the door, and walked straight into Oliver's arms.

"Yeah," I said a few minutes later, still clinging to him, "I should probably have done this the first time round."

He gave me a wholesome cotton pyjama squeeze. "We can work on it."

"Does this mean you'll have me back?"

I was treated to one of his intense stares. "Do you want to come back? I'm only just beginning to understand how much this is asking of you."

"No, Oliver. I came to your house at whatever it is in the morning and spilled my guts all over your bathroom floor because I'm so-so about this."

"I find it oddly comforting that you're feeling well enough to be sarcastic at me."

I risked smiling at him, and he smiled slowly back.

CHAPTER 33

A FEW MINUTES LATER WE were back in Oliver's tiny kitchen, and he was Olivering at the stove because he'd apparently decided that what we really needed now was hot chocolate.

Sitting uselessly at the table, I faffed around with my phone and discovered it was well after five. "You are going to be wrecked at work tomorrow."

"I'm not in court. So I have no intention of actually going in."

"Can you do that?"

"Well, I'm technically self-employed—though the clerks tend not to see it that way—and I haven't had a sick day in...ever."

I flooped. "I'm sorry. Again."

"Don't be. Obviously I'd rather we hadn't had a crisis, but I've come to terms with the idea that there's something I care more about than my job."

I had no idea how to reply to that. Part of me wanted to point out that he probably shouldn't put boys ahead of his career, but since I *was* the boy, that would have been pretty self-defeating. "Yeah, I think I'll be pulling a sickie too."

"I don't think it counts as pulling a sickie if you're actually having a hard time."

"What?" I watched the muscles in his back as he stirred his pan—and couldn't tell if noticing that kind of thing again meant I was getting my shit together or my shit had never been together to begin with. "I should ring them up, and say 'Sorry, I gave myself a nervous breakdown with a *Guardian* article'?"

He came over with a pair of mugs and set them down carefully on coasters. I folded my hands around mine, letting the warmth seep into my palms, as the rich scent of chocolate and cinnamon wafted over the table.

"You've been through a lot today," he said. "There's no need to diminish it."

"Yeah, but if I don't diminish things I have to face them at their normal size, and that's horrible."

"I think it's usually better to face the world as it is. The more we try to hide from something, the more power we give it."

"Don't be wise at me, Oliver." I gave him a look. "It's unsexy."

With the air of someone with a lot on his mind, he turned his hot chocolate a quarter circle, and then back again. "While we're on the topic of—"

"Unsexy?"

"Trying to hide from things."

"Oh."

"You mentioned in the bathroom that our arrangement was no longer feeling quite as artificial as it hitherto had?"

"Are you trying to stop me freaking out by using words you know I'll mock you for using?"

His eyes met mine across the table. "Did you mean it, Lucien?"

"Yes." Was there anything fucking worse than being called on your own sincerity? "I meant it. Can we please go back to what's important here, which is that you actually just said 'hitherto'?"

"As it happens"—he continued adjusting the angle of his mug—"I've been having similar thoughts myself."

At that moment, I couldn't tell whether I'd been waiting desperately to hear that or terrified I might. But it showed how far I'd come, and how seriously committed I was to doing better by Oliver, that I didn't run away screaming. "Okay. Good? That's nice?" In my defence, my voice had only gone up half an octave.

"There's no need to panic. We're just having a conversation."

"Can I go back in the bath—"

"No."

I wheezed. "Look, I … Like I said, I have these feelings. And I'm not used to having these feelings. And every time I have these feelings, I have these other feelings which are…like… When's he going to the press, when's he going to let me down, when's he going to fuck me over."

"Lucien—"

"And"—I ran over him before I could stop myself—"I don't think I could take it. Not from you."

He was quiet for a moment, frowning thoughtfully. "I know the last thing that can possibly help you right now are promises and platitudes. But I do feel quite confident in assuring you that I will never sell your story to the tabloids."

"I'm pretty sure Miles would have said that too."

"But in a different context." His tone was very measured, almost detached, but he also reached across the table and took my limp, damp hand in his. "I'm not asking you to trust in me personally. Obviously, I would be gratified if you could, but I understand that what you've been through renders that difficult."

"I want to trust you, though."

"You don't have to. But you can trust that I have nothing to gain and everything to lose by turning our relationship into a public spectacle. I don't particularly need the money, and I've invested more than a decade in a job that relies on my reputation for discretion."

I gave him a brittle smile. "I'm probably worth a lot more now that my dad's on TV."

"My career means far more to me than any sum of money I could reasonably be offered."

It took me probably too long to Rubik's cube my brain into something that could make sense of this. "Okay. Yes. I see that."

"And, for that matter," he went on, "so are you."

Well, that was a thing. "Thank you. Really. I...fuck, how do we do this?"

"I confess"—Oliver had gone a little pink around the ears—"I hadn't thought that far ahead. This is new territory for both of us."

"Um. I don't want to sound cold-feety, but what if we just... carried on as we were?"

"You mean," he said slowly, "you want us to continue pretending to be in a relationship that we admit feels real to both of us?"

Wow, trying to do the right thing was hard. And seemed very similar to fucking everything up. "I'm worried that if we try to change too much all at once, it'll go wrong somehow and then I'll have let you down and you'll be on your own at your parents' anniversary and it'll be my fault."

"That's kind of you, but I'm not going to put a family party above our relationship."

"You don't have to." I put my other hand over his. "Leaving aside my occasional meltdowns, which I promise I'll learn to deal with, this is working well for us, and will definitely do what we need it to do. Why rush? Or mess with that?"

He was giving me an "I'm not quite sure who you are, but I like it" look. "I'm beginning to think you might be better at relationships than you've claimed."

"I," I announced, "am growing as a person."

"Perhaps I...I could also do better."

I smiled at him, too tired to care how goofy it was. "You don't have to. You're already perfect."

Bed happened pretty soon after that. And, having just exposed the full depth of my emotional wibble, it seemed a bit pointless to worry about what Oliver would think of my boxers or no-pack. As far as I could tell, he wasn't disappointed or repulsed—instead, he pulled me down into his arms, where I lay quiet and cared for, and quickly drifted off to sleep.

We woke late—well, late by Oliver's standards so, like, nine—although I kept him in bed for another hour or so by octopusing myself around him and refusing to let go until he told me very firmly he needed the bathroom. While he was abluting, and probably remembering to floss and all of those other things we're supposed to do but don't, I dug out my phone and called work.

"Coleoptera Research, Protection... Oh no, wait, that's not right." Apparently I'd got Alex. "Coleoptera Research, Reunification, and—bother. Coleoptera Rescue, Research, and—"

"It's me."

"Me who?"

"Me Luc."

"I'm sorry, Luc's not in yet. Alexander Twaddle speaking."

"No, I know who you are, Alex. I'm Luc. Luc is me."

"Oh." I could hear him thinking. "Then why did you say you wanted to speak to Luc?"

"I didn—I'm sorry, I must have misspoken."

"Don't worry, it's easily done, old thing. Only yesterday, I answered the phone with 'Good afternoon' and then realised it was only 11:30."

"Alex," I said slowly, "wasn't yesterday Sunday?"

"Gosh. So it was. I thought it was a bit quiet."

"Anyway." If I didn't stop this now, we'd be here all week. "I called to say I'm not feeling so great and I won't be coming in today."

He made a sound of genuine sympathy. "How beastly for you. Is everything all right?"

"Yeah, just had a rough couple of days."

"I know the feeling. Last month my valet was sick and I could barely keep it together."

"I'm trying to be strong."

"Take all the time you need. A good man is hard to find."

At this moment, Oliver came out the bathroom, stripped to the waist. "I think," I said, "I'll be okay on that front."

"Glad to hear it. Toodle pip."

I hung up and tried not stare too gormlessly at Oliver—which was easier than it might have been, since my phone was trying to notify itself into an embolism. Glancing into WhatsApp—the group was quiet, and currently named You Can Luc (But You Better Not Touch)—I got Bridged in the face by private message:

LUC ARE YOU OKAY

WHAT HAPEPEND WITH OLIVER

LUC

LUC ARE YOU OKAY

LUC

LUC

ARE YOU OKAY

IS EVERYTHING OKAY

Oliver's lips twitched. Given he also knew Bridge, he'd probably also fallen victim to her texting. "I'll be in the kitchen. Come down when you're ready."

Yes, I typed, **sorry for the silence. It's all good. We talked about feelings and Miles and shit**

OMG ARE YOU KSSIING RIGHT NOW??????

No Bridge. I'm texting you
WELLS TOPI T AND GO KISS OLIVER
ANYWAY G2G BEAUSE GEOPOLITICAL UPHEAVEL HAS LED
     TO PULP PAPER SHORTAGE IN TWICKENHAM
AND SO NONE OF OUR BOOKS ARE GETTING PRIPNTED
AHHHHHHHHHHH
Good luck with that. Thank you for last night
ANYTIME G2G

Pulling on Oliver's dressing gown, I headed downstairs. Oliver was eating something scarily healthy-looking from a mason jar, and reading the *Financial Times* on his iPad. God, he was adorable.

"There's toast." He glanced up, looking like some kind of weird and highly specific porno for people who are really into incredibly cut men and funny-coloured newspapers. "Or fruit. Or bircher. I can make porridge if you prefer."

I was still a bit too emotioned out for that much fibre. So I helped myself to a banana, from a bunch that hung from what appeared to be a bespoke banana hanging place, *next to*, but not *in*, the offensively well-stocked fruit bowl.

"What's with the...?" I pointed. "Do you have a problem with bananas?"

"Not personally. But they release ethylene, which is a ripening agent, and can cause other fruit to go bad."

"Oh. Right."

"I'm sorry. Would you rather I'd said that I was concerned about treason in my fruit bowl and strung them from a gibbet pour encourager les autres."

"You remember that time I pretended I spoke to French to impress you? Well, I still can't."

He laughed and pulled me into a kiss—which got me not quite

into his lap but very much lap adjacent. "You don't need to speak French to impress me."

My heart stuttered. But I still wasn't used to all of this... intimacy and okayness. "What are you eating?" I blurted out instead. "It looks like spunk with fruit in it."

"Thank you, Lucien. You always know exactly what to say."

Sheepishly, I nuzzled into his neck and was thrilled by the discovery of his...whatever the opposite of a five-o'clock shadow is. The prickle of hair under my lips a reminder that I was still here. That we both were. Together.

"It's bircher," he went on. "Oats, soaked overnight in almond milk and—as you correctly observe—fruit. But, to the best of my knowledge, no semen, human or otherwise."

"So it's cold porridge?"

"A lot lighter and fresher—but substantial enough to keep me going through a court case. Also I can make it at the start of the week and it sees me through until Saturday, which is convenient."

I was smiling helplessly at him. "Do you put little labels on the jars so you know which is for which day?"

"No." He gave me a stern look that, somehow, wasn't stern at all. "Bircher is fungible."

"Well, if it goes fungible, you probably shouldn't eat it."

He laughed, somewhat indulgently. But, hey, I could get used to being indulged—especially by Oliver.

CHAPTER 34

I'D SPENT THE REST OF Monday with Oliver, feeling fragile but content, in a sort of snow-day haze. We'd talked so much the night before that we didn't have much to say to each other, but that was good somehow. Oliver had mostly sat decorously on his sofa, reading *The Song of Achilles*, and I'd mostly sprawled over him napping. I hoped I wasn't going to keep having emotions, because it would get really tiring really fast. Then in the middle of the afternoon, and despite my protests, he'd insisted that we go for a walk, which had turned out to be far nicer than a walk round Clerkenwell had any right to be.

Of course, taking Monday off meant having to catch up on Tuesday. And since the Beetle Drive was rolling over the hill like a clump of dung under the hind legs of a *Scarabaeus viettei*—wow, I had been working at CRAPP way too long—I had a whole lot to do when I got in the office.

We'd decided that the fundraiser should include a silent auction back when we (that is to say, I) set up the first one a few years ago and I think we'd just thought it sounded good. But it turned out they were a fuckton of work because you needed either a small number of expensive things and a lot of rich people, or a large number of moderately priced things and a reasonable number of rich people, and every time it was touch and go whether the balance was going to shake out right.

It didn't help that Dr. Fairclough insisted on donating a signed copy of her monograph on the distribution of rove beetles in south Devon between 1968 and 1972, which was apparently a wild time for the Devonshire rove beetle. And I wound up having to buy it every year under a series of increasingly unlikely pseudonyms because nobody else would bid on it. The most recent had gone to a Ms. A. Stark of Winterfell Road.

Just as I was securing a helpfully obscene discount on a Fortnum & Mason hamper—which always did well at an auction even though they aren't actually especially hard to get hold of—Rhys Jones Bowen appeared in my doorway with his usual impeccable timing.

"Busy, Luc?" he asked.

"Yes, fantastically."

"Oh, that's okay. I'll only be a moment." He claimed my spare chair with the air of a man who has no intention of only being a moment. "I'm just here to pass on a message from Bronwyn. She said thank you for getting photographed outside her restaurant. It did her the world of good, and she's booked out for the rest of the pop-up. She was going to offer to cook you dinner, but she can't because now she's got too much on."

What with Cam's wanky think piece nearly destroying my relationship with Oliver, I'd taken a break from my Google alerts. "No problem. Honestly, I kind of hadn't noticed."

"It was a lovely article in the end, all about how you were turning over a new healthier leaf, and trying to get your shit together like your dad. And the newspaper man asked Brownyn, and she said you weren't nearly as much of a knobhead as she thought you were going to be. So that's good, isn't it?"

"In an ideal world, my press coverage wouldn't include the word 'knobhead' at all but, yeah. I'll take it."

I waited hopefully for Rhys Jones Bowen to leave, but instead, he sat there stroking his beard. "You know, Luc, I've been think-ing. As what you might call a social media guru, I recently discov-ered that there's this website called Instagram. And apparently, if you're a little bit famous and a bit of a bellend, you can make loads of money on it pretending you like things."

"Are you suggesting"—it took me a moment to even make my head go there—"that I should become a social media influencer?"

"No, no, I'm just saying you should go on the Instagram and help people like Bronwyn. That's what we in the business call leveraging your platform."

"Thanks, but I think I like my platform unleveraged."

"Well, you do you, as they say." He stood up, stretched theat-rically, walked halfway out the door, then stopped and turned. "By the way, you know how much you and your nice boyfriend enjoyed Bronwyn's pop-up dining experience?"

I wasn't sure I liked where this was going. "Yes?"

"Well, I've got this mate Gavin from Merthyr Tydfil, and he's done a series of glass sculptures inspired by the Rising of 1831."

Now, I definitely didn't like where this was going, but for some reason I asked a question about it anyway. "The who? The what?"

"That's so typical of the English. Set the 93rd Highlanders on my countrymen, and then don't even have the decency to teach it in schools. Anyway"—he paused ominously—"you can learn all about it when you go and get your picture taken at Gavin's exhibition."

Call me paranoid, but I was beginning to think Rhys Jones Bowen had an ulterior motive for wanting me on Instagram. I was about to tell him that I had no intention of going to his mate's glass sculpture show, but I did owe him for the whole vegan rescue, and also...I guess...helping people was nice? Besides, it was probably the sort of thing Oliver would actually be into. "Okay," I said. "That sounds interesting. Email me the details, and I'll ask my boyfriend if he's up for it."

"Don't worry, Luc," Rhys said, nodding. "I completely under—oh right. I'll be honest, I expected you to say no to that one."

"Must be Gavin's lucky day. But I really do have to get back to work."

"Tell you what, I'll bring you a coffee."

I thanked him and went back to silent auction hustling. Well, silent auction hustling and texting Oliver: **Want to come with me to an exhibition tonight?**

What sort of exhibition?

Funny you should ask that. Glass sculpture. About—it was while typing this that I realised I'd forgotten what Rhys has said it was about, and even if I could remember, I wouldn't have been able to spell it—**something bad that happened in Wales**

I'm not sure that narrows it down.

An uprising?

There was a pause. Anyone else would have been Googling, but Oliver was just typing. There've been several.

Yes. One of them. Rhys wants me to get some publicity for a friend of his and I said I would because you've made me a better person you bastard

My apologies. I didn't mean to.

It's fine. You can pay for it by making me look like I understand art

I'd love to, Lucien, but I have to work tonight.

Sorry. Not getting out if that easily. It's on all week.

I am genuinely keen to go. Of course he was.

Weekend then?

We have Jennifer's birthday. Followed quickly by: I mean I have Jennifer's birthday, and you are invited to come but should not feel obligated. Followed quickly by: Of course you'll be very welcome. They'd like to meet you.

Calm down. How about Friday?

Works for me.

Okay. On to trying to score some premium tickets for *Harry Potter and the Cursed Child* at a non-exorbitant price. I was beginning to think the box office was never going to get back to me when my phone rang.

"Hello, Luc O'Donnell speaking."

"Hullo, Luc." It was Alex from the front desk. Which meant somebody *was* trying to call me but there was about a 50 percent chance he'd already hung up on them. "Got a slightly queer chappy on the line for you. Okay if I transfer him?"

"Go right ahead."

"Righto. Any idea how I...you know...do that?"

I didn't sigh. I felt very proud of myself for not sighing. "Did you already press Transfer before you called my extension?"

"Yes. I remembered to do it that way around because I've got a clever mnemonic. I just remember the phrase *Sic transit gloria mundi*, then I remember that you press Transfer first because 'transit' is the second word in the old memory aid. Deuced thing is, I can't remember what comes next."

"Hang up."

Alex seemed hurt. "Steady on, old chap, no need to be like that. Just because a fellow has a bit of a tricky time remembering how to use the telephone machine doesn't mean you should just tell him to hang up out of nowhere."

"If you hang up the phone," I explained, "it will transfer automatically."

"Really? That's dashed clever on it. Thanks a jillion."

"No problem. Thanks, Alex."

There was the briefest click of a line reconnecting, and then Jon Fleming's legend-of-rock voice rumbled down the line at me. "Hello, Luc. I don't think Sunday went the way either of us wanted it to."

That was the problem with reaching out to people. Sometimes they reached back. And while I was mostly trying to be a kinder, gentler, nicer person, Jon Fleming was the exception. "No fucking shit."

"I'm back in London. I said I'd look you up."

"Well, you have. Congratulations on partially following through on a commitment."

"So how've you been?"

There was no way I was telling him about, well, anything. "Good, as it happens. Which, I should clarify, has nothing whatsoever to do with you."

There was a slight pause. "I can see you're still carrying a lot of anger with you. I was the sa—"

"Don't even think about telling me you were the same when you were my age."

"As time passes, you learn to be more accepting of things that aren't as you'd wish they were."

"Did you want to talk"—I cradled my office phone awkwardly against my shoulder as I ran down a list of other auction possibilities—"or are you practicing sound bites for the next time you're on *Loose Women?*"

"I was wondering if you'd be free to meet up while I'm in town."

Oh fuck. I'd just about made my peace with the idea that I'd reached out and it hadn't worked and I was never going to see Jon Fleming again. And the fucker hadn't even given me that. "Um. Depends. How long are you here for?"

"There's no hurry. We'll be filming for the next month or so."

I glanced around my office, which was a carnage of pre–Beetle Drive prep. "I don't suppose," I tried, since by all rights there should be some upside to having a famous father, "you want to come to a fundraiser for the charity I work for."

"I was hoping to get a chance to talk to you one-on-one. I'd like an opportunity to set things right."

"Look, I..."

Note to self: Don't start sentences you have no idea how to end. I absentmindedly flicked the release, and my swivel chair sunk about three inches—pretty much matching my mood right down to the weary hiss. Basically, I had no idea what a "setting things right" conversation with Jon Fleming would even begin to look like, but I had a creeping suspicion that it would end with him feeling better and me feeling worse.

I'd obviously left a really audible thinking gap because he said, "You don't have to decide immediately," in this tone that made it sound like he was doing me a massive fucking favour.

"No, it's fine. We can get dinner or something. I'll find out when Oliver's available."

Another pause. From him this time.

"I'm glad Oliver's in your life, but do you not think it'd be easier if it was the two of us?"

Easier for him maybe.

"Besides," he went on, "I know barristers have very busy schedules. It might be difficult to find a window we can both make."

As was so often the case when it came to Jon Fleming: I just couldn't. Was I supposed to be flattered that he wanted me all to himself? Or creeped out that he was acting like someone off *To Catch a Predator*? I mean, nothing good ever began with "and be sure you come alone."

And there was another of my "I'm very conflicted, please talk into this silence" gaps.

Whether out of sensitivity to my needs or a love of his own voice, Jon Fleming talked. "I'm aware I'm being selfish here. Of course you can bring your partner if that's what you feel you need."

Great. Way to make me feel weak and codependent.

"But the truth is"—he hesitated, as if he was sincerely struggling with something—"it's not easy for someone like me to admit when I've done wrong. And it'll be that much harder in front of an audience."

"W-wait. *What?*"

"This isn't the kind of conversation we should be having over the phone."

He was right. But this was the closest I'd ever come to getting *anything* even halfway real from my father. And I didn't know how not to just...grab at it. Except I couldn't. Because how could I be sure he wouldn't disappear like a gateway to Narnia the moment I went looking for him? There'd been a time when I'd wanted this so much, and maybe that made it worth the risk.

Or maybe it really, really didn't.

"Can I..." I asked. "Can I think about it?"

There was a longer-than-I-would-have-liked pause. "Of course you can. I'll send you my personal number, and you can contact me on your own terms. Just remember, I'll be here for you until... until the end."

And with that helpful little reminder he had cancer, Jon Fleming hung up.

CHAPTER 35

OLIVER SEEMED TO GENUINELY ENJOY Gavin's exhibition, although I could have done without his first words as we went through the door being "Ah, so you meant the Merthyr Tydfil Rising of 1831." In any case, while it wouldn't have been my first, second, or indeed twelfth choice for an evening out, I was quite enjoying being the sort of person who took his socially accept-able barrister boyfriend to pop-up dining experiences and indie art events. Also, it gave me a bunch of culture points that I immedi-ately cashed in by treating myself to a Twix McFlurry on the way home. Which, despite his objections to both the contents of the dessert and the business ethics of the company that sold it, I gener-ously shared with Oliver.

It was a bit disorientating getting back to his house and realis-ing that it was Friday night, and I wasn't at home alone being miserable or out at a party being miserable. It was even more disorientating being in bed before one. Then again, Oliver's bed had compensations—Oliver being the most obvious—but I'm pretty sure his sheets were Egyptian cotton, and were usually freshly laundered.

"Um," I said, from where I was tucked under his arm, "you know that thing where I was going to be open and honest about, like, my feelings and stuff?"

"I hope you're making that sound *unnecessarily* ominous."
I cringed. "Sorry. Sorry. It's always ominous in my head."

"What is it, Lucien?"

"My dad rang. He wants to meet up for some one-on-one father-son bonding."

"And what do you want?"

"I don't know, that's the problem." I tried to shrug, but it turned into more of a...nestle? "I told him I needed to think about it."

"Probably wise."

"Yeah, get me with my probable wisdom."

Oliver's fingers drifted soothingly up and down my spine. "Do you have any sense which way you're leaning?"

"Really not. It's one of those things where I want to but I don't want to. Every time I decide to just walk away, I get this little voice in my head saying 'He's got cancer, you knob.' And I know I'd be an idiot to trust him and I know it's probably going to suck. But I think—shit, I might actually be vomiting a little in my mouth as I say this—it's something I've got to do."

"I understand."

Of course he did. "Of course you do."

"I can't work out if I feel appreciated or taken for granted."

"A little of both?" I wriggled down and nuzzled into his neck. "I mean I guess I'm taking it for granted that you're going to be amazing. But that doesn't mean it's not amazing."

He gave an embarrassed little cough. "Thank you. Although I should add I'm not completely unconcerned. I know I've only met your father once, but I can't say he made a good impression."

"I don't think he likes you either."

"I'm sorry if I made things difficult for you."

"Don't be ridiculous." I de-nuzzled and kissed him instead. "You always make things better. And I'm not sure I'd be into anyone Jon Fleming actually got on with."

"Even so, I fear I've burned a bridge that didn't have to be burned."

"It was a shit bridge, Oliver. And I'm still not completely sure which side of it I want to be on."

"I'm sure you don't need to be told this," he said, after a moment, "but there's a chance he could hurt you again."

I twisted my head, gazing up at Oliver with the sort of intensity you could only really get away with when you were both in bed and mostly naked. "It's a very good chance, isn't it?"

"Again, I'm rather stating the obvious here, but I don't want you to be hurt."

"I'm not mad keen on it myself. I guess I just feel like…I'm in a place where even if it goes wrong, I'll be okay. Like it won't utterly wreck me."

"That's"—he gave me a slightly crooked smile—"strangely reassuring."

Sitting on Oliver's freshly made bed the next day, I was starting to think I might have overstated my case utterly-wrecking-me-wise. It had been comparatively easy in my sort-of-a-bit-fake-sort-of-a-bit-real boyfriend's arms to claim I was okay. I was not feeling okay right now. But eventually I got enough of my shit together to phone Jon Fleming on the number he'd had his people send my people. Well, me. I'm kind of my own people.

"Jon here," rumbled my dad, with the confidence of man who knows he's the only Jon that matters.

"Um. Hi. It's me."

"Me who? It's not a good time, I'm about to go on set."

"Me your son. You know, the one you want to connect with."

"Yeah, yeah, I'll be there in a minute." Oh, he wasn't talking to me, was he? "What was that, Luc?"

"I was just ringing to say—"

"Yeah. No. That's great, thanks. Appreciate it." Still not talking to me.

"Look," I said, "if you want to meet up, I'm free sometime this week."

"I'd like that. How about Wednesday? Do you know The Half Moon in Camden?"

"Well, no, but I can Google it."

"I'll see you there at seven. On my way, Jamie."

And he was gone. If I'd been superstitious, I would have said it wasn't the best sign that the last thing he'd said to me was "On my way, Jamie" but I guess I was committed now. And I had an appointment with Jon Fleming. My dad. On my own. So he could maybe tell me he was sorry he left me.

There was no way that was happening, was there?

My first instinct, born from years of practice, was to… Actually, I didn't know. Five years ago, I'd have gone out, got wasted, and got laid. Six months ago I'd have gone home, got drunk, and got under my duvet. Now I just wanted to be with Oliver.

And I could? Because he was downstairs?

This semblance of a healthy lifestyle was going to take some getting used to.

I found him sitting at the kitchen table, elaborately hand-wrapping a wholesale carton of Kinder Happy Hippos.

"I can't believe," I said, "I ever thought you were boring."

He gave me what I'd come to recognise as his "I'm not sure if I'm supposed to be insulted" look. "You mean because when I give somebody a gift, I like to pay attention to its presentation?"

"I'm not being sarcastic, Oliver. This is delightfully strange of you and not what I was expecting to see today."

"I'm wrapping a present. What on earth is strange about that?"

"It's the fact you're going full *Love Actually* cinnamon stick on a job-lot of cheap German chocolate."

He gave a little cough. "Italian."

"What?"

"It's Italian."

"Isn't *Kinder* German for 'child'?"

"Yes, but the company is based in Italy."

"I'm so glad we're focusing on what matters here." I folded myself into a chair opposite him. "What. Are. You. Doing?"

"It's for Jennifer's birthday."

"Oh yes," I affirmed convincingly. "That is a thing I definitely remembered."

He gave me one of those annoying looks that people give when they're not disappointed because they know and care about you, instead of not being disappointed because they have incredibly low expectations. "How was your father?"

"Dick like always." I fiddled pointlessly with the vase of newly refreshed table flowers. "And I know I'm trying to be better at this, but I really don't want to talk about it."

"You don't have to. And I'd understand if you weren't feeling up to the party tonight."

"No, I want to. If only for the expression on your friend's face when she discovers you've bought her five hundred loosely hippo-themed wafer treats filled with a gooey substance that vaguely resembles chocolate."

He blinked petulantly. "It's not chocolate. It's a milk and hazelnut cream. And they're what I always get her."

"And yet somehow you remain friends?"

"She likes them. And it's sort of a tradition."

I ran my toes up his shin. "I somehow thought you'd be too... grown-up or something to have a shit gift ritual."

"I think you'll find I can be just as quirky as you can, Lucien."

He haughtily attached a sprig of lavender to his exquisite creation. "When I choose to be."

"Yeah, but I thought straight people were into, y'know, bottles of wine. Or, I don't know, toast racks."

He covered his mouth with his hand. I wasn't sure if he was laughing or appalled. "Lucien, you work with heterosexuals. Your mother is heterosexual. Bridget is heterosexual."

"Yeah, and I always buy them wine."

"But"—he actually wagged a finger at me—"and please be honest with me when you answer this question: never *toast racks*."

I sank lower in my chair and nearly wound up on the floor. "I...I...panicked, okay? Yes, I know some straight people. But I've never chosen to hang out socially with a large number of them all at once. I'm scared."

"What do you think they're going to do? Put bees on your face?"

"I don't know. What if they don't like me? And think you should go out with a woman or a better gay?"

"They're my friends, Lucien. They'll be happy I'm happy."

I stared at him. "You're...you're happy? I make you happy? That's a thing I do?"

"You know it is. Just maybe don't grill them about their toast racks. They might think you're a tad peculiar."

This opened a whole new chasm of anxieties. "What *do* I talk to them about, then? I don't watch any sports."

"Well, neither do most of them. Jennifer's a human rights lawyer who likes hippos. Peter's a children's illustrator who likes Jennifer. They're just people. I've known them for a long time. And at no point have they threatened to ostracise me if I couldn't tell them...tell them..." He paused for a long moment, frowning. "I was going to cite some obscure piece of sporting information, but, as you can see, I don't know any and that's perfectly all right."

I sighed. "Fine. So I'm being silly."

"You are, but explicably so. And you are being rather charming about it."

"I think," I admitted, "I'm fixating on the straight thing because...these people are important to you. And I don't want to fuck this up."

"The way I see it"—it was Oliver's gravest voice so I braced myself for an onslaught of sincerity—"either you won't, which will be nice. Or you will, which will be funny."

I burst out laughing.

And then, pushing the beautifully wrapped hippos gently aside, leaned over the table to kiss him.

CHAPTER 36

THAT EVENING, I WAS STANDING with Oliver and an over-decorated box of hippos on the doorstep of a very suburban-looking house in Uxbridge. And I already felt incredibly out of place.

"Is this okay?" I asked. "Am I okay? Am I dressed okay?"

"You're fine. This is a nice, relaxed evening. Everyone's going to be very casual and very normal and—"

The door swung open, revealing a stunningly put-together redhead, wearing a full-length evening gown and an actual fucking fascinator. At which point, my mouth also swung open.

"Oliver," she cried. "I'm so happy you could make it. And you've brought Luc. At least, I assume it's Luc." Her eyes widened. "Crap. You are Luc, right?"

I was trying, without much subtlety or success, to hide behind Oliver. This was clearly not the kind of party to wear my artfully ripped jeans to. "Um. Yes. That's me."

"Come in. Come in. Brian and Amanda are already here, because of course they are. And Bridge is running late because of course she is."

We came in, me pulling at Oliver's elbow like a small child at the supermarket in order to signal precisely how little I had signed up for this. A man in full black tie met us at the door to the living room.

"Hi," he said, presenting a silver tray with a teetering pyramid of Ferrero Rocher on it. "And be careful because this is actually quite unstable."

Once again, I tried to safe-word to Oliver with my eyes. But he seemed to be taking this totally in his stride, gently plucking a chocolate from the stack. "Monsieur." It was his driest, most laconic voice which, believe me, was pretty fucking dry and laconic. "With these Rocher, you are really spoiling us."

The guy nearly spilled his tray in excitement. "Thank you. Brian completely fluffed it. And this took hours."

"You know," called a deep voice from within, "you can buy them in pyramids now."

"Shut up, Brian. You have forfeited your right to have an opinion on this."

"Peter," said Oliver, as we were ushered past the Ferrero Rocher and into the living room, "please tell me that this whole evening isn't going to be a sequence of pointlessly elaborate '90s references."

"No." Jennifer gave him a wounded look. "Some of it's pointlessly elaborate '80s references."

Laughing, he hugged her. "Happy birthday, darling. Just no Twister and no Pokémon."

"How do you feel"—her eyes glinted—"about Pogs?"

He glanced at me. "I'm sorry, Lucien. These are my friends. I'm not exactly sure how that happened."

"Hey," protested Jennifer. "It's my birthday. If I want to dress up like an idiot and make you all eat prawn cocktail in celebration of the decades that spawned me, that's my choice, and you will damn well support it."

"You could have at least warned me. I've been trying to convince this man I'm cool."

She sighed. "Oh, Oliver. Even when the word 'cool' was cool, cool people didn't use it."

While she was completely right, I felt I should at least try to defend my ambiguously fake boyfriend from his definitely real friends. "Not true. Bart Simpson said 'cool.'"

"Bart Simpson was a fictional ten-year-old," pointed out the man who had failed to Rocher correctly. Brian, was it?

"I'm not sure," Oliver interjected, "I'm comfortable being compared to Bart Simpson."

I was probably going to get dumped. But there was really no other response. "Don't have a cow, man," I said, at exactly the same time everybody else did.

"You know"—Oliver put his arm around my waist—"Lucien was concerned that he wouldn't have anything in common with you. He clearly failed to account for the fact that mocking me is everybody's favourite pastime."

Jennifer snuck a curious look at me. "Were you, Luc? We were all worried we were going to scare off another of Oliver's boyfriends."

"We don't scare them off." This was Brian, again, in the too jolly tone of someone about to be slightly more insulting than he intends to be. "Oliver does."

"I'll admit"—Oliver had tensed up beside me so I thought it was a good moment to launch myself into the conversation—"that the evening gown did throw me. But I'm totally here for a...a... whatever this is."

Jennifer thought about it for a moment. "Well, I'm not quite sure what it is, actually. It's a sort of celebration of things eight-year-old me thought thirty-year-old me would have in the future. Except I thought we'd be having this party on the moon."

"Now then." Peter clapped his hands in a hosty kind of way. "Can I get either of you a drink? We've got Lambrini, Bacardi Breezers, Cointreau, some things that are actually nice. And Amanda's in the kitchen with mead."

I blinked. "Did I miss the '90s mead boom?"

"We're reenactors," explained Brian. "We *never* don't bring mead. Also they didn't say *which* '90s."

Oliver drifted over to one of the sofas and drew me down next to him. "I'll have one of the things that are actually nice."

"You"—I poked his knee—"are not in the spirit. What flavour breezers do you have?"

Peter perked up. "Good question. I think...some pink ones? And maybe some orange ones? And possibly a slightly different orange one that might be peach?"

"I'll take the slightly different orange one."

"Coming right up. And I'll see what's happened to Amanda."

"And Peter," cried Jennifer, "bring the vol-au-vents. Or is it vols-au-vent?"

"I think technically..." A woman, who looked remarkably like Brian, apart from the beard—as in Brian had the beard, not the woman—appeared in the doorway "...it would be volent-au-vent. Because vol-au-vent is from the French 'to fly in the wind.' And so the plural would be 'they fly in the wind,' which would be 'ils volent au vent.'"

The conversation ricocheted off the way conversations between people who've known each other far too long tend to. And even though I didn't know what the "infamous digger incident" was or what happened at Amanda's twenty-eighth, I felt surprisingly un-left-out. I mean, I did go through a short routine of emotional gymnastics, remembering how I'd freaked out when we'd gone to dinner with Alex and Miffy, and being slightly protective of the closeness I had with Oliver in private. Especially since he tended to be so buttoned up and polite in public. But, actually, it was nice to see him happy and relaxed, and surrounded by people who cared about him.

Eventually the doorbell rang, and Peter took up his Fererro Rocher station. I assumed this was going to be some people I hadn't met because I'd had a message from Bridge saying she was five minutes away, which meant she'd be at least another hour. Voices drifted in from the corridor.

"God, sorry we're late," boomed somebody about two shades posher than me and three shades less posh than Alex. "The twins were absolute shits. Shit, by the way, being the operative... Oh monsieur, with this Rocher you're really spoiling us."

"Suck it, Brian." That was probably Peter.

"Please," continued the posh man, "for Christ's sake, bring me some alcohol. And be careful when you're hanging up my jacket. I think one of the little bastards threw up on it."

"I told you when they were born"—another stranger, a woman this time—"we should have left them on a hillside overnight and kept whichever one survived."

There was a flapping of coats and a shuffling of shoes, and Jennifer and Peter came back into the room, followed by a surprisingly dapper man in a plum waistcoat and a small, round woman in a polka-dot lindy-hop dress.

Oliver—who wasn't so relaxed as to forget his manners—stood to greet them. "Ben, Sophie, this is Luc—he's my boyfriend. Luc, this is Ben, who's a stay-at-home dad, and Sophie, who is Satan."

"I'm not Satan," she huffed. "I'm Beelzebub at worst."

"Jennifer?" Oliver made a slightly imperious gesture. "Who was your last client?"

Sophie rolled her eyes. They'd clearly played this game a lot.

"A refugee from Brunei, who'd have been tortured if he'd been deported." Jennifer lifted her glass of Lambrini in a toast-like gesture. "Yours, Oliver?"

"A barman who stole from an employer who cheated him. Yours, Sophie?"

She mumbled something incoherent.

"What was that? We didn't hear you."

"Fine." She threw her hands in the air. "It was a pharmaceutical company whose drugs, let me be very clear, cannot be proven to have killed any children at all. What can I say? I like clients who can actually pay."

"Just to check," I asked, having slowly come to the realisation that Oliver's friends being straight was not the only thing that made them different from my friends, "am I the only person in this room who isn't either a lawyer or married to a lawyer?"

Peter reverentially returned the wobbly Ferrero Rocher to the Ferrero Rocher table. "Well, you could fix that. It is legal now."

"By which I think he means"—Amanda looked up from the sofa, where she'd been sitting largely on top of her husband—"that it would be legal for you to marry Oliver. Not that it would be legal to kill every lawyer in the room, whatever Shakespeare had to say on the subject."

"What?" cried Peter, comically startled. "Why would you go there? Obviously I meant marriage. Not murder."

"Tell me that again when those three have been talking jurisprudence for three hours."

Oliver cleared his throat—he'd gone a little pink. "I know you're all terribly excited I have a boyfriend. But I think that dropping the M-bomb at this stage in my relationship would be an excellent way to ensure I don't have one for much longer."

"Sorry." Peter hung his head. "I wasn't actually...I didn't mean... please don't break up with him, Luc... Have another Ferrero Rocher."

"And for the record," Oliver went on, "just because I have legal right to do something doesn't mean I actually have to do it. Especially not with someone I've been dating for less than two months. No offence, Luc."

I pulled dramatically out of his arms. "Are you fucking kidding me? What am I going to do with the dress?"

This earned a proportionate laugh and made me feel like I was boyfriending appropriately.

"Shall we not"—Jennifer threw the room a stern look—"attempt to make anyone feel comfortable by suggesting they get married. We're actually thrilled to bits you're here, Luc. And the good news is only some of us are lawyers."

"Yes." Ben was pouring himself a glass of the good wine. "I live off my wife. It's extremely modern and feminist of me."

"And I did law at university," added Brian, "with Morecombe, Slant, and Honeyplace over here. Thankfully, I realised it was fucking awful and I was shit at it, and went into IT."

"As for me—" began Peter, before he was interrupted by the doorbell. "That'll be Bridget."

Jennifer went to let her in and Bridge burst into the front room, still taking off her coat, a few seconds later.

"You are not," she cried, "going to believe what's happened."

The room got about halfway through a chorus of "Careful, Bridge" when the hem of her jacket caught Peter's lovingly stacked pile of Ferrero Rocher and sent them flying, bouncing, and rolling across the floor.

She spun round. "Oh my gosh. What was that?"

"Nothing." Peter sighed. "Don't worry about it."

He, Ben, and Tom—who had followed Bridget in—began to gather up the wreckage of the Ambassador's Reception.

"What's happened?" asked pretty much everyone.

"Well, I can't really talk about it, but we've recently acquired a very promising new author who specialises in high-concept science fiction. And it got a starred review in *Publishers Weekly* and everything, and there were some wonderful pull quotes and the one we decided to run with especially recommended it to fans of another, more famous author of high-concept science fiction. So we put it on all the posters and there's big campaign all over the

Underground and it's on the front of the book and it's too late to change any of it."

Oliver was looking perplexed in a way that made me want to hug him. "That seems unalloyedly positive, Bridget."

"It would be." She threw herself into the nearest free chair. "Except the more famous author in question was Philip K. Dick. And the pull quote was 'If you like Dick, you'll love this.' And no one spotted it until we started getting extremely disappointed reviews on Amazon."

Peter glanced up from the Ferrero Rocher carnage with an expression somewhere between playful and speculative. "Just out of curiosity, how are the sales?"

"Surprisingly good, actually. I think it might have crossover appeal." She spotted me. "Oh, Luc, you're here."

I grinned at her. "I'm a plus-one."

"I don't believe it." Jennifer Wimbledoned between me and Bridge. "Oliver brings his new boyfriend to my party, and I think, finally, I beat you to relationship gossip. Then it turns out you've already met."

Bridge looked, and there's no other word for it, smug. "Of course. Luc's my best friend and Oliver's the only other gay man I know. I've been trying to get them to date for years."

CHAPTER 37

IT TOOK ABOUT TEN MINUTES but eventually we all managed to cram ourselves round a dining table that was strictly designed for six, eight at a push, and taking the piss at ten.

"I will admit," said Jennifer as she wheeled a desk chair in from God knew where, "I was slightly banking on a couple of people cancelling at the last minute."

Brian manoeuvred his mead glass into position amongst the tangles of cutlery. "At the very least, you'd think Oliver would have driven his boyfriend off by now."

"With friends like you, Brian"—Oliver gave a sigh that I worried signalled more than amused exasperation—"who needs opposing counsel."

At which point, Amanda elbowed her husband sharply in the ribs. "Get with the programme, dude. Right now we're in the happy-for-you space. In six to eight days, we'll be in the mocking-you space."

Oliver had just enough room to put his head in his hands. "Please stop helping."

"*Anyway*." That was Jennifer. "Awkward as this is, I like to feel that 'slightly more friends than you can fit around your table' is exactly the right number of friends to have. So I want to thank you all for having managed to avoid work crises, childcare emergencies—"

Some polyphonic bells rang out from Ben's breast pocket and he leapt to his feet, nearly clocking Tom in the head on the way. "Fuck. Babysitter. I bet the little fuckers have burned the house down."

And, with that, he ran out of the room.

"—*mostly* avoid childcare emergencies," Jennifer continued.

Sophie finished her wine. "Darling, that's not an emergency. That's our life now."

"Tell you what." Jennifer made a *fuck this* gesture. "Let's pretend I did a speech. I love you all. Let's eat."

Peter sailed in from the kitchen, bearing a tray of martini glasses full of gunge and lettuce. "To start," he announced in his best *MasterChef* voice, "prawn cocktail. And I'm sorry, Oliver, we thought about you for the main, but we couldn't be buggered to do a veggie starter so we just didn't put the prawns in yours."

"You mean," said Oliver, "I'm starting my evening with a glass of pink mayonnaise."

"Wow. Yes, we really screwed you on that one."

Bridge and Tom had been whispering quietly to one another, but now she looked up in confusion. "Wait a minute. Why are we having prawn cocktail? Nobody's eaten prawn cocktail for twenty years. And, actually, why are we all drinking Bacardi Breezers?"

"Apparently"—Sophie had poured herself yet another glass of the good wine—"this whole party is nonconsensually retro-themed."

Jennifer squirmed sheepishly. "The thing is, I didn't want people to feel pressured to do costumes or, well, make any effort at all. So I decided to make it a surprise. So...*surprise?*"

We settled down to remind ourselves why people stopped eating prawn cocktail. Spoiler: the reason is because it's horrible. Fortunately, we all seemed to agree on that, so nobody felt compelled to politely eat it anyway.

"Don't worry." Peter began to clear up around us. "I think the main course should actually be edible. It's beef Wellington, except

Oliver, who gets mushroom Wellington which, I'll be honest, we sort of made up."

Oliver handed back his largely untouched glass of pink mayonnaise. "Which is to say the main course should be edible for everyone except me."

"I'm sorry, Oliver." Peter gazed at him with mock contrition. "But you should have stuck at being our only gay friend. Trying to be our only vegetarian friend as well is frankly pushing it."

"You know," I said, "the mushrooms sound lovely. If there's enough, I'll have some too."

Bridge actually made a squee noise. "And you used to be so grumpy and unromantic."

"I've never been grumpy and unromantic. I've occasionally been"—I tried to think of something—"brooding and cynical."

"And now Oliver's brought out your inner marshmallow."

"I'm eating a mushroom, not jumping down the bleachers singing, 'I Can't Take My Eyes Off You.'"

Jennifer toasted me with a Smirnoff Ice. "Good on theme reference."

We were just dishing up the Wellingtons, both of which were enormous, when Ben came back looking haggard.

"Drink me." He collapsed next to Sophie. "In the 'give me a drink' sense, not in the *Alice in Wonderland* sense."

She drinked him. "Everything all right, darling?"

"We're going to have to give Eva another raise. Twin A went missing and she looked all over the house for him, and was about to call the police, when she glanced out the window and saw him in next door's kitchen between the cooker and the knife rack."

"I take it he was fine?"

"Sadly yes. Neighbours are a bit traumatised, though."

Sophie rolled her eyes. "We'll send them a gift basket. You know, like the last three times."

We got on with eating for a while. Despite the warnings, the mushroom Wellington was honestly...fine? I mean, it would probably have been improved by the addition of beef but, then, most things are. Unfortunately, this also brought us to my least favourite part of the "meeting other people's social circles" experience: the bit where they decide they've got to take an interest in you for the sake of their friend.

"You're," Brian kicked off, "some kind of...rock star? Is that right?"

I nearly lost a mouthful of Wellington. "No. Very much not. My dad's a rock star. My mum used to be a rock star. I'm, like, the opposite of a rock star."

"A scissors planet?" suggested Amanda after way less thought than it should have taken.

"Um. Yes? Or maybe...no?"

"That makes more sense." Brian gently shifted his beard braids away from the gravy. "I wasn't sure what a rock star would be doing with Oliver."

"What is wrong with you this evening?" This was not Oliver's "you are teasing me and I secretly like it" voice. This was Oliver's "I am properly upset now" voice. "Are you trying to make me look as unattractive as possible in front of a man I actually like?"

"Ignore him, Oliver," said Jennifer. "He's overcompensating for ten years of being the single one."

Oliver still had that prim, icy look about him. "I'm not sure that makes his behaviour acceptable."

"I'm sorry." The table was too small for expansive movements, but it didn't stop Brian from trying. "I really am. It's just you've dated a lot of people and they've never been right for you and I want to know what makes this guy different before you get hurt again."

"I'm not your teenage daughter," snapped Oliver. "And

thinking about it, even if I were your teenage daughter, the way you're acting would still be deeply controlling and weird."

"He's right, dude." Amanda gave her husband a disappointed look. "You're being a prick."

"I ... Sorry."

There was a long silence.

Until Oliver eventually sighed and said, "It's fine. I suppose it's sweet that you care. In a profoundly unhelpful way."

I felt suddenly and intensely shit. Because I was sitting here, eating these people's food and drinking their Bacardi, watching them be all excited and hopeful that their friend—who they obviously cared deeply about, and who'd apparently been more miserable than I'd noticed—was finally happy.

And the whole thing sort of still had an expiration date.

For a while now, I'd been living quietly with the knowledge that I was probably going to be a bit messed up when...if...this ended. It hadn't occurred to me that it might mess Oliver up too.

"So." Sophie changed the subject with the poise and dignity of somebody who'd drunk entirely too much to give a fuck. "If not a rock star, what do you do?"

"I'm a fundraiser for a charity."

"Oh, of course you are. Oliver, why are your boyfriends always so drearily ethical?"

"Don't worry." I slanted a secret grin at Oliver. "I'm not ethical at all. I used to be in PR before I got fired for becoming the story. And now I work for the only people who'll have me."

"That's far better. Keep this one, darling. He's a lot more interesting than the others."

"Yes." Oliver lifted a brow. "Appeasing my evillest friend is exactly what I look for in a boyfriend."

"You joke, but it should be." Her attention flicked back to me. "What's your charity trying to save-slash-prevent?"

"Um. Dung beetles?"

She blinked. "Normally this would be obvious, but saving or preventing?"

"Actually"—Oliver gave my knee a squeeze under the table—"they're extremely ecologically important. They aerate soil."

"My children are six miles away, I've had an awful lot of wine, and Oliver seems to want me to care about dirt. I'm doing my best, but"—Sophie wafted her glass solicitously—"does anybody have a fuck I can borrow because I'm fresh out."

The part of my brain that had actually been showing up to work recently kicked in before I could stop it. "Look, I can absolutely help you find a fuck to give, but I'm very aware that I'm at someone else's birthday party and probably shouldn't be fishing for donors."

"No, please fish Sophie." Jennifer flashed a smile at me across the table. "She's got pots of money and doesn't deserve any of it."

"Excuse me, I work very hard for my morally bankrupt clients. But go on, charity man"—Sophie propped her chin on her palm and gazed at me challengingly—"land me."

I gave Sophie a once-over. Remarkably together despite the truly stupendous amount she'd drunk. From her choice of dress, she liked people to underestimate her and, from the way she spoke, she liked to remind them that they had. There was a strategy that would probably work here, but it was risky.

"Okay," I said. "I'm guessing that you donate to charity for exactly two reasons, which are tax breaks and sticking it to your do-gooder friends. I could try to explain to you why dung beetles are a vital part of the country's ecology, but clearly you don't care. And that's okay. So instead I'll tell you this: any arsehole with a credit card can give money to puppies with cancer or toys for sad children, but nothing says 'I have thought about my charitable donations better than you have' like giving your money to an environmentally vital but fundamentally unattractive insect. In the 'who's best at philanthropy game,' the person with the most obscure charity wins. Always. And you do not get more obscure than us."

There was a pause. A deeply uncomfortable pause that lasted just long enough for me to wonder how badly I'd blown it.

Then Sophie's lips twisted into a gleeful smirk. "Sold. How much do you need?"

Ben burst out laughing.

And I wasn't sure where to go from here. "Um. Great. That's great. But given you're really pissed right now, and you're Oliver's friend, and I don't want him to be cross with me—"

"I'm perfectly happy," he interrupted. "Bleed her dry."

"Even so, I do actually have some professional ethics. You can ring me tomorrow if you want or I can call you or we can set up a lunch or, y'know, there's a big do next week, where you can come and hang out with posh people and throw all your money at us if that's how you're feeling."

"You have a Dung Beetle Do?"

"Yeah, we call it the Beetle Drive. Aren't we adorable?"

Another pause.

"I feel compelled to point out," said Sophie finally, "that you've just refused to take money from me now because I'm drunk. But you've invited me to a party where you presumably try to get a lot of people drunk and then ask them for money."

"Yeah, it's not unethical if you print invitations."

"Then I suppose I'll see you there."

The table broke into only slightly sarcastic applause.

"Anyway"—Jennifer began to help Peter clear the table—"to bring things back to *my birthday*, do people need a pause before dessert?"

Brian stroked his beard. "Very much depends on what dessert is."

"It's a surprise."

"Does that mean it's something we're all going to hate?"

"Ooh." A thought struck Amanda. "Is it Angel Delight?"

A different thought appeared to have struck Ben, who shuddered theatrically. "If it's Black Forest Gateau, I'm leaving."

The frozen dessert banter looked set to continue for a while, which a couple of people seemed to read as a cue to stretch their legs and take bathroom breaks. I was more or less happy where I was, but then Oliver leaned over, and whispered to me that I should come outside a moment.

Oh shit. I shouldn't have tried to develop his friend. What the fuck was wrong with me?

Feeling distinctly chastised, I trailed Oliver into the hall.

"Look," I started, "I'm sorry I—"

At which point he pressed me against the wall and kissed me.

It was fair to say we'd done a decent amount of kissing since putting it on the boyfriend menu, but it hadn't been like this since my *Guardian*-related freak-out. I was beginning to think dumping him had put him off me somehow. And while I'd have really liked to get back to how things had been that night on my sofa—the sweet, sharp certainty of wanting, and being wanted—I'd been wary of pushing my luck. We hadn't managed to see each other for most of the week, and it was hard to expect a guy to look at you as a passionate and intensely sexual being when your last two meetings had involved crying on a bathroom floor and an exhibition of glass sculptures. But, apparently, being moderately supportive at a party and trying to make one of his friends give money to dung beetles had done the job just fine.

In any case, I was here for it. Very, *very* here for it.

As, briefly, was someone else who told us to get a room on his way to the loo.

But fuck it. These weren't *yeah whatever* kisses. They weren't *take it or leave it, get your coat you've pulled* kisses. They were everything I thought I could never have, everything I'd been pretending I never wanted, telling me that I was worth it, that he'd be there for me and put up with me, and wouldn't let me drive him away.

Oliver Blackwood was giving all that to me, and I was giving it right back. In the clutch of hands and the press of bodies and the urgent heat of his mouth on mine.

And when it stopped, it still wasn't over, because he sort of kept staring at me, his eyes all shiny, as his thumbs brushed lightly over my cheeks. "Oh, Lucien."

"I, um, I take it you're not cross about Sophie, then?"

"On the contrary, it was very impressive. I hope you're not having a terrible evening."

"No, it's...really nice.."

"They like you, you know?" He kissed me again, more gently this time. "You can tell by the way they're being total dicks."

I laughed. "I should probably introduce you to my total dicks as well."

"I'd like that. I mean, if you think...I'd reflect positively on you."

"Oliver"—I was feeling way too soppy to give him a withering look but I tried anyway—"my friends know who I am. Of course you'd reflect positively on me."

"Sorry. I just...I'm glad you came with me tonight."

"Me too. I haven't had a Bacardi Breezer in years." I paused, savouring his reaction. "And this bit didn't suck either."

"Well, I'm glad I at least outrank the prawn cocktail."

Pulling him close again, I nipped playfully at the edge of his jaw, where he was all stern and square. "We should go back."

"Actually"—a faint flush darkened his cheeks—"I was rather minded to take you home."

"Why. Are you not feeling... Oh. *Oh.*"

"I mean, if that's agreeable."

It was the wrong time. But I had to. "I thought you said that *wasn't* the title of your sex tape."

"I lied." One of his little coughs. "Now, let's see if we can make our excuses and leave discreetly."

Having met Oliver's friends for all of ten seconds, I did not rate our chances of running home to shag without their knowing exactly what we were up to and commenting on it accordingly.

And I was super right.

CHAPTER 38

THE ETHICALLY SOURCED MINICAB THAT Oliver called to take us home took far too long to take us home. Partly because I was—to use the technical term—horny, but mostly because, the more I thought about it, the more nervous I was getting. Oliver had made it very clear that he did not take sex lightly, and I'd made kind of a lifestyle out of *only* taking it lightly. And, obviously at the back of my mind, I'd been hoping he'd eventually surrender to my naked, animal charisma and give me one, but now that it was happening…it didn't feel quite like I'd thought it would. I mean, yes, it was exciting, and sexy, and he liked me, he really liked me, but what if I fucked it up? What if I wasn't very good? I'd had no complaints but nobody looked a gift blow job in the mouth, so maybe—like every other aspect of my life—I'd just been coasting on other people's low expectations.

The thing about a hookup, the thing I *liked* about hookups, was that it was pretty clear whose job it was to get who off. Those 'whos' being "you" and "yourself" respectively. When you, y'know, cared about someone, you started caring about confusing nonsense like if it was good for them, and how they felt, and what it meant. And what if we got back to Oliver's perfect house and we lay down on his perfect sheets and we did the sex and it was… fine? I'd told him before that fine was all he could expect from me and he'd said fine wasn't enough for him, and now it wasn't enough for me, either, but what if it was all I could manage?

Oliver was far too dignified to actually run for the front door, but he certainly got his hustle on. And we'd barely made it into the hallway before he was on me like I was a vegan brownie, and I was pulling him close, and we were kissing again. Which was great—we'd definitely got the kissing down—but also took everything I'd been stressing about in the taxi and made it horribly real and immediate.

After all, this was supposed to be my bag. I'd spent years getting my debauch on, in and out of the papers, and yet here I was with a guy I was really into and really *really* wanted to be into me, and I was reduced to the sexual sophistication of a teenager in a John Hughes movie. On the admittedly more than a few occasions I'd imagined getting to this point with Oliver, I'd been a creative and considerate lover, and blown his mind with my astounding array of sex moves. Instead, I was clinging and grinding and making, if I'm honest, slightly embarrassing moaning noises. Oh God. Help. This had no right to feel so perfect.

Suddenly, Oliver's weight shifted and, for a handful of awful seconds, I thought I'd put him off somehow. But then he hoisted me into his arms and I was such a weird combination of relieved and lust-addled that—rather than asking what the hell he was playing at—I wrapped my legs around him like a twink in a porno. With a strength I shouldn't have found surprising given his commitment to a healthy lifestyle, he started carrying me towards the bedroom. It was this perfect magical fantasy moment, right up until he pitched forward and dropped me on the stairs.

"Um," I said. "Ow."

Looking flustered and adorable, Oliver reversed off me like a minibus in a cul-de-sac. "I'm so sorry. I don't know what I was thinking."

"No, no, it's cool. It was briefly very sexy and romantic."

"You're not hurt, are you?"

"I'm okay. Bit self-conscious about being too heavy to carry."

I'd been joking but, of course, Oliver got terribly serious in case he'd accidentally body-shamed me as well as accidentally body-slamming me. "It doesn't reflect on you at all. I overestimated my ability to handle the stairs."

"Good to know. Now will you stop being reassuring and fuck me?"

"I will fuck you, Lucien"—he'd gone all stern and, for once, it didn't bother me at all—"in the manner of my choosing."

I stared at him wide-eyed and blatantly into…whatever this was. "Steady on, I didn't sign up for Fifty Shades of Gay."

"No, you signed up for me. Now go upstairs and get on the bed."

I…went upstairs and got on the bed?

A few seconds later, Oliver appeared in the doorway, dropping his coat on the floor. And, I mean, wow. I had never seen him not use a hanger. He must have been really into this. Into me?

"I'm sorry," he said, blushing a little. "I've never thought…I…that is…you…"

"Don't apologise. It's, um, interesting."

He blushed even harder. "I've actually wanted to do this for rather a long time."

"Just throwing this out there"—I scowled at him—"you absolutely could have, at any point."

"I suppose I thought you were worth waiting for."

Shit. I hoped he was right. "I'm not the last After Eight mint."

"Well no." He joined me on the bed, crawling across the covers like a tiger who'd been to Abercrombie and Fitch. "If you were, we'd all be too polite to take you."

"I'd have a witty comeback, but I'm kinda distracted right now."

"You do seem," he said dryly, "to be markedly less intransigent when you have an erection."

"Yes, it's my Achilles' penis."

Laughing, Oliver started unbuttoning my shirt. Which was, on the one hand, good because it got me closer to naked and, therefore, closer to laid. On the other hand, I was about to be topless. And it wasn't like Oliver hadn't seen me topless before, but this was one of those context-is-everything situations. Being naked and being *made* naked felt distinctly and scarily different. Normally, I didn't especially worry what my sexual partners thought about my body, but then normally my sexual partners were strangers.

In an effort to balance the scales, I returned the favour and realised I'd made a tremendous strategic error. Because while I got by on genetics, height, and walking to work, Oliver bothered to take care of himself. It was the sexual equivalent of someone getting you a really thoughtful secret Santa gift when you knew you'd bought them a bath bomb.

"Should I go to the gym?" I asked. "Like, ever? Because otherwise you're going to have to get used to me being monumentally average."

"You are many things, Lucien. But you could never be average."

"No, this is a physical thing and believe me—"

"Stop it." He kissed me, hard enough to smother my protests, his palm gliding over the exposed skin of my torso and leaving a pattern of fresh warmth. "You're beautiful. So beautiful I can't believe I'm finally getting to touch you."

I wanted to say something suave and witty to show I was... suave and witty, and not a pile of melt. But all I managed was, "F-fuck, Oliver."

"God." His voice roughened. "I love how responsive you are. Look..."

His fingertips spiralled up my arm and across my shoulder, goose bumps springing up in his wake like they were doing a stadium wave. I tried to make a noise that, somehow, signalled

Yep, this is how I am with everybody, certainly not just you, but then his mouth got involved, laying pleasure over pleasure over pleasure, and I... Shit. I think I whimpered.

"The things," he murmured, "I've dreamed of doing to you."

I blinked. Maybe I could salvage this before I fell apart. "Why? Are they filthy?"

"Nothing like that." He pushed me onto my back, his hands unbuckling my belt, and pulling off my jeans, boxers and socks in a flurry of very Oliver efficiency. "I just want to be with you. Like this. I want to make you feel things. Good things. For me."

He was gazing at me, with this terrible earnestness, meaning every word. And, y'know, it was fine, I could cope with this, I could have feelings, it was fine. Never mind that there was this sense of nakedness settling over me, strangely independent of the fact that I was actually naked. And never mind that every time he touched me it was like he was unmaking me with tenderness. And definitely never mind that I needed this so badly I wasn't sure how to have it.

Now Oliver was shedding the rest of his clothes, shirt and trousers and everything else, landing messily by the side of the bed. I'd almost forgotten what it was like for a moment like this to mean something—the first time you saw a partner undressed, how they both gained and lost mystery, the truth of them, all their secrets and imperfections, surpassing any fantasy you could have conjured. The strangest thing was that Oliver had seemed so unreal to me at first. I'd wanted him from the beginning—from that horrible encounter at that horrible party—but the way you'd want a watch in a jeweller's shop window. A kind of frustrated admiration for something distant and perfect and just a little bit artificial.

But actually I hadn't seen him at all. Only a reflected bundle of badly thought-out desires. And Oliver was so much more than that: he was kind and complicated, and more anxious than he let on, if his texting style was anything to go by. I knew how to make him angry and how to make him laugh, and I hoped I could make him happy.

Or maybe I couldn't. Maybe I was too fucked up. But Oliver had stuck with me through my dad's bullshit and my mum's curry, he'd held my hand in front of reporters, and let me dump and undump him through a toilet door. He'd become one of the best parts of my life. And so I was fucking well going to try.

"Um," I heard myself say, "I want to be good for you too. I'm just not sure—"

He lowered himself over me, all heat and strength, and the perfect glide of skin. "You are. This is."

"But I—"

"Shhh. You don't have to *do* anything. You're enough. You're…"

I gazed at him, not sure what was coming next. From the look on his face, he probably wasn't either.

"Everything," he finished.

Well, this was…new. Having to deal with sex-feelings and feeling-feelings at the same time, teaming up to leave you all achy and open and hopeful.

His mouth covered mine, half kiss, half groan, and I flung my legs around him to draw him in closer. He seemed to find this encouraging, which was good because he was meant to. And soon he was driving our bodies together in this samba of promise and sensuality, his mouth painting me with shivery little kisses, and this was amazing—like "oh God stop, oh God never stop, oh God" level amazing—except, for whatever reason, I couldn't work out what to do with my hands. And suddenly I had these enormous alien mitts floating around at the end of my arms with no clear instructions. I mean, should I have been trying to get at his cock? Or was it too early? Did he mind having his hair stroked—or was that just weird? Was pulling it a bit much? Wow, his shoulders were really defined.

I'd finally settled on spreading my palms fretfully over Oliver's back when he reared up, caught my wrists, and bore them gently to the pillow on either side of my head. Which, admittedly, wasn't totally unhot.

"Um," I said.

"Sorry." A flush crept down his neck and across his chest. "I...can't seem to help myself."

It was strangely comforting to see Oliver even a little bit out of control. Even if it was in quite a controlling way. And at least I didn't have to worry about my hands anymore, although that might have been cheating. "It's...okay. I think I'm into it. I mean"—I gave a shaky laugh—"not if you're going to pull out your leathers and start telling me to call you Daddy."

He nipped at my throat in playful rebuke. "Oliver will be fine."

His fingers curled around mine, unexpectedly tender given he was on top and holding me down, as he leaned in for another kiss. I pushed against him, not because I wanted to get away, but to feel what it was like to be...inescapably held.

Not awful, as it turned out. When it was Oliver.

My movements turned squirmy. And I heard myself moaning softly. And, God help me, needily. Which was scary and embarrassing and weird.

"Please trust me, Lucien." In that moment, I was sort of relieved and sort of horrified to hear the vulnerability in Oliver's voice. "It's okay to have this."

"Then what are you having?"

"You." He smiled, eyes glinting silver. "I'm rather enjoying having you at my mercy."

And that was when I remembered something—how fucking good it could be, just to be with someone. To let them see you. To be enough.

"How about"—I strained up and kissed him. Well, bit him. Kissily—"less mercy, more having?"

He legit growled.

And things got excitingly rough for a while, my self-consciousness fleeing with Oliver's self-restraint. I made a few token efforts to wriggle free, but he always distracted me, with my name on his lips, or some fresh touch to a place I never knew could be so sensitive, and by the time he stopped holding me down, I was too far gone to notice.

There was only him and me, and the crumpling sheets, and the play of the streetlights through the curtains.

I was pinned by the sheer pleasure of it all—of Oliver's ragged breath and the stream of his caresses. Of his deep, deep kisses, ceaseless as the sky in summer. The drag and press of our bodies, the rub of hair and the glide of sweat.

And the way he was looking at me, tender and fierce, and almost...awestruck, like I was a different, better person.

Although maybe, just then, I was.

CHAPTER 39

WHAT WAS I THINKING? NOT only had I agreed to meet Jon Fucking Fleming at the busiest point in my working year, but now he was taking me away from my gorgeous nearly boyfriend who would otherwise be sexing me silly. I guess I was just that good a person.

To my surprise, The Half Moon turned out to be one of those craft beer places, all exposed brickwork and trying too hard. My dad was late—not that I'd really expected otherwise—so I got myself a pint of Monkey's Butthole, which apparently had notes of mango and pineapple, and a toasty bitterness that lingered right to the end, and found a spare table amongst the beards and ironic lumberjack shirts.

For a while I sat there, feeling like the sort of person who went out on his own to drink artisanal ales which, thinking about it, was probably a perfectly respected pastime in the artisanal-ale-drinking community. Oddly enough, this wasn't very comforting.

Having spent the past half-decade missing deadlines and then telling myself it was fine because my friends knew where they stood with me, I felt at once angry at my dad for pulling the same shit and angry at myself for taking so long to realise what a crappy way that was to treat people, and also for being hypocritical about it.

My phone buzzed. It was nice to know Oliver was thinking of me, but it was less nice that he'd apparently decided to think of me through the medium of an old, bald white man.

What the fuck, I texted. **I assume this is a dick?**

Yes.

Should I have any clue what kind of dick it is?

It's a political dick.

I liked this better when it was a flirty game instead of an actual general knowledge quiz

I'm sorry. Somehow Oliver could even make text come across as genuinely contrite. It's Dick Cheney.

How was I ever supposed to get that?

Contextual clues. I said it was political. How many Dicks are there in politics?

To make the obvious joke. Loads

There was a pause. It's also an I miss you dick.

That's a very specific flavour of dick

"You're here," said Jon Fleming, who was standing over me. "I wasn't sure you would be."

Speaking of, I typed, **Dad's here**

Reluctantly I put my phone away, and found—as ever—I had nothing to say to him. "Yes. Yes, I'm here."

"This has changed." He sounded genuinely peeved about it. "Can I get you anything from the bar?"

I had most of a Monkey's Butthole left, but my father had abandoned me when I was three and making him say "Monkey's Butthole" to a stranger might be the only revenge I'd ever get. I showed him the bottle. "I'll have another of these, thanks."

Heading to the counter, he scored the latest in a string of small, annoying victories by simply pointing at the drinks he wanted, and somehow making the gesture look dignified and commanding, instead of utterly petty. And then, sporting a second Butthole and a pint of Ajax Napalm, he made his way back to me. Given this was so clearly not what he'd been expecting, and that he was the oldest person in the building by a good thirty years, he looked infuriatingly non-out of place. I think it was the combination of everyone else trying to dress like they'd been rock stars in the seventies and that fucking awful charisma that made the world shape itself to him, not the other way around.

Fuck, it was going to be a long evening.

"You wouldn't believe"—he settled himself across from me—"that Mark Knopfler used to perform right over there."

"Oh, I believe it. I just don't care. Honestly, I'm not even"— okay, this was a lie, but I wanted to piss him off the teeniest bit—"completely sure who he is."

I'd definitely misjudged it. Not only did he know I was bullshitting him, but he also wasn't going to let that stop him giving me a long, self-serving rant about the history of the music scene. "When I first met Mark in '76, he and his brother were both on the dole and thinking about starting a band, so I took them to see Max Merritt and the Meteors here at the Moon. Back then, it was part of what we called the toilet circuit."

The problem with my dad—well, one of the many problems with my dad—was that when he talked like this, you really wanted to listen. "The what?"

"Bunch of dingy-as-hell venues up and down the country. Pubs, warehouses, that kind of thing. Places you'd play for the beer, and the exposure, and the love of it. It's where we all got our start in the day. Anyway, I took Mark to see Max Merritt and the Meteors, and what those guys could do with just two acoustic guitars and an electric keyboard… I think that was a real inspiration to him."

"Let me guess: you also said to him, 'Wow, it sounds like you're in dire straits.'"

He smiled. "So you did know who he was."

"Yeah, all right. I had an idea."

"Of course, it's all different now." He paused meditatively and took a swig of Ajax Napalm. "This actually isn't bad. Though in my day what you call craft ales we used to call beer." Another equally meditative pause. "Then the chains took over and the small breweries shut down, and everything was pressurised and standardised. And now we've forgotten where we came from, so a bunch of guys in their twenties are trying to sell back to us something we should have never given away in the first place." A third pause. He was really good at this. "It's a funny thing, the pendulum of the world."

"Is that," I asked, half-sincerely, half not, "what you're going to call your next album?"

He shrugged. "That depends on your mother. Your mother and the cancer."

"So, um, what's up with that? Are you okay?"

"Waiting for tests."

Oh fuck. For a split second, Jon Fleming just looked like a bald, old man drinking IPA from a fancy bottle. "Look, I'm... sorry about... It must be awful."

"It's what it is. And it's made me think about things I haven't in a long time."

A month or so ago I would have said "you mean, like the son you abandoned"? "Like what?" I said instead.

"The past. The future. The music."

I could almost pretend that I fit into "the past" but it wasn't much comfort.

"You see, it's like the beer. When I started out, we were just kids with big ideas playing on borrowed guitars for anyone who'd listen. Rights of Man recorded our first album on a busted-up eight-track in a garage. Then the studios swept in with their bubblegum pop and their bands of plastic children, and all the dirt and the heart went out of the business."

I'd read interviews with Jon Fleming, I'd listened to his songs,

I'd seen him on TV, so I knew that this was just how he talked. But it was different when it was him and you, and those intense blue-green eyes were looking right at you, and making it feel like he was telling you things he'd never tell anybody else.

"And now," he went on, with legendary melancholy, "we're back in the sheds and the bedrooms, and people are making albums on borrowed guitars on busted-up laptops, and putting them on Soundcloud and Spotify and YouTube for anyone who'll listen. And, suddenly, it's real again, and it's where I began, and where I can never go back to."

For once, I wasn't trying to be a dick. But at this stage, against my better judgment, I was genuinely interested. "And how does *The Whole Package* fit into this?"

And for the first time—the first time *ever*—I got a reaction from Jon Fleming. He looked at his beer and closed his eyes for a long moment. "I can't be what I was," he said, "so I have to be something else. Because the other option is being nothing. And I could never be nothing. My agent said *Package* would be a good fit for me—remind my old audience I was there and tell a new audience who I am. It's not a comeback, it's a curtain call. It's standing on the stage with the lights going down and begging the crowd to wait and listen to one last song."

I didn't know what to say. I should have realised I didn't have to say anything. He'd do the talking for both of us.

"Everybody tells you that when you're young, you think you'll live forever. What they don't tell you is that when you're old, you think the same. It's just everything starts reminding you that it's not true."

How the fuck had I got here? What was I supposed to do now? "You'll...you'll never be nothing, Dad."

"Perhaps. Except you look back, and what have you done?"

"Like, nearly thirty studio albums, countless tours, a career spanning five decades, that one time you stole a Grammy from Alice Cooper."

"I didn't steal it. I won it fair and square." He seemed to cheer up slightly. "And we beat the shit out of each other in the carpark afterwards."

"See. You've done loads of important things."

"But when it all comes round again, who will remember?"

"I don't know, people, the internet, me, Wikipedia."

"You could be right." Having downed the last of his IPA, he set the bottle down with a decisive clank. "Anyway, this has been good. I should let you go."

"Oh, you're going?"

"Yeah, I'm expected at Elton's for a party. I'm sure you and... and the boyfriend have a lot to do as well."

Somehow, he was making me resent the ending of a meeting I'd resented the start of. "Okay, well. This was a thing we did."

As he stood, I realised he hadn't even taken his coat off. But, then, he paused and gave me one of those deep, soulful looks that, just for that moment, made it all okay. "I'd like to do this again. While there's still time."

"I'm pretty busy the next couple of weeks. I've got a work do and it's Oliver's parents' anniversary."

"After that then. We'll go to dinner. I'll text you."

Then he was gone. Again. And I did not know how to feel. I mean, I was pretty sure I'd done the right thing. But, apart from that, I wasn't quite sure what I was supposed to be getting out of it. There was no way we'd ever be close. Any chance of that had gone out the window when he'd walked out on me and not come back for twenty-five years. And, now I stopped to think about it, he'd still expressed no remorse about that, and was clearly never going to. Probably we'd never even have a conversation that didn't centre entirely on him.

Not that long ago, it had been a point of pride for me to take the fuck all he was offering me and shove it up his arse. But I didn't really need to do that anymore, and I think I liked not needing to do that. Besides, the man was dying. I could listen to a few stories if it helped him deal. The truth was, Jon Fleming wasn't going to change, and I wasn't going to be important to him in the way I used to think I had to. But I was sort of getting to know him. And I was sort of getting to be there. And that was something.

So why not take it?

CHAPTER 40

THE DAY OF THE BEETLE Drive, I was in the office from eleven and the hotel from three. Insurance and table decorations I had sorted—the insurance by a lot of stressed-out telephone conversations and the table decorations by staying up all night making them with Priya and James Royce-Royce—but I'd come up blank on music. And I was telling myself that no one would mind because posh people mostly just liked the sound of their own voices when Rhys Jones Bowen poked his head into the cubicle where I was frantically pulling on my formalwear.

"I heard," he said, paying absolutely no attention to the fact I was in my underwear, "you were having a spot of bother in the music department."

"It's fine. We'll do without. We had a string quartet last year, and nobody cared."

"Well, if you're sure, I'll tell Uncle Alan we don't need him after all."

"I feel like I've missed the middle of this conversation. Who is Uncle Alan, and why would we need him or otherwise?"

"Oh, you see, I was talking to Becky the volunteer, who was talking to Simon the volunteer, who was talking to Alex, who was talking to Barbara who was saying the band you wanted had pulled out and you couldn't get a replacement. So I thought, why don't I ask Uncle Alan. So I rang him up, and he says to me that he and the boys are in town anyway because they're on *Songs of Praise* and they'd be happy to help us out."

I resigned myself to being trouserless for the rest of the encounter. "Okay, Rhys. One more time: who is Uncle Alan?"

"You know who Uncle Alan is. I've told you about Uncle Alan before. I'm always talking about Uncle Alan."

"Yes, but I'm never listening."

He rolled his eyes. "Ah, there was me forgetting what a bellend you are. Uncle Alan is the managing director of the Skenfrith Male Voice Choir. They're quite big in male voice choir circles."

"And you're only mentioning this now because...?"

"I didn't want to get your hopes up if it wasn't going to come through."

I surrendered to the unstoppable power of Rhys Jones Bowen and his seemingly limitless supply of talented Celts. "Fine. Can you get them settled in and give them whatever they need. And..." I realised with a sinking feeling I was experiencing a moment of genuine gratitude towards Rhys Jones Bowen. Again. "Thank you. Sorry I'm a bellend. I really do appreciate your help."

"Happy to oblige. Nice boxers, by the way. Are they Markses?"

I squinted downward. "I'm not sure I track my pants that closely."

"Right you are then."

And with that, he ambled off, presumably to wrangle a choir. I returned my attention to dressing and had, once again, got into the yoga position necessary to get one leg into my trousers without sitting down, falling over, or dropping anything in the loo. Then Alex burst in.

"For God's sake," I yelled. "I'm not a peep show."

Alex seemed unperturbed. "Um, quick question. You know that one job I had?"

"You mean, the job of not losing the earl?"

"Yes, that job." He paused. "Roughly, how inconvenient would it be if I hadn't a hundred percent discharged it to the full extent of my abilities?"

"Are you trying to tell me you *did* lose the earl?"

"Only a little bit. I don't know exactly where he is, but I have an increasingly comprehensive list of places he isn't."

"Please, Alex." I practiced some calming breathing. "Just find him. Now."

"Rightio. Sorry to, ah, interrupt. Nice boxers, by the way. Very chic."

"Go. Away."

He went. Away. And I began hopping in a small circle, trying to drag my inconveniently clingy trousers over my inconveniently long legs with their inconveniently bendy knees when I heard the door open again behind me.

"Alex," I snapped. "Please will you fuck off for five minutes."

"Oh, I say," said a voice that was much older than Alex's, but not much posher. "I'm terribly sorry. I think the lock must be broken. Though now you mention it, I have misplaced a chap called Alex. Do you know where he is?"

I shuffled back around, still very much under-trousered, to face the patron and primary donor of CRAPP, the Earl of Spitalhamstead. "I'm so sorry, my lord. I thought you were somebody else."

"I gathered that when you called me somebody else's name."

"Ah yes. How very astute of you."

"I enjoyed the swearing, though. I do like a bit of swearing."

"We strive to please. If you give me ten seconds to put my clothes on, I'll take you upstairs and we'll find Alex together."

"It's no bother. I'm sure I'll track him down myself."

"No, no," I insisted. "I'll be with you in a moment."

The Earl of Spitalhamstead was ninety if he was a day, barmy in a way that only the aristocracy were allowed to be, and had a habit of getting into what Alex described as "scrapes." The last time we'd let him wander around unattended at the Beetle Drive, he'd taken a wrong turn into the hotel bar, ordered an obscene amount of champagne "just to be polite," and wound up flying to Vienna with someone he'd completely failed to recognise was a prostitute. Apparently they had a lovely time, but it did rather put a dent in our fundraising.

Ten somewhat hairy seconds later, I was mostly dressed and shepherding a peer of the realm somewhere vaguely in the direction of where he needed to be while he told me a long story about an elephant, a racing monoplane, and the time he slept with Marilyn Monroe.

We found Alex looking very carefully inside a potted plant.

"What," I began, very much aware that I was about to ask a question to which I might not want to hear the answer, "are you doing?"

Alex looked at me like I'd said something deeply foolish. "Looking for the earl. Obviously."

"And you thought you'd find him inside a potted plant?"

"Well, I think you've just made yourself look dashed silly, because that's *exactly* where I found him." He pointed at the Earl of Spitalhamstead, who hadn't moved from my side for the length of the conversation. "See?"

"Hullo, Twaddle," said the earl cheerfully. "How's things?"

"Bally awkward, actually. Meant to be looking after this Earl chappie. Completely lost him."

"What rotten luck. Seems you'll have to make do with me instead."

For a moment, this seemed to trouble Alex. "Well, I was doing this little job for Luc. But…well"—he turned to me helplessly—"Hilary's a jolly old family friend so I'd really probably better take care of him if that's all right with you?"

I patted his shoulder. "You know, I think that might be for the best."

"Huzzah. Victory for common sense." Alex took the earl's arm gently. "Come on, old bean. I've got oodles of chaps—and chappesses for that matter; no need to be sexist, it *is* the twentieth century—simply dying to have a chinwag with you."

"Marvellous," returned the earl. "One so seldom gets to talk about dung beetles to an appreciative audience. You know, they shot me down in the Lords again. Shortsighted bastards..."

I slumped against a pillar as they vanished into the function room—from within which I could already hear the melodious sounds of a male voice choir warming up with the Welsh national anthem. Chances were, this would be the last opportunity I got to droop and catch my breath for the rest of the evening, so I was damn well making the most of it. I did, however, adjust my posture into something approaching respectability because I was fairly close to the lobby, the guests were already beginning to arrive, and "shagged out before you'd even begun" wasn't a confidence-inspiring look in a fundraiser. Which was unfortunate because "shagged out before I'd even begun" was pretty much how I was feeling.

Basically, though, it was fine. Everything had come together. It always kind of did. And, if I was being honest, it was nice seeing the whole team weirdly united in their support for our technically important but thoroughly unglamorous cause. To say nothing of the annual treat that was Rhys Jones Bowen in a suit. And by "treat" I meant "subtle headfuck" because he always managed to look like an undercover Marxist.

Although, speaking of treats of suits, I couldn't quite resist checking out the tuxedo-wrapped piece of manhunkery who'd just come in and was asking the receptionist for directions to the CRAPP fundraiser. And then immediately felt guilty because I had a possibly-actually-real boyfriend now. And then the confused opposite of guilty when I realised the tuxedo-wrapped piece of manhunkery *was* my possibly-actually-real boyfriend.

I lifted my hand in an "I am definitely not overwhelmed by how hot you are" wave. And Oliver came striding over in a flash of black and white and gorgeous.

"You are ridiculously good-looking," I said, attacking him with my eyes, "you know that?"

He smiled at me—all jawlines and cheekbones. "Normally I'd say the same to you, but at the moment you look like you got dressed in a toilet stall."

"Yeah, there's a fairly obvious reason for that."

"Come here."

I came there and Oliver made a number of swift, certain adjustments to my clothing that I found weirdly sexy despite being entirely SFW. He even redid my bow tie. And from the front and everything. You had to admire a man with coordination like that.

"There." He leaned in and kissed me chastely. Apparently, somehow we'd gone from people who needed to practice any sort of physical contact to the ever-challenging appropriate workplace smooch. "Ridiculously good-looking."

I was probably gazing at him pathetically. "Well. Not ridiculous. Maybe slightly absurd. In the right light."

"On the contrary, Lucien. You're always captivating."

"Okay. You're sailing perilously close to the wind here. Because if you keep this up, I'll need to shag you in the nearest closet, and I'm technically supposed to be doing my job here."

"And"—another of his killing-me-to-pieces smiles—"I'm supposed to be helping you with it."

"Got to be honest, I'm fifty-fifty on the job thing right now."

"You know that's not true. You've worked very hard for this."

I sighed. "Yeah, okay. But you better make it up to me later."

"I fully intend to."

Then he slid his arm around my waist and we went in together.

CHAPTER 41

PROFESSOR FAIRCLOUGH'S WELCOME SPEECH ENDED, as it always did: "Please give generously because *Coleoptera* are, by any objective measure, more important than any of you." Which, y'know, was very her and I liked to think it was part of the CRAPP experience. I mean, at what other high-end fundraiser would you be told, to your face, that you were worth less than an insect? She stood down to a polite smattering of applause and then Rhys Jones Bowen's Uncle Alan and the Skenfrith Male Voice Choir took the stage and began singing soulfully in Welsh about, well, I didn't know because it was in Welsh.

"So"—I leaned in to Oliver—"we've got about half an hour to an hour of networking before dinner. The trick, basically, is to never look like you're trying to get money out of people so that they can feel good about themselves when you eventually get money out of them."

He frowned. "That sounds rather outside my skill set. If it's all the same to you, I'll stand next to you and look respectable."

"Yeah, and if you could occasionally talk middle class at people, that'd be helpful too."

"So, *eaten any good quinoa recently*—that kind of thing?"

"Perfect. Just slightly less sarcastic sounding."

We circulated—it was mainly "hello, so glad you could make

it, how's your business/child/novel/horse" type stuff, but occasionally people would want to stop me for a longer conversation, which meant I got to introduce my pointedly appropriate but genuinely wonderful new boyfriend. I was relieved to see that while a couple of our most, how can I put this politely, "traditional" donors had stayed away, we'd still done pretty well, at least in terms of turnout. A handful of new developments, including Ben and Sophie, had shown up, and despite all the posturing, most of the concerned-about-your-values crowd appeared to have backpedalled—either because Alex's plan had somehow worked or because they'd been full of shit from the beginning. So thanks for that, fuckers.

"Adam," I bonhomied, "Tamara. So glad you could make it. Don't you both look lovely."

Adam gave one of his acknowledging nods. "Thank you. The suit's black bamboo hemp."

"And this," added Tamara, indicating her annoyingly gorgeous gold silk caftan, "is by one of my favourite designers. She's very new, so you won't have heard of her yet, but she runs a made-in-Africa social enterprise, working closely with local artisans who specialise in traditional techniques."

I gave her my best smile. "That's so you."

"Well"—Adam almost looked like he'd never been an investment banker—"you know how Tamara and I believe in living our principles."

"Oh, that reminds me," I said, "I haven't introduced you to my partner yet. Oliver, these are Adam and Tamara Clarke. Adam and Tamara, this is Oliver Blackwood."

Handshakes, air-kisses, and entirely one-sided Namastes followed.

"It's a pleasure to meet you." Oliver had his good-at-social-situations face on. "You're the couple behind Gaia, aren't you?"

They both lit up like locally sourced Christmas trees.

"Yes." Tamara's eyes grew soft. "It's been our whole life for five years."

Another of Adam's nods. "Our mission's always been to bring ethical values to the convenience food sector."

I clutched at Oliver's hand in a way that I hoped signalled "I'm in real danger of laughing right now" and he squeezed back in a way that suggested he got it.

"That's very admirable," murmured Oliver, "especially considering how many businesses in that sector have unethical values."

"I know," replied Tamara with absolute sincerity. "It's terrible."

Adam seemed oddly distracted considering that their business, and by extension themselves, had always been the Clarkes' favourite topic of conversation. Then I noticed his gaze kept catching on my hand, still resting in Oliver's. And, y'know, that gave me a bit of a dilemma. Because, from a certain point of view, it was my job to make these people comfortable. But, from a different point of view, fuck him. I'd jumped through a stack of hoops over the past couple of weeks to satisfy the Adam Clarkes of this world, but not holding hands with my boyfriend—my very nice, very respectable boyfriend who nobody could possibly disapprove of—was a hoop too far. And if Adam and Tamara decided to take their chequebook home because they went to a party and saw two guys being mildly affectionate to each other, well, then they could explain that to all their trendy leftie friends.

"So"—he gathered himself—"Oliver. What is it that you do?"

"I'm a barrister."

"What kind?" asked Tamara.

"Criminal."

That earned an indulgent chuckle from Adam. "The sort that locks up innocent people or the sort that puts murderers back on the streets?"

"Well, both, but mainly the murderer sort." Oliver offered a placid smile. "I'd say the money helps me sleep at night, but it's not even that well paid."

"If you ever need help finding peace"—Tamara's earnestness could have stripped bone—"I could put you in touch with a number of excellent yogis."

Before Oliver had to work out how the hell to respond to that, Adam chimed in with "I used to be in a very similar situation myself. I mean, financial sector, obviously, not legal. But Tamara really helped me find my path."

"Thank you," said Oliver, with an impressive air of meaning it. "I'll look you up if I ever feel ready."

They made appreciative, if slightly condescending, noises, congratulated me on the authenticity of the Welsh male voice choir, and finally let us go. I cast Oliver an "I'm sorry, they're the worst" glance but couldn't risk saying it out loud, just in case they—or let's be fair, anybody else—heard me dissing some people who were about to give me a very large sum of money.

"Don't worry." He leaned in, somehow managing to whisper without looking shady. "If I can pretend to respect Justice Mayhew, I can pretend to like the Clarkes."

"You shouldn't have to."

"It's exactly what you needed me for."

Well. Didn't that feel all complicated and confusingey? Because he was right—having someone who could convincingly fake an interest in me and my donors had been the whole plan. But seeing it in action, especially now I genuinely liked him, made the whole thing...icky. "You're better than this."

"Better than what, Lucien?" His eyes gleamed softly at me. "Better than being polite to people I don't particularly care about at my partner's work event?"

"Um, yes?"

He brushed his lips against my brow, hiding his smile. "I've got news for you. For those of us not raised by '80s rock legends, this is just...life. It's fine. I'm happy to be here with you, and later we can go home and laugh about it all."

"When we go home," I told him firmly, "there won't be time for laughing. You have no idea how good you look in those trous—Oh shit." Across the room, I saw to my horror that Dr. Fairclough was interacting with a guest. Which never, ever ended well. I grabbed Oliver by the elbow. "Sorry. This is an emergency. We have to go."

As we drew closer, trying not to look too much like we were staging an intervention, I realised we were even more fucked than I thought. Because Dr. Fairclough was talking to, or rather *at*, Kimberly Pickles. And the problem with Kimberly Pickles—which I knew well from having painstakingly developed her and her wife over the last year and a half—is that she did not give a shit about beetles, and she did give a shit about lots of other things. Things that she felt very strongly her incredibly wealthy partner would be better off spending her money on.

"...can't be sure whether you're being wilfully ignorant," Dr. Fairclough was saying, "or simply ig—"

"Kimberly." I swept in. "How lovely to see you. I don't think you've met my partner, Oliver Blackwood. Oliver, this is Kimberly Pickles, who you might recognise from—"

"Oh, of course," he said, not cutting over me, but kind of gliding in effortlessly. "Your recent miniseries on child sexual exploitation was remarkable."

She beamed, but sadly not in a "totally disarmed" way and said, "Aww, fank you" in the broad Estuary accent that, ten years ago, would definitely have kept her off the BBC.

"And this is my boss"—I indicated Dr. Fairclough warily— "Dr. Amelia Fairclough."

"It's so good to meet you." Oliver didn't bother extending a hand for her to shake, which I initially thought was uncharacteristically impolite. But he must have realised that Dr. Fairclough would have (a) not given a shit and (b) seen the requirement to engage in a pointless social ritual as a waste of time. "Lucien's told me all about your monograph on rove beetles."

She subjected him to her... I was going to say her most intense gaze, but her gazes were all equally intense. "Has he?"

"Yes. I was wondering if you could clear up some of the finer points of their behavioural relationship with ant colonies."

My God. Was this what love felt like?

"I'd be delighted to." Dr. Fairclough looked the closest to happy I'd ever seen her. Which wasn't very. "But it's an intricate subject, and there are too many distractions here."

Oliver drew Dr. Fairclough gently aside in search of a better rove beetle/ant colony interaction discussing location, leaving me awash in gratitude and hopefully better placed to salvage Kimberly Pickles.

"That Dr. Fairclough," she began, "is a right cow."

It wasn't language I would have personally used, but I could see where she was coming from. "I'm afraid academics can be quite single-minded about their interests."

"No fucking kidding. She genuinely finks that dung beetles are more important than people."

I offered a conspiratorial smile. "I'd say you have to get to know her, but no. She genuinely does."

She didn't smile back. "And you really fink it's right, do you? For people to give their money to you instead of a women's shelter in Blackheath or fighting child mortality in sub-Saharan Africa."

Thing is, she wasn't totally wrong. CRAPP wasn't a cool charity, and it wasn't even high up on those effective-giving lists that help nerdy mathlanthropists evaluate exactly how to save the most lives per dollar. But it was my cause, and I'd fight for it, and from what I knew of Kimberly Pickles, she liked a fighter.

"Well," I said, "if I worked for a women's shelter in Blackheath, there'd be people asking me why people should give money to that instead of malaria prevention or de-worming initiatives. And if I worked for a charity that tried to prevent child mortality in sub-Saharan Africa, there'd be people who asked me why they should be sending money overseas when we've got problems enough over here."

She relaxed a bit, but she still wasn't buying it. "It's fucking dung beetles, mate."

"It is." I gave a *you got me* kind of shrug. "And although they *are* ecologically important, I'm not going to pretend we're saving the world here. We're not even saving Bedfordshire. But your missus isn't going to run out of cash any time soon, and she clearly enjoys throwing it at slightly silly things that make her happy."

"She does enjoy laughing at you," Kimberly admitted.

"Yes, so do a surprising number of our donors. It's why we've never changed the acronym. Well, that and because Dr. Fairclough would never let us because she feels it's the most accurate and succinct description of our operation."

That made her cackle like Adele. "Awight, but tell your boss to stop insulting donors' wives."

"Sorry, what was that about insulting my wife?"

Not the best time for Charlie Lewis to rock up. I'd met her through the James Royce-Royces, because she and James Royce-Royce had briefly worked for the same terrifying investment bank doing terrifyingly complicated mathematics with terrifyingly large sums of money. She was built like a fridge, wore her hair like Elvis, and had glasses like Harry Potter. And, right now, did not seem happy with me.

"It's nuffin, babe." Kimberly turned and kissed her wife on the cheek. "Just the professor being weird."

Charlie gave a heavy sigh. "Not again. Why does she bother trying to talk to bipeds?"

"I think," I suggested, "she feels it's expected of her. If it's any consolation, I know for a fact she hates every second of it."

"Maybe I'm not as 'orrible as you, Luc, but it doesn't 'elp."

"I'm helped." Charlie smirked. "I like the idea of people who cross my wife being miserable."

Kimberly whacked her affectionately on the arm. "Will you stop being such a fifties patriarch? Which one of us sits in an office all day moving other people's money around wiv a bunch of prats who went to Oxford? And who spent the last three months interviewing coyotes in Central America?"

"Yes, and you've got back and an annoying woman is being rude to you at a party."

"Yeah, a party *you* made me come to. Because you still want to spend money saving bugs that eat shit."

I hoped this was cute partner banter, not the start of a blowup that was going to jeopardise their relationship or, more relevant to me, our donation. "As a representative of the shit-eating bug community," I said, "we're very glad you're both here."

Kimberly made a conciliatory gesture. "I'm awight really. I like the male voice choir. There's one in Bangor does really good work with disadvantaged teenagers."

Okay, I was pretty sure salvaging had been accomplished. And, actually, from what I knew about her, Kimberly wasn't the sort of person who'd sabotage a charitable donation in a fit of pique. If anything, she was the opposite of that sort of person, and in the interests of maintaining independent identities, she and Charlie tended to very pointedly champion different causes. Even so, there were limits. Of which "insulting your wife to her face about her deeply held beliefs" was a fairly obvious one. Obvious, that is, to everybody except Dr. Fairclough.

"Let me leave you to it for now," I said. "I'd love to catch up after dinner."

Charlie gave me one of those city bastard handshakes. "That'd be splendid. If not, let's do lunch some time. And give my love to James. There's always an opening for him at CB Lewis."

"Will do."

Leaving them bickering happily about their various life choices, I took a meandering route past several other important donors to the nook into which Dr. Fairclough had managed to manoeuvre Oliver. She was still, as far as I could tell, talking about the behavioural relationship between rove beetles and ant colonies and, if I knew her at all, wouldn't have paused for breath in the last ten minutes. I'd been in Oliver's position myself a bunch of times because Dr. Fairclough seemed genuinely unable to comprehend that other people might not find beetles as fascinating as she did, and I'd never mustered even half as much poise, grace, or straight-up sincerity as Oliver was showing right now.

It was just so fucking...heart emoji that I actually had to take a moment.

And then I realised that the longer I stood around in a sea of swoon, the longer Oliver was going to have to talk about bugs. So I went to rescue him.

CHAPTER 42

"...USING PHEROMONE TRAILS," DR. FAIRCLOUGH was saying.

Oliver didn't even flinch. "Oh, how fascinating."

"If you're attempting to employ sarcasm, I assure you I'm quite immune to it."

He thought about it for a moment. "I don't know how to answer that without still sounding like I'm trying to employ sarcasm."

She, too, seemed to think for a moment. "Yes, you appear to have identified a difficult paradox. If it's any help, when I was an undergraduate, my housemates found it convenient to make this signal"—she laid a single finger on her cheek—"to indicate that they were not to be taken seriously."

"I shall endeavour to make use of it. But please do continue."

"*Or*," I said quickly, "we could go and eat because they're serving food now."

Another thoughtful pause from Dr. Fairclough. "No. I'd rather stay here and talk to Oliver."

"Um..."

"I believe..." Once again Oliver slipped into the conversation like...something lubricated. Or maybe a swan. Y'know, graceful and smooth "...Lucien was attempting to politely inform us that we need to go and eat now."

"Well, why didn't he say so?"

"Because not saying exactly what he means is his job. Otherwise he'd have spent the entire evening going up to people and shouting *Give us your money* at the top of his voice."

"It worked for Bob Geldof." She wrinkled her nose disdainfully. "I don't see why everything has to be so complicated."

And with that, she swept off to the staff table with me and Oliver trailing behind.

The food was one of the perks of the Beetle Drive. The donors had paid a lot of money to be here, so you couldn't skimp on the catering, and while Barbara Clench had briefly tried to insist we should make separate arrangements for staff so that we didn't have to waste good food on, well, *ourselves*, that did actually turn out to be more expensive. I had to eat really quickly so I could get back to the guests, but since it was nearly always nouvelle cuisine bullshit, I only had about three mouthfuls to get through on any given course.

Everybody was already settled in, mostly with their plus-ones. Alex had brought Miffy, of course, who was looking ravishing in an ensemble that probably cost more than anything I owned and which she almost certainly hadn't paid for.

"Lovely to see you again, Clara," said Oliver, claiming his seat. "Dior?"

She blinked. "Do my what? Oh, I mean yes. Good eye."

"Fuck." I threw myself exhaustedly down next to Oliver. "I need to do introductions again."

Barbara Clench glared at me across the table. "Language."

"I think I'll stick with English, thanks." To be honest, I should have been nicer to Barbara. Without her, CRAPP would probably have bankrupt. But hating each other was our whole deal, and you didn't mess with a system that worked. I gestured at her. "Oliver, this is Barbara Clench, our office manager. And her husband, Gabriel."

Probably the most impressive thing I'd seen Oliver do that evening was look in no way surprised that Barbara Clench's husband was a six-foot, golden-haired Adonis, about ten years her junior, who seemed genuinely and mythically in love with her. It made no sense. She wasn't rich, and I'd met her so it couldn't be her personality. But, y'know, what? Fair fucking play to her.

"Alex and Miffy you already know. This is Rhys Jones Bowen. And…" Rhys always brought a different date. I had no idea where he got them from. "Sorry, I don't think we've met?"

"This is Tamsin." Rhys did his best game-show pose. "She's from my Zumba class."

I tried to process that. "You're in a Zumba class?"

"It's very good cardio."

"Ahhh." Alex made a sound of slowly dawning comprehension. "I assumed you'd met at work."

"Alex," I said, "we all work in the same building. And none of us have ever seen this woman before in our lives."

"Yes"—Alex was nodding slowly—"it did seem a tad peculiar. But I didn't recognise the one from last year either."

I could feel myself about to step over the precipice of Alex's nitwititude. But, for some reason, I let it go. And maybe I just didn't want to be a dick to my colleagues in front of Oliver but, the truth was, they'd come through for me tonight. They always came through for me. Not in any way anyone else would recognise as helpful, but here we were.

"Look," I began, not quite believing what was coming out of my mouth, "I know I can sometimes be—"

"A total bellend?" That was Tamsin. I'd never even met Tamsin. How did Tamsin know I was a total bellend?

I glared at Rhys Jones Bowen. "Rhys, is that the first thing you tell people about me?"

"Pretty much." He was doing the beard stroking he did when… Actually I'd still not worked out what it meant. "I mean, to be fair, I usually say, 'Apart from that, he's a pretty decent fella' straight after. But people do seem to get stuck on the bellend part. Then again, you don't do yourself any favours."

"Okay. Fine. As I was about to say, despite being *a total bellend*, I'm incredibly proud of all the work we've done, and tonight wouldn't have happened without every single of one of you. So thank you and"—I actually picked up a fucking glass—"here's to you lot."

Everyone joined in with an only slightly reluctant chorus of "to us lot." Except Barbara Clench, who'd been busily making out with her disturbingly attractive husband and looked up afterwards to say, "Sorry, Luc, were you trying to tell me something?"

While I was finishing off my artfully presented pile of seasonal vegetables and foam, and wondering if I could eat anybody else's, Ben and Sophie drifted over as part of the general pre-dessert mill.

"Well." She lifted her wineglass in a toast to me. "You got us."

Oliver stood and kissed her cheek. "Lies. You just wanted another evening away from the kids."

"That too. These days, I'd go to a fundraiser for the Society for the Abolition of Kittens if it got us out the house for five minutes."

"I take it," I said, "you're having a nice time then?"

Sophie cackled gleefully. "Darlings, I'm going to give you all my money. I'm having the best evening. A ninety-year-old earl tried to get me to go to Vienna with him, a very strange woman told me we were all going to die unless we drastically increased our investment in entomology, and—as you quite rightly predicted, Luc—when I told my irritating leftie friends that I was supporting a dung beetle charity, they shit themselves with virtue envy."

"You can also," I offered, "bid on a Fortnum & Mason hamper in the silent auction."

"Fuck that. I'm going for the rove beetle book." She grinned Cheshire cat–style. "I might give it to Bridge for Christmas."

"Oh, Soph." Oliver shook his head. "You're a terrible human being."

"You can't say that to me anymore. I support dung beetles."

Since Sophie and Ben were wandering, that probably meant I should be wandering too. Semireluctantly, I got up and offered Sophie my chair. "I'll leave you to catch up for a bit."

"I'm happy to accompany you," Oliver said. "I see far too much of these two as it is."

Ben's eyes widened in outrage. "You bloody well don't. I know we've been out twice in two weeks, but Jennifer's birthday was my first night off since we forced the grandparents to take the little shits for Boxing Day."

"What about the Alternative Valentine's Day party that Brian still insists on doing even though he's married now?"

"Sophie came to that. I was at home because Twin B had chicken pox and Twin A was about to get chicken pox."

I patted Oliver on the shoulder. "You stay. You've been heroic enough this evening."

"Don't say that." Sophie winced. "He *loves* playing the hero, and the last thing he needs is encouragement."

Oliver shot her a sharp look. "That's not true. I just think it's important to be useful."

"Useful, dear, is for dogs and crescent wrenches. Friends and lovers should care for you even when you're not a blind bit of good to anybody."

"Okay." I gave an exaggerated side step out of an imaginary firing line. "Now I'm *definitely* leaving you to it."

Having given his wife what he clearly considered a sufficient grace period, Ben claimed my chair. "Don't worry. This is how they relate. Can I have your dessert?"

"What?" I spluttered. "How dare you? You're taking advantage of the fact it's my job to be nice to you."

"Yes. I absolutely am. I had to scrub poo out of this tie to be here tonight. I think I deserve another panna cotta."

"Okay. Fine. I can see your need is greater than mine."

He pounced on my spoon in preparation. "Oliver has chosen well. We shall be friends."

I gave Oliver a "you're still my hero" kiss and went to, y'know, work. The rest of the evening unfolded smoothly—funds were raised, things were auctioned silently, nobody was too horribly insulted, and we managed to catch the earl just as he was about to get in a taxi to Heathrow with a companion into whose background we did not look too deeply. By the time we'd cleaned up, packed up, and given up, it was slightly after two and I let Oliver pour me into a taxi and take me home.

"Thank you for tonight," I told him, somewhat slurrily, resting my head against his shoulder.

"You can stop thanking me, Lucien."

"But you were *amazing*. You were nice to everybody, and everybody liked you, and you talked to Dr. Fairclough and you didn't punch the Clarkes..."

"You shouldn't listen to Sophie." He shifted a little uncomfortably. "I don't need you to act like...like this was anything special."

My brain stumbled over something but was too foggy to see what it was. "Why are we talking about Sophie?"

"We're not. I just didn't want you to think that I think that... I don't know."

"I'm really not thinking much at all right now. But this evening went really well for me, and part of that was you." I remembered something else important. "Also you look really hot in black tie. And the moment we get in, I'm going to... I'm going to..."

The next time I was aware of, well, anything, I was in bed, and Oliver was taking off my clothes in a tragically unerotic way.

"Come here." I made a plaintive pawing motion. "We're going to do all of the sex things."

"Yes. Lucien. That's exactly what's happening now."

"Good. Because you're so wonderful...and I really want...and did I mention you look really hot in that..."

Then I opened my eyes and it was dawn and Oliver was fast asleep beside me—looking all peaceful and stubbly and perfect. And, on the one hand, I was annoyed I'd been too knackered to fuck him six ways to, from, or possibly on Sunday. But there he was, warm and curled up against me, holding me tight, in this strangely protective, strangely vulnerable way.

And, y'know, I guess that was okay too.

CHAPTER 43

"KNOCK, KNOCK," I SAID TO Alex.

"Oh, I know this one." He paused. "Who's there?"

"The interrupting cow."

"The interrupt—"

"Moo."

"—ing cow who?" He continued to look at me expectantly. "This is your bit."

"No, no, I did my bit."

"Sorry, did I miss it? Shall we try again?"

"I'm honestly not sure that will help. You see, and"—I was starting to get that sinking feeling—"now that I find myself having to articulate it, I'm beginning to realise that this was probably a poor choice. The interrupting-cow joke is sort of a subversion of the knock-knock joke form."

"Ah. You mean like *Ulysses*?"

"Probably? But more about a cow and less about…I'm going to go out on a limb and say sad Irish people?"

Alex thought about this for a long moment. "And so I'm led by the intrinsic structural features of the knock-knock joke medium to anticipate that the punch line will be delivered following my delivery of the expected reply 'the interrupting cow who' but because the interrupting cow is an interrupting cow, it instead delivers its punch line *during* said response, thus confounding my expectations with hilarious consequences."

"Um. I think so?"

"It's rather good." He leaned sideways. "I say, Rhys. Come in here."

Rhys Jones Bowen's head appeared in the doorway. "What can I do you for, fellows?"

"Knock, knock."

"Who's there?"

Alex shot me a conspiratorial look. "The interrupting cow."

"The interrupting cow who?" asked Rhys Jones Bowen.

"Moo!"

There was a pause. He stroked his beard. "Ooh, I like it. It's rather Dadaist. You see, I was expecting you to interrupt me during the final line because you're an interrupting cow. But you didn't, so I was surprised, and that made it funny. I'll be chuckling about that all day, I will."

They were doing this deliberately, weren't they? They were evil geniuses who'd been playing me for years. Before any of us could go back to what we laughably called our jobs, Dr. Fairclough appeared from upstairs and to my dismay (but not my surprise), Rhys Jones Bowen stopped in the doorway and turned to her.

"Got a joke for you, Doctor F," he announced.

Her reply was wordless and discouraging, but he was not discouraged.

"Knock, knock."

To my surprise, she did in fact reply at once with a curt and formal: "Who's there?"

"The interrupting cow."

"Thank you, but mammals are not my area of interest. Excellent job last night, O'Donnell."

"Moo?" Rhys finished somewhat limply.

"Thank you?" I said, trying and failing not to sound like this was the first remotely supportive thing I'd ever heard her to say.

"Good. I hope you are motivated by this positive reinforcement. If not, I can put a jar of sugar solution in the break room."

"Um, I think I'm okay."

Dr. Fairclough literally checked her phone. I wondered how many seconds she had allocated to taking an interest. "I additionally commend your choice of Mr. Blackwood. He was by far the least insufferable part of Saturday evening. Maintain a relationship with him and bring him next year."

"Just to check"—I did not like the way this was going—"am I fired if I don't?"

"No. But I may suspend your sugar solution privileges." At which point, her phone beeped an alarm. "I hope you all feel valued as employees. I'm done with you now."

Thus reassured of my value as an employee, I wandered back to my office and began to tackle the substantial post-Beetle Drive housekeeping. There were pictures of the event to curate and send to Rhys Jones Bowen, so he could add them to the pile of things he was supposed to be doing social media with. There were donors and, with my more mercenary hat on, donations to follow up. Payments to be made. Apologies and thank-you's to be issued depending on circumstances. Basically a bunch of T's to dot and I's to cross—and, for reasons I couldn't quite articulate but I was sure had very little to do with Dr. Fairclough's new, improved management style, I found myself surprisingly happy to get on with it.

And I also made a sneaky booking at Quo Vadis for the day after Oliver's parents' do. Which, yes, was embarrassingly sentimental. But the alternative was turning to him in the car on the way home and saying "Hi, how about being my fake boyfriend for real?" And that didn't feel like...enough? Of course, this might be *too much*. But given the choice between making Oliver think I didn't care about him and making him think I was a creepy weirdo—actually those were both really bad. Fuck.

This was hard. Romance was hard. How did you romance?

More to the point, how did Oliver want to be romanced? I thought about asking Bridge but she would have told me to take him up the Seine—not a euphemism—in a candlelit rowboat or save his sister from being dishonoured at the hands of a dashing rake. And I wasn't in any position to do either. Besides, I was pretty sure he didn't have a sister.

Wait. Did Oliver have a sister? He'd told me this, but that was back when I didn't give a shit. I think he'd said he had a brother? And that was when I realised how little I actually knew about him. I mean, I knew he was hot and nice and a barrister and he liked it when I... Okay that definitely wasn't helping. But he'd met my mum, and my dad, and seen me cry several times. How did I wind up being the one who did all the intimacy here?

On top of which, I was less than a week away from having to hang out with his family, and what a shitty boyfriend I was going to look if I had no idea who any of them were. And probably Uncle Battenberg was going to come up to me and be all "Ah, you must have met Oliver through his water polo team" and I'd be all "What-er-polo-what?"

Okay. New plan.

Demonstrate how much I care about Oliver by learning a bare minimum of information about his life. Unfortunately, he had a way of distracting me. Well. Several ways of distracting me.

So on Thursday, a little after midnight, I collapsed over Oliver's chest, and with—I'll admit—not the world's best sense of occasion, said "So, tell me about your family."

"Um"—he seemed, I suppose, about as confused as I would have expected—"now?"

"Not necessarily exactly now. But maybe before Sunday? On account of me, y'know, meeting them then?"

He frowned. "How long has this been on your mind? Because I'm a little concerned."

"Couple of days, on and off? And," I added quickly, "we've just been in an off."

"I see."

"It's not... I..." Wow. I really did suck at taking an interest. "I thought it would be nice? To know more about you?"

Normally Oliver was happy for me to sprawl over him as long and as much as I wanted, but he half shifted me, like I was being tucked into a corner. "There's very little to know that you don't already."

"What? You mean you're just an immaculate vegetarian lawyer with a gym routine and a good line in French toast?"

"Is something troubling you, Lucien? I hope you don't feel trapped with me now your event's over."

I sat up like I'd been stung. "No. Not at all. You make me incredibly happy, and I want to be with you. But, like, what are you scared of? When was the last time you cried? What's your favourite place in the world? What's the thing in your life you most regret? Are you on a water polo team?"

He gazed at me warily, monochrome in the half light. "No. I'm not on a water polo team. Where is this coming from?"

Honestly? From liking him way more than I was used to liking anyone. From wanting him to like me back the same sort of way. From a whole wet splat of feels I couldn't put into words. "I guess I'm just nervous. I don't want to make a dick of myself in front of your parents."

"There's nothing to worry about." He drew me back into his arms, and I went gladly enough. "It's a garden party, not a job interview."

"All the same. There are logistics here. You're not going to send me out all unprepared and un-logistics-ed."

I'd thought the logistics thing would be a winner. But he seemed less excited by it than I'd hoped. "Very well. What information do you think is pertinent?"

"I don't know." Way to put me on the spot, Oliver. "Who's going to be there?"

"Well, my parents, obviously—David and Miriam. He's in accountancy. My mother used to be a fellow of the LSE but gave it up when she had me."

This wasn't helping. "You told me that when we first met."

"We can't all be the children of infamous rock legends."

"No, I know. But, like, who are they? Do they have any interests? Or, y'know, personality traits?"

"Lucien"—great, now he sounded borderline narked—"they're my parents. My father's a keen golfer. And my mother does a lot of charitable work."

My heart sank. I was upsetting Oliver and this already sounded awful—but I'd gone too far to back out of either the event or the conversation. "What about your brother? Is your brother coming?"

"Yes. Christopher will be there." He sighed. "As will Mia. I believe they're flying in from Mozambique."

"You..." Here's hoping I didn't make it worse "You don't seem entirely happy about that."

"My brother is very...accomplished. It makes me feel self-conscious."

"You're accomplished," I pointed out. "You're a fucking barrister."

"Yes, but I don't go into war zones and save lives."

"You make sure that people get fair representation in court when they wouldn't otherwise."

"You see? Even you can't make it sound glamorous."

"That's because I'm not you. When you talk about it, your eyes all light up, and you make it seem like the most important thing in the world. And then I want to do you right there."

He blushed. "Please tell me you won't say anything like that at the party."

"Are you kidding? That's *exactly* the sort of thing I'm planning to say at the party. My opening line is going to be 'Hello Miriam, I'm Luc, I really enjoy doing your son.'" I rolled my eyes. "I know how to behave in polite company, Oliver."

"Forgive me, I'm tired. It's getting late, Lucien, and I'm in court tomorrow."

"No, I'm sorry. I'm being weird and keeping you awake."

Despite the mess we'd made—or probably I'd made—of the pillow talk, Oliver wrapped me up and held me like he always did. So I guess we were okay? Except I still felt kind of unsettled, and I wasn't sure why or where it was coming from. Much less what to do about it. And maybe the problem was that there wasn't a problem, and I was just so not used to that, my brain was trying to make one for me.

Fuck you, brain.

I nestled closer to my immaculate vegetarian lawyer and told myself to sleep.

CHAPTER 44

WHEN OLIVER HAD SAID HIS parents lived in Milton Keynes, I'd assumed that they, well, lived in a house in Milton Keynes. Not in a bijou mansionette so far on the outskirts of town that it was surrounded by rolling countryside as far as the eye could see.

Thanks to Oliver's crippling fear of being late, we'd shown up way early and had to sit around in the car for about forty-five minutes in order to arrive at anything like an appropriate time. And I was super mature about it and didn't tell anyone I'd told them so.

But, eventually, we were in a back garden that was just small enough not to qualify as "grounds" but still big enough to hold an absurdly overattended party in. There was bunting, with a tasteful ruby theme, and one of those big fancy tents, to say nothing of waitstaff with trays of champagne and canapes (none of which were vol-au-vents). The booze was clearly expensive, but on that perfectly chosen borderline between noticeable and showy. My tie already felt too tight.

Miriam and David Blackwood looked exactly like you'd expect a couple called Miriam and David Blackwood to look. Which was to say kind of like if the Tesco Finest range did people: basically exactly the same as everyone else, but with a faint air of being slightly better. I reached for Oliver's hand, but somehow missed it, as we trooped over the grass to where his parents were chatting pleasantly to a small knot of people in their late fifties and early sixties.

"Happy anniversary," he said, kissing his mother on the cheek and shaking his father by the hand.

"Oliver." Miriam straightened his tie. "We're so glad you could come." She turned to one of the other guests. "He's been having such a hard time at work lately, we were worried he wouldn't be able to make it."

Oliver shifted slightly at my side. "Work's been fine, Mother."

"Oh, darling, I'm sure you're coping very well. I'm just concerned." Again, a glance to someone else. "He's not like his brother, you know. Christopher thrives under pressure."

"I understand, but I'm all right, really." Oliver didn't quite push me forward but didn't quite not. "This is my boyfriend, Lucien O'Donnell."

"Oliver's gay," Oliver's father explained helpfully to the group.

I shot Oliver a surprised look. "Are you? You never told me."

I'd say my attempt at humour had fallen flat but that suggested it had somewhere to fall from.

"And what is it you do, Lucien?" asked Miriam after an uncomfortably long pause.

"I work for a charity that's trying to save the dung beetle."

"Well"—from the painfully jovial tone I suspected this comment was coming from an uncle—"at least you're not another bloody lawyer."

Miriam subjected the speaker to a cool glance. "Now, now, Jim. Oliver works very hard and we can't all be doctors."

"Works hard putting criminals back on the streets." David's smile said he was joking. His eyes said he wasn't.

I opened my mouth to protest, but then remembered that I was here to be nice and that—having seen him do it before—Oliver could do a much better job defending his profession than I ever could.

"Is Christopher here yet?" he asked. "I should probably say hello to him."

"He's inside with the wife getting changed." David jerked his thumb towards the house. "They've been travelling all day."

"They've been doing disaster relief," added Miriam, for whose benefit I wasn't certain.

David nodded. "In Mozambique."

"Yes, I know." Oliver sounded oddly brittle. "He emailed me."

"Though," David continued cheerfully, "she'll be doing less of that kind of thing now they're starting a family."

Miriam addressed her little audience again. "The truth is, until Christopher met Mia, we despaired of ever having grandchildren."

I opened my mouth and closed it again. Given how well my joke had gone down earlier, I didn't think anyone was going to welcome my pointing out that gay people could have kids, too, thank you very much. Besides, if Oliver could put up with the Clarkes, I could put up with this.

No, really. I could put up with this.

"I...I should go and find Christopher." And, with that, Oliver turned away and started walking towards the house.

I actually had to chase him.

"Are you okay?" I tried.

He cast me a rather impatient look. "Of course. Why wouldn't I be?"

"Um. Because that was... awful?"

"Lucien, please don't be difficult. My parents belong to a different generation. My mother worries about me a lot, and my father tends to be very direct."

I found myself sort of tugging at his sleeve. "Excuse me, my mum belongs to that generation."

"Yes. Well. Your mother is quite an unusual person."

"Yeah but she...but she..." There was something I desperately needed to tell him—something I was sure he needed to understand—but I couldn't quite work out what it was. "She wouldn't talk to anyone like that?"

Oliver stopped walking abruptly. "My parents raised me. My father worked every hour God sent, and my mother gave up her career entirely. I don't want to have an argument with you, especially not here, and especially not now, but I'd thank you not to insult them in their own home."

"I'm sorry, Oliver." I hung my head. "I didn't mean to. I'm here to support you."

"Then …"—he made a this-conversation-is-over gesture—"accept how things are. This is my life. It's not like your life. Please respect it."

I wanted to say that it didn't seem to respect him.

But I didn't quite dare.

We'd just reached the patio when a couple, who I assumed from age and context were Christopher and Mia, stepped through the French windows. He was definitely Oliver-like around the edges though he was slightly taller, his eyes bluer and his hair lighter. The combination of a slightly tousled look and a well-defined three-day stubble gave the impression of somebody who very much wanted you to know that he was too busy saving lives to worry about little details like shaving. His wife, by contrast, was shortish and pretty-ish, in a takes-no-shit way, and sporting a ruthlessly practical pixie cut.

Oliver offered a weird little nod. "Christopher."

"Hi, Ollie." His brother grinned. "How's the law?"

"Much as ever. How's medicine?"

"Right now, intense as fuck. We're exhausted and frankly"— his gaze drifted resentfully over the lawn—"I can't believe they dragged us back here for this."

One of Oliver's eyelids twitched. "Well, of course they want you here. They're extremely proud of you."

"But not so proud that they'll let me stay where I need to be and do the things they're proud of me for doing."

"Yes, yes, we're all very aware how special and important your work is. It's not unreasonable to expect you to make time for your family occasionally."

"Oh for fuck's sake, Ollie. Why do you—"

"Hello," I announced. "I'm Luc. I'm Oliver's boyfriend. I work for a beetle charity. It's nice to meet you."

Mia detached herself from her husband and shook my hand enthusiastically. "Good to meet you too. I'm so sorry. We've been on a plane for thirteen hours, which I know makes it sound like I'm bragging about my exciting jet-setting lifestyle but I really mean I've spent a long time trapped in a metal box."

"God." Christopher ran a hand through his hair. "I'm being a dick, aren't I?"

"Yes," said Oliver. "You are."

A snort from Christopher. "Can I just point out that you're the one who was too busy reaming me out to introduce his own boyfriend?"

"It's fine." I waved my hands in what I hoped was a situation-defusing fashion. "Oliver's told me all about you anyway. I can introduce myself."

"Ollie's told you about us, has he?" Christopher's eyes gleamed wickedly. "Go on then. What's he said?"

Whoops. "Um. You're doctors? That you've been in… I want to say Mumbai but I think that's wrong. And that you're very nice people and he cares about you very much."

"Yeah, I think he maybe said one of those things if you're lucky."

"I'm sorry, Christopher." It was Oliver's coldest voice. "You're not that interesting a topic of conversation."

"I'd be devastated by that comeback, except you never say anything about anyone. You've told us more about Luc than you have about your last six boyfriends, and all you told us about him was his name."

I put a hand to my heart. "I feel so special."

"You should." Mia smuggled a smile across the no-man's-land between the siblings. "He mentioned you without being asked and everything."

Christopher was scrutinising me in a slightly awkward way. "He's not your usual type, Ollie. Which is probably a good thing."

"Hard as it may be for you to believe," Oliver sneered, "I don't choose my romantic partners to please you."

"True." Christopher had good pause game. "You choose them to please Mum and Dad."

There was a deeply nasty silence.

"I hear from Father," said Oliver placidly, "you're starting a family."

There was another somehow even nastier silence.

At the end of which, Mia fixed her brother-in-law with an irate glare. "Fuck off, Oliver. I'm getting a drink."

She fucked off and got a drink.

"What the hell"—Christopher rounded furiously on Oliver—"is wrong with you, you sanctimonious little shit?"

Oliver folded his arms. "It was a perfectly civil question."

"No, it was stirring, and you know it was stirring."

"There wouldn't be anything to stir if you stopped dangling the possibility of grandchildren over our parents."

"That is not—"

"Oh, it absolutely is. You can't bear the idea of them not worshipping you."

Well, this was fun. And I had sort of signed up to have Oliver's back here, but I didn't think that stretched to watching him be a dick to his brother. Who, to be fair, was being equally dickish. But this was getting way too much.

"You know"—I forced myself briefly into the conversation—"I think I need a drink too."

And before anyone could stop me, I made a dash for the big tent.

CHAPTER 45

I FOUND MIA IN A corner, with a glass of champagne in each hand.

"Good plan," I told her, and immediately copied it.

She gave me a rueful look. "Cheers."

We double-clinked. And drank heavily for a few moments in silence.

"I think," said Mia finally, "this might be worse than usual."

God help me. "There's a *usual*?"

"They tend to set each other off."

"I've never seen Oliver act that way."

"And Chris only acts that way around Oliver." She shrugged. "It's kind of their deal."

I finished my backup drink in a single gulp and wondered if I could get away with a third. Truthfully, I was almost angry at how little Oliver had prepared me for this. But, at the same time, I could see why he hadn't—and that alone made me feel sorry for him. "I guess"—I had to play this carefully—"it must be difficult for Oliver because it's pretty clear David and Miriam have a way easier time with Christopher's life choices."

"Hah." Mia drained her glass too.

"Okay, I'm getting the feeling I'm missing something."

"They're definitely supportive." It seemed like Mia was being as careful as I was. "And they make sure he never forgets just how supportive they're being. Anyway, sorry I yelled at your boyfriend. I'm usually not so... Actually I probably am, but fuck it. The Blackwoods bring out the worst in me."

"Yeah, I'm starting to think that's a pattern. Though," I added quickly, "for the record, David really did say the family thing."

She drove her toe into the perfectly kept lawn. "Of course he did. But it was still cheap of Oliver to go there."

"He...he...doesn't seem to be handling today very well."

"I can see how much you like him. Still not feeling particularly forgiving right now."

"I take it...God, I don't even know how to ask this."

"It's not this big sensitive issue. Or at least it's only sensitive because, from where I'm standing, it's crystal fucking clear. We don't want kids. David and Miriam want us to have kids, and they seem to think that their opinion matters as much as ours does."

"Shit. That's...shit."

"Especially because now it's this cold war where they act like it's just a matter of time and Christopher feels guilty for disappointing them and I'm pissed off that he won't shut it down."

"To be fair, they seem like hard people *to* shut down."

She shrugged. "Oh, it's always been like this. And, obviously, the last thing I want is for him to feel he has to choose between his parents and his wife."

"Well"—I risked a grin—"you're clearly a lot better for him than they are, so maybe it would be an improvement."

That made her laugh. "It's a nice idea, but he's been trying to hang onto their approval for nearly thirty years. That's not something you just walk away from."

"I wouldn't know. My dad fucked off when I was three."

"And I'm increasingly glad my parents are normal, well-adjusted human beings."

"Wait. Those exist?"

Before she could answer, Oliver and Christopher stuck their heads into the marquee, looking, I was pleased to see, appropriately sheepish.

"Ollie's got something to say," said Christopher, with a touch more aggression than the statement warranted.

Oliver shuffled. "I'm very sorry, Mia. I was angry and I lashed out, and I shouldn't have done that."

"It's fine." Mia waved a hand. "I know Chris was being a dick to you."

"Hey," protested Christopher. "You're supposed to be on my side."

"For fuck's sake. The fact you think there's sides is the entire fucking problem."

I went gladly back to Oliver and snuck my hand into his. "Do you want to...give me a tour maybe?"

"Of course, Lucien. I'm sorry I've neglected you."

"Actually, I think you'll find I ran away from you. Because it was like *Gunfight at the O.K. Corral* back there, and I thought I was going to get caught in the verbal crossfire."

"I'm... I...I know. I'm very aware I'm behaving badly." He glanced back to his sister-in-law. "Mia, I really do apologise. It won't happen again."

We left the marquee and went for what would, under other circumstances, have been a nice walk around the garden. It was a bright, summery day, and I'd had champagne, and there were flowers and butterflies, but Oliver was vibrating like my gentleman's massager without the fun side.

"I'm sorry," he said, for about the thousandth time. "I shouldn't have brought you here."

"Come on, I'm not doing that badly."

"No, I mean. I'm not at my best. And I don't want you to see me not at my best."

"Oliver, you've seen me having all kinds of freak-outs. I think I can handle you being a bit snarky at a garden party."

He got even more vibratey. "I knew I shouldn't have worn this shirt."

The problem was, he'd said that about every shirt, and he'd tried twelve—nearly making us not ridiculously early in the process. "For the last time, the shirt is fine." I stopped and tugged him round so we were facing each other. "You know, we can go home if you want to?"

He looked at me as if I'd suggested a murder-suicide pact. "We've barely got here. What would my parents think?"

"Right now, I don't really care. All I know is that being here is making you unhappy."

"I'm not unhappy. It's my parents' anniversary. I'm not... handling things very well."

I wasn't sure how to say "You're not handling things very well because your parents are being arseholes to you." I wasn't even sure it was my place. So instead I tried, "I don't think it's you. I mean, Christopher isn't exactly covering himself in glory either."

"Christopher is always covered in glory. At least as far as our parents are concerned."

"You mean, apart from the fact they keep pressuring him to have kids when he clearly doesn't want kids?"

"That's aimed at me, not him. My parents are very understanding about my sexuality, but I can't help but be aware that it has come with attendant disappointments."

"Look"—I flung up my hands—"this is purely hypothetical because it is way too early in the relationship for this conversation, but if you want kids, you can have kids."

"You mean, I could adopt children. That's not the same thing. At least, not from my parents' perspective."

Okay, this was a whole other can of problematic worms. And

now was not the time to open it. "You see, this is why you need queer friends. If you knew more gay people, you could always cut a deal with a lesbian."

"If you're trying to be funny, Lucien, this is in poor taste."

"Sorry, that got flippant. I'm just trying to say that you can live *your* life however *you* want. And your parents' expectations shouldn't factor into that. And I'll bet you any money you like that Chris and Mia are having this exact same conversation right now."

He iced up. "I very much doubt that."

"Oh for—"

A fork tinkled against a glass and we dutifully drifted over the patio, where David and Miriam were standing with about-to-make-a-speech faces on. Joy.

"Thank you," began David, "thank you all for coming to help Miriam and myself celebrate our Ruby Wedding Anniversary. I remember the evening all those years ago when I walked into our common room at the LSE, and I saw the most ravishing woman I'd ever imagined sitting across the way from me. And I said to myself, right then, *that's the lady I'm going to marry.*" A pause. A joke was coming, wasn't it? Rumbling towards us like a disappointing freight train. "And Miriam was two seats away from her."

We all laughed dutifully. Except Uncle Jim, who seemed to find it legitimately hilarious.

"Of course we didn't get on at first, because anybody who knows Miriam knows that she's—shall we say—a woman of strong opinions. But she soon warmed to me once I started pretending to agree with her about everything."

Another round of polite laughter. I thought Uncle Jim might actually piss himself.

"Over our forty years of marriage, we've been blessed with two wonderful sons—"

"*And Oliver and Christopher,*" I murmured under my breath.

"—and Oliver and Christopher. But, seriously, we're tremendously proud of both our boys, one a doctor, one a lawyer, but somehow neither of them making any bloody money."

Laughter again. Uncle Jim literally slapped his thigh.

"Over the years our family has continued to grow, our most recent addition being the lovely Mia, Christopher's wife, and also our last best hope for grandchildren on account of Oliver being a screaming bender."

I stifled a sigh. You see, it's okay because it's the *ironic* kind of homophobia.

"But enough about the boys," David went on. "Because today is about Miriam and myself. And I, for one, couldn't ask for a more beautiful wife. I mean, I could ask, but I probably wouldn't get one." He lofted a glass. "To Miriam."

We obediently *Miriam*ed back.

"To David." Miriam's speech at least had the virtue of being short.

"To David," we echoed.

While I put an arm around Oliver and looked for a hole we could hide in.

CHAPTER 46

THE AFTERNOON, WELL, IT HAPPENED, dragging itself along like a dog with worms. I handled it by standing meekly at Oliver's side while he made polite small talk with various friends and relatives. It was boring as fuck but it would have been okay if I hadn't also had to watch him getting quieter and smaller with every conversation. Maybe I'd had too much champagne but, honestly, it felt like losing him. And all I wanted was to get him back home where he could be prissy or grumpy or funny or secretly wicked. Where he could be my Oliver again.

Eventually, we ended up back on the patio. Miriam and David were holding court from a set of fancy garden furniture, and Oliver and Christopher had just presented them with their joint anniversary gift—a pair of ruby earrings for her, a pair of ruby cuff links for him, which had been offered with an awkward sense of obligation and received with complacent gratitude. Fun times.

"Oliver, darling." Miriam patted the space beside her. "It's so nice to be able to catch up." She glanced to Uncle Jim who, somehow, contrived to always fucking be there. "He hardly speaks to us, you know. At least with Christopher it's because you know he's saving babies in some dreadful malaria-ridden swamp."

Oliver settled in beside her. There was nowhere for me, of course, so I perched on the arm, which drew me an immediate look of disapproval. I briefly considered getting up out of respect, but I'd been on the fast lane to *fuck it* all afternoon and had just crossed the border.

"I'm sorry, Mother," he said. "I know I'm not saving babies, but I have had rather a lot going on."

Miriam's eyes alighted on me very briefly, and then skittered away. "So I see. What happened to the other fellow?"

"Andrew and I broke up."

"Shame. He seemed like such a nice young man."

"It wasn't working out."

"I suppose"—she paused frankly indelicately—"it's more difficult in your situation. I mean, you have to be so careful."

"I'm...I'm not sure that's entirely the case."

"You know best, darling." Apparently it was time for a knee pat. "I just worry because I'm your mother. And you see such horrible stories in the newspapers."

"I'm fine. Really. I think Lucien's been good for me."

"You look very tired."

Yeah, that would be because he hardly slept last night. In the boring tossing, turning, going for a run at 3:00 a.m. way. Rather than the exciting doing sexy things way.

"I told you"—a line had appeared between Oliver's brows— "I'm fine."

Miriam blinked rapidly as if to say "I'm trying not to cry, but it's hard because you're being so horrible to me." "You won't understand this because you'll never have children of your own, but it's very difficult for me to see you boys not taking care of yourselves."

"For God's sake, Oliver," snapped David. "Stop upsetting your mother."

Oliver drooped. "I'm sorry, Mother."

"She gave up a lot for you. Show her some bloody gratitude. And she's right, by the way. When was the last time you had a haircut?"

Before Oliver could reply—I was hoping, in the face of evidence, he was going to tell them all to fuck off—Uncle Jim decided it was time to lighten the mood. Clapping his brother on the back, he unleashed an infuriating chortle. "Probably too busy with his new boyfriend, eh? Eh?"

Somehow Oliver did not punch him in the face. "Lucien's had an important work function so, yes, we have been busy."

"Well, you'd better be careful." Uncle Jim pawed at Oliver in a way that I thought was meant to be affectionate. "Put on any more weight, and he'll dump you like the rest of them."

"I'm not going to dump him," I insisted, probably slightly too loudly. "He looks great. We're very happy."

His mother faffed again with his tie, sighing softly. "Maybe it's this shirt. You know blue isn't your colour, darling."

"I'm sorry." I hadn't thought it would be possible for Oliver to shrink further but he shrank further. "I didn't want to be late so I dressed in a hurry."

"We've still got some of your old things upstairs if you want to change."

Oliver visibly cringed. "I've not lived here since I was seventeen. I don't think anything would fit me anymore."

Another hearty laugh from Uncle Jim. "See, what did I say? You're nearly thirty now. You'll be a fat bastard before you know it."

"Leave the boy alone, James," said David indulgently. Who then totally failed to take his own advice. "Anyway, Oliver. When are you going to start doing something useful with your life?"

I tried to catch Oliver's eye but he was staring fixedly at his clasped hands. "Well, I'm building my reputation in Chambers and we'll see where it goes from there."

"You know we only want you to be happy, darling." That was Miriam. "But is this really where you want to be?"

Oliver glanced up warily. "W-what do you mean?"

"She means," explained David, "that if this was really what you wanted to be doing with your life, you'd be putting a bit more into it. I was talking to Doug at the club, and he was telling me you should be a QC by now."

"That would be almost unprecedented."

"That's not what Doug said. Said he knew a fellow your age got silk last month."

"Sorry?" asked Christopher unexpectedly. "Is this the same Doug who told you we shouldn't take that job in Somalia because we'd get Ebola? Is he an expert on the law now, as well as infectious disease?"

Miriam huffed. "I understand. People your age think people our age can't know anything."

"That's not what I... Oh, forget it."

"In any case," murmured Oliver, "I am looking for more senior positions but they'd probably involve leaving London."

This was news to me. But now was probably not the time to bring that up. Also it was weirdly jarring to think of Oliver being anywhere but, well, where he was. In that absurdly pretty house in Clerkenwell, which always felt like it smelled of French toast, even when it didn't.

David folded his arms. "Didn't think I raised you to be a quitter, Oliver."

Pretty much at the same time his wife said, "What will we do if *both* our sons move away? You're going up north, aren't you? You always said you wanted to go up north."

"I'm not going anywhere," Oliver tried desperately.

If David's sigh of disappointment had been any more exaggerated, he would have passed out from lack of oxygen. "Yes, we're aware of that, son. That's exactly the problem."

"For God's sake. Stop it." Oh help. That was me and I really wished it hadn't been. But everyone was staring so I was kind of committed. "Can't you see you're upsetting him?"

There was one of those silences that made you miss screaming.

Then Miriam was glaring at me with what I was shocked to realise was actual contempt. "How dare you try to tell us how to speak to our own son?"

"I'm not. I'm just pointing out the blindingly fucking obvious. Which is, you're making Oliver feel bad for no reason."

"Step down, Lucien." David stood up, which lacked a certain amount of impact because he was nearly a foot shorter than me. "We've known him a lot longer than you have."

No use turning back now. "Yeah, that doesn't change the fact that you're being arseholes."

Miriam did that you-have-nearly-made-me-cry look again. "Oliver, what on earth possessed you to bring this man into our home?"

There was no answer from Oliver. Which was fair enough because, honestly, I was asking myself the same question.

"Leave him alone." I...shit...I might actually have roared. "Fine, you don't like me. Well, guess what? I don't care. I care about the fact you've invited my boyfriend to a garden party and seem to be getting off on torturing him. And clearly he's too nice or too beaten down from years of this shit to tell you to go fuck yourselves, but I'm not. So...um. Go fuck yourselves."

I'm not sure what reaction I'd been expecting. I mean, obviously it would have nice if they'd turned round and said, "Gosh, you're right, we'll go away and rethink our entire value system," but I think that ship had sailed at around the point I told them to go fuck themselves.

"Get out of my house" was David's predicable and, in context, not unreasonable reply.

I ignored him, and slid off the arm of the bench to plant myself in front of Oliver. He wouldn't look at me. "I'm sorry I've fucked this up. And I'm sorry I've said 'fuck' so many times. Especially when you've been so amazing whenever I've needed you. It's just"—I pulled in a shaky breath—"you're the best man I've ever met. And I can't sit by and watch other people make you doubt that. Even if they're your parents."

Finally, he looked up, his eyes pale and unreadable in the summer sunlight. "Lucien..."

"It's okay. I'm going. And you don't have to come with me. But I want you to know that...that you're great. And I don't know how anyone could think you're not, y'know, great. And...like..." This was impossible. It would have been impossible if we'd been alone in a dark room. And here we were with a half-dozen people staring at us "...your job is...great and you're really...great at it. And you look great in blue. And..." I was getting the feeling this could have gone better. "...I know I'm not your family and I know I'm just some guy but I hope you can believe that I care about you enough that...you can believe...what I'm saying about you now. Because it's...true."

I fully intended to say my piece and walk out of there with my head held high and whatever was left of my dignity. But, yeah. Didn't happen.

I panicked.

And ran like hell.

CHAPTER 47

I HADN'T GOT VERY FAR—NOT even to the point of having to worry how I was going to get out of Milton Keynes—when I heard footsteps. I turned to see Oliver gaining on me rapidly. Seriously, it was embarrassing how fit he was and I wasn't. I had no idea what he was thinking, partly because everyone has the same face while they're running, but mainly because there was no way to tell how he was going to have taken that. The fact he'd come after me was a good sign, right? Well, unless he wanted to have a go at me for being rude to his parents.

"Oliver, I—" I started.

"Let's go home."

Did that mean "let's go home because you've made me see my parents are emotionally abusive and I don't have to stand for it" or "let's go home because you've embarrassed me so much we literally have to leave town"? Even his nonrunning face wasn't helping.

Not really knowing what else to do, I got in the car and had hardly clicked my seat belt into place when Oliver pulled away with the sort of reckless disregard for safety that I usually associated with, well, me. We got halfway to the end of the road with Oliver noticeably exceeding the speed you were supposed to stick to in a built-up area and paying way less attention to lane discipline than even I was comfortable with.

"Um," I tried. "Should you be—"

He swerved to avoid an incoming cyclist and I yelped.

"Okay, getting actually scared now."

With a screech and a grinding of gears, Oliver ploughed the car up the kerb and hit the brakes. Then he folded his arms across the steering wheel, laid his head against them, and burst into tears.

Oh shit. For a second or two, I tried to do that British thing where you pretend nothing untoward is happening in the hope it'll sort itself out quickly and amicably, and then you'll never have to talk about it again. Except Oliver was *crying*, and not stopping crying, and this was definitely a boyfriend job—one that, as an aspiring boyfriend, I was failing hard at.

It didn't help we were in a car, both of us responsibly wearing seat belts, so I couldn't even inadequately hug him. Instead, I was reduced to inadequately petting his shoulder like he'd come third in a primary-school sack race. And I desperately wanted to say something supportive but "don't cry" was toxic bullshit, "it's okay to cry" was patronising, and "there, there" had never made anybody feel better ever in the history of emotions.

Eventually Oliver shook off my hand and turned to face me. He had that red, puffy serious-tears look about him that filled me with a hopeless desire to make everything better for him. "I wish," he said, with a valiant effort to sound Oliver-like, "I wish you hadn't seen that."

"Oh my God, it's okay. Everybody cries."

"Not that. Well, a little bit that. It…it's…everything." He gave a sad little sniff. "I've behaved terribly today."

"You weren't the one telling everyone to go fuck themselves."

"No…I…I'm grateful you tried to speak up for me. But I should never have put you in that position."

I reached across the space between us and smoothed back his

hair from his sticky eyes. "The whole deal was that you'd come to my work thing, and I'd come to your family thing."

"And if I'd...if I'd done better, it would have been...better." He paused. "I knew my mother wouldn't like this shirt."

"Fuck the shirt. And, and I acknowledge out of context this sounds really bad, fuck your mother."

"Please stop saying that. I know today was difficult, but they genuinely want the best for me. And I keep letting them down."

"Oliver, that is the wrongest thing I've ever heard." I made a somewhat futile attempt to sound calm and rational. "Like, okay, I'm just guessing here, but have you ever gone anywhere with your parents without your mum having some complaint or other about what you're wearing?"

"She has very high standards."

"Maybe. Or maybe she's—and I'm having trouble putting this in a nonjudgmental way—maybe she's got into the habit of criticising you and hasn't paid attention to how much that messes you up."

His eyes filled with fresh tears. Go me. "She's not trying to upset me. She's trying to help."

"And, you know what? I believe that. But you don't need that kind of help, and trying to make you think you do is...is...*mean*. And don't even get me started on your dad."

"What's wrong with my father? I mean, I know he's a bit unreformed but he's never been violent, he's always been there, he's supported Christopher through medical school and me through the bar."

"Yeah, none of that gives him the right to call you a screaming bender in front of his friends."

"He was joking. He's always been fine with my sexuality."

"He literally used it as a punch line."

"Lucien, I feel bad enough about this already."

"You shouldn't be the one who's feeling bad," I insisted. "You're a good person."

"But not a very good son."

"Only by the standards of the arseholes you're unfortunate enough to have for parents."

He hid his face, and I had a horrible feeling he was crying again. "I don't want to talk about this anymore."

Wow. I sucked at being comforting. I'd love to pretend that I'd strategically made myself the bad guy so Oliver had someone other than himself to be angry at but, firstly, I hadn't. I'd just fucked up. And, secondly, it wasn't working anyway. I patted him again because it was the most successful thing I'd done that afternoon.

"Sorry." I kept patting. "I'm really sorry. And I'm here for you. And, y'know, feel your feelings. However you need to feel them."

He felt his feelings for…quite a long time.

Eventually he lifted his head. "I wish," he said, "I could have a bacon sandwich."

"That"—my enthusiasm here was probably a little bit inappropriate, but I was just so fucking glad I could actually help somehow—"I can do."

"I meant, except I'm a vegetarian."

I thought about this a moment. "Okay, but in an 'industrial farming is bad, think about your carbon footprint' way?"

"Does that make a difference?"

"Well," I went on, hoping that I was putting this together right. It felt like something Oliver would say, and I thought he'd appreciate that. "If you're avoiding meat because you're trying to reduce the overall negative effect of meat-eating on the world, then what really matters isn't what *you* eat, it's what gets eaten. In fact, it doesn't even matter what gets eaten, it matters what gets *bought*."

He sat up. Turns out being emotionally supportive wasn't

nearly as effective as giving him an intellectual exercise. "I might make the case that one should nevertheless take responsibility for one's own behaviour, but go on."

"Well, I've already *got* bacon in my fridge. Which has already been paid for, so whatever contribution it's making to the—I don't know, the cured meat industrial complex or whatever—has already been made. So now it doesn't technically matter who eats it."

"But if *I* eat your bacon, you'll just buy more."

"I'll promise not to. Pinkie swear."

He gave me a disapproving look. "Pinkie swear? Are you American all of a sudden?"

"Okay, cross my heart, hope to die, stick a sausage in my eye? But you've got to admit I kind of win here. Also it's very good bacon. It's, like, ethical and free range and shit. From Waitrose."

"I'm sure there's a flaw in your argument somewhere. I'm not thinking very clearly right now. Also"—his lips curled upwards very faintly—"I really want some bacon."

"For the record, I make an amazing bacon sandwich. I have a life hack."

"Perhaps I'm showing my age, but I remember when we called life hacks 'ways of doing things.'"

He was definitely on the mend. "Yeah, and I have an excellent way of cooking bacon. Shut up."

"I shouldn't do this…"

"Oh, come on. You want a bacon sandwich. *Please* let me make you a bacon sandwich."

He was silent for a long moment or short minute. I hadn't quite anticipated what a big deal this was going to be for him.

"Well," he said finally, "all right. But you have to promise not to buy any more bacon for a fortnight."

"If that's what it takes…fine."

He dried his eyes and straightened his tie, settling his hands back in the ten-to-two position with the air of someone who'd got past the desire to plough us off the road and into someone's privet hedge. And to my relief, he drove us home very, very sensibly.

As for me, I think I'd been put off Milton Keynes for life. And all the concrete cows in the world couldn't bring me back.

CHAPTER 48

SURPRISINGLY, MY FLAT WAS STILL in pretty good nick. Obviously, not "cleaned all the things" level pristine, but also not a "what the hell is wrong with you" cesspit. It helped that Oliver had stayed over a couple of times and seemed to tidy as he went like some kind of human Roomba. Although I suppose thinking about it, a human Roomba is just a person with a vacuum cleaner.

Oliver was still doing whatever he was doing, dwelling or processing or crying on the inside, when we got in. So I headed for the kitchen and got out my cheap frying pan and my expensive bacon. Some people would probably have had it the other way around. But some people were wrong.

In a minute or two, Oliver—having shed his jacket and tie, but still wearing the ill-fated blue shirt that I maintain he looked fine in—came to join me. Something my kitchen was barely capable of dealing with.

"Why," he asked, smooshing up behind me, "is your bacon underwater?"

"I told you. It's a life hack."

"Lucien, I haven't had bacon in several years. Please don't ruin this for me."

If he hadn't had such a terrible day, I'd have been insulted at his lack of faith. "I'm not going to ruin it. This works perfectly.

I mean, assuming you like your bacon crispy and delicious, not flabby and burned."

"That seems like a false dichotomy."

I hoped the fact he was using the word *dichotomy* in cold blood meant he was feeling at least a little bit better. "I just mean, it's a good way to cook bacon so it doesn't dry out or turn to charcoal." I half turned so that I could catch his eye. "Trust me. If there's one thing I take seriously, it's bacon."

"I do." He kissed my neck, making me shiver. "Trust you, that is. Not take bacon seriously."

"Well, you did come in here to assess my bacon strategy."

"I came in to be close to you."

I ran through a bunch of responses in my head, but decided it wasn't the time to be taking refuge in banter. "I like having you here."

I mean, in abstract I liked having him there. In practice, it was a little bit awkward—but, hey, it was bacon, not the Sistine Chapel. It didn't take that much concentration, and I could watch it cooking almost as effectively with Oliver's arms around me as, well, not. Eventually, the water boiled off, and the bacon had crisped up beautifully. As it always did because the bacon hack is the best thing ever.

Oliver fished my thankfully unmouldy loaf of Hovis Soft White Medium from the bread bin he'd insisted on buying me when he'd discovered that I kept my bread on the side like a normal person, instead of giving it its own special box to go stale in. I buttered it up aggressively, because there's no point trying to make bacon healthy, and offered him his choice of condiments. Well, his choice of ketchup or not ketchup because I hadn't been as prepared as I would have liked to have been to cook emotional-support sandwiches.

Finally, we were on my sofa with plates on our laps, and Oliver was staring at his bacon butty with that confused, yearning look he sometimes got around desserts. And, if I'm honest, me.

"It's okay," I said, "to eat a bacon sandwich."

"I'm a vegetarian."

"Yeah, but you're also human. You can't be perfect all the time."

"I shouldn't do this."

I sighed. "Then don't. I'll eat it. But please don't expect me to talk you into something that you want to do but feel you have to deny yourself. Because that's fucked up."

There was a longish pause. Finally, Oliver took a bite of sandwich. His eyes fluttered closed. "God, that's good."

"I know this is wrong of me"—I dabbed a tiny curl of ketchup from the edge of his mouth with a fingertip—"but, fuck me, you're sexy when you're compromising your principles."

He blushed. "This isn't funny, Lucien."

"I'm not laughing."

We baconed for a while in silence.

"Y'know," I said finally, "I really am sorry that this afternoon didn't go. Um. Anything approaching well. And I'm sorry I got it wrong in the car. I was just... I've never seen you like that."

He was staring at his sandwich with way too much focus. "I'll try to make sure you never have to see me like that again."

"Not what I was going for." I flailed around in vague private guilt. "I wanted to be better for you at the party. Except you didn't... I didn't know what to expect."

"Oh"—Oliver's brows lifted nastily—"so it's my fault you decided to swear at my parents."

I opened my mouth, then closed it again. I had to un-fuck this somehow. "I get that it's not my place to criticise your parents. But it feels like the only way you can believe good things about them is if you believe bad things about yourself. And I'm not... That's not okay with me."

"Lucien, I need you to accept that I had a perfectly normal childhood. You're making Mother and Father out to be monsters."

Reaching out an uncertain hand, I stroked his arm in that

wholly unhelpful way I'd managed to perfect in the car. "I'm not saying they're monsters. They're just people. But people, well, suck sometimes. And while I'm sure they've done lots of good things for you, they've also clearly done some bad things. And... you don't have to bear the burden of that."

"I've never claimed my parents were perfect." He tugged fretfully at the crust on his sandwich. "But they've always encouraged me to push myself, and it's not unreasonable of them to continue to do that."

"Okay," I tried, "but if that's what they're trying to do, why are you sitting on my sofa eating a bacon sandwich and being sad, instead of, like, feeling uplifted and motivated?"

He turned, his eyes meeting mine for a long grey moment. "Because I'm not as strong as you think I am."

"This isn't about strength," I told him. "It's about who you're choosing to make happy."

There was a long silence. During which I picked half-heartedly at my sarnie. Apparently there *were* some situations bacon couldn't make better.

"I keep wondering," Oliver said, "why I brought you today."

"Wow. I know I handled it badly but that's harsh."

He was frowning thoughtfully. Because Oliver. "No—you didn't. Or rather, you handled it as I perhaps, on some level, expected you might. Not that I thought you'd go as far as telling my parents to go fuck themselves in front of Uncle Jim and the vicar. But I think..."

"What?" I asked.

"I think I wanted to do something that was for me, and not for them. To see what it felt like."

"And, um, what *did* it feel like?"

"I...I still don't know."

"That's all right." I moved across and gave him a...well...a sort of nuzzle, I guess, that I probably should have been self-conscious about. "I can live with being for you."

Quietly, he finished his bacon sandwich. Then he ate the rest of mine. But I felt he probably deserved it after everything he'd been through. Trying to stick with my new grown-up lifestyle, I took the plates back to the kitchen and did that half-washing-up thing where you rinse the worst bits off under the tap and dump the rest in the sink, hoping Oliver wouldn't have spiralled into a pit-of-fried-meat-related despair and self-recrimination while I was away.

I found him still on the sofa, still looking a bit blank.

"Are you okay?" I asked.

"I'm not sure."

I settled on the floor in front of him, folding my arms across his knees. "That's all right. You don't have to…um. Anything really."

"I thought I'd feel guiltier. But I just feel…full of bacon."

"Don't knock it. That's a good feeling."

His fingers curled lightly into my hair. "Thank you for doing that for me."

"I'd say I got as much out of it as you did, except you ate my fucking sandwich."

"I'm so sorry."

"I'm teasing, Oliver." I butted his hand with my head. "In two weeks, I'll be able to have all the bacon I like. I'm going to bathe in bacon like that bit in *American Beauty*."

"That is a very disturbing mental image. And also undercuts your original consequentialist argument for why it was okay for me to have this sandwich in the first place."

"Fine. No meat baths then. You're so unreasonable."

He laughed, a bit unsteadily. "Oh, Lucien. I don't know what I would have done without you today."

"Well, probably you wouldn't have had to leave your parents' anniversary."

"From what you've said, that might not have been a good thing."

"See. You're making progress."

There was a pause. "I'm afraid I still can't quite bring myself to think about it properly. I'm not as fearless as you."

"I'm plenty fearful, as you well know."

"It never seems to hold you back."

I caught his wrist and kissed his palm. "You're giving me way too much credit. I was a total mess before I met you."

"Your flat was a total mess. It's not the same."

"Y'know"—I smiled up at him—"I'm not going to sit here and argue with you about whether I suck or not. You just keep believing I don't."

"I'll never believe you're anything less than remarkable."

Oh fuck. I've never been good at this stuff. "Me too. I mean, only like, I think you are. Not that I think I am. I mean, not in a low self-esteem way. Like, that would be really arrogant. Look, can we have sex now?"

"Ever the romantic, Lucien."

"It's how I express myself. It's part of my unique charm."

He snorted, but let me lead him into the bedroom anyway. Where I undressed him slowly and, for some reason, couldn't stop kissing him. And he gave himself up to me, moment by moment, and I lost myself in the rhythm of his body and the hunger of his touch. I came to him like I thought I'd never come to anyone— forgetting to hold back in the need to make him feel as safe and as cherished and as special as he made me. I held him, and he clung to me, and we moved together, and, okay, I gazed into his eyes. And I whispered to him, telling him...stuff. Embarrassing stuff about how much I cared about him and how wonderful he was to me. And I...and we...and.

Look.

It's not the sort of thing you talk about, okay? It was for us. And it was everything.

———————

I was awoken, frankly way too early for a Sunday, by a fully dressed Oliver kissing me lightly on the forehead. This wasn't completely unprecedented because Oliver, being a responsible human adult, didn't share my commitment to the art of the lie-in, but something felt off.

"Goodbye, Lucien," he said.

I was suddenly way more conscious than I liked being at this time of the morning. "Wait. What? Where are you going?"

"Home."

"Why? If you've got work to do, you can do it here. Or give me ten minutes"—well, that was fairly optimistic but what the hell—"and I'll come with you."

"You misunderstand me. I've enjoyed our time together, and I'm grateful for your efforts, but we've done what we set out to do. It's time for us both to move on."

What was even happening right now? "Hang on. What... I... Hey, we had the *this feels real to both of us* talk. There's no takesy-backsies on the *this feels real to both of us* talk."

"And," he said, in this cool, empty voice, "we also agreed that we would wait until the end of the arrangement to make any formal commitments."

"Okay. Then I...formally commit."

"I don't think that's a good idea."

Once again, what was even happening right now? The only thing I was certain about was that I did not want to be having this conversation naked. Not that it was looking like I had a choice. "Why not?"

"Because we were wrong. This isn't real."

"How isn't it real?" Pulling the duvet around me, I struggled into a kneeling position. "We've gone to restaurants, we've talked about our feelings, we've met each other's fucking parents. In what way is this not a relationship?"

"I've had far more of them than you. And I can assure you this has felt nothing like one. It's been a fantasy. That's all."

I stared at him, angry and betrayed and hurt and confused. "You've been in more relationships than me because—by your own admission—you've ballsed so many of them up. Are you honestly trying to claim we're not a couple because we're not miserable or bored of each other?"

"It's easy to be happy," he told me, "when you're pretending."

"Who's fucking pretending? Do you think I'd be like this if I was *pretending*?"

He sat on the edge of the bed, rubbing his brow in that tormented way he had. Except this time it was expressing more than indulgent frustration at my antics. "Please don't make this more difficult than it has to be."

"Of course I'm going to make it fucking difficult. You think I'm just going to let you throw this away? For no reason except... Oh fuck, is this because I made you a bacon sandwich?" I put my head in my hands. "I can't believe I'm about to get dumped over a bacon sandwich."

"It's not about the sandwich. It's"—he sighed—"about you and me. We're different people."

"But we work." That came out sounding slightly more pitiful than I would have wanted. But I guess I had some choices ahead of me, and if it came down to keeping my dignity versus keeping Oliver, things weren't looking so good for dignity. "And I don't understand what I've done wrong. I mean, apart from telling your entire family to fuck off. And, okay, that was probably a biggie, but if it was a deal-breaker, I wish you'd told me that before I made a total fool of myself over you last night."

"It's not that either."

"Then," I yelled, "what the fuck is it? Because from where I'm standing, you spent months telling me I'm wonderful and beautiful and amazing and worth something and now it's just, what, *kthanksbai?*"

"It's not about you, Lucien."

"How is you dumping *me* not about *me?*" Okay. This was good. I could work with this. If I was angry, I wasn't crying. "Like, did you mean a single word you said since this whole thing started?"

"I meant all of it, but being with you isn't right for me. And being with me isn't right for you."

"It felt fucking right yesterday. It's been fucking right for ages."

He wouldn't even look at me. "I've already told you: this hasn't been real. It can't last because, as you've pointed out, my relationships don't, and I'd rather remember what we've had than watch it go cold and die, like it always does."

"Oh, come on. That is the worst reason for breaking up with someone I have ever heard." I made a messy grab for his hand. "I can't promise you forever because that's...not at all how it works. But I literally can't imagine not wanting to be with you. Not wanting this. Whatever we call it."

"That's because you barely know me." With a depressing finality, he untangled his fingers from mine and stood up. "You keep telling me how perfect I am, and must know by now that I'm anything but. In two months you'll realise I'm not that special, and a month after that you'll realise I'm not that interesting either. We'll spend less time together, and mind less about it, and one day you'll tell me things have come to a natural conclusion. You'll move on and I'll be where I always have been: never quite what someone is looking for." He turned his head away. "I'm just not strong enough to go through that with you."

There was a pause.

And then, in a moment of epiphany that deserved a full fucking chorus of angels, or at least the Skenfrith Male Voice Choir, I got it.

"Hang on a second." I actually wagged a finger at him. "I know this because I do it all the time. You like me and you're scared and you've been through something and it's shaken you up and your first instinct is to run. But if I can work through that, then so can you. Because you are way smarter and way less fucked up than me."

Another pause.

"How about," I suggested, somewhere between hope and desperation, "you go into the bathroom for a bit."

A third pause, and definitely the worst yet.

Fuck. Fuck. Fuckity fuck. This was seriously nonideal. I'd legitimately gone all in on this. I'd said some pretty intense things and put myself way out there. And if after all that it blew up in my face, I didn't know how I was going to—

"I can't be what you need me to be," he said. "Goodbye, Lucien."

And by the time I got past the "wait, stop, please don't go" stage he'd already gone.

Which pretty much ruined my Sunday.

And my Monday. And my Tuesday. And possibly my life.

CHAPTER 49

WHEN I'D ARRANGED DAD MEETING 2: Electric Boogaloo, I'd been counting on Oliver not breaking up with me three days earlier and me not having to trog out to the Chiltern Firehouse feeling useless and heartbroken. At the time, I'd been weirdly touched—I mean, it wasn't my sort of place, and to be honest, it probably wasn't his sort of place either, but it was where you went if you were a celebrity or looking for celebrities. So by taking me there, Jon Fleming was publicly upgrading me from "estranged wastrel son" to "legit family member." And while I hadn't snorted quite enough of his Kool-Aid to believe this was totally for my benefit—it would clearly play well as a chapter in the Jon Fleming rehabilitation story—I'd still benefit from it. A bit. To some extent. In the not-nothing sense that I was coming to accept was my relationship with my father.

Of course it struck me that getting something I thought I'd always wanted and losing something I never thought I'd want in the same week was kind of a pisstastic irony. And not the most helpful thing in the world emotional-stability-wise. Anyway, there I was, sitting at a corner table in a converted Victorian fire station, three seats away from someone I was pretty sure had been in One Direction, but wasn't Harry Styles or Zayn Malik. And half an hour later, I was still sitting there, and the waiters were circling like very polite sharks.

After an hour, three unanswered texts, and a straight-to-voicemail call, a very nice young woman had gently informed me that I'd need to order in the next ten minutes or vacate the table. So I was left trying to work out if I'd be more embarrassed slinking away from a Michelin-starred restaurant at eight in the evening or sitting alone, working my way through an expensive three-course meal like this had totally been my plan all along.

So I left, getting heartily papped on my way out, but right then, I did not give two fucks. At least, not until one of them asked if Oliver had got bored of me, at which point I suddenly gave a whole lot of fucks. And, a few months ago, I'd have had one of those embarrassing freak-outs that the paparazzi are constantly baiting you into having so they can photograph you having them. But, apparently, the new mature me was just sad about it.

Being mature sucked.

I put my head down and walked, and this time there was nobody to wrap a coat around me and keep me safe from the flashes and the questions. Mostly I was... Actually, I wasn't sure what I was mostly, especially now Oliver dumping me and my dad dumping me were getting mixed up in my head like a rejection smoothie. As far as Jon Fleming was concerned, I was this frustrating blend of disappointed and not at all surprised. But then there was also this bitter aftertaste, reminding me that if I got pissed off at Jon Fleming for standing me up, and then it turned out he'd tragically died of cancer that afternoon, I'd have felt shitty for possibly the rest of my life. But, apart from checking the internet for obituaries, I didn't have any way of knowing what was really happening with him so I was stuck in this fucked-up quantum state where my dad was simultaneously an arsehole and a corpse. And Oliver...Oliver was gone, and I had to stop thinking about him.

So I rang Mum. And she made some concerned French noises, and then suggested I come over. Which I knew meant it was bad news. The question was, which bad news was it? And an hour or so later, I was getting out of a taxi on Old Post Office Road while my mum hovered anxiously in the doorway.

"He better not be dead," I told her as I marched into the living room. "I'm going to be so annoyed if he's dead."

"Well, then there is good news, mon caneton. Because he is not dead. In fact, he is probably not going to be dead for many years."

I threw myself onto the unusually dog-less but still faintly dog-smelling sofa. There was only one way this was going. There was only one way this had *ever* been going. "He never had cancer, did he?"

"The doctors had said some worrying things, and you know these old men. They are very nervous about their prostates."

I put my head in my hands. I'd have cried but I was cried out already.

"I'm sorry, Luc." She squeezed in beside me and patted me between the shoulder blades like I'd swallowed a penny. "I don't think he was lying exactly. I'm afraid this is what it is like when you are famous. You're surrounded by people who are paid to agree with you, so you get these ideas in your head and you forget they're not necessarily true. Also, don't get me wrong. The man is a total prick."

"So...what? Now he's not dying, he doesn't want to know me anymore?"

"I mean"—she sighed—"yes?"

Turns out, that old saying about expecting the worst and never being disappointed super doesn't work. Jon Fleming behaving exactly like Jon Fleming had no right to hurt this much. "Thanks for not sugarcoating that."

"Well, look on the bright side. Now you know for certain he's a worthless sack of shit that you don't want in your life at all."

"Yeah"—I looked up, slightly wet-eyed and not sure what my expression was doing—"I guess I knew that going in."

"No, you felt it. There's a difference. Now, you'll never wonder. And your father cannot pull this bullshit on you ever again."

"Mum, if that's your idea of a life lesson, it sucks."

"Bof. Sometimes life sucks." She paused. "He still wants to do the album, you know."

I stared at her. "Seriously?"

"He's surprisingly dependable where fame and money are concerned."

Obviously, this was the last thing I wanted. It was bad enough when he'd walked out on *us*. Now, apparently, he was just walking out on *me*. And it was stupid and selfish, but I did not want to share my mum with Jon Fucking Fleming. He did not deserve that. "It...it'd be a great opportunity for you."

"Maybe, but I'm probably going to tell him to go fuck himself."

"Is that," I asked, "a good idea?"

She made another French noise. "I was going to say, 'No but it will be extremely satisfying.' But, actually, yes. It is a good idea. I don't need the money and neither do you. You won't take anything from me as it is. So I'm sure you wouldn't if it had your father's cockprints all over it—"

"Thanks for that image."

"And if I wanted to be making music, I'd be making music. I don't need anyone's permission for that, especially not Jon Fleming's."

"I know it's none of my business, which is why I've never brought it up but, why *did* you never make another album?"

She offered one of her most expressive shrugs. "Lots of reasons. I'm still very rich, I've said what I needed to say. And then I had you, and I had Judy."

"Um." My mouth opened and closed a few times. "Judy? Mum, are you coming out to me? Have you been A Gay all this time?"

"Oh, Luc"—she gazed at me in disappointment—"you are so narrow-minded. Judy is my best friend. And when you have lived the kind of life I have, you realise that the big sexy love is not the kind that really matters. Besides, I'm a famous older French lady. If I want to get laid, I can."

"Please stop. Just stop."

"You were the one who wanted to know if you'd grown up in a secret lesbian fuck palace."

"Okay. Never *ever* say that phrase again."

"The point is, I loved making music. And I loved your father. And I love Judy. And I love you. In very different ways. I have never wanted to have sex with my guitar or watch *Drag Race* with Jon Fleming." She leaned in conspiratorially. "Honestly, I think it would threaten his masculinity. He once said he was going to glass Bowie for looking at him funny. I was very embarrassed. I told him, David's not a gay. He's just pretty."

I covered my mouth with my hands and gave a sobbing sort of laugh. "Oh, Mum, I love you. And I know it's not about me, but if you did change your mind about the album thing, I'd...I'd, y'know...be fine with it."

"Even if I wanted to work with your father again—which I very much do not—he has treated my son incredibly badly, and I am very angry with him about that. Also Judy and I are getting into *Terrace House* so we are going to be extremely busy."

We fell into silence, which was something Mum usually reserved for special occasions so she was probably more concerned about me than she was letting on. Problem was, I wasn't entirely sure what to say. Or, for that matter, how I felt.

Eventually, she nudged her shoulder lightly against mine. "What of you, mon caneton? I am sorry you have had to go through this."

"I'll be okay."

"Are you sure? You do not have to say that if it is not true."

I did something that, on a better day, I would have been

thinking about. "I don't know...it could be. Maybe it's because I half knew it was coming—I mean not the 'oh I'm totally fine, fuck you'—but the being let down. It hurts like hell, but not in the way I thought it would. Not in a way that changes anything."

"That is good. I know it's a cliché, but he really isn't worth it. He's just an old bald man with a leaky prostate who's on TV sometimes."

I grinned. "They should make that his intro package."

"And yet, for some reason, they never even asked me to give them a quote. Though I still get royalties every time they use one of our clips."

We were quiet again for a moment.

"I think," I said finally, "what's weirding me out is that I've spent my whole life wondering why Jon Fleming didn't want me. And now I'm annoyed that I spent such a long time trying to understand this complete arsehole when there are so many people around me who...aren't complete arseholes."

"Yes, it's funny how arseholes do that to you."

"How do you stop them?"

"You don't. You just get on with things and eventually it's... fine. And you're fine. And you feel briefly bitter you spent so long not being fine. But then you're fine."

"I'm...I'm pretty sure I'm in the bitter stage."

"Eh. That's good. It's better than the 'Oh no, what did I do wrong, am I terrible person' stage. And the next step you will hardly notice because you will be fine and you will have a lovely son and a best friend and you can watch *Drag Race* with her dogs. I mean, that's me, obviously, not you. But you can do the you version."

I slumped back on the sofa. "I guess. But what with, y'know, everything, I'm not sure I've ever had a chance to work out what the *me version* is."

"Maybe it's whatever you're doing right now."

Great in principle. But, unfortunately, what I was doing right now was losing someone I actually did care about, not just my wankstain of a father. "Oliver dumped me."

"Oh, Luc." She gave me a genuinely sympathetic look. "I'm sorry. What happened?"

"I don't know. I think we got too close and he got too scared."

"Really? That sounds more like what you would do."

"That's what I said," I complained. "But he still walked out."

"Well, then." Another of Mum's shrugs. "Fuck him."

As advice went, it was surprisingly flexible and worked for my dad, because fuck him. But...but this was different. "Normally I'd agree, but Oliver was good for me, and I don't want to throw that away."

"Then don't."

I blinked a few annoyingly persistent tears from my eyes. "Okay, now you've gone from chill to unhelpful."

"I don't mean to be. But you had a boyfriend, and he made you happy for a while, and now it is over. And if we let happy things make us unhappy when they stopped, there would be no point having happy things."

"That is way more enlightened than I am capable of being right now." There was no point getting angry at my mother, but it was easier than being sad about my ex. "Oliver was pretty much the best part of my life, and I fucked it up, and there's nothing I can do about it, and that feels fucking terrible."

She did the ineffectual shoulder pat, which was somehow way less ineffectual when she did it. "I'm sorry you feel terrible, mon caneton. I am not saying that this will not hurt or that it will be easy. But you did not fuck it up. This Oliver clearly has, as the young people say today, the issues."

"Yeah, and I wanted to help him with them, like he helped me."

"That is his choice, though. Some people, they do not want to be helped."

I was about to protest, but then I remembered that I'd spent five years not wanting to be helped. And it had taken nearly losing my job, dating a guy I would never have considered dating, roping all my friends into a two-day flat-cleaning party, and having some dick from a nightclub feel sorry for me in the *Guardian* for me to realise that I hadn't been as safe as I thought I was. "So where does that leave me? He's still...everything I want, and I can't have him."

"As Mick used to say, 'You can't always get what you want.' And you know, Luc, Oliver was a nice boy and I'm sure he liked you very much and I was wrong about him being engaged to a duke. But I think maybe he just came along at the right time. He is like"—she waved her hand like the world's most raddled fairy godmother—"the feather in that elephant movie."

"Are you trying to tell me that not being a total fuckup was inside me all along?"

"I mean, I used to be a professional songwriter, so I wouldn't say it in such a boring way but...yes? I don't think Oliver changed your life, mon cher. I think he helped you to see it differently. He has gone now, but you still have the job you pretend you don't like, and the friends who have stuck by you through all of your bullshit, and you have me, and Judy, and we love you very much, and will always be here for you until we are both dead."

I squidged along and she put an arm around me. "Thanks, Mum. That was lovely until the crushing reminder of our mortality."

"Since your father is not dying anymore, I thought it was a good time to remind you to appreciate me while you can."

"I love you, Mum." This was embarrassing but, well, sometimes you had to. "Is it okay if I stay tonight?"

"Of course."

Half an hour later, I was lying in my childhood bed, staring at a ceiling whose every crack I already knew by heart. It was weird how, in a month, Jon Fleming had gone from being this idea I'd grown up with to a real person to an idea again—and, while that hurt, my life was already healing around him like skin closing over a cut. Oliver, though, was a whole different kettle of misery fish. But Mum had been right, hadn't she? I couldn't take everything he'd shown me and given me and shared with me and lose it in the…the shittiness of now. He'd helped me see that my life was better than I'd thought it was—that *I* was better than I'd thought *I* was. And I could hold on to that. Even if I couldn't hold on to him.

CHAPTER 50

"OKAY," I SAID TO ALEX.

He glanced up happily. "Oh, are we doing a joke? What larks. We haven't done one in ages."

"Right. What's a pirate's favourite letter of the alphabet?"

"Well, I suppose the average eighteenth-century seaman wouldn't have been literate, so probably most of them wouldn't have had one."

"Fair point. But, that aside, if you were thinking of a generic movie pirate, what would his or her favourite letter of the alphabet be?"

He wrinkled his nose. "I can honestly say I'm not certain."

You sometimes got a guess with this joke. You sometimes didn't. "You might think it'd be *arrrrr*," I explained in my best pirate voice, "but my first love shall always be *the sea*."

There was a long silence.

"Why would you think it would be *r*?" asked Alex. "I mean, *pirate* begins with a *p*. As do *plunder, pillage, purloin, privateer,* and *Port au Prince*."

"*Arrrrrrrrrr*. Like a pirate."

"No, *pirate* begins with *p*."

My phone went. Thank God. I answered on my way back to my office.

"Luc," cried Bridge, "there's a crisis."

What was it this time? Had they accidentally sold a set of film rights for five magic beans? "What's wrong?"

"It's Oliver!"

Suddenly I was paying attention. "Is he all right? What's happened?"

"He's moving to Durham. He's there right now. He's got a job interview tomorrow morning."

We'd broken up. And I'd come to terms with being broken up—okay that was sort of a lie, but I was certainly moving in a termward direction. Even so, my heart still felt like it was going to vomit. "What? Why?"

"He said he wanted a fresh start. Somewhere far away."

I was very inclined to panic. But this did not sound like Oliver. "Bridge, are you completely sure? He loves what he does. And, if I had to pick a word to describe him, it wouldn't be 'impulsive.'"

"He's been weird for ages. I know I'm not supposed to talk about you to each other, but this is an emergency."

"It's certainly odd," I agreed. "But I don't know what I'm supposed to do about it."

"You have to stop him, obviously. I mean, it's your fault for letting him go in the first place."

Ow. Not okay, Bridge. "I did *not* let him go. I begged him to stay. I even talked about my feelings and he dumped me anyway."

She sighed heavily. "Oh, you can both be so hopeless sometimes."

"That is unfair. I really tried."

"Then try again."

"Again? How many times do you want me to throw myself at a guy who doesn't want me?"

"More than once. And you know he wants you. He's always wanted you, Luc."

I collapsed into my desk chair, accidentally activating the tilt so that I nearly slid off under my workstation. "Maybe. But he's convinced himself it can't work, and I don't know how to unconvince him."

"Well, neither do I. But just sitting there while he runs away to the North is probably not a good start."

"So you want me to what? Get on a train to Durham and stand in the city centre shouting 'Oliver, Oliver, I love you' on the off chance he hears me?"

"Or," she suggested, "you could go to Durham and meet him at the hotel he's staying at—which I know because he told me—and then you could say 'Oliver, Oliver, I love you' to his face. Also...oh my gosh, you totally love him. I told you. This is going to be the best thing ever."

"No, it's a terrible idea. And Oliver will think I'm deeply creepy."

She thought about this for a moment. "What if I come with you?"

"I think that will look more creepy."

"I'm coming with you."

My phone buzzed ominously. And the WhatsApp group—now Bridge Over Troubled Waters—flicked into life with a message from the Bridge in question.

WE HAVE TO TAKE LUC TO DYRHAM

*DURHAM

BECAUSE OF TRUE LOVE!!!

This is your way of asking for my truck isn't it?

No, I typed quickly.

YES VERY TRUCK MCUH EMERGENCY WOW

I wish, came James Royce-Royce, someone would teach our Bridget a new meme

This was getting out of hand, and there'd only been seven messages. **Look everythings okay. No one needs to be driven anywhere. Please go about your lives. Thank you and goodnight**

And, of course, an hour later—having taken a personal day that I'd really hoped someone would care about or challenge me on—I was sitting in the back of Priya's truck, with Bridget, Tom, and the James Royce-Royces.

"What are you doing?" I asked. "You've got jobs, some of them quite important. You can't seriously want to drive five hours up to Durham just to watch me get shot down by a barrister."

"Nope"—Priya glanced into the rearview mirror—"we are all up for that. It's because we care-slash-hate you."

"This is the most romantic thing you've ever done, Luc darling," said James Royce-Royce. "We wouldn't miss it for the world."

I gaped at them. "And you're going to...stand around and watch while I...while I..."

"Tell Oliver you *looooooooove him*," offered Bridge.

"While I try and ask a guy who's already turned me down to go out with me."

"You're right." Thank God Tom was on my side. "Standing around and watching would be a bit ridiculous. Let's stop at a Welcome Break and grab some popcorn first."

Priya grinned. "I'd high-five you right now, but I like my truck far too much to take my hands off the wheel."

"I don't even know what I'm going to say to him," I muttered, "and, Bridge, if you tell me to tell him I looooooooove him one more time, I will shove you out of this vehicle."

That earned me a Level Seven Bridget Pout. "Don't be mean. I'm supporting you. And, besides, 'I love you' is all you should have to say."

"I'm pretty sure it doesn't work like that."

"It's all Tom had to say to me."

"For the record"—this was Tom—"I said quite a lot of other things. About how sorry I was for hooking up with your best friend—no offence, Luc."

I rolled my eyes. "It's fine. Tell me to my face what a mistake I am."

"Point is," interrupted Bridget, "it doesn't matter because I wasn't listening to anything after the 'I love you' bit."

Tom laughed and pulled her close. "I *do* love you."

"Oi." Priya banged the wheel. "The only person who's allowed to fuck in my truck is me. I mean me, and whoever I'm fucking."

"Yes, we'd inferred that, darling," remarked James Royce-Royce. "Otherwise you'd just be lying in the back seat having a massive wank."

Priya frowned into the mirror. "Thanks for that speculation into the scale of my masturbatory habits."

"Would you rather I said a tiny wank? A micro wank? A wankette?"

I covered my face with my hands. "I've changed my mind. I'm walking to Durham."

"There, there." Bridget offered me a consoling pat. "It's going to be fine. Oliver really likes you. And you really like him. You've just been really bad at making each other believe that."

"Actually he'd done a great job convincing me. Right up to the point where he said it was over and walked out of my flat."

"He's scared, Luc."

"Yeah, I got that. Credit me with some emotional intelligence."

"But you've also got to understand that he's spent his entire life trying to be the perfect son and the perfect boyfriend, and it never seems to work out for him."

I made an angry noise. "Yes, I got that too. I did pay some attention while we were dating. The difference is, his parents are dicks. And his boyfriends, I assume, have also been dicks."

"Some of them were quite nice. The boyfriends, I mean. His parents are awful and hate me."

"Oh how could anyone hate you, Bridget?" asked James Royce-Royce, with an almost inhuman lack of sarcasm.

She thought about it for a moment. "They seem to get very cross when you're late. And it's not like I'm late on purpose. Things come up. And I once asked for a Malibu and Coke at a party, and they looked at me like I'd asked for a glass of baby's blood."

"Yep." I nodded. "Sounds like them."

"So you can see," Bridge pressed on, "why he's not very good at having relationships."

Even though Oliver wasn't here, and it was the mildest possible criticism, I still felt a strange need to defend him. "He was amazing at them when he was with me. He's the best boyfriend I've ever had."

"That," offered Priya, "is because you're a titanic romantic disaster with incredibly low standards."

I gave her a look. "You know we really do only hang out with you for your truck."

"Stop doing banter." Bridge pounded her fist on the nearest solid object which was, unfortunately, me. "This is important. We're sorting out Luc's love life, and his low standards aren't the problem."

I was about to protest that I didn't have low standards. But I was in this mess because I'd told my friends I needed literally anyone who would go out with me. "So what *is* the problem?"

"You can't feel close to someone," Bridge went on, "when you're spending the whole time trying to be what you think they want."

"But he *is* what I want." Except then I remembered Oliver telling me he wasn't who I thought he was. "Oh fuck. Isn't he?"

Priya's eyebrows did something very aggressive. "We're about a third of the way to Durham, mate. He better fucking had be."

I was so confused. Or maybe I wasn't. Maybe all this stuff

about expectations and pretending and who people really were was so much smoke and bullshit. And maybe I'd just done a terrible job of showing Oliver that what made me happy wasn't the V-cut or the French toast or the socially acceptable career: it was... him. Maybe it *was* that simple.

"Yeah," I said. "He is."

CHAPTER 51

IT PROBABLY SAID SOMETHING ABOUT Oliver's sense of humour—even when he was apparently in the middle of an existential crisis—that he'd chosen to stay in a place called the Honest Lawyer Hotel. Going by my complete lack of historical knowledge or interest, it looked like a converted coaching house, all sash windows, sloping tile roofs, and chimney stacks. There was a blossom tree in full bloom out front, which made it, in theory at least, a great location to try and romance somebody back into your life. And, for that matter, county.

We stuck the truck in their carpark and piled through the front door, looking in no way suspicious.

"Um. Hello," I said to the be-suited man behind the desk—who frankly, and fairly, already seemed to have had enough of my shit.

"Can I help you?" A pause. "Any or all of you?"

"I'm looking for Oliver Blackwood. I think he's staying here."

He got that weary expression that people in service industries got when you were asking them to do things that definitely weren't their jobs. "I'm afraid I can't give you information about guests."

"But," I pounced, "he *is* a guest."

"I can't give you information about whether someone is a guest or not."

"He's not a film star or anything. He's just my ex-boyfriend."

"That doesn't make a difference. I'm not legally allowed to tell you who's staying here."

"Oh. Well. Please?"

"No."

"I've come a really long way."

"And"—to give the receptionist his due, he was being way more patient than I would have been—"you brought all these people with you?"

"We're moral support," Bridget explained.

"If you know this man," said the receptionist slowly, "wouldn't you have his phone number?"

"I guess I was worried he wouldn't pick up."

"But you thought he'd be fine with you showing up at his hotel with no warning and an entourage?"

I turned away from the desk. "Bridge, why did you think this plan would work?"

"It shows you're going above and beyond." She tripped forward to join me. "It shows how much you care."

"Yeah." That was Priya. "I'm coming to the conclusion that it mostly shows you didn't think this through."

"I have to agree," said the receptionist.

Sheepishly, I pulled out my phone and rang Oliver. It went to voicemail, but since there was no message I could conceivably leave, I hung up quickly. "I think he might be screening me."

Desk guy folded his arms in a smug, vindicated way. "You see, this is why we don't give out information about guests."

"But this is, like, love and shit," I tried.

"This is, like"—the receptionist was still visibly unmoved— "my job and shit."

"Don't worry," cried Bridge. "I'll call him. Nobody screens me."

James Royce-Royce struck a despairing pose. "I try to, pumpkin. But you never take no answer for an answer."

"She once left me thirty-seven consecutive voicemails," agreed James Royce-Royce, "about a shop she'd found that was still charging 15p for Freddos."

"Really? Where?" asked the receptionist.

Bridge gave him a haughty glare. "I'm sorry, I'm not at liberty to give that information away."

"Can you please"—I tried very hard to sound calm and in control—"call Oliver for me."

"Don't worry." Bridge was already rummaging in her bag. "I've got this. I'll be incredibly subtle."

"Well," said Priya, "we're fucked."

There was a brief pause as Bridge unlocked her phone. And she'd been right—Oliver wasn't screening her. Which was good under the circumstances but also made me feel like shit.

"Hi," she trilled, not, I'll be honest, entirely convincingly. "I just thought I'd check in for no reason... No, everything's fine... No, no crisis... How's Durham... What do you mean you're not in Durham... Oh. That's nice... Been lovely talking to you. Bye-bye."

"Okay." I stared at Bridget, reminding myself she was my best friend, and you didn't wish your best friend would fall into an open sewer and die. "What was that about him not being in Durham?"

"Apparently"—Bridge squirmed—"he changed his mind. About the job. And, obviously, he must have cancelled his hotel room as well."

"I can neither confirm nor deny that," put in the receptionist. "But please leave."

Priya threw her hands in the air. "You fuckers owe me dinner. Or I'm driving back on my fucking own."

"Can you at least stop saying 'fuck' in the lobby?" asked the receptionist in the plaintive tones of a man who, at this stage, would take what he could get.

"The restaurant here looks perfectly acceptable," piped up James Royce-Royce. "All their ingredients are apparently sourced within twenty miles of the hotel, and I do like a good side of local beef."

"Quick question." I turned back to the receptionist. "Would our going and buying dinner in your restaurant make you less annoyed with us or more annoyed with us?"

The receptionist shrugged. "Right now, I mostly want you away from my desk."

"Yay." Bridge did an actual dance. "Food adventure."

She and I ended up splitting the bill between the two of us since this had been entirely her idea and, theoretically, for my benefit.

After we'd had starters, mains, desserts, and Priya had made a point of ordering coffee, we bundled back into her truck and started the journey home—always the worst part of any road trip, especially one with a gigantic anticlimax in the middle.

"It's a good sign really." As ever, Bridge was the first to break a perfectly satisfying miserable silence.

James Royce-Royce lifted his head from James Royce-Royce's shoulder. "Go on, darling. Spin this one for us."

"Well, don't you see? He was so sad when he broke up with Luc that he had to run away to the other side of the country. But when he thought about the reality of leaving you behind, he couldn't do it."

"Alternatively," I said, "he was in a bad place because he'd just got out of a weird not-quite-fake relationship and his parents had been dicks to him so he thought about doing something dramatic. Then realised it was stupid, because his house, his job, and all his friends are in London. Where he's perfectly happy without me."

Tom had been half dozing in the corner, but now he sat up. "Is it at all possible there's a middle ground here? Like maybe whether Oliver wants to get back with Luc has nothing to do with whether he wants to move to Durham?"

"So you're saying"—I glanced at Tom over Bridge's shoulder— "that Oliver isn't happy or unhappy without me because I'm completely irrelevant?"

"No. I'm saying you might be irrelevant to one very specific set of decisions."

"That's not true," protested Bridge loyally. "I'm sure Oliver wouldn't have been looking for work on the other side of the country if he hadn't broken up with Luc."

I made a fuck-it-all gesture. "In any case, it doesn't matter. I tried to do the big-gesture thing. And all I did was waste about ten hours of everybody's time."

"Time spent with friends," opined James Royce-Royce, "is never wasted. And the beef was excellent, if a trifle under for my taste."

Priya's eyes flashed in the mirror. "My time's been wasted. As has my petrol."

"I'll reimburse you for the petrol."

"And what about the sex I could be having right now?"

"Well..." I blinked. "I'd reimburse you for that as well, but I'm not really qualified. This was your idea, Bridge. Over to you."

She squeaked. "I don't think I'm qualified either."

"Yeah," said Priya, "can we stop talking about my sexuality like it's an entry level position at Deloitte?"

We apologised. After which, Bridge transitioned seamlessly back into my love life. "You'd better not be giving up, Luc."

"He wouldn't even answer my call."

"Yes. That's another good sign. If he didn't care, he'd be fine to talk to you."

"We've been through this. I didn't know what I was going to say in a hotel in Durham. I don't know what I'd have said if he'd answered the phone. And I'm not going to know what to say if I suddenly show up on his doorstep at ten o'clock at night."

"Oh," Bridge gasped. "That's a wonderful idea. Priya, drive to Oliver's house."

Priya scowled again. "Sure. I'll just type 'Oliver's house' into my satnav, shall I?"

"It's fine. I've got his address."

"This is my truck. Not a fucking Uber."

"Oliver didn't like using Uber," I heard myself say. "He thought their business practices were unethical."

"Y'know what else is unethical?" Priya shot back. "Making your only South Asian friend drive you everywhere."

"Ooh"—James Royce-Royce started—"I hadn't thought about the optics of that. I could take a turn at the wheel if you'd like."

Priya shook her head. "Nobody has sex in my truck but me. Nobody drives my truck but me."

"Then stop complaining that we make you drive us places," I complained.

"You could, for example, get your own cars."

"With the congestion charge?" James Royce-Royce looked genuinely shocked. "And parking would be a nightmare. Besides, dear heart, you're the one who chose a career carting scrap metal around."

"I'm a sculptor, not a refuse collector."

I closed my eyes. They could go on like this pretty much indefinitely. And I'd had, to put it mildly, a long day—made longer by its absolute futility. I mean, it was probably for the best that Oliver wasn't randomly upending his entire life in a moment of... whatever it had been a moment of. And, actually, I'd had those kind of moments myself, and they were never a good sign. But, in terms of my relationship, fake or otherwise or lack thereof, it did leave me sort of nowhere. At least if we'd found Oliver in

Durham, I could have been all "No, please don't go, come back with me." Whereas if I tried to talk to him now, I'd just have be like "hi." And I couldn't quite see that being a love story for the ages.

Wow. This sucked.

Resting my head against the window, I let myself doze to the humming of the engine and the comforting white noise of my friends bickering.

CHAPTER 52

"WE'RE HERE." BRIDGET POKED ME excitedly.

I rubbed my eyes, very glad to be home. "Thank fuck. I'm knackered."

"I feel sooooo sorry for you," drawled Priya. "Having to sleep in the back while I ferried you to and from Durham on a wild-goose chase."

"Sorry. Sorry. Next time you have something heavy to lift, I'll make far fewer excuses about helping you." I plopped out of the truck, fumbling in my pocket for my keys. Then I realised I was in Clerkenwell. "Hey, wait. This isn't where I live."

Bridget yanked the door closed again and locked it before winding the window down just far enough that I could hear her. "No, this is Oliver's. Don't you remember? We said we'd take you here."

Yes. Yes, they had. "I did *not* agree to this."

"Tough. It's for your own good. You'll thank us when you're eighty and have a million grandchildren."

I banged on the side of the vehicle. "Let me in, you abject fuckers. This is not funny."

Priya cracked the front window. "You're right. It's not. Hands off the paintwork."

"For fuck's sake." I waved my arms, not quite daring to further risk Priya's wrath. "I'm pretty sure this is legally kidnapping."

"Oooh," cried Bridget. "Oliver's a lawyer. Knock on his door and ask him."

"I am not going to wake him up in the middle of the night to ask a spurious question about whether my friends have committed a felony against me."

"I was just trying to give a plausible cover story you could use to segue into telling him you want to go out with him again."

I was still gesticulating. "Oh so many…many things. Firstly, it is not a plausible cover story. Secondly, it doesn't make up for the fact you've dumped me on the street halfway across London from where I actually live. And, thirdly, most importantly, he doesn't want to go out with me."

"You were willing to do this in Durham. Why aren't you willing to do it here?"

"Because," I yelled, "I've had time to realise what a terrible idea it is. Now let me the fuck back into this van before Oliver's neighbours call the police."

Priya began winding her window back up. "Don't you dare call my truck a van."

"I'm so sorry. Clearly that distinction is what matters most in this moment."

"Lucien," said Oliver, from behind me, "what are you doing?"

Fuck. Fuck. Fuck. Fuck. Fuck.

I turned, trying to look normal and nonchalant. "Just passing? On my way back from…a trip?"

"If you're just passing, why are you standing outside my front door, screaming your head off? And why is there a truck full of people watching you do it?"

I stared at him helplessly for what felt like far too long. He was in stripy pyjama bottoms and one of his plain, excitingly clingy T-shirts, and he had that slightly overchiselled look he'd had when I first met him. It made him feel slightly like a stranger.

"I'm trying to think of a good excuse," I told him. "But I can't."

"Then"—he folded his arms—"why don't you try telling me the truth?"

Well, it couldn't be any worse than "I happened to stop by with all my friends to ask you a legal question." "Bridget told me you were moving to Durham. So I went to Durham. To tell you not to go to Durham. But it turned out you weren't in Durham. You were at your house."

He seemed to be having trouble processing this. Which made two of us. "Is that why you called earlier?"

"Um. Yes."

Long silence.

"I'm...I'm not going to Durham."

"Yes. I figured that out when you weren't in Durham."

More long silence.

"Why," he asked slowly, "do you care?"

"I don't know. I just...didn't want you to be in Durham. I mean, unless you really wanted to be. But, I think...not that it's my place...you probably don't actually...want to, that is. Be in Durham."

He was giving me this "what the hell is wrong with you" look. "Yes, Lucien. That's why I didn't go."

"Yeah, but you applied for an actual job. Booked an actual hotel. Which means you must have been pretty serious for a while there."

"I was. Or rather"—he blushed a little—"I had a moment of wanting to be somewhere else. Far away from everyone I've let down."

"For fuck's sake," I protested, "you haven't let anyone down."

"You didn't seem to feel that way when we last spoke."

I waved my arms in exasperation. "I can't believe you're making me defend your right to dump me. But you didn't let me down. You just made a decision I didn't like. They're not the same thing. I think you made the wrong call but it's not your job to make me, or your parents, or anyone else happy."

A chorus of "kiss, kiss, kiss" rose from the truck. I'm pretty sure Bridge started it.

Wheeling round, I gave them my hardest of hard stares. "Not the time. Really not the time."

"Sorry, Luc, my sweet." James Royce-Royce leaned over from the far passenger side and stuck his head out the window. "It's hard to hear from this position, and we seem to have misread the body language."

"You *definitely* have."

"If it's not too intrusive a question," said Oliver, "why have you brought all your friends to my doorstep?"

"I didn't bring them, they brought me. They've got this idea that if I turned up and told you how much I cared about you that you'd fall into my arms and we'd live happily ever after. But, frankly, they've wildly underestimated how fucked up you are."

His expression Wheel of Fortuned through hurt, relief, and anger, before finally settling on resignation. "Well, I'm glad you're finally seeing me clearly. Can I take it you agree you're better off without me?"

"Fuck a goat, Oliver, no. I know I haven't always got you, and I know there's been a bunch of times where I was a dick to you without meaning to...and also a bunch of times where I was just a dick...but I was never into the guy you think you should be. I'm into the guy you are."

"Is now a good time?" asked Bridget from the truck.

"No," I called back. "Very much not."

"Okay. Sorry. Can you let us know?"

"I really can't. Kind of getting shot down again, actually."

"I'm not shooting you down," interrupted Oliver, making

a valiant effort to ignore the fact I'd accidentally brought an audience. "But you have to understand that I'm not someone people stay with. I try and I try to be a good person, and a good partner, but it's never enough. And it'll never be enough for you."

"Tell him you've got incredibly low standards," suggested Priya.

"I do *not* have incredibly low standards. Well, I do. But it's not relevant here." I put my back firmly to the truck and faced Oliver. "Look, you've got it super wrong. I can't answer for your past relationships, but...what you think pushes people away is what lets them in. And, God I sound like an inspirational Instagram post, but not letting people in is what pushes them away."

"What pushes them away"—Oliver had that tight, frowny expression—"is that I let things slip. My parents see it. You've seen it. When I was with you, I wasn't taking care of myself. I was eating too much, taking too little exercise, I was leaning on you far more than I should have. And God, those scenes I subjected you to with my family and afterwards. That's not who I wanted to be with you."

"Oh, Oliver. Haven't you listened to a word I've said? I wasn't with you because you had a V-cut and no problems." Even as I said, it didn't sound quite right. "Okay, I was at first. But I stayed because you're... Fuck, I was going to say perfect. But you're not perfect and no one's perfect and you don't have to *be* perfect."

"Of course no one's perfect, but I can be better."

"You don't have to be better. You're everything I want right now."

"Can I just remind you that you opened this conversation by telling me how fucked up I am? That cannot be something you want."

"It absolutely can."

"You've seen me have one bad day, Lucien. That doesn't mean you know me."

I laughed. "Oh, you have no fucking idea. When we met, I was too busy drowning in my own shit to pay much attention to yours, but you hide it way less well than you think you do."

"I'm not sure I like where this is going."

"Tough. You literally asked for this. You're prissy and insecure and uptight and use pretentious language because you're afraid of making mistakes. You're so controlling you keep your bananas on a separate hook and such a god-awful people pleaser that it borders on self-destructive. Which is weird because you're also convinced you know what's best for everybody—and it never occurs to you to actually ask them. You're smug, patronising, and adhere rigidly to a set of ethics I don't think you've thought through anywhere near as well as you pretend you have. And I honestly think you might have a little bit of an eating disorder. Which you should probably see someone about, by the way, whether you go out with me or not."

"I thought you came here to try and win me back. Not to elucidate for both of us why I'm the last thing you need."

"Luc, you're doing this all wrong," yelled Bridge. "You're meant to tell him he's wonderful, not that he sucks."

I kept my gaze on Oliver. "You *are* wonderful. But you need to believe that I don't like you in spite of all...all of that. I like you because you're you, and all of that is part of you." In for a penny. "And, anyway, I don't like you—I mean, I do like you, but you probably should know that I love you as well."

Out of the corner of my eye, I saw Bridge literally punch the air. "Yes. Better."

Oliver, however, was silent. Which didn't seem like a good sign.

So I kept talking. Which was probably also a bad sign. "And I know you're in a weird place at the moment. And I was in a weird place when we started this. But I'm in a way better place now, and that's partly because of you, and partly because of these dickheads." I indicated my friends who still had their noses pressed right against the windows like puppies for sale. "The thing is, even then, when I kept fucking up—and let's face it, I fucked up a lot—I knew on some level that we were right. And I kept coming back to you and you kept taking me back. Because you knew it too. And this time, I hate to say it, but you're the one who's fucked up. And I'm still coming back to you because I still think we're right. So, y'know, it's time for you to do your bit."

Okay, even my friends were being quiet. And my stomach felt like it was about to fall to the centre of the earth.

It carried on feeling that way for a very, very long time.

This was it. This was the moment where he got what was I saying, and threw his arms around me, and told me...

"I'm sorry, Lucien," said Oliver. "It's not the same."

Then he turned, walked back into his house, and closed the door.

CHAPTER 53

"YOU KNOW," SAID BRIDGET, AS Priya drove us to Shepherd's Bush, "I really thought that was going to go better."

I sighed and wiped my eyes. "I know you did, Bridge. That's why we love you."

"I don't understand. You're perfect for each other."

"Yeah. We're both *perfectly* messed up."

"In complementary ways."

"If it was complementary, he wouldn't have dumped me, then left me standing on the doorstep when I begged him to undump me."

At which point James Royce-Royce chimed in. "I didn't want to bring this up. But I'm not sure you handled the situation quite as well as you could. I mean, opening with 'Here are all your personal flaws and, by the way, I think you have an eating disorder' is possibly not the best way to strike a romantic tone."

"No." Bridge squidged her face between the headrests. "I thought that at the time, but it was the right thing to do. Oliver needs to know he's loved no matter what."

"I see what you're saying"—James Royce-Royce was nodding sagely—"but I think if what you wanted to communicate was that he was loved no matter what, you should have gone with 'Oliver, you're loved no matter what.'"

I curled further into the corner. "Not massively appreciating the postmortem of my utter romantic failure."

"Bullshit, James." Priya had, of course, chosen to ignore me. But she did seem to be broadly on my side. "People don't believe stuff just because you tell it to them directly. If they did, visual art would be completely worthless. Otherwise I'd go around writing things like 'Capitalism has significant problems' and 'I fancy girls' on walls."

"Stop getting sidetracked." That was Bridge. No surprise. "Point is, we need a new plan."

I closed my eyes. "No. More. Plans."

"But, Luc, you've been so much better since you've been with Oliver. And I don't want you getting all sad and in the tabloids again."

In her defence, it wasn't an unreasonable concern. After all, that was exactly what had happened the last time I'd broken up with someone I cared about. I mean, apart from the minor detail that Oliver hadn't sold me out to a third-rate gossip rag for an insultingly small sum of money. "Thanks for looking out for me, Bridge. But at the risk of sounding like a chick-lit heroine from the '90s, I don't need a man to complete me."

"*You* complete *me*, darling," said James Royce-Royce to James Royce-Royce.

I glared at the backs of their heads. "Way to undercut my point, guys."

"Sorry, I got caught up in the moment."

"The moment of *my* relationship falling apart?"

James Royce-Royce's shoulders hunched in a wincey way. "Oh dear, that does make me sound rather selfish, doesn't it?"

"Look," I said, "being with Oliver has been so good for me. It's helped me sort through a lot. And I'm sure, in the future, I'll be able to have a healthy, functional relationship with someone nice. But, for now, I'm still really upset. So for fuck's sake stop being happy at me."

The message seemed to get through, and everyone remained sympathetically miserable until we got back to my flat. Where I announced my intention to spend the next couple of hours drinking and feeling sorry for myself. "You can join me if you like, but I've been stuck with you all day so I, honestly, don't care if you'd rather just go home."

Priya shrugged. "I'm in. It'll be like the good old days."

"Sorry, darling." James Royce-Royce was already calling an Uber. "My husband and I have to go and be happy somewhere."

"And I've got an early flight," added Tom, "to somewhere I can't talk about to do something I can't talk about."

"I'll stay. It means I'll be late for work tomorrow, but I've got flexi and I'm sure they can survive without me for—" She checked her phone. "Oh shit, I've been fired."

For a moment, I was genuinely not thinking about my own problems. "Fuck. Bridge. I'm so sorry. Was it—"

"False alarm. There's *been* a fire. And half the first print run of *I'm Out of Office at the Moment. Please Forward Any Translation Work to My Personal Email Address* has gone up in smoke. I have to go and deal with this right now."

We all parted ways, except for Priya who followed me up to my flat, made an appropriately rude comment about how surprised she was that I'd managed to keep it clean, and then immediately started raiding the kitchen for booze. I can't say I was good company but it was nice having her there—and she let me cry into my drink without looking awkward or trying to comfort me, which was exactly what I needed right then.

We crawled into bed at three in the morning, because she was in no position to drive and I was in no position to be on my own. Which meant we were both woken up when the buzzer went a couple of hours later.

"Who the fuck is that?" groaned Priya.

The buzzing went on.

"Well"—I rolled over blearily—"I'd normally say you, but you're here. Or Bridge, but she's probably still dealing with a warehouse full of burning books."

The buzzing went on.

She stole my pillow and pressed it over her head. "It's fucking Oliver, isn't it?"

There was no one else it could be. But I couldn't quite work out how to feel about it. This was supposed to make me happy, right? But it was also making me feel crap-the-bed nervous and giving me a headache.

The buzzing went on.

"You have eight seconds to deal with that," Priya told me, "before I put a fucking drill through it."

"I haven't got a drill."

"Then I'll find something heavy and pointy and do the best I can."

"Yeah, I think that would knacker my security deposit."

"Then," she growled, "you better answer the fucking door."

I staggered out of bed and into the living room. "Hello," I said, picking up the handset like I was afraid it might bite me.

"It's me." Oliver's voice was slightly hoarse, though probably less wrecked than mine.

"And?"

"And I...came to see you. Can I come up?"

"Um, there's a tiny, angry lesbian in my bed. So it's not really a good time."

There was a pause. "I'm not sure I want to have this conversation over an intercom."

"Oliver." Tears, alcohol, a ten-hour road trip, and a chronic lack of sleep had turned my brain to cauliflower cheese. "I'm not sure I want to have a conversation at all. Given, y'know, everything."

"I understand that. But"—an anxious, needy little pause—"please?"

Oh fuck. "Fine. I'll come down."

I went down. Oliver was on my doorstep, dressed for work, with dark circles under his eyes.

"Okay," I said. "What?"

He gazed at me for a long moment. "Are you aware that you're wearing nothing but a pair of hedgehog-themed boxer shorts?"

Well, I was now. "I've had a rough night."

"That makes two of us." He took off his big, cashmere lawyer coat and wrapped it round me.

Obviously, pride demanded that I not let him, but—having finally restored my reputation—the last thing I needed was either getting photographed in my underpants or brought up on public indecency charges. Knowing my luck, I'd get stuck with Justice Mayhew.

Oliver drew in a shaky breath. "I'm sorry to wake you. But I...I wanted to tell you I was wrong."

It would have been a good time to say something encouraging and emotionally generous, but I'd just been buzzed out of bed after two hours sleep. "Which bit?"

"All of it. Especially when I said it wasn't the same. Because it was." He stared at the pavement, or possibly my bare feet. "I was shaken and upset and I pulled away, and then I was too ashamed to pull back."

That sounded too familiar for me to be able to condemn it, even though I really wanted to. "I understand. I'm hurt, and I'm mad as hell, but I do understand."

"I wish I hadn't hurt you."

"Me too but"—I shrugged—"here we are."

There was a long silence. Oliver looked kind of uncertain and tormented, but I still wasn't inclined to be particularly helpful.

"Did you mean it?" he asked, finally.

"Mean what?"

"Everything you said."

I was starting to realise he did that a lot—asking you to repeat expressions of affection like he couldn't quite believe he'd heard you right. "Yes, Oliver. I meant it. That's why I said it."

"You think I have an eating disorder?"

He'd better not have come all this way and woken me up and exposed me to the very real possibility that Priya wouldn't let me back in my flat to talk about my perception of his mental health. "I don't know. Maybe. I'm not a medical professional. But you're so committed to being healthy it sometimes seems unhealthy."

"You've also noticed I'm very controlling. Perhaps it's just a symptom of my being generally uptight."

"Is this really what you want to talk about now?"

"No," he admitted, frowning. "I'm being cowardly again. What I really wanted to ask is…did you mean it when you said you…you know."

"When I said"—for someone who didn't like talking about feelings and shit, the words came easily for once—"I loved you?"

He nodded, somewhat abashed.

"Of course I fucking love you. That's why I turned up on your doorstep and made a complete idiot of myself. *Again.*"

"Um." Oliver shuffled. "I'd hope it's obvious, but in case it's not…I'm on your doorstep now. And I'm also feeling rather foolish."

"You're not the one in your underwear." He was looking incredibly lost, and I…I was such a fucking sap I couldn't stand it. "Oliver," I said, "do you have something you want to tell me?"

"So many things, I hardly know where to begin."

"How about you start with the one I clearly need to hear?"

"Then"—he gave me this amazing look, all dignity and

vulnerability mushed up together—"I'm in love with you, Lucien. But it seems hardly adequate."

I'd always figured it was, y'know, ILY that was the important bit. Except any prick could say that and a bunch of them already had. Only Oliver would follow it up with "but it seems hardly adequate." In spite of myself, I smiled. "You've forgotten my incredibly low standards."

"I've still got a lot to figure out in this regard," he murmured, "but you've helped me realise that, very often, standards are bullshit."

Okay. That was even better than "but it hardly seems adequate."

I kissed him. Or he kissed me. I couldn't tell who'd started it. But it didn't matter. All that mattered was that we were kissing. *I missed you* kisses. And *I want you* kisses. And *we're better together* kisses. And kisses that felt like *sorry*. And kisses that felt like promises. And kisses that could be tomorrow and the next day and the next.

Afterwards the sky was bright with new sunlight, pristine and blue and endless. And we sat on my doorstep, knees and shoulders touching, while Shepherd's Bush stirred sleepily around us.

"I should probably tell you," Oliver told me, "that I've thought a lot about what you said. About me and my parents and...how I live my life."

I gave him a slightly worried look. "Don't overdo it. I'm not sure I handled any of that at all well."

"I'm not sure there's a good way to handle it. But I trust you, and that gave me perspective. Of course, I'm still not sure what to *do* with that perspective, but it helps."

"Well, if it takes you less than twenty-eight years, you're doing better than me."

"It's not a competition. And actually"—he gave a soft, slightly bitter laugh—"it's looking like twenty-eight years is about right."

"Family's hard. But you know you've got me, right? Um, not as a replacement. But, like, a bonus."

"You're more than a bonus, Lucien. You're integral."

Oh, be still my beating heart. And I wasn't even being sarcastic.

He stirred nervously at my side. "I'm conscious this could be rather burdensome to hear, but you remain the thing I have most chosen for myself. The thing that's most exclusively mine. The one that brings me the deepest joy."

"Ooof..." The old me would have run a fucking mile. "I'm not sure I feel burdened. I feel...amazed I could be that for you. But I'm up for it."

"I've been attracted to you for a long time. Ever since I saw you at that awful party, and you seemed so impossibly free. Although I do think it was rather pathetic of me to agree to be your fake boyfriend."

"Hey," I pointed out, "I *asked* you to be my fake boyfriend. That's way more pathetic."

"In any case, I wasn't prepared for the truth of you."

I squirmed, sort of delighted, but also incredibly embarrassed. Because I was still not good with feelings and Oliver apparently had a lot of them. And I guess so did I. "Right back atcha, kid."

"Don't diminish this, Lucien. You've done things for me that nobody's ever done before."

"What, you mean—run to Durham for no reason?"

"Seen me. Stood up for me. Fought to keep me."

Through Oliver's eyes, I was starting to sound like a pretty cool person. "Fucking hell. You do not do anything by halves, do you?"

The corners of his lips turned up. "In case you haven't noticed, neither do you."

I tucked my head against his shoulder, and he put an arm around me. "You know, I'm not super sure how we actually boyfriend."

"I suppose we behave much as we did when we were fake boyfriending. It seemed to work for us."

"Okay." That was simpler than I'd anticipated. "Let's do that then."

"I always thought"—Oliver drew me in closer—"my previous relationships failed because I wasn't trying hard enough. But I suspect you were right and I was trying too hard. It felt safe to let my guard down with you because I could tell myself it wasn't real. But now it is and...well...I'm coming to the conclusion I might be unbelievably terrified."

"Me too," I said. "But let's be terrified together."

I slipped my hand into Oliver's and we sat for a while in silence. And I was pretty sure this was how love felt: fuzzy and scary and confusing and light enough to whisk you away like a Tesco's bag on the wind.

ABOUT THE AUTHOR

Alexis Hall is a species of aphodiine beetle native to the United Kingdom. He persists on a diet of leafmould and Jaffa Cakes, and his conservation status was recently upgraded to "least concern" on the IUCN Red List.

Website: quicunquevult.com
Newsletter: quicunquevult.com/contact
Twitter: twitter.com/quicunquevult
Facebook: facebook.com/quicunquevult

ROMANTIC COMEDY AT SOURCEBOOKS CASABLANCA

Boyfriend Material
Wanted: One (fake) boyfriend
Practically perfect in every way

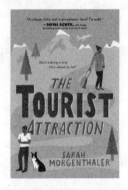

The Tourist Attraction
Welcome to Moose Springs,
Alaska: a small town with a
big heart, and the only world-
class resort where black bears
hang out to look at you!

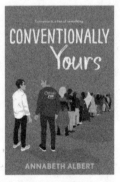

Conventionally Yours
Two infamous rivals.
One epic road trip.
Uncomfortably tight quarters
(why is there only one bed??!!)
And a journey neither
will ever forget.

Bad Bachelor
Everybody's talking about the hot
new app reviewing New York's
most eligible bachelors. But why
focus on prince charming when
you can read the latest dirt on
NYC's most notorious bad boys?